THE EDGAR WINNERS

THE
EDGAR
WINNERS

*33rd Annual Anthology of the
Mystery Writers of America*

Edited by Bill Pronzini

Random House, New York

Library of Congress Cataloging in Publication Data
Main entry under title:
The Edgar winners.
1. Detective and mystery stories, American.
I. Pronzini, Bill.   II. Mystery Writers of
America.
PZ1.E255 [PS648.D4]   813'.0872   79–5546
ISBN 0–394–50830–0

Manufactured in the United States of America
24689753
First Edition

Acknowledgments:

THE ADVENTURE OF THE MAD TEA-PARTY by Ellery Queen Copyright (c) 1934 by Ellery Queen; renewed 1962 by Frederic Dannay and Manfred B. Lee. Reprinted by permission of Frederic Dannay.

AFTER-DINNER STORY by William Irish. Copyright (c) 1937 by Pro-Distributors Publishing Co., Inc. (now Popular Publications, Inc.). Copyright (c) 1965 by William Irish, pseudonym of Cornell Woolrich. First published in *Black Mask.* Reprinted by permission of The Chase Manhattan Bank, N.A., Executor of the Estate of Cornell Woolrich.

CATFISH STORY by Lawrence G. Blochman. Copyright (c) 1948, 1950 by Lawrence G. Blochman. First published in *Collier's* as "Sleepwalker." Reprinted by permission of Mrs. Marguerite Maillard Blochman.

LOVE LIES BLEEDING by Philip MacDonald. Copyright (c) 1952 by Philip MacDonald; from *Something to Hide.* Reprinted by permission of the author.

LAMB TO THE SLAUGHTER by Roald Dahl. Copyright (c) 1953 by Roald Dahl. Reprinted from *Someone Like You,* by Roald Dahl, by permission of Alfred A. Knopf, Inc.

THE HOUSE PARTY by Stanley Ellin. Copyright (c) 1954 by Stanley Ellin. First published in *Ellery Queen's Mystery Magazine.* Reprinted by permission of the author.

THE BLESSINGTON METHOD by Stanley Ellin. Copyright (c) 1956 by Stanley Ellin. First published in *Ellery Queen's Mystery Magazine.* Reprinted by permission of the author.

OVER THERE—DARKNESS by William O'Farrell. Copyright (c) 1958 by William O'Farrell. First published in *Sleuth Mystery Magazine.* Reprinted by permission of Blanche C. Gregory, Inc.

THE LANDLADY by Roald Dahl. Copyright (c) 1959 by Roald Dahl. Reprinted

Contents

Introduction   ix

1947: The Adventure of the Mad Tea-Party •
Ellery Queen   3
1948: After-Dinner Story • William Irish   35
1950: Catfish Story • Lawrence G. Blochman   61
1952: Love Lies Bleeding • Philip MacDonald   79
1953: Lamb to the Slaughter • Roald Dahl   103
1954: The House Party • Stanley Ellin   113
1956: The Blessington Method • Stanley Ellin   133
1958: Over There—Darkness • William O'Farrell   147
1959: The Landlady • Roald Dahl   161
1962: The Sailing Club • David Ely   171
1962: Special Award: This Will Kill You • Patrick
Quentin   183
1964: H as in Homicide • Lawrence Treat   199
1966: The Chosen One • Rhys Davies   213
1967: The Oblong Room • Edward D. Hoch   245
1968: The Man Who Fooled the World • Warner
Law   255
1969: Goodbye, Pops • Joe Gores   293
1970: In the Forests of Riga the Beasts Are Very
Wild Indeed • Margery Finn Brown   301
1971: Moonlight Gardener • Robert L. Fish   311
1972: The Purple Shroud • Joyce Harrington   323
1973: The Whimper of Whipped Dogs • Harlan
Ellison   337
1975: The Jail • Jesse Hill Ford   357
1976: Like a Terrible Scream • Etta Revesz   373
1977: Chance After Chance • Thomas Walsh   383

viii   Contents

1978: The Cloud Beneath the Eaves • *Barbara
     Owens*   397
Edgar and Special Awards   411

Introduction

The Mystery Writers of America was founded in 1945 by such august members of the crime-writing fraternity as Ellery Queen, Anthony Boucher, Judson Philips, and Lawrence G. Blochman. The purposes of the organization were and still are "at least twofold," as Richard Lockridge wrote in his introduction to the first of the MWA annual anthologies, *Murder Cavalcade,* published in 1946. "Its members meet and are addressed by experts in murder—by medical examiners, inspectors of police, students of poison and specialists in the effects of the blunt instrument on the human skull. From such meetings, we learn new ways to chill your blood—and sometimes find our own congealing . . . These experts bring us closer to our subject.

"The second purpose is more immediate to us, but of less importance to the reader . . . We have, as our motto, a simple slogan: 'Crime Does Not Pay—Enough.' One of our main aims is to make it pay more."

That MWA has succeeded in both those goals is evidenced by the continuing popularity of the mystery story, owing in large part to the unflagging ingenuity of old and new members alike, and to the higher royalties those of us writing today are paid by our publishers. MWA's success can also be measured in terms of its growth; from its modest beginnings in 1945, with a handful of well-established professionals largely based in the New York area, it has blossomed into a nationwide organization with a membership of over 700 professional and part-time writers, publishers, editors, critics, mystery scholars, and readers. The annual Edgar Awards banquet, named for our patron, Edgar Allan Poe and held in New York City on the last Friday in April, is regularly attended by more than 400 people, many of them dignitaries in and out of the literary world.

And it is the Edgar Awards that form a third goal of MWA: the honoring of excellence within our field, so as to inspire even better and more ambitious work in the future.

This is one reason why the Edgars are of special importance to MWA's active members, in the same way that the Oscars and Emmys are of special importance to film and television actors. The voting in each of the categories—Novel, First Novel, Short Story, Fact-Crime, etc.—is done by committees comprised of our peers; and there can be no greater honor for any writer, young or old, new or long-established, than to have his work adjudged the best by his peers.

The first Edgars were presented, in that first year of 1945, to Julius Fast for Best First Novel *(Watchful at Night),* to Anthony Boucher for his mystery criticism, and to the classic hard-boiled private-eye film *Murder, My Sweet,* starring Dick Powell. Additional categories were added in later years: Fact-Crime and Short Story in 1947, Novel in 1953, Grand Master (given on an irregular basis to an individual voted by MWA's board of directors to have contributed an important body of work to the genre) in 1954, Juvenile Novel in 1960, Paperback Novel in 1969, and Critical/Biographical Study in 1976. In addition, beginning in 1948, Special Edgars and their sister awards, Ravens, are presented each year for unusual and signatory books, plays, films, and individual services.

This anthology is the thirty-third to be sponsored by MWA. It is, however, totally different from any of the others for three reasons. First, all past anthologies were comprised of stories donated without recompense, for the sole benefit of MWA, by members of the organization; *The Edgar Winners* is comprised of stories donated by MWA members and nonmembers alike. Second, none of the other anthologies, for obvious reasons, contained reference lists of Edgar winners in all major categories; an appendix of such lists is included here. And third and most important, it is the first anthology to bring together in one volume only those stories that have received the coveted Edgar as the Best Mystery Short Story of its year.

(It should be noted here that the first two awards in this category were given for bodies of work, that the third award went to *Ellery Queen's Mystery Magazine,* and that the ensuing four awards were presented to one-volume, single-author collections; it was only in 1954 that the current policy of awarding the Edgar to an individual story was adopted. Those first six award-winners are all of major stature both in and out of the mystery genre—Ellery Queen, William Irish, Lawrence G. Blochman *(Diagnosis: Homicide),* John Collier *(Fancies and Goodnights),* Philip MacDonald *(Something to Hide),* Roald Dahl *(Someone Like You)*—and it would have been criminous, if you'll pardon a pun, to have left out selections by these writers. So I have chosen what I consider to be among the best and most representative stories from the Queen and Irish canons and from three of the four collections.

These twenty-four stories include some of the finest mystery fiction to be published in the past four decades. Moreover, they represent the widest possible variety of types, themes, styles (and authors)—testimony to the fact that the mystery story, contrary to what certain critics would have us believe, is by no means a limited and hidebound genre.

There are traditional tales of detection, stories of pure and psychological suspense, police procedurals, character studies, morality plays, savage social commentaries and gently nostalgic glimpses of the past, even what might be termed an avant-garde literary exercise. There are stories by well known, and by less well known but equally talented, mystery writers: Ellery Queen, William Irish, Lawrence G. Blochman, Philip Mac-Donald, Stanley Ellin, William O'Farrell, David Ely, Lawrence Treat, Edward D. Hoch, Warner Law, Joe Gores, Robert L. Fish, and Thomas Walsh. Stories by newcomers such as Joyce Harrington, Etta Revesz, and Barbara Owens—all three of which, surprisingly and happily enough, were first sales to *Ellery Queen's Mystery Magazine.* Stories by writers of distinction in the literary field—Roald Dahl, Rhys Davies, Margery

Finn Brown, Jesse Hill Ford—and in another genre, science fiction's Harlan Ellison.

Stories by the best in the business of writing fiction, in short. And all of them a winner in more ways than one.

Enjoy.

Bill Pronzini
San Francisco, California
August 1979

THE EDGAR WINNERS

1947:

The Adventure
of the Mad Tea-Party

Ellery Queen

The tall young man in the dun raincoat thought that he had never seen such a downpour. It gushed out of the black sky in a roaring flood, gray-gleaming in the feeble yellow of the station lamps. The red tails of the local from Jamaica had just been drowned out in the west. It was very dark beyond the ragged blur of light surrounding the little railroad station, and unquestionably very wet. The tall young man shivered under the eaves of the platform roof and wondered what insanity had moved him to venture into the Long Island hinterland in such wretched weather. And where, damn it all, was Owen?

He had just miserably made up his mind to seek out a booth, telephone his regrets, and take the next train back to the City, when a lowslung coupé came splashing and snuffling out of the darkness, squealed to a stop, and a man in chauffeur's livery leaped out and dashed across the gravel for the protection of the eaves.

"Mr. Ellery Queen?" he panted, shaking out his cap. He was a blond young man with a ruddy face and sun-squinted eyes.

"Yes," said Ellery with a sigh. Too late now.

"I'm Millan, Mr. Owen's chauffeur, sir," said the man. "Mr.

Owen's sorry he couldn't come down to meet you himself. Some guests—This way, Mr. Queen."

He picked up Ellery's bag and the two of them ran for the coupé. Ellery collapsed against the mohair in an indigo mood. Damn Owen and his invitations! Should have known better. Mere acquaintance, when it came to that. One of J.J.'s questionable friends. People were always pushing so. Put him up on exhibition, like a trained seal. Come, come, Rollo; here's a juicy little fish for you! . . . Got vicarious thrills out of listening to crime yarns. Made a man feel like a curiosity. Well, he'd be drawn and quartered if they got him to mention crime once! But then Owen had said Emmy Willowes would be there, and he'd always wanted to meet Emmy. Curious woman, Emmy, from all the reports. Daughter of some blueblood diplomat who had gone to the dogs—in this case, the stage. Stuffed shirts, her tribe, probably. Atavi! There were some people who still lived in medieval . . . Hmm. Owen wanted him to see "the house." Just taken a month ago. Ducky, he'd said. "Ducky!" The big brute . . .

The coupé splashed along in the darkness, its headlights revealing only remorseless sheets of speckled water and occasionally a tree, a house, a hedge.

Millan cleared his throat. "Rotten weather, isn't it, sir? Worst this spring. The rain, I mean."

Ah, the conversational chauffeur! thought Ellery with an inward groan. "Pity the poor sailor on a night like this," he said piously.

"Ha, ha," said Millan. "Isn't it the truth, though? You're a little late, aren't you, sir? That was the eleven-fifty. Mr. Owen told me this morning you were expected tonight on the nine-twenty."

"Detained," murmured Ellery, wishing he were dead.

"A case, Mr. Queen?" asked Millan eagerly, rolling his squinty eyes.

Even he, O Lord. . . . "No, no. My father had his annual attack of elephantiasis. Poor dad! We thought for a bad hour there that it was the end."

The chauffeur gaped. Then, looking puzzled, he returned his attention to the soggy pelted road. Ellery closed his eyes with a sigh of relief.

But Millan's was a persevering soul, for after a moment of silence he grinned—true, a trifle dubiously—and said: "Lots of excitement at Mr. Owen's tonight, sir. You see Master Jonathan—"

"Ah," said Ellery, starting a little. Master Jonathan, eh? Ellery recalled him as a stringy, hot-eyed brat in the indeterminate years between seven and ten who possessed a perfectly fiendish ingenuity for making a nuisance of himself. Master Jonathan. . . . He shivered again, this time from apprehension. He had quite forgotten Master Jonathan.

"Yes, sir, Jonathan's having a birthday party tomorrow, sir—ninth, I think—and Mr. and Mrs. Owen've rigged up something special." Millan grinned again, mysteriously. "Something very special, sir. It's a secret, y'see. The kid—Master Jonathan doesn't know about it yet. Will he be surprised!"

"I doubt it, Millan," groaned Ellery, and lapsed into a dismal silence which not even the chauffeur's companionable blandishments were able to shatter.

Richard Owen's "ducky" house was a large rambling affair of gables and ells and colored stones and bright shutters, set at the terminal of a winding driveway flanked by soldierly trees. It blazed with light and the front door stood ajar.

"Here we are, Mr. Queen!" cried Millan cheerfully, jumping out and holding the door open. "It's only a hop to the porch; you won't get wet, sir."

Ellery descended and obediently hopped to the porch. Millan fished his bag out of the car and bounded up the steps. "Door open 'n' everything," he grinned. "Guess the help are all watchin' the show."

"Show?" gasped Ellery with a sick feeling at the pit of his stomach.

Millan pushed the door wide open. "Step in, step in, Mr. Queen. I'll go get Mr. Owen. . . . They're rehearsing, y'see. Couldn't do it while Jonathan was up, so they had to wait till he'd gone to bed. It's for tomorrow, y'see. And he was very suspicious; they had an awful time with him—"

"I can well believe that," mumbled Ellery. Damn Jonathan and all his tribe! He stood in a small foyer looking upon a wide brisk living room, warm and attractive. "So they're putting on a play. Hmm. . . . Don't bother, Millan; I'll just wander in and wait until they've finished. Who am I to clog the wheels of Drama?"

"Yes, sir," said Millan with a vague disappointment; and he set down the bag and touched his cap and vanished in the darkness outside. The door closed with a click curiously final, shutting out both rain and night.

Ellery reluctantly divested himself of his drenched hat and raincoat, hung them dutifully in the foyer-closet, kicked his bag into a corner, and sauntered into the living room to warm his chilled hands at the good fire. He stood before the flames soaking in heat, only half-conscious of the voices which floated through one of the two open doorways beyond the fireplace.

A woman's voice was saying in odd childish tones: "No, please go on! I won't interrupt you again. I dare say there may be *one.*"

"Emmy," thought Ellery, becoming conscious very abruptly. "What's going on here?" He went to the first doorway and leaned against the jamb.

An astonishing sight met him. They were all—as far as he could determine—there. It was apparently a library, a large bookish room done in the modern manner. The farther side had been cleared and a home-made curtain, manufactured out of starchy sheets and a pulley, stretched across the room. The curtain was open, and in the cleared space there was a long table covered with a white cloth and with cups and saucers and things on it. In an armchair at the head of the table sat Emmy Willowes, whimsically girlish in a pinafore, her gold-brown hair streaming down her back, her slim legs sheathed in white stockings, and black pumps with low heels on her feet. Beside her sat an apparition, no less: a rabbity creature the size of a man, his huge ears stiffly up, an enormous bow tie at his furry neck, his mouth clacking open and shut as human sounds came from his throat. Beside the hare there was another apparition: a creature with an amiably rodent little face and slow sleepy movements. And beyond the little one, who looked unaccountably like a dormouse, sat the most remarkable of the quartet—a curious creature with shaggy eyebrows and features reminiscent of George Arliss's, at his throat a dotted bow tie, dressed Victorianishly in a quaint waistcoat, on his head an extraordinary tall cloth hat in the band of which was stuck a placard reading: "For this Style 10/6."

The audience was composed of two women: an old lady with pure white hair and the stubbornly sweet facial expression which more often than not conceals a chronic acerbity; and a very beautiful young woman with full breasts, red hair, and green eyes. Then Ellery noticed that two domestic heads were stuck in another doorway, gaping and giggling decorously.

"The mad tea-party," thought Ellery grinning. "I might have known, with Emmy in the house. Too good for that merciless brat!"

"They were learning to draw," said the little dormouse in a high-pitched voice, yawning and rubbing its eyes, "and they drew all manner of things—everything that begins with an M—"

"Why with an M?" demanded the woman-child.

"Why not?" snapped the hare, flapping his ears indignantly.

The dormouse began to doze and was instantly beset by the top-hatted gentleman, who pinched him so roundly that he awoke with a shriek and said: "—that begins with an M, such as mousetraps, and the moon, and memory, and muchness—you know you say things are 'much of a muchness'—did you ever see such a thing as a drawing of a muchness?"

"Really, now you ask me," said the girl, quite confused, "I don't think—"

"Then you shouldn't talk," said the Hatter tartly.

The girl rose in open disgust and began to walk away, her white legs twinkling. The dormouse fell asleep and the hare and the Hatter stood up and grasped the dormouse's little head and tried very earnestly to push it into the mouth of a monstrous teapot on the table.

And the little girl cried, stamping her right foot: "At any rate I'll never go *there* again. It's the stupidest tea-party I was ever at in all my life!"

And she vanished behind the curtain; an instant later it swayed and came together as she operated the rope of the pulley.

"Superb," drawled Ellery, clapping his hands. *"Brava,* Alice. And a couple of *bravi* for the zoological characters, Messrs. Dormouse and March Hare, not to speak of my good friend the Mad Hatter."

The Mad Hatter goggled at him, tore off his hat, and came

running across the room. His vulturine features under the make-up were both good-humored and crafty; he was a stoutish man in his prime, a faintly cynical and ruthless prime. "Queen! When on earth did you come? Darned if I hadn't completely forgotten about you. What held you up?"

"Family matter. Millan did the honors. Owen, that's your natural costume, I'll swear. I don't know what ever possessed you to go into Wall Street. You were born to be the Hatter."

"Think so?" chuckled Owen, pleased. "I guess I always did have a yen for the stage; that's why I backed Emmy Willowes's *Alice* show. Here, I want you to meet the gang. Mother," he said to the white-haired old lady, "may I present Mr. Ellery Queen. Laura's mother, Queen—Mrs. Mansfield." The old lady smiled a sweet, sweet smile; but Ellery noticed that her eyes were very sharp. "Mrs. Gardner," continued Owen, indicating the buxom young woman with the red hair and green eyes. "Believe it or not, she's the wife of that hairy Hare over there. Ho, ho, ho!"

There was something a little brutal in Owen's laughter. Ellery bowed to the beautiful woman and said quickly: "Gardner? You're not the wife of Paul Gardner, the architect?"

"Guilty," said the March Hare in a cavernous voice; and he removed his head and disclosed a lean face with twinkling eyes. "How are you, Mr. Queen? I haven't seen you since I testified for your father in that Schultz murder case in the Village."

They shook hands. "Surprise," said Ellery. "This *is* nice. Mrs. Gardner, you have a clever husband. He set the defense by their respective ears with his expert testimony in that case."

"Oh, I've always said Paul is a genius," smiled the red-haired woman. She had a queer husky voice. "But he won't believe me. He thinks I'm the only one in the world who doesn't appreciate him."

"Now, Carolyn," protested Gardner with a laugh; but the twinkle had gone out of his eyes and for some odd reason he glanced at Richard Owen.

"Of course you remember Laura," boomed Owen, taking Ellery forcibly by the arm. "That's the Dormouse. Charming little rat, isn't she?"

Mrs. Mansfield lost her sweet expression for a fleeting instant; very fleeting indeed. What the Dormouse thought about being publicly characterized as a rodent, however charming, by her husband was concealed by the furry little head; when she took it off she was smiling. She was a wan little woman with tired eyes and cheeks that had already begun to sag.

"And this," continued Owen with the pride of a stock-raiser exhibiting a prize milch-cow, "is the one and only Emmy. Emmy, meet Mr. Queen, that murder-smelling chap I've been telling you about. Miss Willowes."

"You see us, Mr. Queen," murmured the actress, "in character. I hope you aren't here on a professional visit? Because if you are, we'll get into mufti at once and let you go to work. I know *I've* a vicariously guilty conscience. If I were to be convicted of every mental murder I've committed, I'd need the nine lives of the Cheshire Cat. Those damn' critics—"

"The costume," said Ellery, not looking at her legs, "is most fetching. And I think I like you better as Alice." She made a charming Alice; she was curved in her slimness, half-boy, half-girl. "Whose idea was this, anyway?"

"I suppose you think we're fools or nuts," chuckled Owen. "Here, sit down, Queen. Maud!" he roared. "A cocktail for Mr. Queen. Bring some more fixin's." A frightened domestic head vanished. "We're having a dress-rehearsal for Johnny's birthday party tomorrow; we've invited all the kids of the neighborhood. Emmy's brilliant idea; she brought the costumes down from the theatre. You know we closed Saturday night."

"I hadn't heard. I thought *Alice* was playing to S.R.O."

"So it was. But our lease at the *Odeon* ran out and we've our engagements on the road to keep. We open in Boston next Wednesday."

Slim-legged Maud set a pinkish liquid concoction before Ellery. He sipped slowly, succeeding in not making a face.

"Sorry to have to break this up," said Paul Gardner, beginning to take off his costume. "But Carolyn and I have a bad trip before us. And then tomorrow . . . The road must be an absolute washout."

"Pretty bad," said Ellery politely, setting down his three-quarters'-full glass.

"I won't hear of it," said Laura Owen. Her pudgy little Dormouse's stomach gave her a peculiar appearance, tiny and fat and sexless. "Driving home in this storm! Carolyn, you and Paul must stay over."

"It's only four miles, Laura," murmured Mrs. Gardner.

"Nonsense, Carolyn! More like forty on a night like this," boomed Owen. His cheeks were curiously pale and damp under the make-up. "That's settled! We've got more room than we know what to do with. Paul saw to that when he designed this development."

"That's the insidious part of knowing architects socially," said Emmy Willowes with a grimace. She flung herself in a chair and tucked her long legs under her. "You can't fool 'em about the number of available guest-rooms."

"Don't mind Emmy," grinned Owen. "She's the Peck's Bad Girl of show business: no manners at all. Well, well! This is great. How's about a drink, Paul?"

"No, thanks."

"You'll have one, won't you, Carolyn? Only good sport in the crowd." Ellery realized with a furious embarrassment that his host was, under the red jovial glaze of the exterior, vilely drunk.

She raised her heavily lidded green eyes to his. "I'd love it, Dick." They stared with peculiar hunger at each other. Mrs. Owen suddenly smiled and turned her back, struggling with her cumbersome costume.

And, just as suddenly, Mrs. Mansfield rose and smiled her unconvincing sweet smile and said in her sugary voice to no one in particular: "*Will* you all excuse me? It's been a trying day, and I'm an old woman. . . . Laura, my darling." She went to her daughter and kissed the lined, averted forehead.

Everybody murmured something; including Ellery, who had a headache, a slow pinkish fire in his vitals, and a consuming wishfulness to be far, far away.

Mr. Ellery Queen came to with a start and a groan. He turned over in bed, feeling very poorly. He had dozed in fits since one o'clock, annoyed rather than soothed by the splash of the rain against the bedroom windows. And now he was miserably awake, inexplicably sleepless, attacked by a rather surprising insomnia. He sat up and reached for his wrist-watch, which was ticking thunderously away on the night-table beside his bed. By the radium hands he saw that it was five past two.

He lay back, crossing his palms behind his head, and stared into the half-darkness. The mattress was deep and downy, as one had a right to expect of the mattress of a plutocrat, but it did not rest his tired bones. The house was cozy, but it did not comfort him. His hostess was thoughtful, but uncomfortably woebegone. His host was a disturbing force, like the storm. His fellow-guests; Master Jonathan snuffling away in his junior bed —Ellery was positive that Master Jonathan snuffled. . . .

At two-fifteen he gave up the battle and, rising, turned on the light and got into his dressing-gown and slippers. That there was no book or magazine on or in the night-table he had ascertained before retiring. Shocking hospitality! Sighing, he went to the door and opened it and peered out. A small night-light glimmered at the landing down the hall. Everything was quiet.

And suddenly he was attacked by the strangest diffidence. He definitely did not want to leave the bedroom.

Analyzing the fugitive fear, and arriving nowhere, Ellery sternly reproached himself for an imaginative fool and stepped out into the hall. He was not habitually a creature of nerves, nor was he psychic; he laid the blame to lowered physical resistance due to fatigue, lack of sleep. This was a nice house with nice people in it. It was like a man, he thought, saying: "Nice doggie, nice doggie," to a particularly fearsome beast with slavering jaws. That woman with the sea-green eyes. Put to sea in a sea-green boat. Or was it pea-green. . . . "No room! No room!" . . . "There's *plenty* of room," said Alice indignantly. . . . And Mrs. Mansfield's smile did make you shiver.

Berating himself bitterly for the ferment his imagination was in, he went down the carpeted stairs to the living room.

It was pitch-dark and he did not know where the light switch was. He stumbled over a hassock and stubbed his toe and cursed silently. The library should be across from the stairs, next to the fireplace. He strained his eyes toward the fireplace, but the last embers had died. Stepping warily, he finally reached the fireplace wall. He groped about in the rain-splattered silence, searching for the library door. His hand met a cold knob, and he turned the knob rather noisily and swung the door open. His eyes were oriented to the darkness now and he had already begun to make out in the mistiest black haze the unrecognizable outlines of still objects.

The darkness from beyond the door however struck him like a blow. It was darker darkness. . . . He was about to step across the sill when he stopped. It was the wrong room. Not the library at all. How he knew he could not say, but he was sure he had pushed open the door of the wrong room. Must have wandered orbitally to the right. Lost men in the dark forest. . . . He stared intently straight before him into the absolute, unrelieved blackness, sighed, and retreated. The door shut noisily again.

He groped along the wall to the left. A few feet. . . . There it was! The very next door. He paused to test his psychic faculties. No, all's well. Grinning, he pushed open the door, entered boldly, fumbled on the nearest wall for the switch, found it, pressed. The light flooded on to reveal, triumphantly, the library.

The curtain was closed, the room in disorder as he had last seen it before being conducted upstairs by his host.

He went to the built-in bookcases, scanned several shelves, hesitated between two volumes, finally selected *Huckleberry Finn* as good reading on a dour night, put out the light, and felt his way back across the living room to the stairway. Book tucked under his arm, he began to climb the stairs. There was a footfall from the landing above. He looked up. A man's dark form was silhouetted below the tiny landing light.

"Owen?" whispered a dubious male voice.

Ellery laughed. "It's Queen, Gardner. Can't you sleep, either?"

He heard the man sigh with relief. "Lord, no! I was just coming downstairs for something to read. Carolyn—my wife's asleep, I guess, in the room adjoining mine. How she can sleep—! There's something in the air tonight."

"Or else you drank too much," said Ellery cheerfully, mounting the stairs.

Gardner was in pajamas and dressing-gown, his hair mussed. "Didn't drink at all to speak of. Must be this confounded rain. My nerves are all shot."

"Something in that. Hardy believed, anyway, in the Greek unities. . . . If you can't sleep, you might join me for a smoke in my room, Gardner."

"You're sure I won't be—"

"Keeping me up? Nonsense. The only reason I fished about downstairs for a book was to occupy my mind with something.

Talk's infinitely better than Huck Finn, though he does help at times. Come on."

They went to Ellery's room and Ellery produced cigarets and they relaxed in chairs and chatted and smoked until the early dawn began struggling to emerge from behind the fine gray wet bars of the rain outside. Then Gardner went yawning back to his room and Ellery fell into a heavy, uneasy slumber.

He was on the rack in a tall room of the Inquisition and his left arm was being torn out of his shoulder-socket. The pain was almost pleasant. Then he awoke to find Millan's ruddy face in broad daylight above him, his blond hair tragically disheveled. He was jerking at Ellery's arm for all he was worth.

"Mr. Queen!" he was crying. "Mr. Queen! For God's sake wake up!"

Ellery sat up quickly, startled. "What's the matter, Millan?"

"Mr. Owen, sir. He's—he's gone!"

Ellery sprang out of bed. "What d'ye mean, man?"

"Disappeared, Mr. Queen. We—we can't find him. Just gone. Mrs. Owen is all—"

"You go downstairs, Millan," said Ellery calmly, stripping off his pajama coat, "and pour yourself a drink. Please tell Mrs. Owen not to do anything until I come down. And nobody's to leave or telephone. You understand?"

"Yes, sir," said Millan in a low voice, and blundered off.

Ellery dressed like a fireman, splashed his face, spat water, adjusted his necktie, and ran downstairs. He found Laura Owen in a crumpled négligé on the sofa, sobbing. Mrs. Mansfield was patting her daughter's shoulder. Master Jonathan Owen was scowling at his grandmother, Emmy Willowes silently smoked a cigaret, and the Gardners were pale and quiet by the gray-washed windows.

"Mr. Queen," said the actress quickly. "It's a drama, hot off the script. At least Laura Owen thinks so. Won't you assure her that it's all probably nothing?"

"I can't do that," smiled Ellery, "until I learn the facts. Owen's gone? How? When?"

"Oh, Mr. Queen," choked Mrs. Owen, raising a tear-stained face. "I know something—something dreadful's happened. I had a feeling—You remember last night, after Richard showed you to your room?"

"Yes."

"Then he came back downstairs and said he had some work to do in his den for Monday, and told me to go to bed. Everybody else had gone upstairs. The servants, too. I warned him not to stay up too late and I went up to bed. I—I was exhausted, and I fell right asleep—"

"You occupy one bedroom, Mrs. Owen?"

"Yes. Twin beds. I fell asleep and didn't wake up until a half-hour ago. When I saw—" She shuddered and began to sob again. Her mother looked helpless and angry. "His bed hadn't been slept in. His clothes—the ones he'd taken off when he got into the costume—were still where he had left them on the chair by his bed. I was shocked, and ran downstairs; but he was gone. . . ."

"Ah," said Ellery queerly. "Then, as far as you know, he's still in that Mad Hatter's rig? Have you looked over his wardrobe? Are any of his regular clothes missing?"

"No, no; they're all there. Oh, he's dead. I know he's dead."

"Laura, dear, please," said Mrs. Mansfield in a tight quavery voice.

"Oh, mother, it's too horrible—"

"Here, here," said Ellery. "No hysterics. Was he worried about anything? Business, for instance?"

"No, I'm sure he wasn't. In fact, he said only yesterday things were picking up beautifully. And he isn't—isn't the type to worry, anyway."

"Then it probably isn't amnesia. He hasn't had a shock of some sort recently?"

"No, no."

"No possibility, despite the costume, that he went to his office?"

"No. He never goes down Saturdays."

Master Jonathan jammed his fists into the pockets of his Eton jacket and said bitterly: "I bet he's drunk again. Makin' mamma cry. I hope he *never* comes back."

"Jonathan!" screamed Mrs. Mansfield. "You go up to your room this very minute, do you hear, you nasty boy? This minute!"

No one said anything; Mrs. Owen continued to sob; so Master Jonathan thrust out his lower lip, scowled at his grandmother with unashamed dislike, and stamped upstairs.

"Where," said Ellery with a frown, "was your husband when you last saw him, Mrs. Owen? In this room?"

"In his den," she said with difficulty. "He went in just as I went upstairs. I saw him go in. That door, there." She pointed to the door at the right of the library door. Ellery started; it was the door to the room he had almost blundered into during the night in his hunt for the library.

"Do you think—" began Carolyn Gardner in her husky voice, and stopped. Her lips were dry, and in the gray morning light her hair did not seem so red and her eyes did not seem so green. There was, in fact, a washed-out look about her, as if all the fierce vitality within her had been quenched by what had happened.

"Keep out of this, Carolyn," said Paul Gardner harshly. His eyes were red-rimmed from lack of sleep.

"Come, come," murmured Ellery, "we may be, as Miss Willowes has said, making a fuss over nothing at all. If you'll excuse me . . . I'll have a peep at the den."

He went into the den, closing the door behind him, and stood with his back squarely against the door. It was a small room, so narrow that it looked long by contrast; it was sparsely furnished and seemed a business-like place. There was a simple neatness about its desk, a modern severity about its furnishings that were reflections of the direct, brutal character of Richard Owen. The room was as trim as a pin; it was almost ludicrous to conceive of its having served as the scene of a crime.

Ellery gazed long and thoughtfully. Nothing out of place, so far as he could see; and nothing, at least perceptible to a stranger, added. Then his eyes wavered and fixed themselves upon what stood straight before him. That *was* odd. . . . Facing him as he leaned against the door there was a bold naked mirror set flush into the opposite wall and reaching from floor to ceiling —a startling feature of the room's decorations. Ellery's lean figure, and the door behind him, were perfectly reflected in the sparkling glass. And there, above . . . In the mirror he saw, above the reflection of the door against which he was leaning, the reflection of the face of a modern electric clock. In the dingy grayness of the light there was a curious lambent quality about its dial. . . . He pushed away from the door and turned and stared up. It was a chromium-and-onyx clock, about a foot in diameter, round and simple and startling.

He opened the door and beckoned Millan, who had joined the silent group in the living room. "Have you a step-ladder?"

Millan brought one. Ellery smiled, shut the door firmly, mounted the ladder, and examined the clock. Its electric outlet was behind, concealed from view. The plug was in the socket, as he saw at once. The clock was going; the time—he consulted his wrist-watch—was reasonably accurate. But then he cupped his hands as best he could to shut out what light there was and stared hard and saw that the numerals and the hands, as he had suspected, were radium-painted. They glowed faintly.

He descended, opened the door, gave the ladder into Millan's keeping, and sauntered into the living room. They looked up at him trustfully.

"Well," said Emmy Willowes with a light shrug, "has the Master Mind discovered the all-important clue? Don't tell us that Dickie Owen is out playing golf at the Meadowbrook links in that Mad Hatter's get-up!"

"Well, Mr. Queen?" asked Mrs. Owen anxiously.

Ellery sank into an armchair and lighted a cigaret. "There's something curious in there. Mrs. Owen, did you get this house furnished?"

She was puzzled. "Furnished? Oh, no. We bought it, you know; brought all our own things."

"Then the electric clock above the door in the den is yours?"

"The clock?" They all stared at him. "Why, of course. What has that—"

"Hmm," said Ellery. "That clock has a disappearing quality, like the Cheshire Cat—since we may as well continue being Carrollish, Miss Willowes."

"But what can the clock possibly have to do with Richard's— being gone?" asked Mrs. Mansfield with asperity.

Ellery shrugged. *"Je n'sais.* The point is that a little after two this morning, being unable to sleep, I ambled downstairs to look for a book. In the dark I blundered to the door of the den, mistaking it for the library door. I opened it and looked in. But I saw nothing, you see."

"But how could you, Mr. Queen?" said Mrs. Gardner in a small voice; her breasts heaved. "If it was dark—"

"That's the curious part of it," drawled Ellery. "I *should* have seen something *because* it was so dark, Mrs. Gardner."

"But—"

"The clock over the door."

"Did you go in?" murmured Emmy Willowes, frowning. "I can't say I understand. The clock's above the door, isn't it?"

"There is a mirror facing the door," explained Ellery absently, "and the fact that it was so dark makes my seeing nothing quite remarkable. Because that clock has luminous hands and numerals. Consequently I should have seen their reflected glow very clearly indeed in that pitch-darkness. But I didn't, you see. I saw literally nothing at all."

They were silent, bewildered. Then Gardner muttered: "I still don't see—You mean something, somebody was standing in front of the mirror, obscuring the reflection of the clock?"

"Oh, no. The clock's above the door—a good seven feet or more from the floor. The mirror reaches to the ceiling. There isn't a piece of furniture in that room seven feet high, and certainly we may dismiss the possibility of an intruder seven feet or more tall. No, no, Gardner. It does seem as if the clock wasn't above the door at all when I looked in."

"Are you sure, young man," snapped Mrs. Mansfield, "that you know what you're talking about? I thought we were concerned with my son-in-law's absence. And how on earth could the clock not have been there?"

Ellery closed his eyes. "Fundamental. *It was moved from its position.* Wasn't above the door when I looked in. After I left, it was returned."

'But why on earth," murmured the actress, "should any one want to move a mere clock from a wall, Mr. Queen? That's almost as nonsensical as some of the things in *Alice.*"

"That," said Ellery, "is the question I'm propounding to myself. Frankly I don't know." Then he opened his eyes. "By the way, has any one seen the Mad Hatter's hat?"

Mrs. Owen shivered. "No, that—that's gone, too."

"You've looked for it?"

"Yes. Would you like to look yours—"

"No, no, I'll take your word for it, Mrs. Owen. Oh, yes. Your husband has no enemies?" He smiled. "That's the routine question, Miss Willowes. I'm afraid I can't offer you anything startling in the way of technique."

"Enemies? Oh, I'm sure not," quavered Mrs. Owen. "Richard was—is strong and—and sometimes rather curt and contemptuous, but I'm sure no one would hate him enough to—to kill him." She shivered again and drew the silk of her négligé closer about her plump shoulders.

"Don't say that, Laura," said Mrs. Mansfield sharply. "I do declare, you people are like children! It probably has the simplest explanation."

"Quite possible," said Ellery in a cheerful voice. "It's the depressing weather, I suppose . . . There! I believe the rain's stopped." They dully looked out the windows. The rain had perversely ceased, and the sky was growing brighter. "Of course," continued Ellery, "there are certain possibilities. It's conceivable—I say conceivable, Mrs. Owen—that your husband has been . . . well, kidnaped. Now, now, don't look so frightened. It's a theory only. The fact that he has disappeared in the costume does seem to point to a very abrupt—and therefore possibly enforced—departure. You haven't found a note of some kind? Nothing in your letter-box? The morning mail—"

"Kidnaped," whispered Mrs. Owen feebly.

"Kidnaped?" breathed Mrs. Gardner, and bit her lip. But there was a brightness in her eye, like the brightness of the sky outdoors.

"No note, no mail," snapped Mrs. Mansfield. "Personally, I think this is ridiculous. Laura, this is your house, but I think I have a duty. . . . You should do one of two things. Either take this seriously and telephone the *regular* police, or forget all about it. *I'm* inclined to believe Richard got befuddled—he *had* a lot to drink last night, dear—and wandered off drunk somewhere. He's probably sleeping it off in a field somewhere and won't come back with anything worse than a bad cold."

"Excellent suggestion," drawled Ellery. "All except for the summoning of the *regular* police, Mrs. Mansfield. I assure you I possess—er—*ex officio* qualifications. Let's not call the police and say we did. If there's any explaining to do—afterward—I'll do it. Meanwhile, I suggest we try to forget all this unpleasantness and wait. If Mr. Owen hasn't returned by nightfall, we can go into conference and decide what measures to take. Agreed?"

"Sounds reasonable," said Gardner disconsolately. "May I"—he smiled and shrugged—"this *is* exciting!—telephone my office, Queen?"

"Lord, yes."

Mrs. Owen shrieked suddenly, rising and tottering toward the stairs. "Jonathan's birthday party! I forgot all about it! And all those children invited—What *will* I say?"

"I suggest," said Ellery in a sad voice, "that Master Jonathan is indisposed, Mrs. Owen. Harsh, but necessary. You might 'phone all the potential spectators of the mad tea-party and voice your regrets." And Ellery rose and wandered into the library.

It was a depressing day for all the lightening skies and the crisp sun. The morning wore on and nothing whatever happened. Mrs. Mansfield firmly tucked her daughter into bed, made her swallow a small dose of luminol from a big bottle in the medicine-chest, and remained with her until she dropped off to exhausted sleep. Then the old lady telephoned to all and sundry the collective Owen regrets over the unfortunate turn of events. Jonathan *would* have to run a fever when . . . Master Jonathan, apprised later by his grandmother of the *débâcle*, sent up an ululating howl of surprisingly healthy anguish that caused Ellery, poking about downstairs in the library, to feel prickles slither up and down his spine. It took the combined labors of Mrs. Mansfield, Millan, the maid, and the cook to pacify the Owen hope. A five-dollar bill ultimately restored a rather strained *entente*. . . . Emmy Willowes spent the day serenely in reading. The Gardners listlessly played two-handed bridge.

Luncheon was a dismal affair. No one spoke in more than monosyllables, and the strained atmosphere grew positively taut.

During the afternoon they wandered about, restless ghosts. Even the actress began to show signs of tension: she consumed innumerable cigarets and cocktails and lapsed into almost sullen silence. No word came; the telephone rang only once, and then it was merely the local confectioner protesting the cancellation of the ice-cream order. Ellery spent most of the afternoon in mysterious activity in the library and den. What he was looking for remained his secret. At five o'clock he emerged from the den, rather gray of face. There was a deep crease between his brows. He went out onto the porch and leaned against a pillar, sunk in thought. The gravel was dry; the sun had quickly sopped up the rain. When he went back into the house it was already dusk and growing darker each moment with the swiftness of the country nightfall.

There was no one about; the house was quiet, its miserable occupants having retired to their rooms. Ellery sought a chair. He buried his face in his hands and thought for long minutes, completely still.

And then at last something happened to his face and he went to the foot of the stairs and listened. No sound. He tip-toed back, reached for the telephone, and spent the next fifteen minutes in low-voiced, earnest conversation with someone in New York. When he had finished, he went upstairs to his room.

An hour later, while the others were downstairs gathering for dinner, he slipped down the rear stairway and out of the house unobserved even by the cook in the kitchen. He spent some time in the thick darkness of the grounds.

How it happened Ellery never knew. He felt its effects soon after dinner; and on retrospection he recalled that the others, too, had seemed drowsy at approximately the same time. It was a late dinner and a cold one. Owen's disappearance apparently having disrupted the culinary organization as well; so that it was not until a little after eight that the coffee—Ellery was certain later it had been the coffee—was served by the trim-legged maid. The drowsiness came on less than half an hour later. They were seated in the living room, chatting dully about nothing at all. Mrs. Owen, pale and silent, had gulped her coffee thirstily; had called for a second cup, in fact. Only Mrs. Mansfield had been belligerent. She had been definitely of a mind, it appeared, to telephone the police. She had great faith in the local constabulary of Long Island, particularly in one Chief Naughton, the local prefect; and she left no doubt in Ellery's mind of *his* incompetency. Gardner had been restless and a little rebellious; he had tinkered with the piano in the alcove. Emmy Willowes had drawn herself into a slant-eyed shell, no longer amused and very, very quiet. Mrs. Gardner had been nervous. Jonathan, packed off screaming to bed. . . .

It came over their senses like a soft insidious blanket of snow. Just a pleasant sleepiness. The room was warm, too, and Ellery rather hazily felt beads of perspiration on his forehead. He was half-gone before his dulled brain sounded a warning note. And then, trying in panic to rise, to use his muscles, he felt himself slipping, slipping into unconsciousness, his body as leaden and remote as Vega. His last conscious thought, as the room whirled dizzily before his eyes and he saw blearily the expressions of his companions, was that they had all been drugged. . . .

The dizziness seemed merely to have taken up where it had left off, almost without hiatus. Specks danced before his closed eyes and somebody was hammering petulantly at his temples. Then he opened his eyes and saw glittering sun fixed upon the floor at his feet. Good God, all night. . . .

He sat up groaning and feeling his head. The others were sprawled in various attitudes of labored-breathing coma about him—without exception. Someone—his aching brain took it in dully; it was Emmy Willowes—stirred and sighed. He got to his feet and stumbled toward a portable bar and poured himself a stiff, nasty drink of Scotch. Then, with his throat burning, he felt unaccountably better; and he went to the actress and pummeled her gently until she opened her eyes and gave him a sick, dazed, troubled look.

"What—when—"

"Drugged," croaked Ellery. "The crew of us. Try to revive these people, Miss Willowes, while I scout about a bit. And see if anyone's shamming."

He wove his way a little uncertainly, but with purpose, toward the rear of the house. Groping, he found the kitchen. And there were the trim-legged maid and Millan and the cook unconscious in chairs about the kitchen table over cold cups of coffee. He made his way back to the living room, nodded at Miss Willowes working over Gardner at the piano, and staggered upstairs. He discovered Master Jonathan's bedroom after a short search; the boy was still sleeping—a deep natural sleep punctuated by nasal snuffles. Lord, he *did* snuffle! Groaning, Ellery visited the lavatory adjoining the master-bedroom. After a little while he went downstairs and into the den. He came out almost at once, haggard and wild-eyed. He took his hat from the foyer-closet and hurried outdoors into the warm sunshine. He spent fifteen minutes poking about the grounds; the Owen house was shallowly surrounded by timber and seemed isolated as a Western ranch. . . . When he returned to the house, looking grim and disappointed, the others were all conscious, making mewing little sounds and holding their heads like scared children.

"Queen, for God's sake," began Gardner hoarsely.

"Whoever it was used that luminal in the lavatory upstairs," said Ellery, flinging his hat away and wincing at a sudden pain in his head. "The stuff Mrs. Mansfield gave Mrs. Owen yesterday to make her sleep. Except that almost the whole of that large bottle was used. Swell sleeping draught! Make yourselves comfortable while I conduct a little investigation in the kitchen. I think it was the java." But when he returned he was grimacing. "No luck. *Madame la Cuisinière,* it seems, had to visit the bathroom at one period; Millan was out in the garage looking at the cars; and the maid was off somewhere, doubtless primping. Result: our friend the luminalist had an opportunity to pour most of the powder from the bottle into the coffee-pot. Damn!"

"I *am* going to call the police!" cried Mrs. Mansfield hysterically, striving to rise. "We'll be murdered in our beds, next thing we know! Laura, I positively insist—"

"Please, please, Mrs. Mansfield," said Ellery wearily. "No heroics. And you would be of greater service if you went into the kitchen and checked the insurrection that's brewing there. The two females are on the verge of packing, I'll swear."

Mrs. Mansfield bit her lip and flounced off. They heard her no longer sweet voice raised in remonstrance a moment later.

"But, Queen," protested Gardner, "we can't go unprotected—"

"What I want to know in my infantile way," drawled Emmy Willowes from pale lips, "is who did it, and why. That bottle upstairs . . . It looks unconscionably like one of us, doesn't it?"

Mrs. Gardner gave a little shriek. Mrs. Owen sank back into her chair.

"One of us?" whispered the red-haired woman.

Ellery smiled without humor. Then his smile faded and he

cocked his head toward the foyer. "What was that?" he snapped suddenly.

They turned, terror-stricken, and looked. But there was nothing to see. Ellery strode toward the front door.

"What is it now, for heaven's sake?" faltered Mrs. Owen.

"I thought I heard a sound—" He flung the door open. The early morning sun streamed in. Then they saw him stoop and pick up something from the porch and rise and look swiftly about outside. But he shook his head and stepped back, closing the door.

"Package," he said with a frown. "I *thought* someone . . ."

They looked blankly at the brown-paper bundle in his hands. "Package?" asked Mrs. Owen. Her face lit up. "Oh, it may be from Richard!" And then the light went out, to be replaced by fearful pallor. "Oh, do you think—?"

"It's addressed," said Ellery slowly, "to you, Mrs. Owen. No stamp, no postmark, written in pencil in disguised block-letters. I think I'll take the liberty of opening this, Mrs. Owen." He broke the feeble twine and tore away the wrapping of the crude parcel. And then he frowned even more deeply. For the package contained only a pair of large men's shoes, worn at the heels and soles—sport oxfords in tan and white.

Mrs. Owen rolled her eyes, her nostrils quivering with nausea. "Richard's!" she gasped. And she sank back, half-fainting.

"Indeed?" murmured Ellery. "How interesting. Not, of course, the shoes he wore Friday night. You're positive they're his, Mrs. Owen?"

"Oh, he *has* been kidnaped!" quavered Mrs. Mansfield from the rear doorway. "Isn't there a note, b-blood . . ."

"Nothing but the shoes. I doubt the kidnap theory now, Mrs. Mansfield. These weren't the shoes Owen wore Friday night. When did you see these last, Mrs. Owen?"

She moaned: "In his wardrobe closet upstairs only yesterday afternoon. Oh—"

"There. You see?" said Ellery cheerfully. "Probably stolen from the closet while we were all unconscious last night. And now returned rather spectacularly. So far, you know, there's been no harm done. I'm afraid," he said with severity, "we're nursing a viper at our bosoms."

But they did not laugh. Miss Willowes said strangely: "Very odd. In fact, insane, Mr. Queen. I can't see the slightest purpose in it."

"Nor I, at the moment. Somebody's either playing a monstrous prank, or there's a devilishly clever and warped mentality behind all this." He retrieved his hat and made for the door.

"Wherever are you going?" gasped Mrs. Gardner.

"Oh, out for a thinking spell under God's blue canopy. But remember," he added quietly, "that's a privilege reserved to detectives. No one is to set foot outside this house."

He returned an hour later without explanation.

At noon they found the second package. It was a squarish parcel wrapped in the same brown paper. Inside there was a cardboard carton, and in the carton, packed in crumpled tissue-paper, there were two magnificent toy sailing-boats such as children race on summer lakes. The package was addressed to Miss Willowes.

"This is getting dreadful," murmured Mrs. Gardner, her full lips trembling. "I'm all goose pimples."

"I'd feel better," murmured Miss Willowes, "if it was a bloody dagger, or something. Toy boats!" She stepped back and her eyes narrowed. "Now, look here, good people, I'm as much a sport as anybody, but a joke's a joke and I'm just a bit fed up on this particular one. Who's manoevring these monkeyshines?"

"Joke," snarled Gardner. He was white as death. "It's the work of a madman, I tell you!"

"Now, now," murmured Ellery, staring at the green-and-cream boats. "We shan't get anywhere this way. Mrs. Owen, have you ever seen these before?"

Mrs. Owen, on the verge of collapse, mumbled: "Oh, my good dear God. Mr. Queen, I don't—Why, they're—they're Jonathan's!"

Ellery blinked. Then he went to the foot of the stairway and yelled: "Johnny! Come down here a minute."

Master Jonathan descended sluggishly, sulkily. "What you want?" he asked in a cold voice.

"Come here, son." Master Jonathan came with dragging feet. "When did you see these boats of yours last?"

"Boats!" shrieked Master Jonathan, springing into life. He pounced on them and snatched them away, glaring at Ellery.

"My boats! Never seen such a place. My boats! You stole 'em!"

"Come, come," said Ellery, flushing, "be a good little man. When did you see them last?"

"Yest'day! In my toy-chest! My boats! Scan'lous," hissed Master Jonathan, and fled upstairs, hugging his boats to his scrawny breast.

"Stolen at the same time," said Ellery helplessly. "By thunder, Miss Willowes, I'm almost inclined to agree with you. By the way, who bought those boats for your son, Mrs. Owen?"

"H-his father."

"Damn," said Ellery for the second time that impious Sunday, and he sent them all on a search of the house to ascertain if anything else were missing. But no one could find that anything had been taken.

It was when they came down from upstairs that they found Ellery regarding a small white envelope with puzzlement.

"Now what?" demanded Gardner wildly.

"Stuck in the door," he said thoughtfully. "Hadn't noticed it before. This *is* a queer one."

It was a rich piece of stationery, sealed with blue wax on the back and bearing the same pencilled scrawl, this time addressed to Mrs. Mansfield.

The old lady collapsed in the nearest chair, holding her hand to her heart. She was speechless with fear.

"Well," said Mrs. Gardner huskily, "open it."

Ellery tore open the envelope. His frown deepened. "Why," he muttered, "there's nothing at all inside!"

Gardner gnawed his fingers and turned away, mumbling. Mrs. Gardner shook her head like a dazed pugilist and stumbled toward the bar for the fifth time that day. Emmy Willowes's brow was dark as thunder.

"You know," said Mrs. Owen almost quietly, "that's mother's stationery." And there was another silence.

Ellery muttered: "Queerer and queerer. I *must* get this organized. . . . The shoes are a puzzler. The toy boats might be construed as a gift; yesterday was Jonathan's birthday; the boats are his—a distorted practical joke. . . ." He shook his head. "Doesn't wash. And this third—an envelope without a letter in it. That would seem to point to the envelope as the important thing. But the envelope's the property of Mrs. Mansfield. The only other thing—ah, the wax!" He scanned the blue blob on the back narrowly, but it bore no seal-insignia of any kind.

"That," said Mrs. Owen again in the quiet unnatural voice, "looks like our wax, too, Mr. Queen, from the library."

Ellery dashed away, followed by a troubled company. Mrs. Owen went to the library desk and opened the top drawer.

"Was it here?" asked Ellery quickly.

"Yes," she said, and then her voice quivered. "I used it only Friday when I wrote a letter. Oh, good . . ."

There was no stick of wax in the drawer.

And while they stared at the drawer, the front doorbell rang.

It was a market-basket this time, lying innocently on the porch. In it, nestling crisp and green, were two large cabbages.

Ellery shouted for Gardner and Millan, himself led the charge down the steps. They scattered, searching wildly through the brush and woods surrounding the house. But they found nothing. No sign of the bell-ringer, no sign of the ghost who had cheerfully left a basket of cabbages at the door as his fourth odd gift. It was as if he were made of smoke and materialized only for the instant he needed to press his impalpable finger to the bell.

They found the women huddled in a corner of the living room, shivering and white-lipped. Mrs. Mansfield, shaking like an aspen, was at the telephone ringing for the local police. Ellery started to protest, shrugged, set his lips, and stooped over the basket.

There was a slip of paper tied by string to the handle of the basket. The same crude pencil-scrawl. . . . "Mr. Paul Gardner."

"Looks," muttered Ellery, "as if you're elected, old fellow, this time."

Gardner stared as if he could not believe his eyes. "Cabbages!"

"Excuse me," said Ellery curtly. He went away. When he returned he was shrugging. "From the vegetable-bin in the outside pantry, says Cook. She hadn't thought to look for missing *vegetables*, she told me with scorn."

Mrs. Mansfield was babbling excitedly over the telephone to a sorely puzzled officer of the law. When she hung up she was red as a newborn baby. "That will be *quite* enough of this crazy nonsense, Mr. Queen!" she snarled. And then she collapsed in a chair and laughed hysterically and shrieked: "Oh, I knew you were making the mistake of your life when you married that beast, Laura!" and laughed again like a madwoman.

The law arrived in fifteen minutes, accompanied by a howling siren and personified by a stocky brick-faced man in chief's stripes and a gangling young policeman.

"I'm Naughton," he said shortly. "What the devil's goin' on here?"

Ellery said: "Ah, Chief Naughton. I'm Queen's son—Inspector Richard Queen of Centre Street. How d'ye do?"

"Oh!" said Naughton. He turned on Mrs. Mansfield sternly. "Why didn't you say Mr. Queen was here, Mrs. Mansfield? You ought to know—"

"Oh, I'm sick of the lot of you!" screamed the old lady. "Nonsense, nonsense, nonsense from the instant this weekend began! First that awful actress-woman there, in her short skirt and legs and things, and then this—this—"

Naughton rubbed his chin. "Come over here, Mr. Queen, where we can talk like human beings. What the deuce happened?"

Ellery with a sigh told him. As he spoke, the Chief's face grew redder and redder. "You mean you're serious about this business?" he rumbled at last. "It sounds plain crazy to me. Mr. Owen's gone off his nut and he's playing jokes on you people. Good God, you can't take this thing serious!"

"I'm afraid," murmured Ellery, "we must. . . . What's that? By heaven, if that's another manifestation of our playful ghost—!" And he dashed toward the door while Naughton gasped and pulled it open, to be struck by a wave of dusk. On the porch lay the fifth parcel, a tiny one this time.

The two officers darted out of the house, flashlights blinking and probing. Ellery picked up the packet with eager fingers. It was addressed in the now familiar scrawl to Mrs. Paul Gardner. Inside were two identically shaped objects: chessmen, kings. One was white and the other was black.

"Who plays chess here?" he drawled.

"Richard," shrieked Mrs. Owen. "Oh, my God, I'm going mad!"

Investigation proved that the two kings from Richard Owen's chess-set were gone.

The local officers came back, rather pale and panting. They had found no one outside. Ellery was silently studying the two chessmen.

"Well?" said Naughton, drooping his shoulders.

"Well," said Ellery quietly. "I have the most brilliant notion, Naughton. Come here a moment." He drew Naughton aside and began to speak rapidly in a low voice. The others stood limply about, twitching with nervousness. There was no longer any pretense of self-control. If this was a joke, it was a ghastly one indeed. And Richard Owen looming in the background . . .

The Chief blinked and nodded. "You people," he said shortly, turning to them, "get into that library there." They gaped. "I mean it! The lot of you. This tomfoolery is going to stop right now."

"But, Naughton," gasped Mrs. Mansfield, "it couldn't be any of us who sent those things. Mr. Queen will tell you we weren't out of his sight today—"

"Do as I say, Mrs. Mansfield," snapped the officer.

They trooped, puzzled, into the library. The policeman rounded up Millan, the cook, the maid, and went with them. Nobody said anything; nobody looked at anyone else. Minutes passed; a half-hour; an hour. There was the silence of the grave from beyond the door to the living room. They strained their ears. . . .

At seven-thirty the door was jerked open and Ellery and the Chief glowered in on them. "Everybody out," said Naughton shortly. "Come on, step on it."

"Out?" whispered Mrs. Owen. "Where? Where is Richard? What—"

The policeman herded them out. Ellery stepped to the door of the den and pushed it open and switched on the light and stood aside.

"Will you please come in here and take seats," he said dryly; there was a tense look on his face and he seemed exhausted.

Silently, slowly, they obeyed. The policeman dragged in extra chairs from the living room. They sat down. Naughton drew the shades. The policeman closed the door and set his back against it.

Ellery said tonelessly: "In a way this has been one of the most remarkable cases in my experience. It's been unorthodox from every angle. Utterly nonconforming. I think, Miss Willowes, the wish you expressed Friday night has come true. You're about to witness a slightly cock-eyed exercise in criminal ingenuity."

"Crim—" Mrs. Gardner's full lips quivered. "You mean—there's been a crime?"

"Quiet," said Naughton harshly.

"Yes," said Ellery in gentle tones, "there has been a crime. I might say—I'm sorry to say, Mrs. Owen—a major crime."

"Richard's d—"

"I'm sorry." There was a little silence. Mrs. Owen did not weep; she seemed dried out of tears. "Fantastic," said Ellery at last. "Look here." He sighed. "The crux of the problem was the clock. The Clock That Wasn't Where It Should Have Been, the clock with the invisible face. You remember I pointed out that, since I hadn't seen the reflection of the luminous hands in that mirror there, the clock must have been moved. That was a tenable theory. But it wasn't the *only* theory."

"Richard's dead," said Mrs. Owen, in a wondering voice.

"Mr. Gardner," continued Ellery quickly, "pointed out one possibility: that the clock may still have been over this door, but that something or someone may have been standing in front of the mirror. I told you why that was impossible. But," and he went suddenly to the tall mirror, "there was still another theory which accounted for the fact that I hadn't seen the luminous hands' reflection. And that was: that when I opened the door in the dark and peered in and saw nothing, the clock was still there but the *mirror* wasn't!"

Miss Willowes said with a curious dryness: "But how could that be, Mr. Queen? That—that's silly."

"Nothing is silly, dear lady, until it is proved so. I said to myself: How could it be that the mirror wasn't there at that instant? It's apparently a solid part of the wall, a built-in section in this modern room." Something glimmered in Miss Willowes's eyes. Mrs. Mansfield was staring straight before her, hands clasped tightly in her lap. Mrs. Owen was looking at Ellery with

glazed eyes, blind and deaf. "Then," said Ellery with another
sign, "there was the very odd nature of the packages which
have been descending upon us all day like manna from heaven.
I said this was a fantastic affair. Of course it must have occurred
to you that someone was trying desperately to call our attention
to the secret of the crime."

"Call our at—" began Gardner, frowning.

"Precisely. Now, Mrs. Owen," murmured Ellery softly, "the
first package was addressed to you. What did it contain?" She
stared at him without expression. There was a dreadful silence.
Mrs. Mansfield suddenly shook her, as if she had been a child.
She started, smiled vaguely: Ellery repeated the question.

And she said, almost brightly: "A pair of Richard's sport oxfords."

He winced. "In a word, *shoes*. Miss Willowes," and despite
her nonchalance she stiffened a little, "you were the recipient
of the second package. And what did that contain?"

"Jonathan's toy boats," she murmured.

"In a word, again—*ships*. Mrs. Mansfield, the third package
was sent to you. It contained what, precisely?"

"Nothing." She tossed her head. "I still think this is the purest
drivel. Can't you see you're driving my daughter—all of us—
insane? Naughton, are you going to permit this farce to continue? If you know what's happened to Richard, for goodness'
sake tell us!"

"Answer the question," said Naughton with a scowl.

"Well," she said defiantly, "a silly envelope, empty, and
sealed with our own wax."

"And again in a word," drawled Ellery, *"sealing-wax.* Now,
Gardner, to you fell the really whimsical fourth bequest. It
was—?"

"Cabbage," said Gardner with an uncertain grin.

"Cabbages, my dear chap; there were two of them. And
finally, Mrs. Gardner, you received what?"

"Two chessmen," she whispered.

"No, no. Not just two chessmen, Mrs. Gardner. Two *kings.*"
Ellery's gray eyes glittered. "In other words in the order named
we were bombarded with gifts . . ." He paused and looked at
them, and continued softly, *"'of shoes and ships and sealing-
wax, of cabbages and kings.'"*

. . .

There was the most extraordinary silence. Then Emmy Willowes gasped: "The Walrus and the Carpenter. *Alice's Adventures in Wonderland!*"

"I'm ashamed of you, Miss Willowes. Where precisely does Tweedledee's Walrus speech come in Carroll's duology?"

A great light broke over her eager features. *"Through the Looking Glass!"*

"Through the Looking Glass," murmured Ellery in the crackling silence that followed. "And do you know what the subtitle of *Through the Looking Glass* is?"

She said in an awed voice: *"And What Alice Found There."*

"A perfect recitation, Miss Willowes. We were instructed, then, to go through the looking glass and, by inference, find something on the other side connected with the disappearance of Richard Owen. Quaint idea, eh?" He leaned forward and said brusquely: "Let me revert to my original chain of reasoning. I said that a likely theory was that the mirror didn't reflect the luminous hands because the mirror wasn't there. But since the wall at any rate is solid, the mirror itself must be movable to have been shifted out of place. How was this possible? Yesterday I sought for two hours to find the secret of that mirror—or should I say . . . looking glass?" Their eyes went with horror to the tall mirror set in the wall, winking back at them in the glitter of the bulbs. "And when I discovered the secret, I looked *through the looking glass* and what do you suppose I—a clumsy Alice, indeed!—found there?"

No one replied.

Ellery went swiftly to the mirror, stood on tiptoe, touched something, and something happened to the whole glass. It moved forward as if on hinges. He hooked his fingers in the crack and pulled. The mirror, like a door, swung out and away, revealing a shallow closet-like cavity.

The women with one breath screamed and covered their eyes.

The stiff figure of the Mad Hatter, with Richard Owen's unmistakable features, glared out at them—a dead, horrible, baleful glare.

Paul Gardner stumbled to his feet, choking and jerking at his collar. His eyes bugged out of his head. "O-O-Owen," he gasped. "Owen. He *can't* be here. I b-b-buried him myself under the big rock behind the house in the woods. Oh, my God." And he smiled a dreadful smile and his eyes turned over and he collapsed in a faint on the floor.

Ellery sighed. "It's all right now, De Vere," and the Mad Hatter moved and his features ceased to resemble Richard Owen's magically. "You can come out now. Admirable bit of statuary histrionics. And it turned the trick, as I thought it would. There's your man, Mr. Naughton. And if you'll question Mrs. Gardner, I believe you'll find that she's been Owen's mistress for some time. Gardner obviously found it out and killed him. Look out—there *she* goes, too!"

"What I can't understand," murmured Emmy Willowes after a long silence late that night, as she and Mr. Ellery Queen sat side by side in the local bound for Jamaica and the express for Pennsylvania Station, "is—" She stopped helplessly. "I can't understand so many things, Mr. Queen."

"It was simple enough," said Ellery wearily, staring out the window at the rushing dark countryside.

"But who is that man—that De Vere?"

"Oh, he! A Thespian acquaintance of mine temporarily 'at liberty.' He's an actor—does character bits. You wouldn't know him, I suppose. You see, when my deductions had led me to the looking glass and I examined it and finally discovered its secret and opened it, I found Owen's body lying there in the Hatter costume—"

She shuddered. "Much too realistic drama to my taste. Why didn't you announce your discovery at once?"

"And gain what? There wasn't a shred of evidence against the murderer. I wanted time to think out a plan to make the murderer give himself away. I left the body there—"

"You mean to sit there and say you knew Gardner did it all the time?" she demanded, frankly skeptical.

He shrugged. "Of course. The Owens had lived in that house barely a month. The spring on that compartment is remarkably well concealed; it probably would never be discovered unless you knew it existed and were looking for it. But I recalled that Owen himself remarked Friday night that Gardner had designed 'this development.' I had it then, naturally. Who more likely than the architect to know the secret of such a hidden closet? Why he designed and had built a secret panel I don't know; I suppose it fitted into some architectural whim of his. So it had to be Gardner, you see." He gazed thoughtfully at the dusty ceiling of the car. "I reconstructed the crime easily enough. After we retired Friday night Gardner came down to have it out with Owen about Mrs. Gardner—a lusty wench, if I ever saw one. They had words: Gardner killed him. It must have been an unpremeditated crime. His first impulse was to hide the body. He couldn't take it out Friday night in that awful rain without leaving traces on his night-clothes. Then he remembered the panel behind the mirror. The body would be safe enough there, he felt, until he could remove it when the rain stopped and the ground dried to a permanent hiding-place; dig a grave, or whatnot. . . . He was stowing the body away in the closet when I opened the door of the den; that was why I didn't see the reflection of the clock. Then, while I was in the library, he closed the mirror-door and dodged upstairs. I came out quickly, though, and he decided to brazen it out; even pretended he thought I might be 'Owen' coming up.

"At any rate, Saturday night he drugged us all, took the body out, buried it, and came back and dosed himself with the drug to make his part as natural as possible. He didn't know I had found the body behind the mirror Saturday afternoon. When, Sunday morning, I found the body gone, I knew of course the reason for the drugging. Gardner, by burying the body in a place unknown to anyone—without leaving, as far as he knew, even a clue to the fact that murder had been committed at all —was naturally doing away with the primary piece of evidence in any murder-case . . . *the corpus delicti.* . . . Well, I found the opportunity to telephone De Vere and instruct him in what he had to do. He dug up the Hatter's costume somewhere, managed to get a photo of Owen from a theatrical office, came down here. . . . We put him in the closet while Naughton's man was detaining you people in the library. You see, I had to build up suspense, make Gardner give himself away, break down his moral resistance. He had to be forced to disclose where he had buried the body; and he was the only one who could tell us. It worked."

The actress regarded him sidewise out of her clever eyes.

Ellery sighed moodily, glancing away from her slim legs outstretched to the opposite seat. "But the most puzzling thing of all," she said with a pretty frown. "Those perfectly fiendish and fantastic packages. Who sent them, for heaven's sake?"

Ellery did not reply for a long time. Then he said drowsily, barely audible above the clatter of the train: "You did, really."

"*I?*" She was so startled that her mouth flew open.

"Only in a manner of speaking," murmured Ellery, closing his eyes. "Your idea about running a mad tea-party out of *Alice* for Master Jonathan's delectation—the whole pervading spirit of the Reverend Dodgson—started a chain of fantasy in my own brain, you see. Just opening the closet and saying that Owen's body had been there, or even getting De Vere to act as Owen, wasn't enough. I had to prepare Gardner's mind psychologically, fill him with puzzlement first, get him to realize after a while where the gifts with their implications were leading. . . . Had to torture him, I suppose. It's a weakness of mine. At any rate, it was an easy matter to telephone my father, the Inspector; and he sent Sergeant Velie down and I managed to smuggle all those things I'd filched from the house out into the woods behind and hand good Velie what I had. . . . He did the rest, packaging and all."

She sat up and measured him with a severe glance. "Mr. Queen! Is that cricket in the best detective circles?"

He grinned sleepily. "I had to do it, you see. Drama, Miss Willowes. You ought to be able to understand that. Surround a murderer with things he doesn't understand, bewilder him, get him mentally punch-drunk, and then spring the knock-out blow, the crusher. . . . Oh, it was devilish clever of me, I admit."

She regarded him for so long and in such silence and with such supple twisting of her boyish figure that he stirred uncomfortably, feeling an unwilling flush come to his cheeks. "And what if I may ask," he said lightly, "brings that positively lewd expression to your Peter Pannish face, my dear? Feel all right? Anything wrong? By George, how *do* you feel?"

"As Alice would say," she said softly, leaning a little toward him, "curiouser and curiouser."

1948:

After-Dinner Story

William Irish

MacKenzie got on the elevator at the thirteenth floor. He was a water-filter salesman and had stopped in at his home office to make out his accounts before going home for the day. Later on that night he told his wife, half-laughingly, that that must have been why it happened to *him*, his getting on at the thirteenth floor. A lot of buildings omit them.

The red bulb bloomed and the car stopped for him. It was an express, omitting all floors, both coming and going, below the tenth. There were two other men in it when he got on, not counting the operator. It was late in the day, and most of the offices had already emptied themselves. One of the passengers was a scholarly looking man with rimless glasses, tall and slightly stooped. The time came when MacKenzie learned all their names. This was Kenshaw. The other was stout and cherubic-looking, one of two partners in a struggling concern that was trying to market fountain pens with tiny light bulbs in their barrels—without much success. He was fiddling with one of his own samples on the way down, clicking it on and off with an air of proud ownership. He turned out to be named Lambert.

The car was very efficient looking, very smooth running, sleek with bronze and chromium. It appeared very safe. It stopped at the next floor down, the twelfth, and a surly looking individual with bushy brows stepped in, Prendergast. Then the number 11 on the operator's call board lit up, and it stopped there too. A man about MacKenzie's own age and an older man with a trim white mustache were standing there side by side when the door opened. However, only the young man got on; the elder man gripped him by the arm in parting and turned away remarking loudly, "Tell Elinor I was asking for her." The younger answered, " 'By, Dad," and stepped in. Hardecker was his name. Almost at the same time 10 was flashing.

The entry from 11 had turned to face the door, as all passengers are supposed to do in an elevator for their own safety. MacKenzie happened to glance at the sour-pussed man with the bushy brows at that moment; the latter was directly behind the newest arrival. He was glaring at the back of Hardecker's head with baleful intensity; in fact MacKenzie had never seen such a hundred-watt glower anywhere before except on a movie "heavy." The man's features, it must be admitted, lent themselves to just such an expression admirably; he had a swell headstart even when his face was in repose.

MacKenzie imagined this little by-play was due to the newcomer's having inadvertently trodden on the other's toe in turning to face forward. As a matter of fact, he himself was hardly conscious of analyzing the whole thing thus thoroughly; these were all just disconnected thoughts.

Ten was still another single passenger, a bill collector judging by the sheaf of pink, green, and canary slips he kept riffling through. He hadn't, by the gloomy look he wore, been having much luck today; or maybe his feet hurt him. This one was Megaffin.

There were now seven people in the car, counting the operator, standing in a compact little group facing the door, and no more stops due until it reached street level. Not a very great crowd; certainly far from the maximum the mechanism was able to hold. The framed notice, tacked to the panel just before MacKenzie's eyes, showed that it had been last inspected barely ten days before.

It never stopped at the street floor.

MacKenzie, trying to reconstruct the sequence of events for his wife that night, said that the operator seemed to put on added speed as soon as they had left the tenth floor behind. It was an express, so he didn't think anything of it. He remembered noticing at this point that the operator had a boil on the back of his neck, just above his uniform collar, with a Maltese cross of adhesive over it. He got that peculiar sinking sensation at the pit of his stomach many people get from a too-precipitate drop. The man near him, the young fellow from the eleventh, turned and gave him a half-humorous, half-pained look, so he knew that he must be feeling it too. Someone farther back whistled slightly to show his discomfort.

The car was a closed one, all metal, so you couldn't see the shaft doors flashing up. They must have been ticking off at a furious rate, just the same. MacKenzie began to get a peculiar ringing in his ears, like when he took the subway under the East River, and his knee-joints seemed to loosen up, trying to buckle under him.

But what really first told him—and all of them—that something had gone wrong and this was not a normal descent, was the sudden, futile, jerky way the operator was wangling the control lever to and fro. It traveled the short arc of its orbit readily enough, but the car refused to answer to it. He kept slamming it into the socket at one end of the groove, marked Stop for all eyes to read, and nothing happened. Fractions of seconds, not minutes, were going by.

They heard him say in a muffled voice, "Look out! We're going to hit!" And that was all there was time for.

The whole thing was a matter of instants. The click of a camera-shutter. The velocity of the descent became sickening; MacKenzie felt as if he were going to throw up. Then there was a tremendous bang like a cannon, an explosion of blackness, and of bulb-glass showering down as the light went out.

They all toppled together in a heap, like a bunch of ninepins. MacKenzie, who had gone over backward, was the luckiest of the lot; he could feel squirming bodies bedded under him, didn't touch the hard-rubber floor of the car at all. However, his hip and shoulder got a bad wrench, and the sole of his foot went numb, through shoe and all, from the stinging impact it got flying up and slapping the bronze wall of the car.

There was no opportunity to extricate one's self, to try to regain one's feet. They were going up again—on springs or something. It was a little sickening too, but not as bad as the coming down had been. It slackened, reversed into a drop, and they banged a second time. Not with the terrific impact of the first, but a sort of cushioned bang that scrambled them up even more than they were already. Somebody's shoe grazed MacKenzie's skull. He couldn't see it but quickly caught it and warded it aside before it kicked him and gave him a fracture.

A voice near him was yelling, "Stop it! Cut it out!" half-hysterically, as though the jockeying up and down could be controlled. Even MacKenzie, badly frightened and shaken up as he was, hadn't lost his head to that extent.

The car finally settled, after a second slight bounce that barely cleared the springs under it at all, and a third and almost unnoticeable jolt. The rest was pitch darkness, a sense of suffocation, a commingling of threshing bodies like an ant heap, groans from the badly hurt and an ominous sigh or two from those even beyond groaning.

Somebody directly under MacKenzie was not moving at all. He put his hand on him, felt an upright, stiff collar, and just above it a small swelling, crisscrossed by plaster. The operator was dead. There was an inertness that told MacKenzie, and the rubber matting beneath the operator's skull was sticky.

He felt then for the sleek metal wall of the enclosure that had buried them all alive, reached up it like a fly struggling up glass, with the heels of his hands and the points of his elbows. He squirmed the rest of his body up after these precarious grips. Upright again, he leaned against cold bronze.

The voice, there's always one in every catastrophe or panic, that had been pleading to "Cut it out!" was now begging with childish vehemence: "Get me outa here! For the love of Mike, I've got a wife and kids. Get me outa here!"

MacKenzie had the impression it was the surly-looking fellow with the bushy eyebrows. The probabilities, he felt, were all for it. Such visible truculence and toughness are usually all hollow inside, a mask of weakness.

"Shut up," he said, "I've got a wife too. What's that got to do with it?"

The important thing, he recognized, was not the darkness, nor their trapped position at the bottom of a sealed-up shaft, nor even any possible injuries any of them had received. But the least noticeable of all the many corollaries of their predicament was the most dangerous. It was that vague sense of stuffiness, of suffocation. Something had to be done about that at once. The operator had opened the front panel of the car at each floor, simply by latchmotion. There was no reason why that could not be repeated down here, even though there was no accompanying opening in the shaft wall facing it. Enough air would filter down the crack between the jammed-in car and the wall, narrow though it was, to keep them breathing until help came. They were going to need that air before this was over.

MacKenzie's arms executed interlocking circles against the satiny metal face of the car, groping for the indented grip used to unlatch it. "Match," he ordered. "Somebody light a match. I'm trying to get this thing open. We're practically airtight in here."

The immediate, and expected, reaction was a howl of dismay from the tough-looking bird, like a dog's craven yelp.

Another voice, more self-controlled, said, "Wait a minute." Then nothing happened.

"Here I am; here, hand 'em to me," said MacKenzie, shoveling his upturned hand in and out through the velvety darkness.

"They won't strike, got all wet. Glass must have cut me." And then an alarmed "My shirt's all covered with blood!"

"All right, it mayn't be yours," said MacKenzie steadyingly. "Feel yourself before you let loose. If it is, hold a handkerchief to it. That bulb glass isn't strong enough to pierce very deep." And then in exasperation he hollered out, "For the love of—! Six men! Haven't any of you got a match to give me?" Which was unfair, considering that he himself had run short just before he left his office, and had been meaning to get a folder at the cigar store when he got off the car. "Hey, you, the guy that was fiddling with that trick fountain pen coming down, how about that gadget of yours?"

A new voice, unfrightened but infinitely crestfallen, answered disappointedly: "It—it broke." And then with a sadness that betokened there were other, greater tragedies than what had happened to the car: "It shows you can't drop it without breakage. And that was the chief point of our whole advertising campaign." Then an indistinct mumble: "Fifteen hundred dollars capital! Wait'll Belman hears what a white elephant we've got on our hands." Which, under the circumstances, was far funnier than was intended.

At least he's not yellow, whoever he is, thought MacKenzie. "Never mind," he exclaimed suddenly. "I've got it." His fingertips had found the slot at the far end of the seamless cast-bronze panel. The thing didn't feel buckled in any way but if the concussion had done that to it, if it refused to open. . . .

He pulled back the latch, leaning over the operator's lifeless body to do so, and tugged at the slide. It gave, fell back about a third of its usual orbit along the groove, then stalled unmanageably. That was sufficient for their present needs, though there was no question of egress through it. The rough-edged bricks of the shaft wall were a finger's width beyond the lips of the car's orifice; not even a venturesome cat could have gotten a paw between without jamming it. What mattered was that they wouldn't asphyxiate now, no matter how long it took to free the mechanism, raise it.

"It's all right, fellows," he called reassuringly to those behind him, "I've got some air into the thing now."

If there was light farther up the shaft, it didn't reach down this far. The shaft wall opposite the opening was as black as the inside of the car itself.

He said, "They've heard us. They know what's happened. No use yelling at the top of your voice like that, only makes it tougher for the rest of us. They'll get an emergency crew on the job. We'll just have to sit and wait, that's all."

The nerve-tingling bellows for help, probably the tough guy again, were silenced shamefacedly. A groaning still kept up intermittently from someone else. "My arm, oh, Gawd, it hurts!" The sighing, from an injury that had gone deeper still, had quieted suspiciously some time before. Either the man had fainted, or he, too, was dead.

MacKenzie, matter-of-factly but not callously, reached down for the operator's outflung form, shifted it into the angle between two of the walls, and propped it upright there. Then he sat himself down in the clear floor space provided, tucked up his legs, wrapped his arms around them. He wouldn't have called himself a brave man; he was just a realist.

There was a momentary silence from all of them at once, one of those pauses. Then, because there was also, or seemed to be, a complete stillness from overhead in the shaft, panic stabbed at the tough guy again. "They gonna leave us here all night?" he whimpered. "What you guys sit there like that for? Don't you wanna get out?"

"For Pete's sake, somebody clip that loud-mouth on the chin!" urged MacKenzie truculently.

There was a soundless indrawn whistle. "My arm! Oh, my arm!"

"Must be busted," suggested MacKenzie sympathetically. "Try wrapping your shirt tight around it to kill the pain."

Time seemed to stand still, jog forward a few notches at a time every so often, like something on a belt. The rustle of a restless body, a groan, an exhalation of impatience, an occasional cry from the craven in their midst, whom MacKenzie sat on each time with increasing acidity as his own nerves slowly frayed.

The waiting, the sense of trapped helplessness, began to tell on them, far more than the accident had.

"They may think we're all dead and take their time," someone said.

"They never do in a case like this," MacKenzie answered shortly. "They're doing whatever they're doing as fast as they can. Give 'em time."

A new voice, that he hadn't heard until then, said to no one in particular, "I'm glad my father didn't get on here with me."

Somebody chimed in, "I wish I hadn't gone back after that damn phone call. It was a wrong number, and I coulda ridden down the trip before this."

MacKenzie sneered, "Ah, you talk like a bunch of ten-year-olds! It's happened; what's the good of wishing about it?"

He had a watch on his wrist with a luminous dial. He wished that he hadn't had, or that it had gone out of commission like the other man's trick fountain pen. It was too nerve-racking; every minute his eyes sought it, and when it seemed like half an hour had gone by, it was only five minutes. He wisely refrained from mentioning it to any of the others; they would have kept asking him, "How long is it now?" until he went screwy.

When they'd been down twenty-two and one-half minutes from the time he'd first looked at it, and were all in a state of nervous instability bordering on frenzy, including himself, there was a sudden unexpected, unannounced thump directly overhead, as though something heavy had landed on the roof of the car.

This time it was MacKenzie who leaped up, pressed his cheek flat against the brickwork outside the open panel, and funneled up the paper-thin gap: "Hello! Hello!"

"Yeah," a voice came down, "we're coming to you, take it easy!"

More thumping for a while, as though somebody were jigging over their heads. Then a sudden metallic din, like a boiler factory going full blast. The whole car seemed to vibrate with it, it became numbing to touch it for long at any one point. The confined space of the shaft magnified the noise into a torrent of sound, drowning out all their remarks. MacKenzie couldn't stand it, finally had to stick his palms up flat against his ears. A blue electric spark shot down the narrow crevice outside the door from above. Then another, then a third. They all went out too quickly to cast any light inside.

Acetylene torches! They were having to cut a hole through the car roof to get at them. If there was a basement opening in the shaft, and there must have been, the car must have plunged down even beyond that, to sub-basement level, wound up in a dead end cul-de-sac at pit bottom. There was apparently no other way.

A spark materialized eerily through the ceiling. Then another, then a semicircular gush of them. A curtain of fire descended halfway into their midst, illuminating their faces wanly for a minute. Luckily it went out before it touched the car floor.

The noise broke off short and the silence in its wake was deafening. A voice shouted just above them: "Look out for sparks, you guys below, we're coming through. Keep your eyes closed, get back against the walls!"

The noise came on again, nearer at hand, louder than before. MacKenzie's teeth were on edge from the incessant vibration. Being rescued was worse than being stuck down there. He wondered how the others were standing it, especially that poor guy with the broken wing. He thought he heard a voice scream: "Elinor! Elinor!" twice, like that, but you couldn't be sure of anything in that infernal din.

The sparks kept coming down like a dripping waterfall; MacKenzie squinted his eyes cagily, kept one hand shielded up over them to protect his eyesight. He thought he saw one spark shoot across horizontally, instead of down vertically, like all the others; it was a different color too, more orange. He thought it must be an optical illusion produced by the alternating glare and darkness they were all being subjected to; either that, or a detached splinter of combusted metal from the roof, ricocheting off the wall. He closed his eyes all the way, just to play safe.

There wasn't much more to it after that. The noise and sparks stopped abruptly. They pried up the crescent-shaped flap they had cut in the roof with crowbars, to keep it from toppling inward and crushing those below. The cool, icy beams of torches flickered through. A cop jumped down into their midst and ropes were sent snaking down after him. He said in a brisk, matter-of-fact way: "All right, who's first now? Who's the worst hurt of yez all?"

His torch showed three forms motionless at the feet of the others in the confined space. The operator, huddled in the corner where MacKenzie had propped him; the scholarly looking man with the rimless glasses (minus them now, and a deep gash under one eye to show what had become of them) lying senseless on his side; and the young fellow who had got on at the eleventh, tumbled partly across him, face down.

"The operator's dead," MacKenzie answered as spokesman for the rest, "and these two're out of their pain just now. There's a guy with a busted arm here, take him first."

The cop deftly looped the rope under the armpits of the ashen-faced bill collector, who was knotting the slack of one sleeve tightly in his other hand and sweating away like a fish in the torchlight.

"Haul away!" the cop shouted toward the opening. "And take your time, the guy's hurt."

The bill collector went up through the ceiling, groaning, legs drawn up under him like a trussed-up fowl.

The scholarly looking man went next, head bobbing down in unconsciousness. When the noose came down empty, the cop bent over to fasten it around the young fellow still on the floor.

MacKenzie saw him change his mind, pry open one eyelid, pass the rope on to the tough-looking mug who had been such a cry-baby, and who was shaking all over from the nervous reaction to the fright he'd had.

"What's the matter with him?" MacKenzie butted in, pointing to the floor.

"He's dead," the cop answered briefly. "He can wait, the living come first."

"Dead! Why, I heard him say he was glad his father didn't get on with him, long after we hit!"

"I don't care what you heard him say!" the cop answered. "He coulda said it, and still be dead now! Nuts. Are you telling me my business? You seem to be pretty chipper for a guy that's just come through an experience like this!"

"Skip it," said MacKenzie placatingly. He figured it was no business of his anyway, if the guy had seemed all right at first and now was dead. He might have had a weak heart.

He and the disheartened fountain pen entrepreneur seemed to be the only two out of the lot who were totally unharmed. The latter, however, was so brokenhearted over the failure of his appliance to stand up under an emergency, that he seemed hardly to care whether he went up or stayed down or what became of him. He kept examining the defective gadget even on his way up through the aperture in the car roof, with the expression of a man who has just bitten into a very sour lemon.

MacKenzie was the last one up the shaft, except the two fatalities. He was pulled in over the lip of the basement opening, from which the sliding doors had been taken down bodily. It was a bare four feet above the roof of the car; in other words the shaft continued on down past it for little more than the height of the car. He couldn't understand why it had been built that way, and not ended flush with the basement, in which case their long imprisonment could have been avoided. It was explained to him later, by the building superintendent, that it was necessary to give the car additional clearance underneath, else it would have run the risk of jamming each time it came down to the basement.

There were stretchers there in the basement passageway, and the bill collector and the studious-looking man were being given first aid by a pair of interns. The hard-looking egg was gulping down a large glass of spirits of ammonia between clicking teeth. MacKenzie let one of the interns look him over, at the latter's insistence; was told what he knew already, that he was O.K. He gave his name and address to the lieutenant of police in charge, and walked up a flight of stairs to the street level, thinking, "The old-fashioned way's the best after all."

He found the lobby of the building choked with a milling crowd, warded off a number of ambulance chasers who tried to tell him how badly hurt he was. "There's money in it, buddy, don't be a sucker!" MacKenzie phoned his wife from a nearby booth to shorten her anxiety, then he left the scene for home.

His last fleeting impression was of a forlorn figure standing there in the lobby, a man with a trim white mustache, the father of the young fellow lying dead below, buttonholing every cop within reach, asking over and over again, "Where's my son? Why haven't they brought my son up yet?" And not getting any answer from any of them—which was an answer in itself. MacKenzie pushed out into the street.

Friday, that was four days later, the doorbell rang right after supper and he had a visitor. "MacKenzie? You were in that elevator Monday night, weren't you, sir?"

"Yes," MacKenzie grinned, he sure was.

"I'm from Police Headquarters. Mind if I ask you a few questions? I've been going around to all of 'em checking up."

"Come in and sit down," said MacKenzie interestedly. His first guess was that they were trying to track down labor sabotage, or some violation of the building laws. "Matter, anything phony about it?"

"Not for our money," said the dick, evidently because this was the last leg of what was simply a routine questioning of all the survivors, and he refused to differ from his superiors. "The young fellow that was lying dead there in the bottom of the car —not the operator but young Wesley Hardecker—was found by the examiner to have a bullet embedded in his heart."

MacKenzie, jolted, gave a long-drawn whistle that brought his Scotty to the door questioningly. "Whew! You mean somebody shot him while we were all cooped up down there in that two-by-four?"

The dick showed, without being too pugnacious about it, that he was there to ask the questions, not answer them. "Did you know him at all?"

"Never saw him in my life before, until he got on the car that night. I know his name by now, because I read it in the papers next day; I didn't at the time."

The visitor nodded, as though this was the answer he'd gotten from all the others too. "Well, did you hear anything like a shot while you were down there?"

"No, not before they started the blowtorches. And after that, you couldn't have heard one anyway. Matter of fact, I had my hands over my ears at one time. I did see a flash, though," he went on eagerly. "Or at least I remember seeing one of the sparks shoot *across* instead of dropping down, and it was more orange in color."

Again the dick nodded. "Yeah, a couple of others saw that too. That was probably it, right there. Did it light up anyone's face behind it, anything like that?"

"No," MacKenzie admitted, "my eyes were all pinwheels, between the coal blackness and these flashing sparks coming down through the roof; we'd been warned, anyway, to keep them shut a minute before." He paused thoughtfully, went on: "It doesn't seem to hang together, does it? Why should anyone pick such a time and place to—"

"It hangs together beautifully," contradicted the dick. "It's his old man, the elder Hardecker, that's raising a stink, trying to read something phony into it. It's suicide while of unsound mind, and has been all along; and that's what the findings of the coroner's inquest are going to be too. We haven't turned up anything that throws a doubt on that. Old man Hardecker himself hasn't been able to identify a single one of you as having ever known or seen his son—or himself—before six o'clock last Monday evening. The gun was the fellow's own, and he had a license for it. He had it with him when he got in the car. It was under his body when it was picked up. The only fingerprints brought out on it were his. The examiner finds the wound a contact wound, powder burns all around it."

"The way we were crowded together down there, any kind of a shot at anyone would have been a contact," MacKenzie tried to object.

The dick waved this aside. "The nitrate test shows that his fingers fired the shot. It's true that we neglected to give it to anyone else at the time, but since there'd been only one shot fired out of the gun, and no other gun was found, that don't stack up to much. The bullet, of course, was from that gun and no other, ballistics has told us. The guy was a nervous, high-strung young fellow. He went hysterical down there, cracked up, and when he couldn't stand it any more, took himself out of it. And against this, his old man is beefing that he was happy, he had a lovely wife, they were expecting a kid and he had everything to live for."

"Well, all right," objected MacKenzie mildly, "but why should he do it when they were already working on the roof over us, and it was just a matter of minutes before they got to us. Why not before? That don't sound logical. Matter of fact, his voice sounded calm and unfrightened enough while we were waiting."

The detective got up, as though the discussion were ended, but condescended to enlighten him on his way to the door: "People don't crack up at a minute's notice; it was after he'd been down there twenty minutes, half an hour, it got him. When you heard him say that, he was probably trying to hold himself together, kid himself he was brave or something. Any psychiatrist will tell you what noise'll do to someone already under a strain or tension. The noise of the blowtorches gave him the finishing touch; that's why he did it then, couldn't think straight any more. As far as having a wife and expecting a kid is concerned, that would only make him lose his head all the quicker. A man without ties or responsibilities is always more cold-blooded in an emergency."

"It's a new one on me, but maybe you're right. I only know water-filters."

"It's my job to be right about things like that. Good night, Mr. MacKenzie."

The voice on the wire said, "Mr. MacKenzie? Is this the Mr. Stephen MacKenzie who was in an elevator accident a year ago last August? The newspapers gave—"

"Yes, I was."

"Well, I'd like you to come to dinner at my house next Saturday evening, at exactly seven o'clock."

MacKenzie cocked his brows at himself in the wall mirror. "Hadn't you better tell me who you are, first?"

"Sorry," said the voice, crisply. "I thought I had. I've been doing this for the past hour or so, and it's beginning to tell on me. This is Harold Hardecker, I'm head of the Hardecker Import and Export Company."

"Well, I still don't place you, Mr. Hardecker," MacKenzie said levelly. "Are you one of the men who was on that elevator with me?"

"No, my son was. He lost his life."

"Oh," said MacKenzie. He remembered now. A man with a trim white mustache, standing in the milling crowd, buttonholing the cops as they hurried by. . . .

"Can I expect you then at seven next Saturday, Mr. MacKenzie? I'm at—Park Avenue."

"Frankly," said MacKenzie, who was a plain soul not much given to social hypocrisy, "I don't see any point to it. I don't believe we've ever spoken to one another before. Why do you single me out?"

Hardecker explained patiently, even good-naturedly, "I'm not singling you out, Mr. MacKenzie. I've already contacted each of the others who were on the car that night with my son, and they've all agreed to be there. I don't wish to disclose what I have in mind beforehand; I'm giving this dinner for that purpose. However, I might mention that my son died intestate, and his poor wife passed away in childbirth in the early hours of the following morning. His estate reverted to me, and I am a lonely old man, without friends or relatives, and with more money already than I know what to do with. It occurred to me to bring together five perfect strangers, who shared a common hazard with my son, who were with him during the last few moments of his life." The voice paused, insinuatingly, to let this sink in. Then it resumed, "If you'll be at my house for dinner Saturday at seven, I'll have an announcement of considerable importance to make. It's to your interest to be present when I do."

MacKenzie scanned his water-filter-salesman's salary with his mind's eye, and found it altogether unsatisfactory, as he had done not once but many times before. "All right," he agreed, after a moment's consideration. . . .

Saturday at six he was still saying, "You can't tell me. The guy isn't in his right mind, to do a thing like this. Five people that

he don't know from Adam, and that don't know each other. I
wonder if it's a practical joke?"

"Well, if you feel that way, why didn't you refuse him?" said
his wife, brushing off his dark blue coat.

"I'm curious to find out what it's all about. I want to see
what the gag is." Curiosity is one of the strongest of human
traits. It's almost irresistible. The expectation of getting something for nothing is no slouch either. MacKenzie was a good
guy, but he was a guy after all, not an image on a stained glass
window.

At the door she said with belated anxiety, "Steve, I know you
can take care of yourself and all that, but if you don't like the
looks of things, I mean if none of the others show up, don't stay
there alone."

He laughed. He'd made up his mind by now, had even spent
the windfall ahead of time, already. "You make me feel like one
of those innocents in the old silent pictures, that were always
being invited to a big blowout and when they got there they
were alone with the villain and just supper for two. Don't
worry, Toots, if there's no one else there, I turn around and
come back."

The building had a Park Avenue address, but was actually on
one of the exclusive side streets just off that thoroughfare. A
small ultra-ultra co-operative, with only one apartment to a
floor. "Mr. Harold Hardecker?" asked Mr. MacKenzie in the
lobby. "Stephen MacKenzie."

He saw the hallman take out a small typed list of five names,
four of which already had been penciled out, and cross out the
last one. "Go right up, Mr. MacKenzie. Third floor."

A butler opened the single door in the elevator foyer for him,
greeted him by name and took his hat. A single glance at the
money this place spelled would have been enough to restore
anyone's confidence. People that lived like this were perfectly
capable of having five strangers in to dinner, subdividing a dead
son's estate among them, and chalking it off as just that evening's little whimsey. The sense of proportion alters above a
certain yearly income.

He remembered Hardecker readily enough as soon as he saw
him coming toward him along the central gallery that seemed

to bisect the place like a bowling alley. It took him about three and a half minutes to get up to him, at that. The man had aged appreciably from the visual snapshot that was all he'd had of him at the scene of the accident. He was slightly stooped, very thin at the waist, looked as though he'd suffered. But the white mustache was as trim and needle-pointed as ever, and he had on one of the new turned-over soft collars under his dinner jacket, which gave him a peculiarly boyish look in spite of the almost blinding white of his undiminished hair, cropped close as a Prussian's.

Hardecker held out his hand, said with just the right mixture of dignity and warmth, "How do you do, Mr. MacKenzie, I'm very glad to know you. Come in and meet the others and have a pickup."

There were no women present in the living room, just the four men sitting around at ease. There was no sense of strain, of stiffness; an advantage that stag gatherings are apt to have over mixed parties anyway, not through the fault of women, but through men's consciousness of them.

Kenshaw, the scholarly looking man, had a white scar still visible under his left eye where his glasses had broken. The cherubic Lambert had deserted the illuminated fountain pen business, he hurriedly confided, unasked, to MacKenzie, for the ladies' foundation-girdle business. No more mechanical gadgets for him. Or as he put it, unarguably, "A brassiere they gotta have, or else. But who needs a fountain pen?" The hard-bitten mug was introduced as Prendergast, occupation undisclosed. Megaffin, the bill collector, was no longer a bill collector. "I send out my own now," he explained, swiveling a synthetic diamond around on his pinky.

MacKenzie selected Scotch, and when he'd caught up with the rest the butler came to the door, almost as though he'd been timing him through a knothole. He just looked in, then went away again.

"Let's go and get down to business now, gentlemen, shall we?" Hardecker grinned. He had the happy faculty, MacKenzie said to himself, of making you feel perfectly at home, without overdoing it, getting in your hair. Which looks easier than it is.

.   .   .

No flowers, candles, or fripperies like that were on the table set for six; just good substantial man's board. Hardecker said, "Just sit down anywhere you choose, only keep the head for me." Lambert and Kenshaw took one side, Prendergast and Megaffin on the other. MacKenzie sat down at the foot. It was obvious that whatever announcement their host intended making was being kept for the end of the meal, as was only fitting.

The butler had closed a pair of sliding doors beyond them after they were all in, and he stayed outside. The waiting was done by a man. It was a typical bachelor's repast, plain, marvelously cooked, without dainty or frivolous accessories to detract from it, salads, vegetables, things like that. Each course had its vintage corollary. And at the end no cloying sweets—Roquefort cheese and coffee with the blue flame of Courvoisier flickering above each glass. It was a masterpiece. And each one, as it ended, relaxed in his chair in a haze of golden daydreams. They anticipated coming into money, money they hadn't had to work for, maybe more money than they'd ever had before. It wasn't such a bad world after all.

One thing had struck MacKenzie, but since he'd never been waited on by servants in a private home before, only in restaurants, he couldn't determine whether it was unusual or customary. There was an expensive mahogany buffet running across one side of the dining room, but the waiter had done no serving or carving on it, had brought in each portion separately, always individually, even the roast. The coffee and the wines, too, had been poured behind the scenes, the glasses and the cups brought in already filled. It gave the man a lot more work and slowed the meal somewhat, but if that was the way it was done in Hardecker's house, that was the way it was done.

When they were already luxuriating with their cigars and cigarettes, and the cloth had been cleared of all but the emptied coffee cups, an additional dish was brought in. It was a silver chalice, a sort of stemmed bowl, holding a thick yellowish substance that looked like mayonnaise. The waiter placed it in the exact geometrical center of the table, even measuring with his eye its distance from both sides, and from the head and foot, and shifting its position to conform. Then he took the lid off and left it open. Threads of steam rose sluggishly from it. Every eye was on it interestedly.

"Is it well mixed?" they heard Hardecker ask.

"Yes, sir," said the waiter.

"That will be all, don't come in again."

The man left by the pantry door he had been using, and it clicked slightly after it had closed behind him.

Somebody—Megaffin—asked cozily: "What's *that* got in it?" evidently on the lookout for still more treats.

"Oh, quite a number of things," Hardecker answered carelessly, "whites of eggs, mustard, as well as certain other ingredients all beaten up together."

MacKenzie, trying to be funny, said, "Sounds like an antidote."

"It is an antidote," Hardecker answered, looking steadily down the table at him. He must have pushed a call button or something under the table, for the butler opened the sliding doors and stood between them, without coming in.

Hardecker didn't turn his head. "You have that gun I gave you? Stand there, please, on the other side of those doors and see that no one comes out of here. If they try it, you know what to do."

The doors slipped to again, effaced him, but not before MacKenzie, facing that way, had seen something glimmer in his hand.

Tension was slow in coming on, the change was too abrupt, they had been too steeped in the rosy afterglow of the meal and their own imminent good fortune. Then too, not all of them were equally alert mentally, particularly Megaffin, who had been on such a fourth dimensional plane of unaccustomedness all evening he couldn't tell menace from hospitality, even when a gun was mentioned.

Its first focal point was Hardecker's own face—that went slowly white, grim, remorseless. From there it darted out to MacKenzie and Lambert, caught at them, paled them too. The rest grew allergic to it one by one, until there was complete silence at the table.

Hardecker spoke. Not loudly, not angrily, but in a steely, pitiless voice. "Gentlemen, there's a murderer in our midst."

Five breaths were sharply indrawn together, making a fearful "Ffff!" sound around the table. Not so much aghast at the statement itself, as aghast at the implication of retribution that lurked just behind it. And behind that was the shadowy suspicion that it had already been exacted.

No one said anything.

The hard, remorseless cores of Hardecker's eyes shot from face to face. He was smoking a long slim cigar, cigarette-thin. He pointed it straight out before him, indicated them all with it without moving it much, like a dark finger of doom. "Gentlemen, one of you killed my son." Pause. "On August 30, 1936." Pause. "And hasn't paid for it yet."

The words were like a stone going down into a deep pool of transparent water, and the ripples spreading out from them spelled fear.

MacKenzie said slowly, "You setting yourself above the properly constituted authorities? The findings of the coroner's inquest were suicide while of unsound mind. Why do you hold them incompe—"

Hardecker cut him short like a whip. "This isn't a discussion. It's"—a long pause, then very low, but very audible—"an execution."

There was another of those strangling silences. They took it in a variety of ways, each according to his temperament. MacKenzie just kept staring at him, startled, apprehensive. Apprehensive, but not inordinately frightened, any more than he had been that night on the elevator. The scholarly looking Kenshaw had a rebuking look on his face, that of a teacher for an unruly pupil, and the scar on his cheek stood out whitely. Megaffin looked shifty, like some small weasel at bay, planning its next move. The pugnacious-looking guy was going to cave in again in a minute, judging by the wavering of his facial lines. Lambert pinched the bridge of his nose momentarily, dropped his hand, mumbled something that sounded like, "*Oy*, I give up my pinochle club to come here, yet!"

Hardecker resumed, as though he hadn't said anything unusual just now. "I know who the man is. I know which one among you the man is. It's taken me a year to find out, but now I know, beyond the shadow of a doubt." He was looking at his cigar now, watching the ash drop off of its own weight onto his coffee saucer. "The police wouldn't listen to me, they insisted it was suicide. The evidence was insufficient to convince them the first time, and for all I know it still may be." He raised his eyes. "But I demand justice for the taking of my son's life." He took an expensive, dime-thin, octagonal watch out of his pocket, placed it face up on the table before him. "Gentlemen, it's now nine o'clock. In half an hour, at the most, one of you will be dead. Did you notice that you were all served separately just now? One dish, and one alone out of all of them, was deadly. It's putting in its slow, sure work right as we sit here." He pointed to the silver tureen, equidistant from all of them. "There's the answer. There's the antidote. I have no wish to set myself up as executioner above the law. Let the murderer be the chooser. Let him reach out and save his life and stand convicted before all of you. Or let him keep silent and go down to his death without confessing, privately executed for what can't be publicly proved. In twenty-five minutes collapse will come without warning. Then it will be too late."

It was Lambert who voiced the question in all their minds. "But are you sure you did this to the right—"

"I haven't made any mistake, the waiter was carefully rehearsed, you are all perfectly unharmed but the killor."

Lambert didn't seem to derive much consolation from this. "Now he tells us! A fine way to digest a meal," he brooded aloud. "Why didn't you serve the murderer first, so then the rest of us could eat in peace at least?"

"Shut up," somebody said, terrifiedly.

"Twenty minutes to go," Hardecker said, tonelessly, as a chime signal over the radio.

MacKenzie said, without heat, "You can't be sane, you know, to do a thing like this."

"Did you ever have a son?" was the answer.

Something seemed to snap in Megaffin. His chair jolted back. "I'm gettin' out of here," he said hoarsely.

The doors parted about two inches, silently as water, and a black metal cylinder peered through. "That man there," directed Hardecker. "Shoot him where he stands if he doesn't sit down."

Megaffin shrank down in his seat again like a whipped cur, tried to shelter himself behind Prendergast's shoulder. The doors slipped together again into a hairline crack.

"I couldn't," sighed the cherubic-faced Lambert, "feel more at home if I was in the Brown House at Munich!"

"Eighteen minutes," was the comment from the head of the table.

Prendergast suddenly grimaced uncontrollably, flattened his forearms on the table, and ducked his head onto them. He sniveled aloud. "I can't stand it! Lemme out of here! *I* didn't do it!"

A wave of revulsion went around the table. It was not because he'd broken down, analyzed MacKenzie, it was just that he didn't have the face for it. It should have been Lambert with his kewpie physiognomy, if anyone. The latter, however, was having other troubles. He touched the side of his head, tapped himself on the chest. "Whoof!" he murmured. "What heartburn! He should live so long, I don't take this up with my lawyer!"

"This is no way," said MacKenzie surlily. "If you had any kind of a case—"

"This is my way," was Hardecker's crackling answer. "I've given the man his choice. He needn't have it this way; he has his alternative. Fourteen minutes. Let me remind you, the longer the antidote's delayed, the more doubtful its efficiency will be. If it's postponed too long, it may miss altogether."

Conscious of a sticking sensation in his stomach, as though a mass of concrete had lodged there, MacKenzie felt a burning sensation shoot out from it. There is such a thing as nervous indigestion, he knew, but. . . . He eyed the silver goblet reflectively.

But they were all doing that almost incessantly. Prendergast had raised his head again, but it remained a woebegone mask of infantile fretfulness. Megaffin was green in the face and kept moistening his lips. Kenshaw was the most self-controlled of the lot; he had folded his arms and just sat there, as though waiting to see which one of the others would reach for the salvation in the silver container.

MacKenzie could feel a painful pulsing under his solar plexus now, he was in acute discomfort that verged on cramp. The thought of what this might be was bringing out sweat on his forehead.

Lambert reached out abruptly, and they all quit breathing for a minute. But his hand dodged the silver tureen, plunged into a box of perfectos to one side of it. He grabbed up two, stuck one in his breast pocket, the other between his teeth. "On you," he remarked resentfully to Hardecker.

Somebody gave a strained laugh at the false alarm they had all had. Kenshaw took off his glasses, wiped them ruefully, as though disappointed it hadn't been the payoff after all.

MacKenzie said, "You're alienating whatever sympathy's due you, by pulling a stunt like this."

"I'm not asking for sympathy," was Hardecker's coldly ferocious answer. "It's atonement I want. Three lives were taken from me: My only son, my daughter-in-law, their prematurely born child. I demand payment for that!"

Lambert said aloud, for his own benefit, "Jennie wouldn't believe this when I tell her."

Prendergast clutched his throat all at once, whimpered: "I can't breathe! He's done it to *me,* so help me!"

MacKenzie, hostile now to Hardecker, tried to steady him just on general principle. "Gas around the heart, maybe. Don't fall for it if you're not sure."

"Don't fall for it," was the ungrateful yelp, "and if I drop dead are *you* gonna bring me back?"

"He ought to be arrested for this," said Kenshaw, displaying emotion for the first time. His glasses had clouded over, giving him a peculiarly sightless look.

"Arrested?" snapped Lambert. He wagged his head from side to side. "He's going to be sued like no one was ever sued before! When I get through with him he'll go on relief."

Hardecker threw him a contemptuous look. "About ten minutes," he said. "He seems to prefer the more certain way. Stubborn, eh? He'd rather die than admit it."

MacKenzie gripped the seat of his chair, his churning insides heaving. He thought, "If this is the McCoy that I'm feeling now, I'm going to bash his head in with a chair before I go. I'll give him something to poison innocent people about!"

Megaffin was starting to swear at their tormentor, in a whining, guttural singsong.

"*Mazel tov,*" seconded Lambert, with a formal nod of approval. "Your breath, but my ideas."

"Five minutes. It will almost certainly fail if it's not downed within the next thirty seconds." Hardecker pocketed his watch,

as though there were no further need for consulting it.
MacKenzie gagged, hauled at the knot of his tie, undid his
collar-button. A needle of suffocating pain had just splintered
into his heart.

Only the whites of Prendergast's eyes showed, he was going
off into some fit or fainting spell. Even Lambert quit pulling at
his cigar, as though it sickened him. Kenshaw took off his glasses
for the third time in five minutes, to clear them.

A pair of arms suddenly shot out, grasped the silver bowl,
swung it. It was uptilted over someone's face and there was a
hollow, metallic groaning coming from behind it, infinitely
gruesome to hear. It had happened so quickly, MacKenzie
couldn't be sure who it was for a minute, long as he had been
sitting at the macabre table with all of them. He had to do it by
a quick process of elimination. Man sitting beside Lambert—
Kenshaw, the scholarly-looking one, the man who had had least
to say since the ordeal had begun! He was gulping with a con-
vulsive rising and falling of his Adam's apple, visible in the
shadow just below the lower rim of the bowl.

Then suddenly he flung it aside, his face was visible again, the
drained receptacle clanged against the wall where he'd cast it,
dropped heavily to the floor. He couldn't talk for a minute or
two, and neither could anyone else, except possibly Hardecker,
and he didn't. Just sat staring at the self-confessed culprit with
pitiless eyes.

Finally Kenshaw panted, cheeks twitching, "Will it—will it—
save me?"

Hardecker folded his arms, said to the others, but without
taking his eyes off Kenshaw: "So now you know. So now you see
whether I was right or not."

Kenshaw was holding his hands pressed tightly to the sides of
his head. A sudden flood of words was unloosed from him, as
though he found it a relief to talk now, after the long unbearable
tension he'd been through. "Sure you were right, and I'd do it
over again! I'm glad he's gone. The rich man's son that had
everything. But that wasn't enough for him, was it? He had to
show off how good he was—Horatio Alger stuff, paddle your
own canoe from riches to more riches! He couldn't take a job
with your own firm, could he? No, people might say you were
helping him. He had to come to the place *I* worked and ask for

a job. Not just anonymously. No, he had to mention whose son
he was, to swing the scales in his favor! They were afraid to
offend you, they thought maybe they'd get a pull with you,
through him. It didn't count that I'd been with them all the best
years of my life, that I had someone home too, just like he had,
that I couldn't go anywhere else and mention the name of an
influential father! They fired me."

His voice rose shrilly. "D'you know what happened to me?
D'you know or care how I tramped the streets in the rain, at my
age, looking for work? D'you know my wife had to get down on
her knees and scrub dirty office corridors? D'you know how I
washed dishes, carried sandwich-boards through the streets,
slept on park benches, all on account of a smart-aleck with
Rover Boy ideas? Yes, it preyed on my mind, why wouldn't it?
I suppose you found the threatening letters I wrote him, that's
how you knew."

Hardecker just shook his head slightly in denial.

"Then he got on the elevator that day. He didn't see me,
probably wouldn't have known me if he had, but I saw him. I
knew him. Then we fell—and I hoped he was dead, I hoped
he was dead! But he wasn't. The idea took hold of me slowly,
waiting down there in the dark. The torches started making
noise, and I grabbed him, I was going to choke him. But he
wrenched himself free and took out his gun to defend himself
against what I guess he thought was a fear-crazed man. I
wasn't fear-crazed, I was revenge-crazed, I knew what I was
doing!

"I grabbed his hand. Not the gun, but the hand that was
holding it. I turned it around the other way, into his own heart.
He said 'Elinor, Elinor!' but that didn't save him; that was the
wrong name, that was *his* wife not mine. I squeezed the finger
he had on the trigger with my own, and he fired his own
weapon. So the police were right, it was suicide in a way.

"He leaned against me, there wasn't room enough in there
to fall. I flung myself down first under him, so they'd find us that
way, and eased him down on top of me. He bled on me a little
while and then he quit. And when they came through I pretended I'd fainted."

Hardecker said, "Murderer. Murderer." Like drops of ice
water. "He didn't *know* he'd done all that to you; oh, why didn't

you give him a chance at least, why weren't you a man? Murderer! Murderer!"

Kenshaw started reaching downward to the floor, where he'd dropped his glasses when he had seized the antidote. His face was on a level with the table top. He scowled: "No matter what they've all heard me say just now, you'll never be able to prove I did it. Nobody saw me. Only the dark."

A whisper sounded: "And that's where you're going. Into the dark."

Kenshaw's head vanished suddenly below the table. The empty back of his chair whirled over sidewise, cracked against the floor.

They were all on their feet now, bending over him. All but Hardecker. MacKenzie got up from his knees. "He's dead!" he said. "The antidote didn't work in time!"

Hardecker said, "That wasn't the antidote, that was the poison itself. He hadn't been given any until he gulped that down. He convicted himself and carried out sentence upon himself with one and the same gesture. I hadn't known which one of you it was until then. I'd only known it hadn't been my son's own doing, because, you see, the noise of those torches wouldn't have affected him much, he was partly deaf from birth."

He pushed his chair back and stood up. "I didn't summon you here under false pretenses; his estate will be divided in equal parts among the four of you that are left. And now I'm ready to take my own medicine. Call the police, let them and their prosecutors and their courts of law decide whether I killed him or his own guilty conscience did!"

1950:

Catfish Story

Lawrence G. Blochman

Max Ritter, the youngest, smartest, thinnest, darkest and homeliest lieutenant of detectives on the Northbank police force, came to work as usual at seven o'clock. When he saw the message on his desk, he did not even wait for the morning line-up, but drove directly to 2214 Kanold Street.

He stopped his car in front of a small, two-story stucco house which, like every other two-story stucco house in the street, had a patch of lawn, an elm tree, and a hydrangea bush beside the miniature front stoop. The two plainclothesmen sitting on the front steps got up when Ritter approached.

"The Coroner hasn't showed up yet," one of them said. "The body's still on the stairs. His name was Robert Arlington. He was a house guest of the Smiths."

Ritter pushed open the front door, glanced briefly about the overstuffed early 1939 Grand Rapids interior, then devoted himself to the late Robert Arlington.

The dead man was sprawled head down, near the bottom of the stairway. He was young, probably in his late twenties. He wore only a suit of silk underwear, the shirt of which had been ripped up the front.

"The Smiths are upstairs," said one of the plainclothesmen.

61

Ritter found a tall, athletically built man in woolly pajamas sitting on the edge of a bed, solemnly studying his big hands. A diminutive blonde in a blue silk negligee stood in front of a mirror, nervously applying lipstick. As the man arose, Ritter noted that he had patient, mastiff jowls, and a broad forehead that reached well up into his thinning, graying hair.

"I'm Jonathan Smith," he said. "This is my wife, Monica. I suppose you want to hear the story all over again."

"You'll tell it a hundred times before we're through," Ritter said. "Shoot."

Monica Smith glided into the protective circle of her husband's arm, like a frightened bird seeking cover. She came scarcely to her husband's shoulder, and seemed at least fifteen years his junior. She had big, baby-blue eyes of incredible innocence, and a rosebud mouth that seemed incapable of melting butter. Some of her other features, however, chastely suggested by the lines of the blue negligee, might well melt many things including the granite heart of a police detective.

"There's not much to tell, really," Smith said. "I walk in my sleep. I've had a recurring dream for the past year—usually about an intruder that I must overcome and throw out of my home. I've been meaning to see a psychiatrist about it, but you know how one puts off those things. Well, when I have that dream I walk in my sleep, and last night I dreamed I was fighting with a burglar. I woke up to find myself standing at the top of the stairs. Monica was standing beside me, shaking my arm and crying. Poor Arlington was lying on the steps, just where you see him now."

Smith moistened his lips. He looked at the detective with clear, gray, frank, inquiring eyes as though to say, I know this sounds implausible, but you do believe it, don't you?

"Go on," said Ritter.

"Well, I was horrified, of course. It was obvious that I must have grappled with Arlington in my sleep—that I made him part of my dream and threw him downstairs. I rushed down to help him, but he was obviously dead. He must have struck his head on a step. I immediately phoned the police."

"What time was this?" Ritter asked.

"Exactly three minutes to four," Monica Smith volunteered. "I looked at my watch while Jonathan was phoning." She did not look at the detective as she spoke. Her eyes were fixed on her husband's rugged features in frightened adoration. Smith's arm tightened reassuringly about her shoulders.

"How long was this guy Arlington staying with you folks?" Ritter pursued.

"Three days." Smith's voice rumbled pleasantly.

"And how long have you known him?"

"Three days." Jonathan Smith smiled.

"Then he was Mrs. Smith's friend?"

"No. Oh, no." Still looking at her husband, Monica Smith shook her head so violently that a silken wisp of hair slid wantonly across one eye.

Then Jonathan Smith explained that Arlington had come to Northbank especially to consult him; that he was doing some research in ichthyology, and, having read Professor Smith's *Mutations of Teleostean Fishes,* wanted his help on a scientific problem. So, as they had room, Smith had asked him to stay at the house. . . .

"What did you say your profession was?" the detective asked.

"I'm an ichthyologist."

"Spell that," Ritter said.

Smith did, and Ritter wrote on the back of a dogeared envelope.

"Where did Arlington sleep?" the detective asked.

"Downstairs, just off the kitchen. We can't afford a maid, so we've turned the maid's room into a guest room."

"Then what the hell was Arlington doing on the stairs at four in the morning, if he slept downstairs?" Ritter demanded.

"I don't suppose we'll ever know—now," said Jonathan Smith. He lifted his hand from his wife's shoulder and gently brushed the wanton lock of hair back from her forehead. He smiled sadly. "I don't know why all this is necessary," he said. "There's no mystery. I killed Arlington. It was completely involuntary, but I did kill him. And I suppose you'll have to arrest me on some homicide charge or other, won't you?"

"Can't say till the Coroner comes," Ritter said. "Mind if I look around a little in the meantime?"

Without waiting for a reply, the detective opened a closet door, ran an appraising eye over a row of expensive-looking high-heeled shoes, poked into a rack of dresses. The dresses were not new, but they were cut with distinction and made of first-class materials. Some of them bore New York and Miami labels. But the Smiths could not afford a maid. . . .

Ritter found nothing of interest in the bathroom, nor in what was obviously Professor Smith's study. So he went downstairs.

The small room off the kitchen, occupied by the late Mr. Arlington, appeared to have been previously visited either by a freak windstorm or a man packing to go somewhere in a hurry. Two suitcases stood open on the floor, and there was clothing on the bed, the floor, and all the chairs. Max Ritter noted seven more suits of silk underwear, two tweed suits and three gabardines bearing the labels of Hollywood and Miami tailors, and a dozen expensive sport shirts of bright colors not usually associated with the academic life.

The death of Robert Arlington presented a problem that cried out for scientific police procedure. Yet the Northbank police possessed no laboratory, and Northbank was still burdened with the coroner system which placed a premium on skill in politics rather than in forensic medicine. So Max Ritter picked up the telephone and called his friend Dr. Daniel Webster Coffee, pathologist for Pasteur Hospital, who was probably just finishing his breakfast.

"Hi, Doc? Max Ritter. Say, Doc, what's a—" Ritter consulted his dog-eared envelope. "What's an ichthyologist? . . . Expert on fishes? . . . I ain't surprised. His story sounds fishy to me. . . . Yeah, I got an ichthyologist here who's mixed up in a homicide—an ichthyologist that walks in his sleep. Say, Doc, can you rush your breakfast and stop off here at 2214 Kanold Street on your way to the hospital? I'd like you to look at the dead man before the Coroner gets here and puts the evil eye on him. . . . I'll be waiting, Doc."

Dan Coffee did not like to hurry through breakfast. In fact he disliked hurrying through any meal, unless he happened to be engrossed in a laboratory problem which made him forget about food altogether. Ordinarily Dan Coffee liked to eat as much as he disliked wearing a vest, even in the dead of winter. He had a closet full of virgin vests. He was, in fact, the despair of some of Northbank's best tailors because of his genius for making the most skillful sartorial job resemble a ready-made one-flight-up suit of clothes in less than a week. But a call from Max Ritter was a little like the clang of the alarm bell to an old-time fire horse. Dr. Coffee did rush through his kipper. He spurned a second cup from the percolator, kissed his wife good-bye, and climbed into his tired, wind-broken, pre-war coupe.

As Dr. Coffee pulled up in front of 2214 Kanold Street, he saw Max Ritter on the sidewalk, arguing with a stocky, red-faced man in overalls. The red-faced man had a coil of garden hose over his arm and a spade and rake on his shoulder.

"But Mrs. Smith told me to come today," he told the detective. "She told me to spade up the—"

"I don't care what she told you," Ritter said. "There's going to be no gardening around this place today."

"If you'll let me talk to Mrs. Smith—"

"Tomorrow," said Ritter, turning the gardener around, and starting him on his way with a firm hand on his back. "Come back tomorrow. . . . Hi, Doc. The Coroner ain't showed up yet. He had to go to Boone Point last night on a suicide, and since this is election year, he stayed overnight to straddle a few political fences. Shall we go inside to have a look at the stiff?"

"Sure," said Dr. Coffee. "Why?"

While Dr. Coffee was examining the mortal remains of Robert Arlington, Ritter told him the story of the ichthyologist who walked in his sleep, of his pretty blonde wife who couldn't possibly be as innocent as she looked—nobody could be that innocent—and of his discoveries in Mrs. Smith's clothes closet that made him think that the ichthyology business must have been pretty good at one time. Dr. Coffee, as he listened, contemplated the corpse lying head down on the staircase and decided that the late Mr. Arlington was a handsome young man, even in death. The dead man seemed to be smiling at some private roguery that he had carried with him into eternity. It was a worldly, disillusioned smile, a little sad, perhaps because the universe was so full of wickedness, but tolerant withal because of a thorough understanding of all aspects of that wickedness.

Suddenly Dr. Coffee realized that the late Mr. Arlington's waxen features were clear and unmottled. He took three quick steps upstairs to examine the bare feet and legs with intent interest. Then, backing downward, he re-examined the entire body. He noted the torn silk undershirt. He was also interested in Mr. Arlington's hands—soft, white, graceful hands which had apparently never known manual labor, but which had conspicuous black crescents under the well-manicured fingernails. Then, gently if illegally, he lifted the head to examine the damage to the skull, partly concealed by the wavy brown hair. His lower jaw protruded pugnaciously as he made a short, rude noise with his lips.

"They've been lying to you, Max," Dr. Coffee said. "The man didn't die in this position."

"How do you figure that one, Doc?" the detective asked.

"Look at the purple patches on the feet and legs. If the man had been lying head downward for as long as you say, the post-mortem lividity would have appeared on the face and shoulders instead of on the feet. The fact that we have lividity in the lower extremities indicates that the man was sitting up —or was propped up—for some time after death. The body wasn't moved to this head-down position for several hours after the blood stopped circulating."

The detective snorted. "Ichthyologist!" he said. "Sleep walker! My eye!"

"Furthermore," Dr. Coffee continued, "the skull fracture which caused the man's death seems to be parallel to the spine. If he had struck his head by falling backward, the wound should be roughly at right angles."

"Let's go up and talk to the Smiths," Max Ritter said.

Professor Smith patiently told his story all over again. This time Monica did not warm her nervousness against her husband's shoulder. Although Dr. Coffee's eyes never left Smith's placid face as he spoke, the Doctor could not help seeing Monica's reflection in the mirror. She sat behind Dr. Coffee, her hands tightly clasped in her lap, the blue silk of her negligee taut across the provocative rhythm of her breathing.

"Now tell it again," Ritter said, when Smith had finished. "Only this time don't leave out anything."

"But I've told you everything."

"You didn't tell us who moved the body," the detective said.

Monica Smith's hands came unclasped like a spring catch opening. There was a moment of silence. Then Smith's rumbling voice declared calmly: "The body wasn't moved, Lieutenant. The poor fellow has been right on the stairs where I first saw him. And the police came five minutes later."

"Dr. Coffee here says the body was moved," Ritter said. "Doc, tell these folks how you know it."

Dr. Coffee explained the mechanics of post-mortem lividity.

"Convincing, indeed," said Smith. "I wish I could explain the apparent contradiction. But when I woke up—"

"Okay, skip it," Ritter said. "Just tell us exactly what you're doing in Northbank, Professor—if you can."

Professor Smith certainly could—and in learned detail. He had been brought to Northbank, he said, to make a survey for the Barzac Cannery. After the fall tomato pack was in, the cannery had several idle months and was seeking a suitable fresh-water fish that might be put up during the slack season, if it could be planted in the streams and lakes of the region. The cannery people were much interested in the possibility of canning catfish, if the Amiurus Nigricans of the Great Lakes, or the Amiurus Ponderosus of the Mississippi, which grew to a hundred pounds, could be transplanted to the region. Or even a smaller but sweeter catfish such as the Ictalurus Punctatus . . .

"Okay, that's fine," Max Ritter interrupted. "Now about your gardener that I just tossed out of your yard: Is this his regular day to work?"

"Gardener?" Smith asked.

"Oh yes, the gardener," Monica said. "I told him to come today."

"Well, I told him to come tomorrow," said Ritter. "I don't want him tramping around the place till we've finished our investigation. Now, if Mrs. Smith could come down and brew a little caffeine for the doc and me—"

"I usually make the coffee in the morning," Smith said. "I'll be glad to—"

"You stay here and shave," Ritter said. "I want to talk to Mrs. Smith alone."

Max Ritter seemed in no hurry to talk. He sat on the kitchen table, pushed his soft gray hat to the back of his head, fished two cigarettes from his pocket, offered one to Dr. Coffee, and lit them both. He let Monica Smith bustle about the stove for a full minute before he asked suddenly:

"Mrs. Smith, when did you and this guy Arlington go to Florida together?"

Monica Smith dropped a coffee cup. Her baby-blue eyes stared at the detective with dismay, then with defiance. Dr. Coffee noted the quick metamorphosis from kitten to tigress and wondered which was the basic personality.

"I don't know what you mean," Monica said.

"Sure, you do," Ritter said. "And so do I. Who was Arlington?"

"I thought you knew everything." The tigress was still speaking.

"We want to hear you tell it," Ritter said.

Monica got a dustpan and swept up the pieces of cup. It was a fairly complicated operation because one hand was periodically busy correcting the tendency of her negligee to yawn. When she spoke, it was the kitten purring again. "I'll tell you everything," she said, "if you promise not to tell my husband. I want him to hear it from me first. Please."

"Cross my heart," Ritter said. "What about Miami?"

"I was there with Bob Arlington two years ago last winter. We lived together before I married Jonathan."

"Nice gal," said Ritter, "bringing the boy friend home to hubby disguised as a—as a fish expert."

"I didn't bring him here. I didn't even know he was in Northbank until Jonathan brought him home. Bob Arlington was a fast talker."

"Don't tell me this guy Arlington just came here to talk about catfish."

"Of course not. He said he'd been hunting me for months. He wanted me to come back to him."

"Begin at the beginning," Max Ritter said.

Monica Smith resumed her interrupted coffee-making as she told her story. It was a commonplace, tawdry, rather pitiful story—the pretty girl who didn't quite make the grade in Hollywood; the flashy young man with a sympathetic ear, a smooth manner, and a generous bankroll; the quick infatuation, the trusting first love that denied nothing. She had loved him wildly and recklessly, even after she found out he was a professional gambler. She didn't care. When he was in the chips, they lived high; they traveled and drank champagne and she wore jewelry. When he was down in his luck, they lived in furnished rooms, drank water, and pawned her jewelry to give him working capital. She was very happy—until Arlington left her for another woman. Even then she forgave him and took him back when he returned two weeks later, because she loved him. She took him back the second time, too, but she didn't forgive him, because he was drunk and abusive for days after he came back.

After a year of this, a year in which she lost twenty pounds, most of her sanity, and all of her self-respect, she packed up and left. He had been gone three weeks this time, and she left because she was afraid he might still return. And she was afraid she would take him back, because she still loved him. So she ran away to some friends who had a cabin in the Sierras, to try to regain her health, her sanity, and her self-respect.

It was in the Sierras that she met Jonathan Smith. He was working on a California State Fisheries project; stocking trout, she thought. Two weeks after they met, he asked her to marry him.

"I told Jonathan the truth," Monica said. She poured the coffee. "I told him I'd been through an unhappy love affair, and that I didn't feel as though any decent man should even look at me—not for a long time. I didn't tell him Bob Arlington's name, and he's never asked it. I just told him that he couldn't possibly want me, particularly as I didn't love him. Jonathan said that didn't matter; that he loved me and that he would take a chance. He was so kind and patient, and I was so completely demoralized, that—Well, I married him. I needed him, to bring me back to life. It was selfish of me, I guess, but I've tried to make it up to him. I've tried hard to make him a good wife. I didn't want him to regret anything. And now this . . . this . . ."

"Weren't you afraid Arlington might run to your husband with the truth unless you went away with him?"

"I was frantic."

"Did you threaten to kill Arlington unless he left you alone?"

"Why? Bob wasn't afraid of me."

And with reason, Dan Coffee decided. The tigress wasn't real. Monica was all kitten, even when she showed her claws. There was something warm and human and helpless about this girl that appealed to him. And yet—

"I've got one question, Mrs. Smith," Dr. Coffee said. "How could a professional gambler pose as an ichthyologist and fool an expert like your husband?"

"Bob Arlington had a photographic memory," Monica replied. "He could read the *Racing Form* through just once and tell you how Mogul performed against Pickled Beets and Galorette at Aqueduct last year. He could recite the record of every horse that ever ran six furlongs and up, at Bowie or Hialeah or Churchill Downs. Remembering the names of fishes would be just the same to Bob as remembering race horses. He probably read Jonathan's book on the train coming here."

"Did you write to Arlington since you got married?" Ritter asked.

"No."

"Then how did he track you to Northbank?"

"I don't know." Monica bit her lip. "Unless Eddie Drake told him. Eddie was Bob Arlington's partner, on and off. When I left Bob they had a gambling joint together—the Canyon Casino at Los Juegos, Nevada. Last time Bob was broke, I pawned a little ring that my mother gave me before she died. It wasn't very valuable—there were three little diamonds in it—but I wanted it back for sentimental reasons. So I sent Eddie Drake the money and the ticket and my address. I asked Eddie not to mention it to Bob, but maybe Bob saw the letter."

"Now tell us why you moved the body," Ritter said.

"But I didn't. I woke up a little before four and—"

"Sure, we know. You found your husband standing at the top of the stairs," the detective mocked. "You know what I think happened? I think you killed Arlington to keep his mouth shut, and then went to bed and worried about it until your husband started sleepwalking. You came back downstairs, dragged your ex-boy friend to the steps so it would look like an accident. Then you woke up your husband and let him think he did it."

Monica Smith hesitated a long time before she replied.

"All right," she said at last. "Let's say that's what happened. You know, Lieutenant, there was one fine thing about these terrible three days: I found out I really love Jonathan. You can't know what it meant to me to be able to look at Bob Arlington and not get all hot and cold inside, with my knees turning to jelly—to know that all I ever felt for Bob was over and dead and would stay dead, even if he stayed around for years, saying the same flattering things he used to say, with the same charming smile. I'm grateful to him for that—for letting me know that I love Jonathan deeply and sincerely, that I'd do anything in the world for Jonathan. Anything. Why don't you arrest me for the murder of Bob Arlington, Lieutenant? I certainly should have killed him. Why don't you arrest me?"

"Maybe I will," Max Ritter said, "after I find out what you used to crack his skull with. But first—Hello, Brody, what's up?"

The plainclothesman who had just come into the kitchen said: "There's a guy out here with a story you ought to hear, Max. He says he lives next door."

"Bring him in, Brody," Ritter said. "Mrs. Smith, go upstairs and take your husband a cup of coffee, so he'll stay awake. I don't want him walking around in his sleep while I'm in the house."

The man from next door said his name was Pelham. He had come home from a card game shortly after midnight, he said, and thought he saw a shadow moving about in the shrubbery of the Smiths' yard. He had said, "Good evening, Professor," but there was no reply, and the man—if it was a man—had disappeared. He worried about it as he undressed for bed, and half an hour later, as he opened his bedroom window, he looked out again—and again he saw a shadow moving in the shrubbery. This time he got a flashlight and shone the beam into the Smiths' yard, but he did not see the prowler, if it was a prowler. A moment later a car which he had not noticed before drove away from in front of the Smiths' house. The tail light was out and he could not see the license plates. Then he noticed the lights were on in the Smiths' living room, so he thought no more of it—until he saw all the police cars out front this morning.

Ritter thanked Mr. Pelham and promised to call on him again. Then he took Dr. Coffee upstairs again to confront the Smiths with their neighbor's story.

The Smiths could offer no explanation. They had had no visitors. They had heard no car drive away from the house after midnight. The living room lights were out when they went upstairs, because Arlington had already retired to his room.

"We went to bed at ten-thirty," said Jonathan Smith.

"I'd slept very badly for two nights," said Monica Smith. "I just couldn't keep my eyes open last night. I must have been fast asleep by eleven. And I didn't wake up—"

"We know, we know. Till nearly four o'clock." Max Ritter raised his hands in a gesture of surrender, but there was no surrender in the set of his tight lips. "Get dressed, you two. We're going downtown. I'm going to hold you as material witnesses."

On the stairs, Dr. Coffee said to the detective: "Max, I've got to go upstate to do an autopsy for an insurance company. I probably won't be back until tomorrow. But if you find anything, take it right to my lab. Dr. Mookerji will be there."

"The Swami?"

"The Swami did all right on the Starkey case," Dr. Coffee said.

"And the Gable case," Ritter agreed. "What do you think I might find, Doc?"

"Since Arlington probably died sitting up, examine all the chairs for stains. Send the stained fabric to Dr. Mookerji and ask him to test for blood. He may even be able to type the blood for you, in which case he'll want blood samples from your suspects and from the victim. You might also make scrapings from under Arlington's fingernails. They're pretty black for a man who obviously sees a manicurist regularly."

"I noticed that," Ritter said. "I'm likewise a little inquisitive about why his undershirt was ripped."

"Another thing, Max. The body wasn't dragged. I didn't see any marks on the rug or floors. So look for possible bloodstains on the clothes of whoever could have carried him."

"I'll look," the detective said. "See you tomorrow, Doc."

Dr. Coffee returned to Northbank by the early morning train. He went directly to his laboratory in Pasteur Hospital, where he found Dr. Motilal Mookerji, the rotund little Hindu who was his resident pathologist, extremely busy. The Hindu's pink turban bobbed excitedly as he carried a rack of test tubes across the laboratory. He did not see Dr. Coffee come in. Neither did Max Ritter, who sat on a tall stool, his back to the door, watching

Dr. Mookerji drip liquid from a glass rod onto squares of white blotting paper.

As green stains appeared on the blotting paper, a broad smile appeared simultaneously on Mookerji's round face. Dr. Coffee put down his bag. The Hindu and the detective both looked up.

"Welcome, Doctor Sahib! Five times welcome!" Dr. Mookerji exclaimed. "Am just now becoming assistant detective to Leftenant Ritter."

Dan Coffee watched the green stains spread and darken. He asked: "Benzidine test?"

"Leuco-malachite," the Hindu replied. "Am happy to announce positive reaction for presence of blood."

"Hi, Doc," Ritter said. "I found a flatiron in the Smiths' kitchen. It had a couple of hairs sticking to it, and a brown spot that's maybe rust and maybe not. The Swami here says it's blood. So we found the weapon. I also cut a piece of fabric from the back of a big chair in the Smiths' living room. The Swami says that's got blood on it, too."

"Two bloods," Dr. Mookerji amended. "Was able to make extract from stain sufficient for agglutination, and procured splendid double reaction for AB type blood cells, plus O type cells. Having previously classified blood of late deceased Mr. Arlington as O type, can state that person of AB type likewise mingled blood on furniture."

"So it looks like our killer maybe got a finger caught under a corner of the iron when he smacked Arlington," Ritter said.

"The fact that he's in the AB group is going to narrow your field considerably," said Dr. Coffee. "Only one person in twenty has AB type blood. Did you take a sample from Professor Smith?"

"Have offered to do so," Dr. Mookerji said. "Would greatly enjoy blood relationship with such distinguished ichthyologist as Jonathan Smith."

"You didn't tell me you knew this guy Smith," Ritter said.

"Acquaintanceship to date is only vicarious." The Hindu sighed. "Before opting for medical profession, was contemplating career in fisheries department of Indian Civil Service. Was then on intimate terms with Professor Smith's book on *Mutations of Teleostean Fishes*, which is extremely monumental and scientific work. Am informed Professor Smith is currently engaged in surveying catfish situation in Northbank. Would therefore greatly welcome opportunity for comparing American catfishes with Hindu species entitled *Mahsur,* which inhabit unsalted waters of Indian mountain streams and are somewhat delicious when eaten by non-Brahmans. Would—"

"We won't need any more samples," the detective interrupted. "I think I already know who killed Arlington."

"Mister or Missus?" Dr. Coffee asked.

"Come along and see for yourself." Ritter looked at his watch. "I'm going to make the pinch now. But we'll have to make it snappy, because my pinch is strictly by timetable."

On the way to Kanold Street, Dan Coffee asked: "Did you give Dr. Mookerji a look at the fingernail scrapings, Max?"

"I did," Ritter said, "and the Swami says it's good rich topsoil, with just a soupsong of fertilizer."

"You know, Max, I've been wondering why the Smiths didn't jump at the chance of pinning Arlington's death on an outsider," Dr. Coffee said. "The chance was offered on a silver platter when their neighbor told the story of the prowler at midnight. Why didn't they take it? Aside from the fact that each of them suspects the other, they're both probably telling the truth when they say they were asleep at midnight—which must have been the time that Arlington was killed."

"Doc, you've got the makings of a detective," Ritter said. "That's exactly my line of thinking since you left yesterday. If it's a third party, I ask myself, who is it? Well, I get to thinking about little Monica's story yesterday, and I telephone the Chief of Police at Los Juegos, Nevada. I ask him about the Canyon Casino. The Chief says the Canyon Casino is closed down since about two weeks, and that it is the general belief among the stoolies in Los Juegos that the Casino is closed because one of the partners skipped with the bank. And since Partner Eddie Drake is around town for a couple-three days after the Casino closes, dead drunk until he jumps in his car and takes a powder, it is the general belief that Partner Bob Arlington is the guy who skips with the money. So I get Eddie Drake's description from the Chief, and I put it on the ticket with a ten-state alarm to pick up a car with his Nevada license plates. One hour later my own boys pick up a car with Nevada plates in a downtown parking lot, right here in Northbank."

"Interesting," said Dr. Coffee.

"Damned interesting," the detective said. "Because if Eddie Drake kills Arlington, why is Eddie Drake's car still in Northbank? The only answer I come up with is this: Drake doesn't find what he kills Arlington to get. And what does he kill Arlington to get if it isn't the bank from the Canyon Casino which Arlington is supposed to elope with? So maybe the open suitcases and the clothes that clutter up Arlington's room ain't Arlington getting ready to pack, but Drake looking for frog-skins. And maybe the torn undershirt is Eddie Drake looking for a money belt. And maybe—Hey, here we are."

The car stopped in front of the Smith house and the two men got out. The plainclothesman sitting on the front steps waved a smoking cigarette at Ritter.

"What gives, Brody?" Ritter asked.

"Nothing," Brody said. "Except that gardener came back. You said it was okay to let him work today, so he's around back, gardening his head off."

Ritter led Dr. Coffee to the back of the house where a red-faced man in overalls was spading in a dahlia bed.

"You can quit digging now," Ritter said. "I already found what you're digging for."

The man in overalls looked up from his spade and wiped the perspiration from his red face. "Who the hell are you?" he demanded.

"It don't make much difference who I am," Ritter replied. "But it makes a hell of a lot of difference that you're Eddie Drake from Los Juegos, Nevada. How'd you hurt your little finger, Eddie?"

"I caught it in a door," said the man in overalls. "And my name's not Eddie. I'm the gardener here. Mrs. Smith told me to spade up the backyard. You can ask Mrs. Smith."

"Maybe Monica will cover for you," the detective said. "And maybe she won't. In any case, I'm going to pinch you for the murder of Robert Arlington."

"Who's Arlington?"

"He's the guy that buried sixty thousand dollars here in this yard, night before last, when he got wind that you were in town," Ritter said. "He buried it with his bare hands, and you guessed it when you saw the dirt under his fingernails after you conked him with a flatiron. So when you couldn't find the money on or about Arlington's person, you went out to do a little digging yourself, until the next-door neighbor put a flashlight on you and scared you off. Then you decided to do a little daylight gardening, figuring that Monica Smith wouldn't have the heart to put a finger on you when she recognized you."

"I don't get it," said the man in overalls.

"You didn't get the sixty G's either," Ritter went on, "because I noticed the black nails myself, and I did my own digging last night. The money's down at the station now, and I think we ought to go down and look at it. We'll also look for a parking-lot stub that maybe you got in your pocket. And since you got a smashed little finger, we'll take a sample of your blood so Doc Coffee can tell us if you're an AB type." Ritter looked at his watch. "Come on, Eddie," he said.

Another police car was pulling up as the trio reached the front of the house. Monica Smith was the first to get out of the car. Her feet seemed to freeze to the sidewalk when she saw the man in overalls. She blanched.

"That double-take is identification enough for me, Eddie," Ritter said. "Mrs. Smith, why didn't you tell me Eddie Drake was in Northbank?"

"I didn't know he was in Northbank," Monica said.

"Let's quit playing games," Ritter said, "or you'll talk yourself into jail as an accomplice after the fact, Mrs. Smith. Eddie Drake wouldn't be hanging around this house full of cops unless he was damned sure you'd cover for him. When did you talk to Eddie last, Mrs. Smith?"

"He telephoned night before last," Monica said, "but I didn't know he was in Northbank. He said he was calling long-distance."

"Why did he phone?"

"He said he heard Bob Arlington was here, so he was coming to town to pay him a visit—and that I'd better keep my mouth shut, or he'd open his wide to Jonathan. He told me if he showed up as a plumber or a handyman or anything like that, I'd better say I sent for him—or else."

"So when I mentioned the gardener yesterday, you knew it was Eddie."

"I thought so. But I thought he'd just arrived."

"Mrs. Smith, Eddie's going to think you're mighty ungrateful for spilling the truth like this," Ritter said, "because he probably figures he did you a big favor by killing Arlington."

"Eddie killed—?" The shock of surprise gave way to the shock of realization and relief. Monica folded into a pretty little heap on the sidewalk. Jonathan Smith lifted her gently and carried her into the house.

"I guess that's all, Eddie," said Max Ritter, reaching for his handcuffs.

Max Ritter and Dr. Coffee were sitting in the living room of the Smith house, talking to the ichthyologist.

"I think your sleepwalking nights are ended, Professor," Dan Coffee said. "I don't think you'll have any more nightmares about fighting an intruder in your home. But you may have to explain in court why you moved Arlington's body."

"Why do you think I moved it?" Smith asked.

"Arlington was killed while sitting right there." Dr. Coffee pointed to a chair from which a big piece of upholstery had been cut. "He continued to sit there long enough for post-mortem lividity to settle in his legs, so he couldn't have walked to the stairway. And your wife, much as she loves you, isn't big enough or strong enough to have carried the body. That leaves you. You must have wakened three or four hours after the murder. You saw a light downstairs, got up to investigate, and found Arlington dead in the chair. You were afraid that your wife had killed him, so you put out the lights, carried the body to the stairs, and staged your sleepwalking act. So you must have suspected that Arlington was your wife's former boy friend. When, Professor?"

Smith smiled sheepishly. "Almost immediately," he said. "Arlington was remarkably familiar with my book, but when we talked of matters not in the book, he was obviously faking. He didn't know, for instance, that the Gronias, the Leptops, and the Noturus are also genera of catfish. When I realized he was an impostor, I had an overwhelming desire to see him together with Monica. I deliberately brought him into my home. I was glad I did. Monica was uneasy and a little frightened by the situation, but it was quite apparent that her old love for Arlington was quite dead. That's why I thought she may have killed him—because he had threatened her, perhaps, if she did not come back to him. And of course I had to protect her. By the way, what is the penalty under the law for moving a dead body before the arrival of the coroner?"

"None, maybe," Max Ritter said, "if a fellow did it in his sleep and dropped the body on the stairs when he woke up."

1952:

Love Lies Bleeding

Philip MacDonald

Cyprian didn't like rushing over dinner, so they had eaten early. And now, at eight o'clock, he was alone with coffee in Astrid's living room while Astrid herself was in the bedroom out of sight and sound, changing into some frock suitable for the rather tedious party they were going to together.

It was very quiet in Astrid's apartment, very comfortable. The maid had gone as soon as they had finished eating, so there weren't even sounds of movement from dining room and kitchen to disturb the peace. And there was plenty of time. Plenty. Because they needn't arrive at the Ballards' before nine-thirty at the earliest.

Cyprian stretched luxuriously. He picked his coffee cup from the mantel and drained it and set it down again, his fingers momentarily caressing the delicate texture of the thin china.

He strolled about the room, thinking how well Astrid had done with it, taking pleasure in the blendings and contrasts of color under the soft lights, the balance and position of furniture, the choice and subject of the few paintings.

He went back to the mantel, and took the fragile, thistle-shaped liqueur glass from beside his empty coffee cup. He couldn't remember what was in it, and sniffed at it, his thin sensitive nostrils quivering a little as the sharp, bitter-orange aroma stung them pleasantly. He smiled; he should have known that Astrid wouldn't make mistakes.

He sipped slowly, letting the hot stringency slide over his tongue. He turned his back to the room and faced himself in the big mirror over the mantel and was pleased by what he saw. He could find this evening nothing at variance with the appearance of Cyprian Morse as he wished it to be. With absorbed interest he studied Cyrpian—the graceful, high-shouldered slenderness so well set off by the dinner jacket of midnight blue; the fine-textured pallor of the odd, high-cheekboned face with its heavy-lidded eyes and chiseled mouth which seemed to lift at one corner in satire perpetual but never overstressed; the long slim fingers of the hand which twitched with languid dexterity at the tie which so properly enhanced the silken snowy richness of the shirt and its collar.

The blue gleam of the carved lapis lazuli in his signet ring made him think of Charles, and the time when Charles had given it to him. He turned away from the mirror and sipped at the liqueur again and wished Charles were here and wondered how long it would be before Charles returned from Venezuela. He was looking forward to Charles and Astrid meeting, though he wasn't too sure what Charles's initial reaction would be. Astrid would be all right, of course—and, after all, Charles would very soon find out what she was like, just an awfully nice girl, and a great, an inspired designer. He toyed with visions of making Charles work too. With Astrid doing the sets, and Charles letting himself go on weird, macabre décor, Cyprian Morse's *Abanazar* could well be the most sensational production ever seen in the theater.

Cyprian finished the liqueur, and set down the glass. Still musing on the possibilities of *Abanazar,* he dropped into a big low chair, and found himself—his eyes almost level with a coffee table—looking straight at a photograph of Astrid he hadn't seen before. It was an excellent portrait, oddly and interestingly lighted, and the camera had caught and registered that somehow astringent little smile which some people said spoiled her looks, but which had always been for Cyprian a sort of epitome of why he liked her. He went on looking at it now, and thought, as he had thought many times looking at her in life, how necessary a smile it was. Without it there would be no way of knowing that the full-blown and almost aggressive femininity of Astrid's structure was merely an accident in design; no way of telling that in fact she had no nonsense about her but was simply the best of designers and—he was beginning to believe more and more as their association developed—the best of friends.

He stretched again and relaxed in the chair. He was in the after-dinner mood which he liked best, and which only seemed to come when he had had exactly the right amount of a-little-too-much-to-drink. All his senses, all his perceptions, were sharpened to a fine edge beneath a placid sheath of contentment. There was a magazine lying on the table near the photograph, and he reached out a lazy arm and picked it up. It was last month's *Manhattan,* and it fell open in his hands to the theatrical page and the beginning of Burn Heyward's long glowing review of *The Square Triangle.* He knew it nearly by heart, but nevertheless began to read and savor it afresh, starting with the headline, Cyprian Morse Does It Again, and going through its delicious paeans to the shiny super-plum of the very last paragraph, "*. . . There is no doubt left that, despite his youth and (in this instance at least) his dubious choice of subject, Morse is one of the really important playwrights of the day, certainly the most significant in America . . .*"

He heard the door open behind him, and let the magazine fall shut on his knee and said, "Ready?" without turning around.

"*Cyprian!*" said Astrid's voice.

There was something strange about the sound, a quality which inexplicably, as if it had been some dreadful psychic emanation, seemed to change the shape of his every thought and sensation, so that where he had been relaxed and warmly content, he was now tense and chill with formless apprehension.

"*Cyprian!*" said the voice again, and he came to his feet in a single spasmodic movement, turning to face Astrid as he rose.

He stared at her in stunned amazement and a useless hope of disbelief. His flesh crept, and he seemed to feel the hairs on his neck rising like the hackles on a dog.

She came toward him, slowly—and he backed away. She mustn't touch him, she mustn't touch him.

She drew inexorably closer. She held out her arms to him. He didn't know he was still moving away until the edge of the mantelshelf came hard against his shoulders. He could feel sweat clammy-cold on his forehead, his upper lip, his neck. Desperately, his mind struggled for mastery over his body. His mind knew that, in reality, this was merely a distressing incident hardly removed from the commonplace. His mind knew that a few simple words, a curl of the lip, a lift of the shoulders —any or all of these would free him not only now but forever. But the words had to be uttered, the gestures made—and his body refused the tasks.

She was close now. Very close. She was going to touch him. She said, in the same thick voice, "Cyprian! Don't look at me like that." And she said, "I love you, Cyprian, you must know that . . ."

There was a ringing in his ears, and the tight grip of nausea in his stomach. His throat worked as he tried to speak, but no words came from his mouth.

She touched him. She was close against him. His body could feel the dreadful soft warmness of her. There was a mist over his eyes and he could hardly see her through it.

And then her arms were around his neck, soft but implacably strong. His mind screamed something, but the arms tightened their hold. She was speaking, but he couldn't hear through the roaring in his head. Somehow, he tore himself free. Forgetting, he tried to retreat, and thudded against the brick of the mantel. With a scrabbling lunge, he went sideways—and almost fell.

He clutched wildly. His left hand caught the edge of the mantelshelf and checked his fall. His right hand, swinging, struck against something metallic and closed around it.

"Cyprian—" said the voice. "*Cyprian!*"

She was going to touch him again. Through the haze he could see her, the arms reaching.

There was a clatter of metal as the rest of the fire irons fell, and his right hand, still grasping the log pick it had closed around, raised itself above his head and swung downward, with more than all his force.

Through the rushing in his ears, through the red-flecked haze over his eyes, he heard the sick dull crushing of the first blow, saw the slender shape crumple and collapse . . .

The haze and the roaring faded, and he found himself standing half crouched over the thing on the floor—striking down at it again and again. It was as if some outside power had taken charge of him, so that the blows came without his conscious volition—thudding with the broadside of the heavy bar, then thrusting, slashing, tearing with the sharp point of the spike . . .

Then, piercing the haze and thrusting him back into knowledge of himself, there was a sharp pain in his shoulder as a muscle twisted and cramped.

The log pick fell from his hands, thudding onto the thick carpet. He looked down at what he had done—and then, an arm flung across his eyes, he turned and ran, stumbling and wavering, for the outer door of the apartment.

He smashed into it—scrabbled with shaking hands for the latch—tore it open—plunged out into the corridor—and, sightless, witless, came into heavy collision with a man and a woman just passing the door.

The woman lurched against the opposite wall. Cursing, the man snarled at Cyprian and caught him by the shoulder and straightened his slim bent body and thrust him back against the door jamb. The woman took one horrified look at Cyprian and screamed. The man stared and said, "What in the name of—"

Cyprian swayed. Everything—the figures facing him, the walls and doors, the lights overhead, the pattern of the corridor carpet—all swung crazily together before his eyes; swung and tilted so that he reeled, and clutched vainly for support—and slid down against the jamb to sit sprawled and ungainly on the floor, clutching at his whirling head.

The woman said, "Look at him. *Look* at him!" in a shaking voice. "That's *blood!*"—And the man said heavily, "What goes on around here?"

Cyprian moaned—and began to vomit. Above him the man said, "I'm going to take a look in there," and moved through the open doorway.

The woman went after him, and there glowed in Cyprian's mind the first sudden and frightful awareness of his danger. Even as another spasm shook him, a tiny self-preservatory spark was born, and when the woman began to scream just inside the door, he was already mumbling to himself, "*. . . there was a man . . . he went through the window . . .*"

And then the beginning of the long nightmare.

The man and woman rushing out of the apartment. Shouting.
Doors opening. People. More screaming. Trying to get to his
feet and failing. More men, one in shirt sleeves, another in a
robe, standing over him like guards. Sirens wailing outside.
Whistles. Noise. Voices. Elevator doors clanging and heavy feet
tramping down the corridor. New voices, harsh and different.
Men in uniform. The other faces going, the new faces staring
down at him, looming behind the harsh voices. A hand as ruthless as God's pulling him to his feet . . .

He wanted help. He craved succor. *". . . there was a man
. . . he went through the window . . ."*

He wanted a friend. He wanted Charles. Charles would know
what to do. Charles would deal with these bullying louts.

*". . . there was a man . . . he went through the win-
dow . . ."*

And Charles was thousands of miles away.

The nightmare went on. The questions. First in the room
where men—not in uniform now—worked over the horror on
the floor, muttering to each other, measuring, flashing lights,
pointing cameras, scribbling in notebooks.

Then in another room, after a hellish, siren-screaming journey in a crowded car. Questions, questions. All framed with the
certainty, the *knowledge,* that he had done what he must not
admit having done.

Questions. And the white light aching in his eyes. His throat
stiff and his lips unmanageable. His whole body shaking, shaking. The inside of his head shaking too.

—Why did you kill her?

—What time did you kill her?

—What did you kill her for? What had she done?

—How long after ya killed her before you run out?

—*I didn't. I didn't . . . there was a man . . . he went through
the window . . .*

—All right—so there was a man. An' he went outa the window. Whaddud he do? Jump? Fly?

—You don't expect us to swallow that, do you?

—Yeah. How d'ya figure this sorta hooey's goin' to help?

—*I tell you there was a man . . . he went through the window
. . . Down the fire escape . . .*

—He did? Leavin' your prints all over the poker?

—Yeah. An' splashin' her blood all over ya?

—Now, listen, Mr. Morse: it's completely certain that you killed this woman. The evidence is overwhelming. Can't you realize that you're doing yourself no good by your attitude?

—*I'm telling the truth. There was a man. I—I was in the bathroom. I heard a noise. I ran in. I saw Astrid. There was a man. He climbed out of the window. I'm telling the truth.*

—Very well. So you're telling the truth. Which window did this man go out?

—Yeah? And how come he locked it behind him?

—Never mind that, Mr. Morse. Answer the other question. Which window?

—*I—I don't know . . . The window in the—the end wall. . . . Next the fire escape. . . .*

—Which window? The right as you face? Or the left?

—Yeah. Which? One of 'em was locked, bud. Which?

Questions. And the light. Questions all around him. Questions from faces. Coarse, brutal faces. Sharp fox faces. They began to associate themselves with the voices.

And another face with wise gray eyes that watched him always. A face with no voice. A face in the corner. A face more to be feared than all the faces with voices.

Questions. And the light. Time standing still, immobilized. He had always been here. He would always be here. "*. . . there was a man . . . he went through the window . . .*"

It was a pattern, diabolic and infinite: Fear—questions—fear fear—light—fear fear fear—fatigue.

Fatigue. First a dull dead core of exhaustion, but now beginning to reach out all around itself, encroaching more and more on all other feeling.

Until even fear was going . . . going . . . almost gone——

—Why don't we wind this up, Morse?

—Yes. We know you killed her, and you know we know. Why not get it over with?

—Yeah. How's about it, fella? Why doncha come clean, so's we can let up on ya?

Fear flickering again, momentarily reborn.

—*I didn't I didn't I didn't . . . There was a man. When I ran in, he was climbing out of the window . . .*

For an instant a picture forming behind his eyes. An image of Charles—tall, tough, elegant, dangerous, one shoulder lifting higher than the other, a cigarette jutting from the corner of his long mouth, his creased face creasing more in a mastering smile. Charles coming through the door, being suddenly framed in the doorway, standing and looking down at the faces, the stupid crafty animal faces——

Then his eyes closing. His head falling forward. Then nothing. Except the hard scratched feeling of the table top against his cheek. And a ghost smell of soap and pencils and agony.

A rough hand biting into his shoulder. Shaking. His head lolling, jerking back and forward like a marionette's——

Then a new voice, quiet, sharp, charged with authority.

—That's enough. Let him alone. Schraff, you go find Doctor Innes. This isn't any Bowery bum you're handling.

His head resting on the table again. The voices muttering all around him, not thrusting at him now.

Conscious of someone standing over him. Not touching him. Just standing.

Opening his eyes. Forcing muscles to roll up the ton-weight lids. Seeing the wise gray eyes looking down at him, contemplating him, understanding everything.

Staring dully up into the gray eyes for a moment, dully wondering. Then letting the heavy lids fold down over his own eyes again.

The door opening, and brisk footsteps. And quick impersonal hands upon him. Doctor's hands. Feeling at his temples, his wrist. Tilting back his unbearably heavy head, with a deft thumb rolling back those eyelids.

Then muttering above his head. His coat being eased off, shirt sleeve rolled up.

Indefinite pause—and then the fingers on his arm, and the sting of the needle . . .

When he waked it was to grayness. A gray blanket over him; gray walls; a door of gray bars; gray light filtering through a small grilled window.

For some timeless interval the drug held memory in check. But at last, with a sick gray emptiness in his stomach, recollection came. And fear again, all the worse because its edges were dulled now and instead of it being so intense that there was no room in him for other emotions, it was now entangled and heightened by remorse and shame and horror.

He threw off the blanket and swung his feet to the floor and propped his elbows on his knees and dropped his face into his hands.

There was a clanging sound, and he started convulsively and raised his head and saw a uniformed guard coming into the cell. The man was carrying a big suitcase which he put down as he closed the barred door. On the side of the case were the initials *C.M.*, and Cyprian saw with dull surprise that it was his own, the one Charles had given him in London. He heard himself saying, "Where did you get that?" and the fellow looked at him and said, "Came from y'r apartment. There's clothes an' shaving tack an' setra." He had a strange manner, at once meaning and noncommittal, official and yet faintly sycophantic.

He came closer to Cyprian and looked down at him. He said, "Mr. Friar fixed it. An' about sendin' out for what you want."

A little faint glow of warmth came to life somewhere in Cyprian's coldness. Trust John Friar, he thought.

The guard said, "You like anything now? Breakfast? Or just coffee?"

Cyprian went on staring at him: it was as if his mind was so full that he didn't hear words until long after they had been spoken.

"Coffee," he said at last. "Just coffee."

The man nodded, and went to the door and opened it again, and paused. "Like to see the papers?" he said over his shoulder.

This time the words penetrated fast. Cyprian recoiled from them as if they were blows. "No!" he said. "No—*no!*"

He closed his eyes and held them screwed shut until he had heard the door open and clang shut, and then receding footsteps echoing. A shudder shook him at the thought of newspapers, and once more he covered his face with his hands. Headlines—as if on an endless ticker tape—began to unroll behind his eyes, running the gamut from the sober through the sensational to the nadir of the tabloid—

—FAMOUS PLAYWRIGHT HELD ON MURDER CHARGE. DESIGNER SLAIN . . .

—CYPRIAN MORSE ARRAIGNED FOR MURDER. GIRL

ASSOCIATE BRUTALLY BATTERED TO DEATH . . .
—PARK AVENUE LOVE-FIEND MURDER. NUDE THEA-
TER BEAUTY SLASHED. MORSE, BROADWAY FIGURE,
JAILED . . .

He groaned and twisted his body this way and that and desperately pressed the heels of his palms against his eyes until a
spark-shot red mist seemed to swim under the lids. But the tape
went on unrolling—a ceaseless stream of words.

He jumped up and began to pad about the cell—and then
mercifully heard footsteps in the corridor again and mastered
himself and was sitting on the edge of the gray cot when the
guard reappeared with a tray.

He mumbled thanks and reached for the coffee pot. But his
hand trembled so badly that, without speaking, the man filled
a cup for him.

He drank greedily, and felt strength coming back to him. He
looked up and said, "Can I—would—is it allowed to send a
cablegram?"

"Could be. With an okay from the Warden's office." The
fellow reached into a pocket, produced a little memo pad and
a stump of pencil. "Want to write it down?"

Cyprian took the things. Once more he mumbled thanks. He
didn't look at the man; he didn't like his eyes. He began to
write, not having to think, letting the pencil print the words—

*Charles de Lastro Hotel Castilia Venezuela In terrible trouble
need you desperately please come Reply care John Friar Cyprian.*

He handed the pad and pencil back, and watched while what
he had written was read. He said, "Well——?" and met the eyes
again as they flickered over him.

"Seems like this'll be okay." The guard turned a blue-clad
back and went to the door. "I'll look after it."

Once more the clanging, the footsteps dying away—and Cyprian was alone again. His hand steadier now, he poured himself
more coffee. Anything, any action, to keep him from thought.

He drained the cup. He picked up the suitcase and set it on
the cot and opened it. Forcing himself to activity, he washed
and shaved and put on the clothes he found packed. A suit of
dark blue flannel—a white silk shirt—a plain maroon tie.

He felt a little better. It was easier to believe that this was

Cyprian Morse—and he gave silent thanks to John Friar.

But there was nothing to do now—and if he weren't careful he might have to start thinking. He lit a cigarette from the box in the suitcase and began to pace the cell. There were five steps one way and six the other . . .

So this was Cyprian Morse. Perhaps he did feel better after all. Perhaps——

Footsteps in the corridor again. One, two, three sets.

John Friar himself, with another man and the guard. Who opened the door, and stood aside to let the visitors in, and clanged the door shut again and stood outside, his back to it.

John Friar took Cyprian's hand in both of his and gripped hard. He was white-faced, strained. He looked less like a successful producer than ever, and more like a truncated and careworn Abe Lincoln. The man with him towered over him, a lank, loose-limbed, stooping giant with a thatch of white hair and a seamed, unlikely face which was neither saint's nor gargoyle's but something of both.

John Friar said, "Cyprian!" in a voice which wasn't quite steady. He made a gesture including the third man. He said, "Julius, meet Cyprian Morse . . . Cyprian, this is Julius Magnussen."

Again Cyprian's hand was taken, and enveloped in a vast paw which gripped firmly but with surprising gentleness. And Cyprian found himself looking up, tall though he was, into dark unreadable eyes which seemed jet black under the shaggy white brows.

John Friar said, "Julius is taking on your def—your case, Cyprian. And you know what that means!"

"I most definitely do!" Cyprian hoped they wouldn't hear the trembling in his throat. "Is there anyone in America who doesn't?"

Magnussen grunted. He turned away and folded his length in the middle and sat on the edge of the gray bed. He looked at Cyprian and said, "Better tell me about it," then moved a little and added, "Sit down here."

Cyprian found himself obeying. But he couldn't keep on meeting the dark eyes, and gave up trying to. He looked up at John Friar and essayed a smile. He said, "Of course," in Magnussen's direction—and then, faintly, all the fear and horror of memory breaking loose in his head again, "Where—where—d'you want me to start?"

"At the beginning, Mr. Morse," Magnussen said, and Cyprian drew a deep breath to still the quaking inside him. But it wouldn't be stilled. It spread from his body to his mind. He was being thrust into nightmare again——

—I can't . . . I can't . . .

—Would it be easier if I asked you questions?

Questions. The pattern returning. Fear—questions—fear fear—fatigue. But worse now. Hiding from friends not enemies.

—I have to ask you this: did you kill this woman Astrid Halmar?

—No—no—no! . . . *There was a man . . . he went through the window* . . .

—You know of no enemies Miss Halmar might have had?

—No. How should I? I——

—So you think the murderer was a stranger, a prowler?

—How—how do I know what he was! Or who! I don't know anything . . .

Questions. Questions. Fear. Thinking furiously before each answer without letting the pause be evident. Trying to screen the vortex of his mind with caution. Time standing still again. He had always been here. He would always be here.

—So you were in the bathroom for more than an hour?

—Yes—yes. I went there just after dinner. Just as—just after the maid left the apartment.

—Were you feeling unwell? Is that why you stayed so long? Had something you ate upset your stomach?

A straw. A solid straw. Snatch it!

—Yes. That's right. I was sick . . . It was the oysters. . . .

More questions. More fear. Feeling the dark eyes always on his face. Not meeting them.

—And you were just about to come out of the bathroom when you heard a cry. Am I right?

Another straw. Snatch it!

—Yes. Yes. Astrid screamed . . .

—And you ran out, and along the passage to the living room?

—Yes.

—While you were running along the passage, did you happen to notice Miss Halmar's robe, lying on the floor?

—Robe? What—no, I don't think——

—Her robe was found by the door to the living room. The killer—however he gained entry to the apartment—must have struggled with her, snatched at her, in the passageway there, pulling off the robe as she fled into the living room. I am wondering—did you notice it?

A straw?

—I think I did. There was something—soft on the floor. It caught my shoe. . . .

—Now, Mr. Morse, as you entered the living room, you saw the figure of a man just disappearing out of the window?

—Yes. Yes.

—And you saw Miss Halmar's body on the floor and ran to it?

—Yes. Of course I did. I—I had to try and help her . . .

—Naturally. Now, as your fingerprints are on the log pick, Mr. Morse, you must have handled it? Maybe you touched it— picked it up—when you went to her? It was in your way, was it?

A sudden lightening. As if some frightful pressure were easing. Fear actually receding. Knowing now that these were no accidental straws, but material for a raft. A life raft.

—Yes. That was it. I remember now. It—it was lying across her body. I—I picked it up and—threw it down, away from her.

—And in your shock and horror, when you found she was dead, you forgot the telephone and ran blindly out to seek help, and then collapsed?

—Yes. Yes. That's it—exactly.

Questions. Questions. But not minding them now. Being eager for them. And being able to meet the dark eyes, keeping his own eyes on them.

The pattern had changed. Fear was there, as a permanent lowering background, but in front of it was hope . . .

The hope persisted, even when he was alone once more. It seemed to widen the cell, and raise its roof. It set the blood flowing through his head again, so that his brain worked fast and clear and he started to elaborate on the structure Julius Magnussen had begun to build for him.

This work—and work it was—carried him through the dragging days and weeks with a surprising minimum of anguish. It even fortified him to some extent against the shock of the answering cablegram from Charles, which didn't arrive until several days after he had expected it.

The cable ran: *Hospitalized bad kickup malaria Flying back immediately released maybe two weeks Hang on Charles.*

And that, of course, was bad news. Bad from two angles—that he would have to wait before Charles could get to him, that poor Charles was sick.

But whereas, before the first meeting with Julius Magnussen, Cyprian would have been crushed almost to extinction by these twin misfortunes, now they seemed merely to serve as a spur to his fortitude and his hope and his labor. So that he clenched his teeth and redoubled his efforts to produce appropriate "memories"—until he reached the point of being sure that at least Friar and Magnussen believed him, that he almost believed himself.

But it was as well for him that he wasn't present at any of the several meetings between Julius Magnussen and John Friar alone, or he would have heard talk which would have turned his hope-lightened purgatory into hopeless hell.

—A bad case, John. Don't hide it from yourself. We'll need a miracle.

—Good God, Julius, d'you mean you yourself don't believe—

—Stop. That's not a question I want to be asked. Or answer. Leave it at what I said. A bad case. No case at all.

—But the evidence against him's all circumstantial!

—And therefore the best, in spite of what they say in novels.

—But surely it's all open to two interpretations! Like—like his fingerprints on that poker.

—*And* the splashes of blood on him and his clothing? Have you thought of that, John? *Splashes.* Not smears, which are what should be there from raising her, examining her, trying to help her . . .

—But the boy's *gentle,* Julius! There's no violence in him. He couldn't even kill a fly that was pestering him.

—Maybe not. And don't think that's not going to be used. For more than all it's worth. For God's sake, it's practically all we have! You know the young man, John: tell me, how would he react to the suggestion of an alternative plea?

—You mean "not guilty, or guilty by reason of insanity"!—

that gag! Good God, Julius—he wouldn't go for that if you tortured him.

—H'mm. I was afraid that would be the answer.

—Look now, what is all this? What are you trying to do—tell me you won't take the case after all? Is that it?

—Cool off, John. I'm trying to save your prodigy's life, that's all.

—I don't get this! Julius Magnussen, of all people, scared of a setup like this! . . . Remember that police photograph you showed me? Well, think of it. Not the head wounds, the others. Think of 'em! Cyprian could not have been responsible for that frightful *sort* of brutality. Think of what was done to that girl, man! . . . Can't you see—can't you?

—Oh, yes, John, I can see. A great many things . . .

But Cyprian knew nothing of such conversations, and it seemed to him, every time he saw his counsel, that more and more confidence radiated from that towering, loose-limbed figure; that the penetrating dark eyes looked always more cheerful.

So he rode out the rest of the dragging days and nights and came in good enough order to the morning when the trial was to open. It was a Thursday, and he liked that because he had had a fancy, since an episode in his boyhood, that Thor's was his lucky day. Further, a bright autumnal sun was glittering over New York and even—a rare occurrence in the weeks he had been there—pushing rays through the bars of the small window high up in the wall of the cell.

He dressed with great, almost finicking care. He drank a whole pot of coffee and then sent for more. He even ate a little of his breakfast.

He was ready and waiting a full half hour before they came for him. He spent it pacing the cell, smoking too much and too fast, glancing occasionally toward the pile of letters which he hadn't read and had no more intention of ever reading than he had of looking in court at any of the reporters' faces. He didn't think of what was before him today. He daren't think of that, in the same way—only infinitely multiplied—that he never thought about what was coming on a first night.

So he considered, with furious intensity, anything and everything except what was coming. The sure hope at the back of his mind must be kept inviolate.

He came naturally to thoughts of Charles. Every day he had been sure this must be the day when he would hear again—and every day he had been disappointed. He had wired again, and he had written—just a note which John Friar had air mailed for him. But still no answer. Charles must be very ill indeed. Or— a wonderful idea which he dare not dwell upon for more than one delicious instant—Charles was well again and had arrived in New York, and was on his way here.

The third alternative he shuddered away from. The thought of Charles dead was so black, so bleak, so dreadful, that it would have driven him back in escape to thoughts of the immediate future if he hadn't been saved by the arrival of his guard.

For once he was glad to see the fellow. He said, "Do we start now?" and moved towards the door.

But the man shook his head. "They ain't here yet," he said. "Take it easy." He drew a folded yellow envelope from a pocket and held it out to Cyprian. "Sent over from Friar's," he said. "He reckoned you might like to have it right away."

Cyprian almost snatched it from the outstretched hand. His heart was pounding, and sudden color had tinged his pallid face. With fingers which he didn't know were shaking, he fumbled at the flimsy envelope, ripped it open at last, and unfolded the sheet it contained.

And read: *Better Out next Wednesday will fly arriving Thursday Charles.*

The new color deepened in Cyprian's face. He read the cable again—and again. Here was the best of all possible omens. Almost as good as his wild daydream of a few moments before—that perhaps Charles would arrive in person. On second thought, perhaps better. Because now he was supremely confident, and he would so far prefer to have all this ugliness behind him when Charles returned; out of sight and wrapped up and put away, to be disinterred and examined, if ever, at a safe distance in time and then only for personal historic interest.

He moved his shoulders unconsciously, as if in reflex to the removal of a heavy weight. He folded the strip of paper carefully, and stowed it away in his breast pocket. And then looked at the guard and smiled, and said softly, "Thank you. Thank you very much. . . ."

There was a tramping of feet in the corridor—and two uniformed men he had never seen before. One of them pushed the cell door wide and looked at him with no expression and said, "All set?"

Cyprian smiled at this man too, and walked out into the corridor quickly, lightly, almost jauntily . . .

But there was no lightness in him when he came back eight hours later, and no square of sunshine from the barred window. There was only night outside and here the hard cold light of the single bulb overhead.

His face was lined and wax white. His shoulders sagged and his body seemed not to fill his clothes. He lurched on his feet while they opened the door of the cell, and one of the men gripped his arm and said, "Take it easy."

They put him inside and he dropped on the edge of his cot and sat there limp and head hanging, his eyes wide and staring at the floor and not seeing it.

The escort went away and his own guard came, and sometime later the doctor. He couldn't get food down, and they put him to bed and gave him a sedative. He slept almost at once, and they left him.

He lay like a log for three hours, until the deadly numbness of fatigue had gone and the drug had eased its grip. And then he began to murmur and thrash around on the cot—and in a moment gave a harsh choked cry and sat upright, awake.

He remembered. He tried not to, he fought, but he couldn't stop memory from working. He remembered everything—at first in jumbled pictures, then in echoing phrases; at last, concentrated upon the gray-haired, gray-eyed figure of the District Attorney, he recalled the whole of the clear and ruthlessly dispassionate opening for the Prosecution. The speech which, period by period, point by careful point, had not only stripped Cyprian Morse of all cover but had shattered all remnant of hope in him.

What had happened after the speech didn't matter. The irreparable damage to Cyprian Morse, the conviction of Cyprian Morse, had been brought about; those witnesses, the silly endless procession of them who answered silly endless questions, they were just so many more nails in his coffin. After the speech, which showed such complete, such eerie knowledge and understanding, as if the speaker had not only seen everything that had happened but had seen it with Cyprian's mind and Cyprian's eyes—after that, all else seemed time-prolonging and sadistic anticlimax . . .

He didn't move. He sat as he was, and stared into the abyss . . .

Morning came, and daylight, and people he heard and saw as if from a long distance. He moved then but was almost unconscious of moving. It was as if his body were an automaton and his mind a separate entity outside it, which had no concern with the robot movements.

The automaton clothed itself, and ate and drank, and went with his mind and the uniformed men and sat in the crowded courtroom in the same place as his undivided self had sat the day before.

The automaton sat still and went through motions—of listening to friends and Counsel, of answering them when necessary, of looking attentive to the gabber-jab of the unending witnesses, of considering thoughtfully the closing speech for the Prosecution, of hearing the crabbed Judge rule that the Court, this being Friday, should recess until the morning of Monday . . .

But his mind, his actual self, was in hell without a permit. For sixty-two hours the automaton made all the foolish gestures of living; for uncountable stages of distorted time his mind gazed into the pit.

The Monday came, and the automaton moved accordingly. But the clean-cut edges of the schism between body and mind began to waver before the two parts of him left the cell, as if something had happened which demanded they should be joined again. Resisting the pull, his mind began to wonder what had caused it. His refusal to see John Friar or Magnussen during the recess? The odd, almost excited manner of his guard on bringing a newspaper to the cell and trying to insist on the automaton reading it? The looks which both his escorts cast at the automaton in the car on the way to court?

He didn't want the union. He would break, he felt, if he

couldn't keep up the separation. But the pull grew stronger with every foot of the way, and almost irresistible as he entered the courtroom itself, and his mind felt a difference—a strange, disturbing, agitated alteration—in the other minds behind the faces staring at him.

And then, with a shivering, nauseating shock, his resistance went and he was swept back into his body once more, so that he was stripped and next to the world again with no transparent armor between.

It was the face of Magnussen's wizened clerk which brought it about, a face which always before had been harassed and grave and filled with foreboding, but which now was gay and eager and irradiated by a tremendous gnomelike smile. As Cyprian was about to take his seat, this smile was turned full on him, and his hand was surreptitiously taken and earnestly squeezed, and through the smile a voice came whispering something which couldn't be distinguished but all the same was pregnant with the most extreme importance.

Cyprian sat down, weakly. Once again, he had no strength. He looked up into the little clerk's face and muttered something—he wasn't sure of the words himself.

An astonished change came over the puckered visage. "Mr. Morse!" The voice cracked in amazement. "Do you mean to say you haven't *heard!*"

Dumbly Cyprian shook his head, the small movement leaving him exhausted.

"Not about the—the other killings! . . . Mr. Morse! There have been two more murders of unfortunate girls! In every respect the same as Miss Halmar's—even the—the mutilations identical . . . On Saturday night the first victim was found; and another discovered in the early hours of this morning!"

Cyprian went on staring up into the excited, agitated face.

"D-don't you realize what this m-means!" The voice was stammering now. "All three deaths must be linked. *You* couldn't have caused the others! They're the work of a maniac —a Jack the Ripper!" Fluttering hands produced a newspaper, unfolded it, waved it. "Look here, Mr. Morse!"

There were black heavy headlines. They wavered in front of Cyprian's eyes, then focused sharply and made him catch at his breath.

POLICE CLUELESS IN NEW FIEND SLAYINGS! MORSE RELEASE DEMANDED BY PUBLIC!
"Oh," said Cyprian, his lips barely moving. "Oh, I see . . ." His whole body began to tingle, as if circulation had been withheld from it until now. He said, a little louder, "What—what will happen?"

The clerk sat down beside him. His hoarse whispering was as clear now as a shout in Cyprian's ears. "What will happen? I'll tell you, Mr. Morse. I'll tell you exactly. The D.A. will withdraw —and not long after Mr. Magnussen's opened. He'll withdraw, Mr. Morse, you mark my words!"

The words coincided with a stentorian bellow from the back of the courtroom, followed by a stamping rustle as everyone stood up—and Justice swept to its throne in a dusty black robe . . .

And Cyprian, life welling up in him, found himself caught in a whirling timeless jumble of fact and feeling and emotion, a maelstrom which was in effect the precise opposite of the long nightmare succeeding his arrest——

Julius Magnussen towering on his feet, speaking of Cyprian Morse's innocence with an almost contemptuous certainty. Julius Magnussen examining detectives on the witness stand, forcing them to prove all three killings had been identical. Julius Magnussen calling more witnesses, then looking around haughtily at the Prosecution when the Court was asked to hear a statement. The District Attorney himself, gray eyes not understanding now but puzzled and confused, muttering that the state withdrew its case against Cyprian Morse. The Judge speaking, bestowing commiseration on Cyprian Morse, laudation on Julius Magnussen, censure upon their opponents——

Then bedlam breaking loose, himself the center. Friends. Strangers. Acquaintances. Reporters. All crowding, jabbering, laughing. Women weeping. Flashbulbs exploding. John Friar pumping both his hands. Magnussen clapping him on the shoulder. Himself the center of a wedge of policemen, struggling for the exit. An odd little instant of comparative quiet in the hallway, and hearing Magnussen say to John Friar behind him, "An apology, John, you were right."

Then John's big car, and the soft-cushioned seat supporting him. And quietness, with the tires singing on the road and time to draw breath—and taste freedom . . .

. . .

All horror was behind him and it was Wednesday evening and Charles was coming home. From John Friar's house in Westchester, in John Friar's car, driven by John Friar's chauffeur.

It was deepening dusk when they pulled into the parking lot behind the apartment house. Cyprian peered, and saw no sign of any human being and was pleased. He got out and smiled at the chauffeur and said warmly, "Thank you, Maurice. Thank you very much . . ." and thrust a lavish tip into the man's gloved hand and waved a cheerful salute and walked off toward the rear entrance of the building. His footsteps rang crisply on the concrete, and a faint, wreathlike mist from his breathing hung on the autumn air. He suppressed an impulse to stop and crane his neck to look up to the penthouse and see the warm lights glowing out from it. He knew they were there, because he had heard John Friar telephoning to his servant, telling him when Mr. Morse was to be expected.

Good old John, he thought. Thoughtful John! And then forgot John completely as he entered the service door, and still met no one and found one of the service elevators empty and waiting.

He forgot John. He forgot everyone and everything—except Charles.

And Charles would be here tomorrow. That was why Cyprian had insisted upon coming home tonight—so that he could supervise preparation.

He hurried the elevator with his mind, and when it reached the rear hallway of his penthouse, threw open the gate—and was faced, not by light and an open door and Walter's white-smiling black face, but by cold unwelcoming darkness.

He stepped out of the elevator and groped for the light switch and pressed it and blinked at the sudden glare. Frowning, he tried the door to the kitchen. It wasn't locked, but when he opened it there was more darkness. And no sound. No sound at all.

A chill settled on his mind. The warm excited glow which had been growing inside him evaporated with unnerving suddenness. He switched on more lights and went quickly through the bright-tiled neatness and threw open an inner door and called,

"Walter! Walter, where are you?" into more darkness still.

Not such absolute darkness this time, but the more disturbing for that. The curtains across the big windows at the west side of the living room had not been drawn and there was still a sort of gray luminosity in the air.

Cyprian took two or three paces into the room. He called, "Walter!" again, and heard his own voice go up too high at the end of the word.

And another voice spoke from behind him—a cracked and casual voice.

"I sent him out for an hour or two," it said. "Hope you don't mind."

Cyprian started violently. He gasped, *"Charles!"* And wheeled around and saw a tall figure looming in the grayness. His heart pounded in his ears and he felt a swaying in his head.

There was no answering sound—and he said, "Charles!" again and moved toward a table near the figure and reached out for the lamp he knew was on it.

But his shoulder was caught in a grip which checked him completely. Long fingers strong as steel bit into his flesh, and Charles's voice said, "Take it easy. We don't need light just yet."

Cyprian felt cold. His head still whirled. He couldn't understand, and the grip on his shoulder seemed to be paralyzing him and he was afraid with that worst of all fears which hasn't any shape.

He said wildly, "Charles, I don't understand—I——" and couldn't get out any more words. He contorted all the muscles in his face in a useless attempt to see Charles's face.

"You will," said Charles's voice. "Do you remember once telling me you'd never lie to me again?"

"Yes," Cyprian whispered—and then, his mouth drying with fear, "Let me go. You're hurting me . . ."

"Did you mean it?" The hand didn't relax its grip.

"Of course . . . And I never have lied to you since! I don't understand——"

"You will." The grip tightened and Cyprian caught his breath. "I want a truthful answer to one question. Will you give it?"

"Yes. Yes. Of course I will . . ."

"Did you kill that Halmar woman?"

"No—no—*there was a man . . . he went through the window . . ."*

"I thought you weren't going to lie to me. Did you kill her?"

"No! I——" The steel fingers bit deeper and Cyprian sobbed.

"Did you kill her? Don't lie to me."

"Yes! *Yes!"* Cyprian's face was writhing. His eyes stung with tears and his lips were trembling. "Yes, I killed her! I killed her —*I killed her! . . ."*

The grip eased. The hand lifted from his shoulder. He tottered on uncertain feet, and the lamp on the table jumped suddenly into life and through the mist over his eyes he saw Charles for the first time—and then heard Charles's voice say, easily and softly and with the old-time chuckle hidden somewhere in it:

"Well, that's that. Just so long as we know . . . I'd like a drink."

He turned away from Cyprian and crossed with his lounging walk to the bar—the lounging walk which always reminded Cyprian of the stalking of a cat——

And suddenly Cyprian knew.

He knew, and in the same moment that understanding flooded his mind, he thought—for the first time actively thought—of those other two deaths which had saved him from death.

A scream came to his throat and froze there. He shrank into himself as he stood there—and Charles turned, glass in hand, and looked at him.

His eyes burned in his head. He couldn't move their gaze from Charles's face. He said:

"You did it. You killed those two women. You weren't ill. You got someone else to send those cables. You heard about Astrid and you flew back without anyone knowing. And you plotted and planned and stalked—and did that. As if they were animals. You did that!"

His voice died in his throat. All strength went out of him and he tottered to a chair and doubled up in it and sat crumpled.

"Don't fret, my dear Cyprian." Charles drank, looking at him over the rim of the glass. "We sit tight—and live happily ever after . . ."

Cyprian dropped his head into his hands.

"Oh, my God!" he said. "Oh, my God!"

1953:

Lamb to the Slaughter

Roald Dahl

The room was warm and clean, the curtains drawn, the two table lamps alight—hers and the one by the empty chair opposite. On the sideboard behind her, two tall glasses, soda water, whiskey. Fresh ice cubes in the Thermos bucket.

Mary Maloney was waiting for her husband to come home from work.

Now and again she would glance up at the clock, but without anxiety, merely to please herself with the thought that each minute gone by made it nearer the time when he would come. There was a slow smiling air about her, and about everything she did. The drop of the head as she bent over her sewing was curiously tranquil. Her skin—for this was her sixth month with child—had acquired a wonderful translucent quality, the mouth was soft, and the eyes, with their new placid look, seemed larger, darker than before.

When the clock said ten minutes to five, she began to listen, and a few moments later, punctually as always, she heard the tires on the gravel outside, and the car door slamming, the footsteps passing the window, the key turning in the lock. She laid aside her sewing, stood up, and went forward to kiss him as he came in.

"Hullo darling," she said.

"Hullo," he answered.

She took his coat and hung it in the closet. Then she walked over and made the drinks, a strongish one for him, a weak one for herself; and soon she was back again in her chair with the sewing, and he in the other, opposite, holding the tall glass with both his hands, rocking it so the ice cubes tinkled against the side.

For her, this was always a blissful time of day. She knew he didn't want to speak much until the first drink was finished, and she, on her side, was content to sit quietly, enjoying his company after the long hours alone in the house. She loved to luxuriate in the presence of this man, and to feel—almost as a sunbather feels the sun—that warm male glow that came out of him to her when they were alone together. She loved him for the way he sat loosely in a chair, for the way he came in a door, or moved slowly across the room with long strides. She loved the intent, far look in his eyes when they rested on her, the funny shape of the mouth, and especially the way he remained silent about his tiredness, sitting still with himself until the whiskey had taken some of it away.

"Tired, darling?"

"Yes," he said. "I'm tired." And as he spoke, he did an unusual thing. He lifted his glass and drained it in one swallow although there was still half of it, at least half of it left. She wasn't really watching him, but she knew what he had done because she heard the ice cubes falling back against the bottom of the empty glass when he lowered his arm. He paused a moment, leaning forward in the chair, then he got up and went slowly over to fetch himself another.

"I'll get it!" she cried, jumping up.

"Sit down," he said.

When he came back, she noticed that the new drink was dark amber with the quantity of whiskey in it.

"Darling, shall I get your slippers?"

"No."

She watched him as he began to sip the dark yellow drink, and she could see little oily swirls in the liquid because it was so strong.

"I think it's a shame," she said, "that when a policeman gets to be as senior as you, they keep him walking about on his feet all day long."

He didn't answer, so she bent her head again and went on with her sewing; but each time he lifted the drink to his lips, she heard the ice cubes clinking against the side of the glass.

"Darling," she said. "Would you like me to get you some cheese? I haven't made any supper because it's Thursday."

"No," he said.

"If you're too tired to eat out," she went on, "it's still not too late. There's plenty of meat and stuff in the freezer, and you can have it right here and not even move out of the chair."

Her eyes waited on him for an answer, a smile, a little nod, but he made no sign.

"Anyway," she went on, "I'll get you some cheese and crackers first."

"I don't want it," he said.

She moved uneasily in her chair, the large eyes still watching his face. "But you *must* have supper. I can easily do it here. I'd like to do it. We can have lamb chops. Or pork. Anything you want. Everything's in the freezer."

"Forget it," he said.

"But darling, you *must* eat! I'll fix it anyway, and then you can have it or not, as you like."

She stood up and placed her sewing on the table by the lamp.

"Sit down," he said. "Just for a minute, sit down."

It wasn't till then that she began to get frightened.

"Go on," he said. "Sit down."

She lowered herself back slowly into the chair, watching him all the time with those large, bewildered eyes. He had finished the second drink and was staring down into the glass, frowning.

"Listen," he said. "I've got something to tell you."

"What is it, darling? What's the matter?"

He had now become absolutely motionless, and he kept his head down so that the light from the lamp beside him fell across the upper part of his face, leaving the chin and mouth in shadow. She noticed there was a little muscle moving near the corner of his left eye.

"This is going to be a bit of a shock to you, I'm afraid," he said.

"But I've thought about it a good deal and I've decided the only thing to do is tell you right away. I hope you won't blame me too much."

And he told her. It didn't take long, four or five minutes at most, and she sat very still through it all, watching him with a kind of dazed horror as he went further and further away from her with each word.

"So there it is," he added. "And I know it's kind of a bad time to be telling you, but there simply wasn't any other way. Of course I'll give you money and see you're looked after. But there needn't really be any fuss. I hope not anyway. It wouldn't be very good for my job."

Her first instinct was not to believe any of it, to reject it all. It occurred to her that perhaps he hadn't even spoken, that she herself had imagined the whole thing. Maybe, if she went about her business and acted as though she hadn't been listening, then later, when she sort of woke up again, she might find none of it had ever happened.

"I'll get the supper," she managed to whisper, and this time he didn't stop her.

When she walked across the room she couldn't feel her feet touching the floor. She couldn't feel anything at all—except a slight nausea and a desire to vomit. Everything was automatic now—down the steps to the cellar, the light switch, the deep freeze, the hand inside the cabinet taking hold of the first object it met. She lifted it out, and looked at it. It was wrapped in paper, so she took off the paper and looked at it again.

A leg of lamb.

All right then, they would have lamb for supper. She carried it upstairs, holding the thin bone-end of it with both her hands, and as she went through the living-room, she saw him standing over by the window with his back to her, and she stopped.

"For God's sake," he said, hearing her, but not turning round. "Don't make supper for me. I'm going out."

At that point, Mary Maloney simply walked up behind him and without any pause she swung the big frozen leg of lamb high in the air and brought it down as hard as she could on the back of his head.

She might just as well have hit him with a steel club.

She stepped back a pace, waiting, and the funny thing was

that he remained standing there for at least four or five seconds, gently swaying. Then he crashed to the carpet.

The violence of the crash, the noise, the small table overturning, helped bring her out of the shock. She came out slowly, feeling cold and surprised, and she stood for a while blinking at the body, still holding the ridiculous piece of meat tight with both hands.

All right, she told herself. So I've killed him.

It was extraordinary, now, how clear her mind became all of a sudden. She began thinking very fast. As the wife of a detective, she knew quite well what the penalty would be. That was fine. It made no difference to her. In fact, it would be a relief. On the other hand, what about the child? What were the laws about murderers with unborn children? Did they kill them both —mother and child? Or did they wait until the tenth month? What did they do?

Mary Maloney didn't know. And she certainly wasn't prepared to take a chance.

She carried the meat into the kitchen, placed it in a pan, turned the oven on high, and shoved it inside. Then she washed her hands and ran upstairs to the bedroom. She sat down before the mirror, tidied her hair, touched up her lips and face. She tried a smile. It came out rather peculiar. She tried again.

"Hullo Sam," she said brightly, aloud.

The voice sounded peculiar too.

"I want some potatoes please, Sam. Yes, and I think a can of peas."

That was better. Both the smile and the voice were coming out better now. She rehearsed it several times more. Then she ran downstairs, took her coat, went out the back door, down the garden, into the street.

It wasn't six o'clock yet and the lights were still on in the grocery shop.

"Hullo Sam," she said brightly, smiling at the man behind the counter.

"Why, good evening, Mrs. Maloney. How're *you?*"

"I want some potatoes please, Sam. Yes, and I think a can of peas."

The man turned and reached up behind him on the shelf for the peas.

"Patrick's decided he's tired and doesn't want to eat out tonight," she told him. "We usually go out Thursdays, you know, and now he's caught me without any vegetables in the house."

"Then how about meat, Mrs. Maloney?"

"No, I've got meat, thanks. I got a nice leg of lamb from the freezer."

"Oh."

"I don't much like cooking it frozen, Sam, but I'm taking a chance on it this time. You think it'll be all right?"

"Personally," the grocer said, "I don't believe it makes any difference. You want these Idaho potatoes?"

"Oh yes, that'll be fine. Two of those."

"Anything else?" The grocer cocked his head on one side, looking at her pleasantly. "How about afterwards? What you going to give him for afterwards?"

"Well—what would you suggest, Sam?"

The man glanced around his shop. "How about a nice big slice of cheesecake? I know he likes that."

"Perfect," she said. "He loves it."

And when it was all wrapped and she had paid, she put on her brightest smile and said, "Thank you, Sam. Goodnight."

"Goodnight, Mrs. Maloney. And thank *you.*"

And now, she told herself as she hurried back, all she was doing now, she was returning home to her husband and he was waiting for his supper; and she must cook it good, and make it as tasty as possible because the poor man was tired; and if, when she entered the house, she happened to find anything unusual, or tragic, or terrible, then naturally it would be a shock and she'd become frantic with grief and horror. Mind you, she wasn't *expecting* to find anything. She was just going home with the vegetables. Mrs. Patrick Maloney going home with the vegetables on Thursday evening to cook supper for her husband.

That's the way, she told herself. Do everything right and natural. Keep things absolutely natural and there'll be no need for any acting at all.

Therefore, when she entered the kitchen by the back door, she was humming a little tune to herself and smiling.

"Patrick!" she called. "How are you, darling?"

She put the parcel down on the table and went through into the living room; and when she saw him lying there on the floor with his legs doubled up and one arm twisted back underneath his body, it really was rather a shock. All the old love and longing for him welled up inside her, and she ran over to him, knelt down beside him, and began to cry her heart out. It was easy. No acting was necessary.

A few minutes later she got up and went to the phone. She knew the number of the police station, and when the man at the other end answered, she cried to him, "Quick! Come quick! Patrick's dead!"

"Who's speaking?"

"Mrs. Maloney. Mrs. Patrick Maloney."

"You mean Patrick Maloney's dead?"

"I think so," she sobbed. "He's lying on the floor and I think he's dead."

"Be right over," the man said.

The car came very quickly, and when she opened the front door, two policemen walked in. She knew them both—she knew nearly all the men at that precinct—and she fell right into Jack Noonan's arms, weeping hysterically. He put her gently into a chair, then went over to join the other one, who was called O'Malley, kneeling by the body.

"Is he dead?" she cried.

"I'm afraid he is. What happened?"

Briefly, she told her story about going out to the grocer and coming back to find him on the floor. While she was talking, crying and talking, Noonan discovered a small patch of congealed blood on the dead man's head. He showed it to O'Malley, who got up at once and hurried to the phone.

Soon, other men began to come into the house. First a doctor, then two detectives, one of whom she knew by name. Later, a police photographer arrived and took pictures, and a man who knew about fingerprints. There was a great deal of whispering and muttering beside the corpse, and the detectives kept asking her a lot of questions. But they always treated her kindly. She told her story again, this time right from the beginning, when Patrick had come in, and she was sewing, and he was tired, so tired he hadn't wanted to go out for supper. She told how she'd put the meat in the oven—"it's there now, cooking"—and how she'd slipped out to the grocer for vegetables, and come back to find him lying on the floor.

"Which grocer?" one of the detectives asked.

She told him, and he turned and whispered something to the other detective, who immediately went outside into the street.

In fifteen minutes he was back with a page of notes, and there was more whispering, and through her sobbing she heard a few of the whispered phrases—". . . acted quite normal . . . very cheerful . . . wanted to give him a good supper . . . peas . . . cheesecake . . . impossible that she . . ."

After a while, the photographer and the doctor departed and two other men came in and took the corpse away on a stretcher. Then the fingerprint man went away. The two detectives remained, and so did the two policemen. They were exceptionally nice to her, and Jack Noonan asked if she wouldn't rather go somewhere else, to her sister's house perhaps, or to his own wife, who would take care of her and put her up for the night.

No, she said. She didn't feel she could move even a yard at the moment. Would they mind awfully if she stayed just where she was until she felt better? She didn't feel too good at the moment, she really didn't.

Then hadn't she better lie down on the bed? Jack Noonan asked.

No, she said. She'd like to stay right where she was, in this chair. A little later perhaps, when she felt better, she would move.

So they left her there while they went about their business, searching the house. Occasionally one of the detectives asked her another question. Sometimes Jack Noonan spoke at her gently as he passed by. Her husband, he told her, had been killed by a blow on the back of the head administered with a heavy blunt instrument, almost certainly a large piece of metal. They were looking for the weapon. The murderer may have taken it with him, but on the other hand he may've thrown it away or hidden it somewhere on the premises.

"It's the old story," he said. "Get the weapon, and you've got the man."

Later, one of the detectives came up and sat beside her. Did she know, he asked, of anything in the house that could've been used as the weapon? Would she mind having a look around to see if anything was missing—a very big spanner, for example, or a heavy metal vase.

They didn't have any heavy metal vases, she said.

"Or a big spanner?"

She didn't think they had a big spanner. But there might be some things like that in the garage.

The search went on. She knew that there were other policemen in the garden all around the house. She could hear their footsteps on the gravel outside, and sometimes she saw the flash of a torch through a chink in the curtains. It began to get late, nearly nine she noticed by the clock on the mantle. The four men searching the rooms seemed to be growing weary, a trifle exasperated.

"Jack," she said, the next time Sergeant Noonan went by. "Would you mind giving me a drink?"

"Sure I'll give you a drink. You mean this whiskey?"

"Yes please. But just a small one. It might make me feel better."

He handed her the glass.

"Why don't you have one yourself," she said. "You must be awfully tired. Please do. You've been very good to me."

"Well," he answered. "It's not strictly allowed, but I might take just a drop to keep me going."

One by one the others came in and were persuaded to take a little nip of whiskey. They stood around rather awkwardly with the drinks in their hands, uncomfortable in her presence, trying to say consoling things to her. Sergeant Noonan wandered into the kitchen, came out quickly and said, "Look, Mrs. Maloney. You know that oven of yours is still on, and the meat still inside."

"Oh *dear* me!" she cried. "So it is!"

"I better turn it off for you, hadn't I?"

"Will you do that, Jack? Thank you so much."

When the sergeant returned the second time, she looked at him with her large, dark, tearful eyes. "Jack Noonan," she said.

"Yes?"

"Would you do me a small favor—you and these others?"

"We can try, Mrs. Maloney."

"Well," she said. "Here you all are, and good friends of dear Patrick's too, and helping to catch the man who killed him. You must be terribly hungry by now because it's long past your suppertime, and I know Patrick would never forgive me, God bless his soul, if I allowed you to remain in his house without offering you decent hospitality. Why don't you eat up that lamb that's in the oven? It'll be cooked just right by now."

"Wouldn't dream of it," Sergeant Noonan said.

"Please," she begged. "Please eat it. Personally I couldn't touch a thing, certainly not what's been in the house when he was here. But it's all right for you. It'd be a favor to me if you'd eat it up. Then you can go on with your work again afterwards."

There was a good deal of hesitating among the four policemen, but they were clearly hungry, and in the end they were persuaded to go into the kitchen and help themselves. The woman stayed where she was, listening to them through the open door, and she could hear them speaking among themselves, their voices thick and sloppy because their mouths were full of meat.

"Have some more, Charlie?"

"No. Better not finish it."

"She *wants* us to finish it. She said so. Be doing her a favor."

"Okay then. Give me some more."

"That's a hell of a big club the guy must've used to hit poor Patrick," one of them was saying. "The doc says his skull was smashed all to pieces just like from a sledgehammer."

"That's why it ought to be easy to find."

"Exactly what I say."

"Whoever done it, they're not going to be carrying a thing like that around with them longer than they need."

One of them belched.

"Personally, I think it's right here on the premises."

"Probably right under our very noses. What you think, Jack?"

And in the other room, Mary Maloney began to giggle.

1954:

The House Party

Stanley Ellin

"He's coming around," said the voice.

He was falling. His hands were outflung against the stone-cold blackness of space, and his body tilted head over heels, heels over head, as he fell. If there were only a way of knowing what was below, of bracing himself against the moment of impact, the terror might not have been so great. This way he was no more than a lump of terror flung into a pit, his mind cowering away from the inevitable while his helpless body descended toward it.

"Good," the voice said from far away, and it sounded to him as if someone were speaking to him quite calmly and cheerfully from the bottom of the pit. "Very good."

He opened his eyes. A glare of light washed in on him suddenly and painfully, and he squinted against it at the figures standing around him, at the faces, partly obscured by a sort of milky haze, looking down at him. He was lying on his back, and from the thrust of the cushions under him he knew he was on the familiar sofa. The milky haze was fading away now, and with it the panic. This was the old house at Nyack, the same living room, the same Utrillo on the wall, the same chandelier glittering over his head. *The same everything,* he thought bitterly, even to the faces around him.

That was Hannah, her eyes bright with tears—she could turn on tears like a faucet—and her hand was gripping his so hard that his fingers were numb under the pressure. Hannah with the overdeveloped maternal instinct, and only a husband to exercise it on . . . That was Abel Roth chewing on a cigar—even at a time like this, that reeking cigar!—and watching him worriedly. Abel with his first successful production in five years, worrying about his investment . . . And that was Ben Thayer and Harriet, the eternal bumpkins . . . And Jake Hall . . . And Tommy McGowan . . . All the old familiar faces, the sickening familiar faces.

But there was a stranger, too. A short, stout man with a look of amiable interest on his face, and splendidly bald, with only a tonsure of graying hair to frame his gleaming scalp. He ran his fingers reflectively over his scalp and nodded at Miles.

"How do you feel now?" he asked.

"I don't know," Miles said. He pulled his hand free of Hannah's and gingerly tried to raise himself to a sitting position. Halfway there he was transfixed by a shocking pain that was driven like a white-hot needle between his ribs. He heard Hannah gasp, and then the stranger's blunt fingers were probing deep into the pain, turning it to liquid, melting it away.

"See?" the man said. "It's nothing. Nothing at all."

Miles swung his legs around so that he sat erect on the sofa. He took a deep breath, then another. "For a second I thought it was my heart," he said. "The way it hit me—"

"No, no," the man said. "I know what you thought. You can believe me when I say it is of no concern." And then, as if it explained everything, he said, "I am Dr. Maas. Dr. Victor Maas."

"It was a miracle, darling," Hannah said breathlessly. "Dr Maas was the one who found you outside and brought you in. And he's been an absolute angel. If it weren't for him—"

Miles looked at her, and then looked at all the others standing there and watching him with concern. "Well," he demanded, "what *did* happen? What was it? Heart? Stroke? Amnesia? I'm not a child, for God's sake. You don't have to play games with me."

Abel Roth rolled his cigar from the left-hand corner of his mouth to the right-hand corner. "You can't blame him for feeling that way, can you, doc? After all, the man is out cold for fifteen minutes, he wants to know where he stands. Maybe there's some kind of checkup you could give him, like blood pressure and stuff like that. Maybe we'd all feel better for it."

Miles relished that, and relished even more the thought of what he had in store for Abel Roth. "Maybe we would, Abel," he said. "Maybe we've got a theater sold out sixteen weeks in advance, and the SRO sign up every night. Maybe we've got a real little gold mine to dig so long as I can keep swinging the shovel eight performances a week."

Abel's face turned red. "Ah, now, Miles," he said. "The way you talk—"

"Yes?" Miles said. "What about the way I talk?"

Ben Thayer shook his head slowly and solemnly. "If you'd only take the chip off your shoulder for one minute, Miles," he drawled. "If you'd try to understand—"

"Please!" Dr. Maas said sharply. "Gentlemen, please!" He frowned at them. "There is one thing I must make clear. Actually, I am not a medical physician. My interests, so to speak, lie more in the field of psychiatrics, and while I am, perhaps, qualified to make the examination of Mr. Owen that you suggest, I have no intention of doing so. For Mr. Owen's benefit I will also say that there is no need for me or anyone else to do so. He has my word on that."

"And Dr. Maas, I am sure," said Miles, "is an honorable man." He stood up flexing his knees gingerly, and noting the relief on the faces around him. "If you want to make yourself at home, doctor, go right ahead. There seems to be some kind of buffet over there, and while I can't vouch for the food I can promise that the liquor is very, very good."

The doctor's grin gave him a surprising resemblance to a plump and mischievous boy. "A delightful suggestion," he said, and immediately made his way toward the buffet. Abel followed, and, Miles observed, before the doctor had even reached the buffet, the cigar was perilously close to his ear. Abel spent three hours a week on a psychoanalyst's couch, and at least as much time pouring out lists of frightening and inconsequential symptoms to a sleek and well-fed Park Avenue practitioner. Dr. Maas, Miles thought with a wry sympathy, was in for some heavy going, whether he knew it or not.

The rest of the circle around the sofa broke up and eddied off, until only Hannah was left. She caught his arm in a panicky grip. "Are you *sure* you're all right?" she demanded. "You know you can tell me if there's anything wrong."

There was something wrong. Every time she caught hold of him like that, tried to draw him close, he had the feeling of a web ensnaring him, closing over him so that he had to fight it savagely.

It had not been like that at the start. She had been so beautiful that he thought in her case it might be different. The rising together, the eating together, the talking together, the endless routine of marriage looked as if it might somehow be bearable as long as it was shared with that loveliness. But then after a year the loveliness had become too familiar, the affection too cloying, the routine too much of a crushing burden.

He had been unconscious for fifteen minutes. He wondered if he had babbled during that time, said something about Lily that could be seized on as a clue. It wasn't of much concern if he had; in fact, it might have been a good way of preparing Hannah for the blow. It was going to be quite a blow, too. He could picture it falling, and it wasn't a pleasant picture.

He shrugged off Hannah's hand. "There's nothing wrong," he said, and then could not resist adding, "unless it's this business of your throwing a house party the one time of the week when I might expect a little peace and quiet."

"I?" Hannah said uncertainly. "What did *I* have to do with it?"

"Everything, as long as you've got that damn yen to be the perfect hostess and everybody's friend."

"They're *your* friends," she said.

"You ought to know by now that they're not my friends either. I thought I made it clear a hundred different ways that I hate them all, individually and collectively. They're nobody's friends. Why is it my obligation to feed them and entertain them the one time of the week I can get rid of them?"

"I don't understand you," Hannah said. She looked as if she were about to break into tears. "I know you bought the house up here so you could get away from everybody, but you were the one—"

The web was closing in again. "All *right,*" he said. "All *right!*" The whole thing didn't matter, anyhow. After he cleared out she could throw a house party every night of the week if she wanted to. She could burn the damn house down if that suited her. It wasn't of any concern to him. He'd had enough of this country-squire life between every Saturday and Monday performance to last him the rest of his life, and, as Lily had once remarked, Central Park had all the trees she wanted to see. Just the realization that he would soon be packed and out of here made any arguments pointless.

He shouldered his way to the buffet past Bob and Liz Gregory, who were mooning at each other as if doing it on the radio six mornings a week wasn't enough; past Ben Thayer, who was explaining to Jake Hall the trouble he was having with the final act of his new play; past Abel, who was saying something to Dr. Maas about psychosomatic factors. The doctor had a tall glass in one hand, and a sandwich in the other. "Interesting," he was saying. "Very interesting."

Miles tried to close his ears to all of them as he poured down two fingers of bourbon. Then he looked at his glass with distaste. The stuff was as flat as warm water, and as unpleasant to the palate. Obviously, one of the local help who took turns cleaning up the house had found the key to the liquor cabinet, and, after nearly emptying the bottle, had done a job on it at the kitchen tap. Damn fool. If you're going to sneak a drink, do it and forget it. But to ruin the rest of the bottle this way . . .

Abel poked him in the ribs. "I was just telling the doctor here," Abel said, "if he gets an evening off I'll fix him up with a house seat for *Ambuscade.* I was telling him, if he hasn't seen Miles Owen in *Ambuscade* he hasn't seen the performance of all time. How does that sound to you, Miles?"

Miles was lifting another bottle after making sure its seal was unbroken. He looked at Abel, and then set the bottle down with great care.

"As a matter of fact," he said, "I don't know how it sounds to me, Abel. It's something I've wanted to talk to you about, and maybe this is as good a time as any."

"Talk about what?" said Abel cheerfully, but there was a sudden worry in his eyes, a flickering of premonition on his face.

"It's private business, Abel," Miles said, and nodded to Dr. Maas, who stood by interestedly. "That is, if the doctor will excuse us."

"Of course, of course," the doctor said quickly. He waved his glass enthusiastically toward Miles. "And you were altogether right about the liquor, Mr. Owen. It is superb."

"Fine," Miles said. "This way, Abel."

He pushed his way through the crowd and crossed the room to the library, Abel trailing after him. When he closed the door of the library and switched on a lamp, the chill dampness of the room seemed to soak right into him, and he shivered. Logs and kindling had been laid on the fireplace, and he held a match to it until the wood crackled and caught. Then he lit a cigarette and drew deeply on it. He looked at the cigarette in surprise. There was a flatness about it, a lack of sensation which made him run his tongue over his lips questioningly. He drew again on the cigarette, and then flung it into the fire. First the liquor, he thought, and now this. Dr. Maas might be a handy man with Freudian complexes, but the first thing Monday an honest-to-God M.D. would be checking up on this little problem. It is discomforting to find out suddenly that you've lost your capacity to taste anything. Ridiculous maybe, but still discomforting.

Abel was standing at the window. "Look at that fog, will you. When I brought *Coxcomb* over to London I thought I saw the real thing there, but this makes it look like nothing. You could cut your way through this with a shovel."

The fog was banked solidly outside the window, stirring in slow waves, sending threads of damp smoke against the glass. Where the threads clung, little beads of water trickled down the pane.

"You get that around here a couple of times a year," Miles said impatiently. "And I didn't come in here to talk about the weather."

Abel turned away from the window and sat down reluctantly in an armchair. "No, I guess you didn't. All right, Miles, what's bothering you?"

"Ambuscade," Miles said. *"Ambuscade* is what's bothering me."

Abel nodded wearily. "It figured. It figured. Well, what particular thing? Your billing? We're using the biggest letters they make. Your publicity? All you have to do is name the time and you have your pick of any TV or radio guest spot in town. Remember what I told you after opening night, Miles? You name it, and if I can get it for you, I will."

Miles found himself suddenly enjoying the scene. Ordinarily, he had a genuine horror of such scenes. "Funny," he said. "I didn't hear you say anything about money just now, did I? I mean, in all that pretty speech it couldn't have slipped past me, could it?"

Abel sank down in his chair and sighed like a man deeply stricken. "I thought it would come down to this. Even if I'm paying you twice as much as the biggest star I ever had, I could see it coming, Miles. All right, what's the beef?"

"As a matter of fact," Miles said, "there's no beef."

"No?"

"None at all."

"What are you getting at?" Abel demanded. "What's all this about?"

Miles smiled. "I'm not getting *at* anything, Abel. I'm getting *out.* I'm leaving the show."

Miles had seen Abel meet more than one crisis before; he could have predicted every action before it took place. The face becoming an impassive mask, the hand searching for a match, the thumbnail flicking the match into a light, the elaborate drawing on the cigar stump, the neat flick of the match across the room. Abel fooled him. The match was snapped with sudden violence between the fingers, and then slowly rolled back and forth, back and forth.

"You're a cute boy, Miles," Abel said. "This wouldn't be your idea of a joke, would it?"

"I'm getting out, Abel. Tonight was positively the last appearance. That gives you all day tomorrow to line up another boy for the Monday-night curtain."

"What other boy?"

"Well, you've got Jay Welker on tap, haven't you? He's been understudying me for five months, and hoping I'd break a leg every night of it."

"Jay Welker couldn't carry *Ambuscade* one week, and you

know it, Miles. Nobody can carry that show but you, and you know that, too."

Abel leaned forward in his chair and shook his head from side to side unbelievingly. "And knowing that, you don't give a damn. You'd close the biggest thing on Broadway just like that, and to hell with the whole world, is that it?"

Miles felt his heart starting to pound heavily, his throat tightening. "Wait a second, Abel, before you start on the dirty words. One thing has already come through pretty well. In all this, you haven't yet asked me why I'm leaving. For all you know I might have some condition that's going to kill me an hour from now, but that would bother you less than keeping your show running! Have you thought about that side of it?"

"What side of it? I was standing right there when the doctor said you were in good shape. What am I supposed to do now? Get affidavits from the American Medical Association?"

"Then it's your idea that I'm pulling out because of a whim?"

"Let's not kid each other, Miles. You did this to Barrow five years ago, you did it to Goldschmidt after that, you did it to Howie Freeman last year, and I know, because that's how I got my chance to grab you for *Ambuscade*. But all the time I figured these others didn't know how to handle you, they didn't see just how much you meant to a show. Now I tell you they were right all along, and I was a prize sucker. They told me you would be going along fine, and then all of a sudden you would get a bug in your ear, and that was it. Bug in your ear, Miles. That's my low, ignorant way of saying whim, which is what it adds up to."

Abel paused. "The difference between me and them, Miles, is that I didn't take chances, and that's why you signed the first run-of-the-play contract you ever got since you were a nobody. You think you're walking out on that contract? Think again, my friend."

Miles nodded. "All right," he said thickly, "I'm thinking. Do you want to know about what?"

"They're your dice, my friend."

"I'm thinking about eight performances a week, Abel. Eight times a week I say the same lines, walk the same steps, make the same faces. I've done it for five months, which is the biggest break you ever got in your life, but if you had your way I'd be doing it for five years! Right now it's turned into one of those nightmares where you do the same thing over and over without being able to stop, but you wouldn't know about that because *you're* a guy in love with routine! But *I'm* not! After a while it's like being in jail with the key thrown away. What do you tell a man when he can walk out of jail? To stay there and like it?"

"Jail!" Abel cried. "Tell me somebody in this country who wouldn't give his right eye to be in the kind of jail you're in!"

"Listen," Miles said. He leaned forward urgently. "Do you remember before the show opened when we were rehearsing that kitchen scene? Do you remember when we ran through it that night ten times, fifteen times, twenty times? Do you know how I felt then? I felt as if I was plunked right down in hell, and all I would do for eternity was just play that scene over and over again. That's my idea of hell, Abel: a sweet little place where you do the same thing over and over, and they won't even let you go nuts at it, because that would spoil the fun for them. Do you get that? Because if you do, you can see just how I feel about *Ambuscade!*"

"I get it," Abel said. "I also get a certain little run-of-the-play contract tucked away in my safe deposit box. If you think rehearsing a scene a few times is hell you'll find out different when Equity lands on you. They look at this a little different from you."

"Don't try to scare me, Abel."

"Scare you, hell. I'm going to sue you black and blue, and I'm going to make it stick. I'm dead serious about that, Miles."

"Maybe. But isn't it hard to sue a man who's too sick to work?"

Abel nodded with grim understanding. "I figured you'd get around to that angle. I'm the patsy, because to the rest of the world you're sick." His eyes narrowed. "And that explains something else, too. That little business of your little blackout on the front doorstep, with a doctor handy, and twenty witnesses to swear to it. I have to hand it to you, Miles, you don't miss a trick. Only it'll take more than a smart trick and a quack doctor to work things your way."

Miles choked down the rage rising in him. "If you think that was a trick—!"

"What was a trick?" Harriet Thayer's voice said gaily behind him. Harriet and Ben were standing in the doorway, regarding him with a sort of cheerful curiosity. They made an incongruous couple, Ben's gauntness towering high over Harriet's little-girl fragility, and they had an eager, small-town friendliness that grated on Miles's nerves like a fingernail drawn down a slate. "It sounds terribly exciting and interesting," Harriet said. "Don't let us stop you."

Abel pointed at Miles with a shaking forefinger. "This'll stop you all right," he said, "and I'll give it to you in one line. Our friend here is walking out on *Ambuscade*. Maybe *you* can do something to change his mind!"

Ben stared with slow incredulity, and Miles had to marvel, as he had done so many times before, that any man who could write even the few good lines to be found in *Ambuscade* could be so slow on his feet.

"But you can't," Ben said. "Your contract runs as long as the play does."

"Sure," Abel jeered, "but he's a sick man. He falls down and has fits. You saw him, didn't you?"

Harriet nodded dumbly. "Yes, but I never thought—"

"And you were right," Abel said. "He's faking it. He's just fed up with making all that money and having all those nice things printed about him, so he's going to close the show. That's all. Just fold it up tight."

Miles slammed his hand down hard on the arm of Abel's chair. "All right," he said, "now that you've made everything so clear I'll ask you something. Do you think if *Ambuscade* was really a good play that any one person could close it up? Did it ever strike you that no one comes to see your crummy play; they come to see me walk through it? If you gave me *Jabberwocky* to read up there they'd come to see me! Who's to tell a one-man show that he has to keep playing when he doesn't want to!"

"It *is* a good play!" Harriet shouted at him. "It's the best play you ever acted in, and if you don't know that—"

Miles was shouting himself now. "Then get someone else to play it! It might be even better that way!"

Ben held his hands out, palms up, in a pleading gesture. "Now, Miles, you know you've been identified with that part so no one else could take it over," he said. "And try to see it my

way, Miles. I've been writing fifteen years, and this is the first
real break—"

Miles walked up to him slowly. "You clown," he said softly.
"Don't you have any self-respect at all?"

When he walked out of the library he quickly slammed the
door behind him to forestall any belated answer to that.

The party had broken into several small knots of people scattered around the room, a deafening rise and fall of voices, a
haze of blue smoke which lay like a transparent blanket midway
between floor and ceiling. Someone, Miles observed, had overturned a drink on the piano; the puddle ran down in a glittering
string along the side of the mahogany and was leaving a damp
stain on the Wilton rug beneath. Tommy McGowan and his
latest, an overripe blonde—Norma or Alma or something—sat
on the floor shuffling through piles of phonograph records, ar-
ranging some into a dangerously high stack and carelessly tossing the others aside. The buffet looked as if a cyclone had hit
it; only some empty platters and broken pieces of bread remained amidst the wreckage. From the evidence, Miles
thought sardonically, the party would have to be rated a roaring
success.

But even the sense of heat and excitement in the room could
not erase the chill that he seemed to have brought with him
from the library. He rubbed his hands together hard, but this
didn't help any, and he felt a small pang of fright at the realization. What if there really were something wrong with him? Lily
was not the kind of woman to take gracefully to the role of
nursemaid to an invalid. Not that she was wrong about that, as
far as he was concerned; if the shoe were on the other foot he
couldn't see himself playing any Robert Browning to her Elizabeth Barrett either. Not for Lily or anyone else in the world. In
that case it was better not to even bother about a checkup. If
there was something, he didn't even want to know about it!

"You are disturbed about something, I think."

It was Dr. Maas. He was leaning casually against the wall, not
an arm's length away, his hands thrust into his pockets, his eyes
fixed reflectively on Miles. Taking in everything, Miles thought
angrily, like some damn scientist looking at a bug under a microscope.

"No," Miles snapped. Then he thought better of it. "Yes," he said. "As a matter of fact, I am."

"Ah?"

"I don't feel right. I know you told me I was fine, but I don't feel fine."

"Physically?"

"Of course, physically! What are you trying to tell me? That it's all in my mind, or some claptrap like that?"

"I am not trying to tell you anything, Mr. Owen. You are telling me."

"All right. Then I want to know what makes you so sure of yourself. No examination, no X-ray, no anything; and you come up with your answer just like that. What's the angle here? Do we somehow get around to the idea that there's nothing wrong physically, but if I put myself in your hands for a nice long expensive psychoanalysis—"

"Stop right there, Mr. Owen," Dr. Maas said coldly. "I will take for granted that your manners are abominable because you are clearly under some pressure. But you should rein in your imagination. I do not practice psychoanalysis, and I never said I did. I am not a healer of any sort. The people I deal with are, unfortunately, always past the point of any cure, and my interest in them, as you can see, must be wholly academic. To be taken for some kind of sharper seeking a victim—"

"Look," Miles said abruptly, "I'm sorry. I'm terribly sorry. I don't know what made me go off like that. Maybe it's this party. I hate these damn parties; they always do things to me. Whatever it is, I'm honestly sorry for taking it out on you."

The doctor nodded gravely. "Of course," he said. "Of course." Then he nervously ran his fingers over his shining scalp. "There is something else I should like to say. I am afraid, however, I would risk offending you."

Miles laughed. "I think you owe it to me."

The doctor hesitated, and then gestured toward the library. "As it happens, Mr. Owen, I heard much of what went on in there. I am not an eavesdropper, but the discussion got a little —well, heated, shall we say?—and it was impossible not to overhear it from outside the door here."

"Yes?" Miles said warily.

"The clue to your condition, Mr. Owen, lies in that discussion.

To put it bluntly, you are running away. You find what you call routine unbearable, and so you are fleeing from it."

Miles forced himself to smile. "What do you mean, what *I* call routine? Is there another word for it in your language?"

"I think there is. I think I would call it responsibility. And since your life, Mr. Owen—both your professional and your private life—are very much an open book to the world, I will draw on it and say that most of this life has also been spent fleeing from responsibility of one sort or another. Does it strike you as strange, Mr. Owen, that no matter how far and fast you run you always find yourself facing the same problem over and over again?"

Miles clenched and unclenched his fist. "After all," he said, "it's my problem."

"That is where you're wrong, Mr. Owen. When you suddenly leave your role in a play, it affects everyone concerned with that play, and, in turn, everyone concerned with those people. In your relations with women you may move on, but they do not stay motionless either. They move on, too, dangerous to themselves and perhaps to others. Forgive me if I seem sententious, Mr. Owen, but you cannot cast pebbles in the water without sending ripples to the far shore.

"That is why when you say *routine,* it is because you are thinking only of yourself caught in a situation. And when I say *responsibility,* I am thinking of everyone else concerned with it."

"And what's the prescription, Doctor?" Miles demanded. "To stay sunk in a private little hell because if you try to get away you might step on somebody's toes in the process?"

"Get away?" the doctor said in surprise. "Do you really think you can get away?"

"You've got a lot to learn, Doctor. Watch me and see."

"I am watching you, Mr. Owen, and I do see. In a wholly academic way, as I said. It is both fascinating and bewildering to see a man trying to flee, as he calls it, his private little hell, while all the time he is carrying it with him."

Miles's hand was half raised, and then it dropped limp at his side. "In other words, Doctor," he said mockingly, "you're replacing the good old-fashioned sulphur-and-brimstone hell with something even bigger and better."

The doctor shrugged. "Of course, you don't believe that."

"No," Miles said. "I don't."

"I have a confession to make, Mr. Owen." The doctor smiled, and suddenly he was the plump and mischievous boy again. "I knew you wouldn't. In fact, that is why I felt free to discuss the matter with you."

"In an academic way, of course."

"Of course."

Miles laughed. "You're quite a man, Doctor. I think I'd like to see more of you."

"I am sure you will, Mr. Owen. But right now I believe that someone is trying to attract your notice. There, by the door."

Miles followed the doctor's gesturing finger, and his heart stopped. All he could do was pray that no one else had noticed, as he swiftly crossed the room and blocked off the woman who was entering it from the hallway that led to the front door. He thrust her back against the door, and catching hold of her shoulders he shook her once, sharply and angrily.

"Are you crazy?" he demanded, "Don't you have any more sense than to show up here like this?"

She twisted her shoulders away from his grasp, and carefully brushed at the collar of her coat with her fingertips. The coat had cost Miles a month's pay.

"Aren't you sweet, Miles. Do you invite all your guests in this way?"

Even in the dimness of the hallway she was startling to look at. The sulky lips against the gardenia pallor of the face, the high cheek bones, the slanted eyes darting fire at him. He quailed.

"All right, I'm sorry. I'm sorry. But, my God, Lily, there are two dozen of the biggest mouths on Broadway in that room. If you want the whole world to know about this, why don't you just tip off Winchell?"

She knew when she had him beaten. "I don't like that, darling. I don't like that at all. I mean, to make it sound as obscene and disgusting as all that. It really isn't supposed to be like that, is it?"

"You know damn well it isn't like that, Lily. But use your head, will you? There is such a thing as discretion."

"There's also such a thing as working a word to death, darling.

And I don't mind telling you that in the last two months you've filled me up to here with that one."

Miles said angrily, "I've been trying to make it clear that we'd work this thing out in the right way at the right time. I've already told Abel I was leaving the show. I was going to talk to Hannah, too, but this party has fouled everything up. Tomorrow, when I can be alone with her—"

"Ah, but tomorrow may be a long time away, darling. Much longer than you realize."

"What exactly does that mean?"

She fumbled through her purse and drew an envelope from it. She waved the envelope back and forth under his nose with a fine air of triumph.

"It means this, Miles. Two pretty little reservations, outward bound, for tomorrow's sailing. You see, you don't have nearly as much time as you thought, do you, darling?"

"Tomorrow! The agent said he couldn't possibly have anything for us within a month!"

"He didn't count on cancellations. This one came through just two hours ago, which is exactly how long it took me to get here. And if it wasn't for that awful fog on the road I would have been here that much sooner. I have the car outside, Miles. You can pack whatever is handy, and get the rest of what you need on the boat. When I go back I expect you to be with me, Miles, because whether you are or not I'll be sailing tomorrow. You can't really blame me for that, can you, darling? After all, none of us are getting any younger."

He tried to straighten out the aching confusion of his thoughts. He wanted to escape Hannah's web, and now it seemed, somehow or other, there was another waiting to be dropped around him. Running, the doctor had said. Always running and never getting anywhere. There was a great weight of weariness in his arms, his legs, his whole body. Running did that to you.

"Well," Lily said, "make up your mind, darling."

He rubbed his hand over his forehead. "Where's the car?"

"Right across the road."

"All right," Miles said, "you wait in it. Just stay there, and don't blow the horn for me, or anything like that. I'll be down in ten minutes. Fifteen minutes at the most. Most of my stuff is in town, anyhow. We'll pick it up on the way to the boat."

He opened the door and gently pushed her toward it.

"You'll have to feel your way to the car, Miles. I've never seen anything like what's outside."

"I'll find it," he said. "You just wait there."

He closed the door, then leaned against it fighting the sickness that kept rising to his throat. The loud voices in the next room, the shrieks of idiot laughter that now and then cut through it, the roar of music from the phonograph tuned at its greatest volume—everything seemed conspiring against him, not allowing him to be alone, not allowing him to think things out.

He went up the stairs almost drunkenly, and into the bedroom. He pulled out his valise, and then at random started cramming it full. Shirts, socks, the contents of the jewel case on his dresser. He thrust down hard with all his weight, making room for more.

"What are you doing, Miles?"

He didn't look up. He knew exactly what the expression on her face would be, and he didn't want to meet it then. It would have been too much.

"I'm leaving, Hannah."

"With that woman?" Her voice was a vague, uncomprehending whisper.

He had to look at her then. Her eyes stared at him, enormous against the whiteness of her skin. Her hand fumbled with the ornament at her breast. It was the silver mask of comedy he had picked up for her on Fifth Avenue a week before their marriage.

She said wonderingly, "I saw you with her in the hallway. I wasn't prying or anything like that, Miles, but when I asked the doctor where you were—"

"Stop it!" Miles shouted. "What do you have to apologize for!"

"But she's the one, isn't she?"

"Yes, she's the one."

"And you want to go away with her?"

His hands were on the lid of the valise. He rested his weight on them, head down, eyes closed.

"Yes," he said at last. "That's what it comes to."

"No!" she cried with a sudden fervor. "You don't really want to. You know she's not good for you. You know there's nobody in the whole world as good for you as I am!"

He pressed the lid of the valise down. The lock caught with a tiny click.

"Hannah, it would have been better for you not to have come up just now. I would have written to you, explained it somehow—"

"Explained it? When it would be too late? When you'd know what a mistake you'd made? Miles, listen to me. Listen to me, Miles. I'm talking to you out of all my love. It would be a terrible mistake."

"I'll have to be the judge of that, Hannah."

He stood up, and she came toward him, her fingers digging into his arms frantically. "Look at me, Miles," she whispered. "Can't you see how I feel? Can't you understand that I'd rather have the both of us dead than to have you go away like this and leave the whole world empty for me!"

It was horrible. It was the web constricting around him so hard that it was taking all his strength to pull himself free. But he did, with a brutal effort, and saw her fall back against the dresser. Then she suddenly wheeled toward it, and when she faced him again he saw the pistol leveled at him. It shone a cold, deadly blue in her hand, and then he realized that her hand was trembling so violently that the gun must be frightening her as much as it did him. The whole grotesquerie of the scene struck him full force, melting away the fear, filling him with a sense of outrage.

"Put that thing down," he said.

"No." He could hardly hear her. "Not unless you tell me that you're not going."

He took a step toward her, and she shrank farther back against the dresser, but the gun remained leveled at him. She was like a child afraid someone was going to trick her out of a toy. He stopped short, and then shrugged with exaggerated indifference.

"You're making a fool of yourself, Hannah. People are paid for acting like this on the stage. They're not supposed to make private shows of themselves."

Her head moved from side to side in a slow, aimless motion. "You still don't believe me, do you, Miles?"

"No," he said. "I don't."

He turned his back on her, half expecting to hear the sudden explosion, feel the impact between his shoulder blades, but there was nothing. He picked up the valise and walked to the door. "Good-bye, Hannah," he said. He didn't turn his head to look at her.

The weakness in his knees made each step a trial. He stopped at the foot of the staircase to shift the valise from one hand to the other, and saw Dr. Maas standing there, hat in hand, a topcoat thrown over his arm.

"Ah?" said the doctor inquiringly. "So you, too, are leaving the party, Mr. Owen?"

"Party?" Miles said, and then laughed short and sharp. "Leaving the nightmare, if you don't mind, Doctor. I hate to tell this to a guest, but I think you'll understand me when I say that this past hour has been a nightmare that gets thicker and thicker. That's what I'm leaving, Doctor, and you can't blame me for being happy about it."

"No, no," said the doctor. "I quite understand."

"The car is waiting for me outside. If I can give you a lift anywhere—?"

"Not at all," the doctor said. "I really do not have far to go."

They went to the doorway together and stepped outside. The fog moved in on them, cold and wet, and Miles turned up his jacket collar against it.

"Rotten weather," he said.

"Terrible," the doctor agreed. He glanced at his watch, and then lumbered down the steps to the walk like a walrus disappearing into a snowbank. "I'll be seeing you, Mr. Owen," he called.

Miles watched him go, then lifted the valise and went down the steps himself, burying his nose in his collar against the smothering dampness all around him. He was at the bottom step when he heard the sibilance of the door opening behind him, the faraway whisper of danger in his bones.

He turned, and, as he knew it would be, there was Hannah standing at the open door, still holding the gun. But the gun was gripped tightly in both hands now, and the menace of it was real and overwhelming.

"I tried to make you understand, Miles," she said, like a child saying the words. "I tried to make you understand."

He flung his arms out despairingly.

"No!" he cried wildly. "No!"

And then there was the roar of the explosion in his ears, the gout of flame leaping out toward him, the crushing impact against his chest, and the whole world dissolving. In it, only one thing stood sharp and definable: the figure of the doctor bending over him, the face strangely Satanic in its cruel indifference.

For that single moment Miles understood everything. He had been here before. He had lived this hour a thousand times before, and would live it again and again for all eternity. The curtain was falling now, but when it rose again the stage would be set once more for the house party. Because he was in Hell, and the most terrible thing of all, the terror which submerged all others, was this moment of understanding given him so that he could know this, and could see himself crawling the infinite treadmill of his doom. Then the darkness closed in with a rush, blotting out all understanding—until next time . . .

"He's coming around," said the voice.

He was falling. His hands were outflung . . .

1956:

The Blessington Method

Stanley Ellin

Mr. Treadwell was a small, likable man who worked for a prosperous company in New York City, and whose position with the company entitled him to an office of his own. Late one afternoon of a fine day in June a visitor entered this office. The visitor was stout, well-dressed, and imposing. His complexion was smooth and pink, his small, near-sighted eyes shone cheerfully behind heavy horn-rimmed eyeglasses.

"My name," he said, after laying aside a bulky portfolio and shaking Mr. Treadwell's hand with a crushing grip, "is Bunce, and I am a representative of the Society for Gerontology. I am here to help you with your problem, Mr. Treadwell."

Mr. Treadwell sighed. "Since you are a total stranger to me, my friend," he said, "and since I have never heard of the outfit you claim to represent, and, above all, since I have no problem which could possibly concern you, I am sorry to say that I am not in the market for whatever you are peddling. Now, if you don't mind—"

"Mind?" said Bunce. "Of course, I mind. The Society for Gerontology does not try to sell anything to anybody, Mr. Treadwell. Its interests are purely philanthropic. It examines case histories, draws up reports, works toward the solution of one of the most tragic situations we face in modern society."

"Which is?"

"That should have been made obvious by the title of the organization, Mr. Treadwell. Gerontology is the study of old age and the problems concerning it. Do not confuse it with geriatrics, please. Geriatrics is concerned with the diseases of old age. Gerontology deals with old age as the problem itself."

"I'll try to keep that in mind," Mr. Treadwell said impatiently. "Meanwhile, I suppose, a small donation is in order? Five dollars, say?"

"No, no, Mr. Treadwell, not a penny, not a red cent. I quite understand that this is the traditional way of dealing with various philanthropic organizations, but the Society for Gerontology works in a different way entirely. Our objective is to help you with your problem first. Only then would we feel we have the right to make any claim on you."

"Fine," said Mr. Treadwell more amiably. "That leaves us all even. I have no problem, so you get no donation. Unless you'd rather reconsider?"

"Reconsider?" said Bunce in a pained voice. "It is you, Mr. Treadwell, and not I who must reconsider. Some of the most pitiful cases the Society deals with are those of people who have long refused to recognize or admit their problem. I have worked months on your case, Mr. Treadwell. I never dreamed you would fall into that category."

Mr. Treadwell took a deep breath. "Would you mind telling me just what you mean by that nonsense about working on my case? I was never a case for any damned society or organization in the book!"

It was the work of a moment for Bunce to whip open his portfolio and extract several sheets of paper from it.

"If you will bear with me," he said, "I should like to sum up the gist of these reports. You are forty-seven years old and in excellent health. You own a home in East Sconsett, Long Island, on which there are nine years of mortgage payments still due, and you also own a late-model car on which eighteen monthly payments are yet to be made. However, due to an excellent salary you are in prosperous circumstances. Am I correct?"

"As correct as the credit agency which gave you that report," said Mr. Treadwell.

Bunce chose to overlook this. "We will now come to the point. You have been happily married for twenty-three years, and have one daughter who was married last year and now lives with her husband in Chicago. Upon her departure from your home your father-in-law, a widower and somewhat crotchety gentleman, moved into the house and now resides with you and your wife."

Bunce's voice dropped to a low, impressive note. "He's seventy-two years old, and, outside of a touch of bursitis in his right shoulder, admits to exceptional health for his age. He has stated on several occasions that he hopes to live another twenty years, and according to actuarial statistics which my Society has on file *he has every chance of achieving this*. Now do you understand, Mr. Treadwell?"

It took a long time for the answer to come. "Yes," said Mr. Treadwell at last, almost in a whisper. "Now I understand."

"Good," said Bunce sympathetically. "Very good. The first step is always a hard one—the admission that there *is* a problem hovering over you, clouding every day that passes. Nor is there any need to ask why you make efforts to conceal it even from yourself. You wish to spare Mrs. Treadwell your unhappiness, don't you?"

Mr. Treadwell nodded.

"Would it make you feel better," asked Bunce, "if I told you that Mrs. Treadwell shared your own feelings? That she, too, feels her father's presence in her home as a burden which grows heavier each day?"

"But she can't!" said Mr. Treadwell in dismay. "She was the one who wanted him to live with us in the first place, after Sylvia got married, and we had a spare room. She pointed out how much he had done for us when we first got started, and how easy he was to get along with, and how little expense it would be—it was she who sold me on the idea. I can't believe she didn't mean it!"

"Of course, she meant it. She knew all the traditional emotions at the thought of her old father living alone somewhere, and offered all the traditional arguments on his behalf, and was sincere every moment. The trap she led you both into was the pitfall that awaits anyone who indulges in murky, sentimental thinking. Yes, indeed, I'm sometimes inclined to believe that

Eve ate the apple just to make the serpent happy," said Bunce, and shook his head grimly at the thought.

"Poor Carol," groaned Mr. Treadwell. "If I had only known that she felt as miserable about this as I did—"

"Yes?" said Bunce. "What would you have done?"

Mr. Treadwell frowned. "I don't know. But there must have been something we could have figured out if we put our heads together."

"What?" Bunce asked. "Drive the man out of the house?"

"Oh, I don't mean exactly like that."

"What then?" persisted Bunce. "Send him to an institution? There are some extremely luxurious institutions for the purpose. You'd have to consider one of them, since he could not possibly be regarded as a charity case; nor, for that matter, could I imagine him taking kindly to the idea of going to a public institution."

"Who would?" said Mr. Treadwell. "And as for the expensive kind, well, I did look into the idea once, but when I found out what they'd cost I knew it was out. It would take a fortune."

"Perhaps," suggested Bunce, "he could be given an apartment of his own—a small, inexpensive place with someone to take care of him."

"As it happens, that's what he moved out of to come live with us. And on that business of someone taking care of him—you'd never believe what it costs. That is, even allowing we could find someone to suit him."

"Right!" Bunce said, and struck the desk sharply with his fist. "Right in every respect, Mr. Treadwell."

Mr. Treadwell looked at him angrily. "What do you mean—right? I had the idea you wanted to help me with this business, but you haven't come up with a thing yet. On top of that you make it sound as if we're making great progress."

"We are, Mr. Treadwell, we are. Although you weren't aware of it we have just completed the second step to your solution. The first step was the admission that there was a problem; the second step was the realization that no matter which way you turn there seems to be no logical or practical solution to the problem. In this way you are not only witnessing, you are actually participating in, the marvelous operation of The Blessington Method which, in the end, places the one possible solution squarely in your hands."

"The Blessington Method?"

"Forgive me," said Bunce. "In my enthusiasm I used a term not yet in scientific vogue. I must explain, therefore, that The Blessington Method is the term my co-workers at the Society for Gerontology have given to its course of procedure. It is so titled in honor of J. G. Blessington, the Society's founder, and one of the great men of our era. He has not achieved his proper acclaim yet, but he will. Mark my words, Mr. Treadwell, some day his name will resound louder than that of Malthus."

"Funny I never heard of him," reflected Mr. Treadwell. "Usually I keep up with the newspapers. And another thing," he added, eyeing Bunce narrowly, "we never did get around to clearing up just how you happened to list me as one of your cases, and how you managed to turn up so much about me."

Bunce laughed delightedly. "It does sound mysterious when you put it like that, doesn't it? Well, there's really no mystery to it at all. You see, Mr. Treadwell, the Society has hundreds of investigators scouting this great land of ours from coast to coast, although the public at large is not aware of this. It is against the rules of the Society for any employee to reveal that he is a professional investigator—he would immediately lose effectiveness.

"Nor do these investigators start off with some specific person as their subject. Their interest lies in *any* aged person who is willing to talk about himself, and you would be astonished at how garrulous most aged people are about their most intimate affairs. That is, of course, as long as they are among strangers.

"These subjects are met at random on park benches, in saloons, in libraries—in any place conducive to comfort and conversation. The investigator befriends the subjects, draws them out—seeks, especially, to learn all he can about the younger people on whom they are dependent."

"You mean," said Mr. Treadwell with growing interest, "the people who support them."

"No, no," said Bunce. "You are making the common error of equating *dependence* and *finances*. In many cases, of course, there is a financial dependence, but that is a minor part of the picture. The important factor is that there is always an *emo-*

tional dependence. Even where a physical distance may separate the older person from the younger, that emotional dependence is always present. It is like a current passing between them. The younger person by the mere realization that the aged exist is burdened by guilt and anger. It was his personal experience with this tragic dilemma of our times that led J. G. Blessington to his great work."

"In other words," said Mr. Treadwell, "you mean that even if the old man were not living with us, things would be just as bad for Carol and me?"

"You seem to doubt that, Mr. Treadwell. But tell me, what makes things bad for you now, to use your own phrase?"

Mr. Treadwell thought this over. "Well," he said, "I suppose it's just a case of having a third person around all the time. It gets on your nerves after a while."

"But your daughter lived as a third person in your home for over twenty years," pointed out Bunce. "Yet, I am sure you didn't have the same reaction to her."

"But that's different," Mr. Treadwell protested. "You can have fun with a kid, play with her, watch her growing up—"

"Stop right there!" said Bunce. "Now you are hitting the mark. All the years your daughter lived with you you could take pleasure in watching her grow, flower like an exciting plant, take form as an adult being. But the old man in your house can only wither and decline now, and watching that process casts a shadow on your life. Isn't that the case?"

"I suppose it is."

"In that case, do you suppose it would make any difference if he lived elsewhere? Would you be any the less aware that he was withering and declining and looking wistfully in your direction from a distance?"

"Of course not. Carol probably wouldn't sleep half the night worrying about him, and I'd have him on my mind all the time because of her. That's perfectly natural, isn't it?"

"It is, indeed, and, I am pleased to say, your recognition of that completes the third step of The Blessington Method. You now realize that it is not the *presence* of the aged subject which creates the problem, but his *existence.*"

Mr. Treadwell pursed his lips thoughtfully. "I don't like the sound of that."

"Why not? It merely states the fact, doesn't it?"

"Maybe it does. But there's something about it that leaves a bad taste in the mouth. It's like saying the only way Carol and I can have our troubles settled is by the old man's dying."

"Yes," Bunce said gravely, "it is like saying that."

"Well, I don't like it—not one bit. Thinking you'd like to see somebody dead can make you feel pretty mean, and as far as I know it's never killed anybody yet."

Bunce smiled. "Hasn't it?" he said gently.

He and Mr. Treadwell studied each other in silence. Then Mr. Treadwell pulled a handkerchief from his pocket with nerveless fingers and patted his forehead with it.

"You," he said with deliberation, "are either a lunatic or a practical joker. Either way, I'd like you to clear out of here. That's fair warning."

Bunce's face was all sympathetic concern. "Mr. Treadwell," he cried, "don't you realize you were on the verge of the fourth step? Don't you see how close you were to your solution?"

Mr. Treadwell pointed to the door. "Out—before I call the police."

The expression on Bunce's face changed from concern to disgust. "Oh, come, Mr. Treadwell, you don't believe anybody would pay attention to whatever garbled and incredible story you'd concoct out of this. Please think it over carefully before you do anything rash, now or later. If the exact nature of our talk were even mentioned, you would be the only one to suffer, believe me. Meanwhile, I'll leave you my card. Anytime you wish to call on me I will be ready to serve you."

"And why should I ever want to call on you?" demanded the white-faced Mr. Treadwell.

"There are various reasons," said Bunce, "but one above all." He gathered his belongings and moved to the door. "Consider, Mr. Treadwell: anyone who has mounted the first three steps of The Blessington Method inevitably mounts the fourth. You have made remarkable progress in a short time, Mr. Treadwell —you should be calling soon."

"I'll see you in hell first," said Mr. Treadwell.

Despite this parting shot, the time that followed was a bad one for Mr. Treadwell. The trouble was that having been introduced to The Blessington Method he couldn't seem to get it out of his mind. It incited thoughts that he had to keep thrusting away with an effort, and it certainly colored his relationship with his father-in-law in an unpleasant way.

Never before had the old man seemed so obtrusive, so much in the way, and so capable of always doing or saying the thing most calculated to stir annoyance. It especially outraged Mr. Treadwell to think of this intruder in his home babbling his private affairs to perfect strangers, eagerly spilling out details of his family life to paid investigators who were only out to make trouble. And, to Mr. Treadwell in his heated state of mind, the fact that the investigators could not be identified as such did not serve as any excuse.

Within very few days Mr. Treadwell, who prided himself on being a sane and level-headed businessman, had to admit he was in a bad way. He began to see evidences of a fantastic conspiracy on every hand. He could visualize hundreds—no, thousands—of Bunces swarming into offices just like his all over the country. He could feel cold sweat starting on his forehead at the thought.

But, he told himself, the whole thing was *too* fantastic. He could prove this to himself by merely reviewing his discussion with Bunce, and so he did, dozens of times. After all, it was no more than an objective look at a social problem. Had anything been said that a *really* intelligent man should shy away from? Not at all. If he had drawn some shocking inferences, it was because the ideas were already in his mind looking for an outlet.

On the other hand—

It was with a vast relief that Mr. Treadwell finally decided to pay a visit to the Society for Gerontology. He knew what he would find there: a dingy room or two, a couple of under-paid clerical workers, the musty odor of a piddling charity operation —all of which would restore matters to their proper perspective again. He went so strongly imbued with this picture that he almost walked past the gigantic glass and aluminum tower which was the address of the Society, rode its softly humming elevator in confusion, and emerged in the anteroom of the Main Office in a daze.

And it was still in a daze that he was ushered through a vast and seemingly endless labyrinth of rooms by a sleek, long-legged young woman, and saw, as he passed, hosts of other young women, no less sleek and long-legged, multitudes of brisk, square-shouldered young men, rows of streamlined machinery clicking and chuckling in electronic glee, mountains of stainless-steel card indexes, and, over all, the bland reflection of modern indirect lighting on plastic and metal—until finally he was led into the presence of Bunce himself, and the door closed behind him.

"Impressive, isn't it?" said Bunce, obviously relishing the sight of Mr. Treadwell's stupefaction.

"Impressive?" croaked Mr. Treadwell hoarsely. "Why, I've never seen anything like it. It's a ten-million-dollar outfit!"

"And why not? Science is working day and night like some Frankenstein, Mr. Treadwell, to increase longevity past all sane limits. There are fourteen million people over sixty-five in this country right now. In twenty years their number will be increased to twenty-one million. Beyond that no one can even estimate what the figures will rise to!

"But the one bright note is that each of these aged people is surrounded by many young donors or potential donors to our Society. As the tide rises higher, we, too, flourish and grow stronger to withstand it."

Mr. Treadwell felt a chill of horror penetrate him. "Then it's true, isn't it?"

"I beg your pardon?"

"This Blessington Method you're always talking about," said Mr. Treadwell wildly. "The whole idea is just to settle things by getting rid of old people!"

"Right!" said Bunce. "That is the exact idea. And not even J. G. Blessington himself ever phrased it better. You have a way with words, Mr. Treadwell. I always admire a man who can come to the point without sentimental twaddle."

"But you can't get away with it!" said Mr. Treadwell incredulously. "You don't really believe you can get away with it, do you?"

Bunce gestured toward the expanses beyond the closed doors. "Isn't that sufficient evidence of the Society's success?"

"But all those people out there! Do they realize what's going on?"

"Like all well-trained personnel, Mr. Treadwell," said Bunce reproachfully, "they know only their own duties. What you and I are discussing here happens to be upper echelon."

Mr. Treadwell's shoulders drooped. "It's impossible," he said weakly. "It can't work."

"Come, come," Bunce said not unkindly, "you mustn't let yourself be overwhelmed. I imagine that what disturbs you most is what J. G. Blessington sometimes referred to as the Safety Factor. But look at it this way, Mr. Treadwell: isn't it perfectly natural for old people to die? Well, our Society guarantees that the deaths will appear natural. Investigations are rare—not one has ever caused us any trouble.

"More than that, you would be impressed by many of the names on our list of donors. People powerful in the political world as well as the financial world have been flocking to us. One and all, they could give glowing testimonials as to our efficiency. And remember that such important people make the Society for Gerontology invulnerable, no matter at what point it may be attacked, Mr. Treadwell. And such invulnerability extends to every single one of our sponsors, including you, should you choose to place your problem in our hands."

"But I don't have the right," Mr. Treadwell protested despairingly. "Even if I wanted to, who am I to settle things this way for anybody?"

"Aha." Bunce leaned forward intently. "But you do want to settle things?"

"Not this way."

"Can you suggest any other way?"

Mr. Treadwell was silent.

"You see," Bunce said with satisfaction, "the Society for Gerontology offers the one practical answer to the problem. Do you still reject it, Mr. Treadwell?"

"I can't see it," Mr. Treadwell said stubbornly. "It's just not right."

"Are you sure of that?"

"Of course I am!" snapped Mr. Treadwell. "Are you going to tell me that it's right and proper to go around killing people just because they're old?"

"I am telling you that very thing, Mr. Treadwell, and I ask you to look at it this way. We are living today in a world of progress, a world of producers and consumers, all doing their best to improve our common lot. The old are neither producers nor consumers, so they are only barriers to our continued progress.

"If we want to take a brief, sentimental look into the pastoral haze of yesterday we may find that once they did serve a function. While the young were out tilling the fields, the old could tend to the household. But even that function is gone today. We have a hundred better devices for tending the household, and they come far cheaper. Can you dispute that?"

"I don't know," Mr. Treadwell said doggedly. "You're arguing that people are machines, and I don't go along with that at all."

"Good heavens," said Bunce, "don't tell me that you see them as anything else! Of course, we are machines, Mr. Treadwell, all of us. Unique and wonderful machines, I grant, but machines nevertheless. Why, look at the world around you. It is a vast organism made up of replaceable parts, all striving to produce and consume, produce and consume until worn out. Should one permit the worn-out part to remain where it is? Of course not! It must be cast aside so that the organism will not be made inefficient. It is the whole organism that counts, Mr. Treadwell, not any of its individual parts. Can't you understand that?"

"I don't know," said Mr. Treadwell uncertainly. "I've never thought of it that way. It's hard to take in all at once."

"I realize that, Mr. Treadwell, but it is part of The Blessington Method that the sponsor fully appreciate the great value of his contribution in all ways—not only as it benefits him, but also in the way it benefits the entire social organism. In signing a pledge to our Society a man is truly performing the most noble act of his life."

"Pledge?" said Mr. Treadwell. "What kind of pledge?"

Bunce removed a printed form from a drawer of his desk and laid it out carefully for Mr. Treadwell's inspection. Mr. Treadwell read it and sat up sharply.

"Why, this says that I'm promising to pay you two thousand dollars in a month from now. You never said anything about that kind of money!"

"There has never been any occasion to raise the subject before this," Bunce replied. "But for some time now a committee of the Society has been examining your financial standing, and it reports that you can pay this sum without stress or strain."

"What do you mean, stress or strain?" Mr. Treadwell retorted. "Two thousand dollars is a lot of money, no matter how you look at it."

Bunce shrugged. "Every pledge is arranged in terms of the sponsor's ability to pay, Mr. Treadwell. Remember, what may seem expensive to you would certainly seem cheap to many other sponsors I have dealt with."

"And what do I get for this?"

"Within one month after you sign the pledge, the affair of your father-in-law will be disposed of. Immediately after that you will be expected to pay the pledge in full. Your name is then enrolled on our list of sponsors, and that is all there is to it."

"I don't like the idea of my name being enrolled on anything."

"I can appreciate that," said Bunce. "But may I remind you that a donation to a charitable organization such as the Society for Gerontology is tax-deductible?"

Mr. Treadwell's fingers rested lightly on the pledge. "Now just for the sake of argument," he said, "suppose someone signs one of these things and then doesn't pay up. I guess you know that a pledge like this isn't collectible under the law, don't you?"

"Yes," Bunce smiled, "and I know that a great many organizations cannot redeem pledges made to them in apparently good faith. But the Society for Gerontology has never met that difficulty. We avoid it by reminding all sponsors that the young, if they are careless, may die as unexpectedly as the old . . . No, no," he said, steadying the paper, "just your signature at the bottom will do."

When Mr. Treadwell's father-in-law was found drowned off the foot of East Sconsett pier three weeks later (the old man fished from the pier regularly although he had often been told by various local authorities that the fishing was poor there), the event was duly entered into the East Sconsett records as Death By Accidental Submersion, and Mr. Treadwell himself made the arrangements for an exceptionally elaborate funeral. And it was at the funeral that Mr. Treadwell first had the Thought. It was a fleeting and unpleasant thought, just disturbing enough to make him miss a step as he entered the church. In all the confusion of the moment, however, it was not too difficult to put aside.

A few days later, when he was back at his familiar desk, the Thought suddenly returned. This time it was not to be put aside so easily. It grew steadily larger and larger in his mind, until his waking hours were terrifyingly full of it, and his sleep a series of shuddering nightmares.

There was only one man who could clear up the matter for him, he knew; so he appeared at the offices of the Society for Gerontology burning with anxiety to have Bunce do so. He was hardly aware of handing over his check to Bunce and pocketing the receipt.

"There's something that's been worrying me," said Mr. Treadwell, coming straight to the point.

"Yes?"

"Well, do you remember telling me how many old people there would be around in twenty years?"

"Of course."

Mr. Treadwell loosened his collar to ease the constriction around his throat. "But don't you see? I'm going to be one of them!"

Bunce nodded. "If you take reasonably good care of yourself there's no reason why you shouldn't be," he pointed out.

"You don't get the idea," Mr. Treadwell said urgently. "I'll be in a spot then where I'll have to worry all the time about someone from this Society coming in and giving my daughter or my son-in-law ideas! That's a terrible thing to have to worry about all the rest of your life."

Bunce shook his head slowly. "You can't mean that, Mr. Treadwell."

"And why can't I?"

"Why? Well, think of your daughter, Mr. Treadwell. Are you thinking of her?"

"Yes."

"Do you see her as the lovely child who poured out her love to you in exchange for yours? The fine young woman who has just stepped over the threshold of marriage, but is always eager to visit you, eager to let you know the affection she feels for you?"

"I know that."

"And can you see in your mind's eye that manly young fellow who is her husband? Can you feel the warmth of his handclasp as he greets you? Do you know his gratitude for the financial help you give him regularly?"

"I suppose so."

"Now, honestly, Mr. Treadwell, can you imagine either of these affectionate and devoted youngsters doing a single thing —the slightest thing—to harm you?"

The constriction around Mr. Treadwell's throat miraculously eased; the chill around his heart departed.

"No," he said with conviction, "I can't."

"Splendid," said Bunce. He leaned far back in his chair and smiled with a kindly wisdom. "Hold on to that thought, Mr. Treadwell. Cherish it and keep it close at all times. It will be a solace and comfort to the very end."

1958:

Over There—Darkness

William O'Farrell

Everything that Miss Fox owned was of the finest quality. She was a middle-aged woman with delicate features and soft, graying hair who lived alone in self-contained elegance. She dressed beautifully, spending a great deal of thought and money on her clothes. Her only companion was a dog named Vanessa, a pedigreed black poodle who, unlike her mistress, was a little overweight.

Miss Fox was as graceful and slim as she had ever been. She had a sizable income from a trust fund and her own lovely furniture in a four-room apartment. The apartment was in a huge, well-managed building which was located, incongruously, in a rowdy neighborhood of the Chelsea district in New York.

She was hardly aware of the neighborhood. She had signed a long-term lease during the housing shortage, and the management had considerately insulated her from any outside crudeness from the day she had moved in. There was a supermarket on the ground floor of the building. There was also a rental library, a beauty salon and an excellent restaurant. Theoretically, she could have remained inside the apartment house indefinitely, and in effect that is what she did. But twice a day she walked the poodle along West Twenty-third Street. Six times a week, her favorite elevator boy took the dog for longer walks at night.

Once, in the spring of 1943, a captain in the Quartermaster Corps had asked Miss Fox to marry him. He had given her the ring of her selection, and two weeks later entered a hospital in Virginia. The captain had died there of a kidney complaint, and she had not seen him again before his death. Wartime travel was difficult and Miss Fox preferred to remember him as he had been, unwasted by illness. She had telegraphed flowers, relying on her florist to send something suitable. He was a member of the American Florists Association and had good taste.

The ring was exquisite, a diamond solitaire surrounded by emeralds, and Miss Fox still wore it. Her ring, her dog and Eddie McMahon—the last in a different way and on a lower level—were the only things capable of stirring in her more than casual interest. All three were beautiful and Eddie McMahon was very useful, too.

Eddie was the nighttime dog walker. He was young—not tall, but well proportioned—and he had long-lashed blue eyes and wavy brown hair that turned black under the dim lights of the elevator. He wore a neat navy blue uniform with a gold stripe down the trousers and had good manners. As men go, he was nice.

She paid him five dollars a week. That was above the going rate for dog walking, but she did not begrudge the extra money. The arrangement might have continued for as long as he kept his job and she stayed on in the apartment, if she had not made one small mistake.

That happened just before Christmas, and at the time she did not recognize it as a mistake. As in past years, she handed the doorman an envelope containing money to be divided among the other employees and himself, but in a separate envelope on which Eddie's name was written she put a twenty-dollar bill. It seemed to her that from that time on his attitude sharply changed.

He was as respectful as ever, but in early January, he asked for his five dollars before it was due. The same thing happened in March and, although she gave him the money on both occasions, Miss Fox was disturbed. She lived within her income and expected other people to be as provident as herself. Then, about the middle of April, he appeared unexpectedly at her apartment on his day off.

There was a knock on the door. She opened it and Eddie came in without being asked. Such a thing was unprecedented. It was necessary occasionally to admit a repair man or an employee of the gas company, but their visits were always preceded by a call on the house telephone and Miss Fox kept the door open while they were inside. Eddie closed the door. He also leaned against it, breathing heavily.

"Climbed the stairs," he explained. "Fourteen flights. Not supposed to hang around the building my day off."

It was the first time she had seen him out of uniform. His suit was clean, but badly cut. It changed his whole appearance. He seemed older and heavier—a stranger, and an unprepossessing one.

"Then what are you doing here?" she asked.

"Miss Fox"—his breathing was a little easier—"I have to talk to you. Just for a minute, please?"

He was almost pleading, and Miss Fox felt distaste. She walked through the small foyer into the living room.

"Come in," she said. Then, hearing his footsteps following her too closely, on impulse she called, "Vanessa!"

The poodle lay in its basket in a corner. It looked at her and immediately went to sleep again. Miss Fox walked to the windows overlooking the avenue, and stood there with her back turned to the room.

"Yes, Eddie?" She had always been proud of her gentle voice. It was a relief to hear it now, in perfect control.

Eddie took two more forward steps. When next he spoke, she judged that he was standing beside the coffee table on which she had just placed a cup of tea. The tea was getting cold and that annoyed her. She liked it steaming hot.

"Miss Fox, will you let me take fifty dollars? I need it bad. I'll pay you back. It'll take three, four weeks, but today I have to send this money order . . ."

His voice dwindled into silence. Miss Fox stood quietly, unshocked by the preposterous request. She felt, rather, an odd sense of satisfaction, as though having known that something like this was bound to come, she was glad to have it in the clear at last.

"You say this money is important to you?"

"Yes, ma'am. Very important."

"Why come to me?" she asked.

"Because I've already tried everywhere else. My watch is in hock. The union gave me a loan, but that's all gone. You couldn't unscrew an advance from the management here with a Stillson wrench. And because"—he hesitated—"because you're kind."

She turned. "Sit down, Eddie." She waited until he was sitting stiffly on the couch. "Why is it necessary to send a money order in such a rush? To whom?"

"To my girl." He saw her lips tighten and added quickly, "She's in this sanitarium. The state pays half the expenses, see, and I promised to pay the other half. I done it so far, too, but now there's this extra—"

"You're engaged?"

"I guess you could call it that," he said.

But there had been a pause before he spoke and obviously the idea was new to him. New and strange. Miss Fox glanced at the ring on her left hand. Her own romance had not been conducted in so casual a manner. There had been the short, but proper courtship, the proposal, the betrothal kiss. Marriage would have been the next orderly step if tragedy had not intervened.

She sighed and shook her head. "I can't lend you fifty dollars, Eddie. Don't you earn a good salary?"

"Seventy a week," he said morosely, "but that's not take-home pay."

"No matter how little you actually take home, it's merely a question of planning, Eddie. I live on a fixed income and every cent is budgeted. Fifty dollars?" She shrugged. "I couldn't possibly spare an amount as large as that,"

Eddie was no longer listening. His eyes were fixed on something behind her back. She looked over her shoulder and saw her white gloves and alligator bag.

They were lying on the living room table. Miss Fox grew hot, then cold—which was ridiculous, because there was no earthly way for Eddie to have learned that she had cashed a fairly large check only a few hours before.

"I'm sorry," she said firmly. "It's impossible."

His eyes had left the table. They were focused on her ring. For a moment he was silent. Then he rose.

"Yes, ma'am. My fault for asking. Excuse me, please." He went out and closed the door.

A vague unrest covered the remainder of her day. She couldn't read. The laundry was delivered at four o'clock, and after she had put it away there was nothing more to do until six. At two minutes before the hour she turned on the television.

The program was a good one, but this evening nothing could have held her interest. The memory of Eddie's bland presumption kept creeping back into her mind. She snapped off the television and poured a glass of sherry. It was infuriating to think that, because he was vulgarly good-looking and a few years younger than herself, the boy had actually believed that he could take her in.

She drank her sherry, went into the bedroom. When she came back, she had changed her dress and was wearing a light spring coat. A bright scarf was tied around her head. It was a fetching ensemble and made her look ten years younger, but she hardly glanced at the mirror as she picked up her bag, pulled on her gloves. She went downstairs to dinner a full three quarters of an hour earlier than she usually did. She had an excellent dinner, which she did not enjoy, and was back in her apartment before eight o'clock.

At a quarter to ten, when the dog whimpered to go out, Miss Fox attached a leash of shocking pink to the poodle's matching collar and once more pulled on her gloves, picked up her alligator bag.

The weather was freakishly warm for April, so warm that the doorman had propped open the front doors of the apartment house. It had rained earlier, and the street lamps were reflected from the still-wet pavement like little moons put there to guide her feet. There was an exhilarating quality about the night. It called for adventure and Miss Fox responded to it. She walked west instead of, as she usually did, in the direction of the well-lighted avenue toward the east.

On her right, as she strolled along, were the amber windows of her own apartment house. These extended west for a hundred yards. The building ended there and was succeeded by a long row of old brownstone fronts—respectable once, but fallen now into almost sinister disrepair. The demarcating line was like a frontier between light and darkness, and she determined to go only as far as the end of the building and then turn back.

Reaching the predetermined spot, she pulled gently at Vanessa's leash. But the poodle had scented something beyond the dark frontier and strained forward. After a token struggle, Miss Fox let the dog have her way.

"Oh, very well," she said aloud, "but only as far as the next tree, dear."

They never reached the tree. Halfway there, a rough arm encircled Miss Fox's throat. She was bent over backwards and a hand was clasped across her mouth. Blood pounded in her ears as above her she saw, for just an instant, a man's shadowed face. She tried to scream and couldn't, and the last thing she heard was Vanessa's frantic yelp. Then the black world tilted up on end and slid away. When she regained consciousness, she was lying on the sidewalk, the doorman from the apartment house was kneeling beside her, the glove had been stripped from her left hand, and her diamond and emerald ring was gone.

So was her alligator bag containing a hundred and eighty dollars, but as she explained to Detective Sergeant Kirby in her apartment a half hour later, the money wasn't important. What she wanted, what she demanded in fact, was the immediate return of her ring.

Sergeant Kirby assured her that everything possible would be done. "We don't have a lot to work on, though. You say you wouldn't know the man if you saw him again."

Miss Fox thoughtfully fingered the bandage around her throat. The policeman was trying to be helpful, but he was going about it in such a plodding way. The fact that she had glimpsed her assailant only for an instant and in deep shadow meant very little. He had brutally manhandled her. She would be able to pick him out of any crowd.

"I did say that," she admitted, "but now I'm beginning to remember how he looked."

"Description?"

"He had dark hair and—let me think—he was strong, but not especially tall . . ."

"Clothes?"

"I didn't notice. His sleeve was of some coarse material."

"Did he say anything?"

"No. I heard nothing, but the dog. Now that I think of it," Miss Fox said, "it's odd that she didn't bark until after the attack."

"I've thought of that." Kirby got up from his chair. "Another point is that the mugger only tore the glove off your left hand. It's almost as though he knew about the ring."

Eddie! The abrupt revelation caused Miss Fox no surprise. It was only logical. That afternoon he had tried to borrow fifty dollars. Refused, he had stared at her ring—as now it came to her quite clearly—with unconcealed cupidity. There could be no doubt about it. Eddie was the thief.

But she said nothing. If, employing their own means, the police found and arrested him, that was their business. Her business was to get the ring back. That, she believed, she knew how to do.

Sergeant Kirby was leaving and she rose to say good-bye. "Thank you so much. I may expect to hear from you?"

"Probably very soon. If it isn't soon it may be never. That's how these things work." He rubbed Vanessa's ears. "You can thank your dog for spreading the alarm, Miss Fox."

"Yes. Goodnight, Sergeant."

She went to bed, but could not fall asleep. After a tortured half-hour, she had to take a capsule. It worked, but just as she was dozing off, she was aroused by the ringing of the telephone.

"Hope I didn't wake you," Sergeant Kirby said. "We've picked up a man who may have done the job. Can you come down?"

Miss Fox was half-doped and thoroughly exasperated. There was no reason why this unpleasant business of identification could not have been postponed until the morning. "At this hour? Come down where?"

He gave her the station house address. "It's only one o'clock."

"Does he have my ring?"

"Not on him. But if you make a positive I.D., I'll get it back."

"Very well. As soon as I can find a taxi, I'll be there."

The station house was only a few blocks away. The taxi

rounded a corner and pulled up at the curb. Miss Fox saw a dreary-looking building with a green light beside its wide front door. "Here you are, lady," the taxi driver said.

Then she was in a functionally furnished room and Sergeant Kirby was telling her that the suspect had been arrested in a Tenth Avenue bar. "Within a block of where it happened and only twenty minutes later. He was half-drunk and flashing a wad of bills he can't account for. Bad record, too. Looks like we wound this up in record time."

"If you have," Miss Fox said, "no one will be happier than I, Sergeant Kirby."

But she was disappointed. The man shoved through the doorway by a uniformed policeman was not Eddie. He was Eddie's height and had dark hair, but there was no resemblance otherwise. His hands were filthy. It was unthinkable that she had been touched by such grimy hands.

"No." She shook her head. "It is not he."

"You're sure?" Kirby sounded disappointed.

"Quite sure," she said, avoiding the man's eyes.

His eyes were insolent. He wore a flashy suit, black shirt and yellow tie, but Miss Fox paid no attention to his clothes. She was too agitated by his dirty hands and bullying stare.

"Well, thanks for coming," Kirby said. "Be seeing you."

Miss Fox went home and slept until ten the following morning. Eddie's shift on the elevator started at noon. She took the dog out at eleven and told the doorman that she wanted to see Eddie as soon as he came in. He knocked on her door a few minutes before twelve.

She opened it. "Come in."

"Say, Miss Fox, I heard about what happened!"

"Come in, Eddie, and sit down," she said.

His expression, as he obeyed, was one of puzzled innocence. It was a pity, she thought, that so handsome a face should conceal a mind so devious. She stood erectly, steeling herself to a distasteful task.

"So you've heard."

"Yes, ma'am. I always said this neighborhood ain't safe."

"You know I was robbed of some money and my ring?"

"That's what they say."

"Very well. Now listen carefully. I want to be quite sure you understand. I don't care about the money, but I want my ring. Its description has been circulated. Trying to sell it would be dangerous."

"That's right. It's plenty hot."

"So it might as well be returned to me. Particularly if I promise to forget the hundred and eighty dollars that I've lost, and say no more about the matter. Don't you agree?"

Eddie appeared to be thinking deeply. "Well, I don't know. This guy that mugged you—there is a couple of things he could do. He could break the ring up, get rid of the stones that way. Or he could wait until the heat's off and sell it somewheres out of town."

"He would still be taking a risk. I have a better idea. I'm prepared to pay five hundred dollars for its return. Five hundred dollars, Eddie, and no questions asked."

He got up slowly. "I sure hope you get it back. Excuse me— I got to go to work." He walked toward the door, but stopped before he reached the foyer. "Look, Miss Fox, don't count too much on that plan of yours. What would you do—advertise? Chances are the guy would never see your ad, and if he did he'd be dumb to stick his neck out."

"You don't think I'll get my ring back?" There was an edge to Miss Fox's normally soft voice.

"No, ma'am. Not that way, I don't."

"You may go, Eddie," Miss Fox said.

The doorman announced Sergeant Kirby an hour later. He entered briskly and came directly to business.

"You have an arrangement with an elevator boy named McMahon to walk your dog. Yesterday was his day off, but he was seen leaving your apartment about two in the afternoon. Is that correct?"

Miss Fox walked to the window and stood with her back turned, as she had done the day before. "Why do you ask?"

"Routine. McMahon has a good record and he's a steady worker. On the other hand, he needs money. Why did he come here?"

She did not move. Her voice was cool and impersonal as she replied. "You seem to have ferreted out almost everything. You might as well know the rest. He wanted me to lend him fifty dollars."

"Did you do it?"

"Of course not."

There was a silence. Then Kirby asked quietly, "Was it McMahon?"

She turned and looked directly into the detective's eyes. "I had hoped it wouldn't come to this. I gave him his chance. I even offered him money to return the ring. He refused."

"You positively identify him?"

Unconsciously, she had already passed her own personal line of demarcation between light and darkness. "Yes, it was Eddie," Miss Fox said.

She did not look at Eddie during the trial. She kept her eyes averted as she testified. It was a short trial. He had no alibi. They brought him in and tried him, and sent him to prison for three years.

Or maybe it was for one year with the other two suspended. Miss Fox wasn't sure. She had her own problems now that Eddie was no longer on the elevator. She had to find someone else to walk Vanessa, and the other boys had suddenly become very busy. They seemed curiously indifferent as to whether or not they made extra money every week.

Eventually she was forced to hire a professional. He was unsatisfactory. The third night he called, Miss Fox smelled liquor on his breath. From then on she took the dog out every night herself.

At first she shunned the sidewalk west of the apartment house. She never even approached it until, in the heat of summer, the streets became more crowded and consequently safe. Then she found that her dread of the dark frontier had lessened greatly. Fear was now no more than a rather pleasurable titillation of her senses. She sometimes permitted Vanessa to pull her right up to the line, and she would stand within inches of it peering into unexplored darkness.

Summer passed and was succeeded by the fall, and in all that time she had no news of her ring. Sergeant Kirby told her that Eddie still insisted he was innocent, but of course Eddie would do that. She telephoned Kirby several times and he was always courteous, until one day in November two policemen came to her apartment and brusquely told her that the sergeant wanted to see her at the station house.

She was indignant. "Why doesn't he come here?"

"Couldn't tell you, lady. Just said he wanted to talk to you."

Miss Fox graciously agreed to go.

Kirby met her in the bare room she had been in once before. He looked grim. "We've found your ring," he said.

She displayed none of the emotion she was feeling. "I knew that sooner or later Eddie would tell the truth."

"McMahon never had it." The grimness in the detective's face was reflected in his voice. "Remember the man you didn't identify? We got him on another charge and the ring was in his room. He confessed."

Something was wrong. Something was so drastically wrong that Miss Fox couldn't absorb it immediately. "But I saw him! I saw Eddie!"

"Did you?"

"Well, I thought I did. I was so sure!"

"You certainly succeeded in giving that impression. As a result, I look like a fool and an innocent man's in jail."

Miss Fox said angrily, "I may have made a mistake, but it was an honest one. I believe it's the duty of the police to check these things. Could it have been that you were so anxious to arrest someone that you didn't care whether or not he was guilty?"

Kirby shrugged, looking past her at a blank space on the wall.

"If you have nothing further to say, give me my ring."

He wouldn't do it. He showed it to her, and there was no question about it being hers, and he said it would be returned in due time. Meanwhile, it was evidence and must be held. He wouldn't even tell her when Eddie would be released.

"I don't know," he said. "Why should you care?"

Miss Fox did care. She foresaw a period of strain when and if Eddie returned to his old job, and she wanted to avoid that by finding another apartment first. She disliked friction of any kind, and so she bought a box of expensive cigars and sent them to Sergeant Kirby. After that she was able to dismiss the detective from her mind.

During the weeks that followed she inspected a number of apartments, but none of them met her fastidious standards. She flinched from the ordeal of moving anyway, and at last was forced to the realization that she was better off where she was. Having accepted this, she made a generous gesture. She spoke personally to the manager of the apartment house and was surprised to learn that her request had been anticipated. He had already written Eddie, offering to take him back.

"But it's thoughtful of you, Miss Fox," he said. "I must say I'm relieved."

She left his office satisfied he would tell Eddie what she'd done. Eddie would be grateful. What might have been a tense situation had been eased.

Eddie came back to work the week before Christmas. One morning she buckled on Vanessa's leash and pushed the elevator bell. With a minimum of delay the elevator door slid open, and there he was. Everything was as it had been, including his respectful smile.

"Good morning, Miss Fox."

"Eddie!" she said. "I can't tell you how happy I am."

He took her down to the lobby. By the time she had walked the dog, riding up in the elevator again, she had recovered from her surprise. "Hold the car a moment," she said, stepping out on the fourteenth floor. "There's something I must say to you."

He held the door open, waiting. She turned in the softly lighted corridor to study him. He had changed. His smile was fixed and meaningless, and there was a glassy quality in his eyes.

Never mind. It was in her power to change that, and she would. "I want you to know that it wasn't easy for me to testify against you, Eddie. I only told the court what I believed to be the truth."

"Sure, Miss Fox."

"It was a terrible experience for both of us. I think the best thing we can do is to forget it and start afresh."

"Yes, ma'am."

"Good," she said. "Vanessa will be waiting when you finish work tonight." She started down the corridor.

He stopped her. "Miss Fox, I won't be walking your dog any more."

She turned, incredulous and a little piqued. "You want more money, I suppose?"

"It isn't that," he said. "It's just that I can get along now on my pay. I don't have any extra expenses now."

"How about your fiancée?"

"She died," he said.

The elevator door slid shut. Miss Fox was alone.

She let herself into the apartment, sat down and thought about it rationally. Everything had worked out for the best. The girl had been ill. Eddie would have found her an intolerable burden. He would get over her death. She had gone through the same natural sequence of suffering and recuperation when the captain died. She told herself these things, but still remained unsatisfied, sensing that somewhere there was something she had overlooked. At two o'clock she put on her coat again, walked to an elevator at the far end of the building and went down to her bank.

When she returned, she told the doorman that she wanted to see Eddie during his coffee break. He came to her apartment at four o'clock. Miss Fox did not invite him to come in.

"I've been thinking about you," she said. "I want to help you —well, to rehabilitate yourself. As I once told you, I was prepared to pay five hundred dollars for my ring. I had the money set aside, and I can think of no better use for it than to give it to you." She handed him an envelope. "Shall we call it a Christmas present, Eddie? Five one-hundred-dollar bills."

There was a long moment while he stood holding the white envelope, looking at the floor. Then he put the envelope in his pocket. "Thank you very much, Miss Fox," he said.

Miss Fox was greatly relieved as she shut the door. It was a pity that Eddie had not accepted the five hundred dollars when she'd offered it to him eight months before. It would have been so simple. He could have taken the money and returned her ring—

But Eddie had not stolen the ring, she suddenly remembered. She shrugged. Anyway, it was finished now. She drank a cup of steaming tea and had a nice, long nap.

When she went out with the dog at ten that night, Eddie had already gone off duty. It was snowing, and she had always enjoyed the first snowfall of the season. Vanessa pulled to the right and Miss Fox humored her by walking west, mildly exhilarating by the drifting flakes.

She came to the end of the lighted apartment house and stood, as she had often stood before, on the very edge of darkness. A few yards ahead was the spot where the man had thrown her down. She smiled nervously, telling herself that she was glad now it had happened. It was rather thrilling to look back from her present security to a danger safely passed.

"Let's go home, dear," she told Vanessa, and turned back.

A man blocked her way. He had come up behind her silently. Miss Fox gasped. Then her shrill scream echoed down the street.

He raised his arm. His open palm found and covered her face. He pushed. Miss Fox staggered backward, tripped and fell. She had time to scream once more before he stopped the noise at its source. The last thing she heard was the far off yelping of her dog.

This time when the doorman found her, he was too late. She lay on her back, snowflakes falling in her open eyes. Between her rapidly stiffening fingers were five one-hundred-dollar bills.

1959:

The Landlady

Roald Dahl

Billy Weaver had travelled down from London on the slow afternoon train, with a change at Reading on the way, and by the time he got to Bath it was about nine o'clock in the evening and the moon was coming up out of a clear starry sky over the houses opposite the station entrance. But the air was deadly cold and the wind was like a flat blade of ice on his cheeks.

"Excuse me," he said, "but is there a fairly cheap hotel not too far away from here?"

"Try The Bell and Dragon," the porter answered, pointing down the road. "They might take you in. It's about a quarter of a mile along on the other side."

Billy thanked him and picked up his suitcase and set out to walk the quarter-mile to The Bell and Dragon. He had never been to Bath before. He didn't know anyone who lived there. But Mr. Greenslade at the Head Office in London had told him it was a splendid town. "Find your own lodgings," he had said, "and then go along and report to the Branch Manager as soon as you've got yourself settled."

Billy was seventeen years old. He was wearing a new navy-blue overcoat, a new brown trilby hat, and a new brown suit, and he was feeling fine. He walked briskly down the street. He was trying to do everything briskly these days. Briskness, he had decided, was *the* one common characteristic of all successful businessmen. The big shots up at Head Office were absolutely fantastically brisk all the time. They were amazing.

There were no shops on this wide street that he was walking along, only a line of tall houses on each side, all of them identical. They had porches and pillars and four or five steps going up to their front doors, and it was obvious that once upon a time they had been very swanky residences. But now, even in the darkness, he could see that the paint was peeling from the woodwork on their doors and windows, and that the handsome white façades were cracked and blotchy from neglect.

Suddenly, in a downstairs window that was brilliantly illuminated by a street-lamp not six yards away, Billy caught sight of a printed notice propped up against the glass in one of the upper panes. It said BED AND BREAKFAST. There was a vase of yellow chrysanthemums, tall and beautiful, standing just underneath the notice.

He stopped walking. He moved a bit closer. Green curtains (some sort of velvety material) were hanging down on either side of the window. The chrysanthemums looked wonderful beside them. He went right up and peered through the glass into the room, and the first thing he saw was a bright fire burning in the hearth. On the carpet in front of the fire, a pretty little dachshund was curled up asleep with its nose tucked into its belly. The room itself, so far as he could see in the half-darkness, was filled with pleasant furniture. There was a baby-grand piano and a big sofa and several plump armchairs; and in one corner he spotted a large parrot in a cage. Animals were usually a good sign in a place like this, Billy told himself; and all in all, it looked to him as though it would be a pretty decent house to stay in. Certainly it would be more comfortable than The Bell and Dragon.

On the other hand, a pub would be more congenial than a boarding-house. There would be beer and darts in the evenings, and lots of people to talk to, and it would probably be a good bit cheaper, too. He had stayed a couple of nights in a pub once before and he had liked it. He had never stayed in any boarding-houses, and, to be perfectly honest, he was a tiny bit frightened of them. The name itself conjured up images of watery cabbage, rapacious landladies, and a powerful smell of kippers in the living-room.

After dithering about like this in the cold for two or three minutes, Billy decided that he would walk on and take a look at The Bell and Dragon before making up his mind. He turned to go.

And now a queer thing happened to him. He was in the act of stepping back and turning away from the window when all at once his eye was caught and held in the most peculiar manner by the small notice that was there. BED AND BREAKFAST, it said. BED AND BREAKFAST, BED AND BREAKFAST, BED AND BREAKFAST. Each word was like a large black eye staring at him through the glass, holding him, compelling him, forcing him to stay where he was and not to walk away from that house, and the next thing he knew, he was actually moving across from the window to the front door of the house, climbing the steps that led up to it, and reaching for the bell.

He pressed the bell. Far away in a back room he heard it ringing, and then *at once*—it must have been at once because he hadn't even had time to take his finger from the bell-button —the door swung open and a woman was standing there.

Normally you ring the bell and you have at least a half-minute's wait before the door opens. But this dame was like a jack-in-the-box. He pressed the bell—and out she popped! It made him jump.

She was about forty-five or fifty years old, and the moment she saw him, she gave him a warm welcoming smile.

"Please come in," she said pleasantly. She stepped aside, holding the door wide open, and Billy found himself automatically starting forward. The compulsion or, more accurately, the desire to follow after her into that house was extraordinarily strong.

"I saw the notice in the window," he said, holding himself back.

"Yes, I know."

"I was wondering about a room."

"It's *all* ready for you, my dear," she said. She had a round pink face and very gentle blue eyes.

"I was on my way to The Bell and Dragon," Billy told her. "But the notice in your window just happened to catch my eye."

"My dear boy," she said, "why don't you come in out of the cold?"

"How much do you charge?"

"Five and sixpence a night, including breakfast."

It was fantastically cheap. It was less than half of what he had been willing to pay.

"If that is too much," she added, "then perhaps I can reduce it just a tiny bit. Do you desire an egg for breakfast? Eggs are expensive at the moment. It would be sixpence less without the egg."

"Five and sixpence is fine," he answered. "I should like very much to stay here."

"I knew you would. Do come in."

She seemed terribly nice. She looked exactly like the mother of one's best school-friend welcoming one into the house to stay for the Christmas holidays. Billy took off his hat, and stepped over the threshold.

"Just hang it there," she said, "and let me help you with your coat."

There were no other hats or coats in the hall. There were no umbrellas, no walking-sticks—nothing.

"We have it *all* to ourselves," she said, smiling at him over her shoulder as she led the way upstairs. "You see, it isn't very often I have the pleasure of taking a visitor into my little nest."

The old girl is slightly dotty, Billy told himself. But at five and sixpence a night, who gives a damn about that? "I should've thought you'd be simply swamped with applicants," he said politely.

"Oh, I am, my dear, I am, of course I am. But the trouble is that I'm inclined to be just a teeny weeny bit choosy and partic-ular—if you see what I mean."

"Ah, yes."

"But I'm always ready. Everything is always ready day and night in this house just on the off-chance that an acceptable young gentleman will come along. And it is such a pleasure, my dear, such a very great pleasure when now and again I open the door and I see someone standing there who is just *exactly* right." She was halfway up the stairs, and she paused with one hand on the stair-rail, turning her head and smiling down at him with pale lips. "Like you," she added, and her blue eyes travelled slowly all the way down the length of Billy's body, to his feet, and then up again.

On the second-floor landing she said to him, "This floor is mine."

They climbed up another flight. "And this one is *all* yours," she said. "Here's your room. I do hope you'll like it." She took him into a small but charming front bedroom, switching on the light as she went in.

"The morning sun comes right in the window, Mr. Perkins. It *is* Mr. Perkins, isn't it?"

"No," he said. "It's Weaver."

"Mr. Weaver. How nice. I've put a water-bottle between the sheets to air them out, Mr. Weaver. It's such a comfort to have a hot water-bottle in a strange bed with clean sheets, don't you agree? And you may light the gas fire at any time if you feel chilly."

"Thank you," Billy said. "Thank you ever so much." He noticed that the bedspread had been taken off the bed, and that the bedclothes had been neatly turned back on one side, all ready for someone to get in.

"I'm so glad you appeared," she said, looking earnestly into his face. "I was beginning to get worried."

"That's all right," Billy answered brightly. "You mustn't worry about me." He put his suitcase on the chair and started to open it.

"And what about supper, my dear? Did you manage to get anything to eat before you came here?"

"I'm not a bit hungry, thank you," he said. "I think I'll just go to bed as soon as possible because tomorrow I've got to get up rather early and report to the office."

"Very well, then. I'll leave you now so that you can unpack. But before you go to bed, would you be kind enough to pop into the sitting-room on the ground floor and sign the book? Everyone has to do that because it's the law of the land, and we don't want to go breaking any laws at *this* stage in the proceedings, do we?" She gave him a little wave of the hand and went quickly out of the room and closed the door.

Now, the fact that his landlady appeared to be slightly off her rocker didn't worry Billy in the least. After all, she not only was harmless—there was no question about that—but she was also quite obviously a kind and generous soul. He guessed that she had probably lost a son in the war, or something like that, and had never gotten over it.

So a few minutes later, after unpacking his suitcase and washing his hands, he trotted downstairs to the ground floor and entered the living-room. His landlady wasn't there, but the fire was glowing in the hearth, and the little dachshund was still sleeping soundly in front of it. The room was wonderfully warm and cosy. I'm a lucky fellow, he thought, rubbing his hands. This is a bit of all right.

He found the guest-book lying open on the piano, so he took out his pen and wrote down his name and address. There were only two other entries above his on the page, and, as one always does with guest-books, he started to read them. One was a Christopher Mulholland from Cardiff. The other was Gregory W. Temple from Bristol.

That's funny, he thought suddenly. Christopher Mulholland. It rings a bell.

Now where on earth had he heard that rather unusual name before?

Was it a boy at school? No. Was it one of his sister's numerous young men, perhaps, or a friend of his father's? No, no, it wasn't any of those. He glanced down again at the book.

Christopher Mulholland   231 Cathedral Road, Cardiff
Gregory W. Temple   27 Sycamore Drive, Bristol

As a matter of fact, now he came to think of it, he wasn't at all sure that the second name didn't have almost as much of a familiar ring about it as the first.

"Gregory Temple?" he said aloud, searching his memory. "Christopher Mulholland? . . ."

"Such charming boys," a voice behind him answered, and he turned and saw his landlady sailing into the room with a large silver tea-tray in her hands. She was holding it well out in front of her, and rather high up, as though the tray were a pair of reins on a frisky horse.

"They sound somehow familiar," he said.

"They do? How interesting."

"I'm almost positive I've heard those names before some-where. Isn't that odd? Maybe it was in the newspapers. They weren't famous in any way, were they? I mean famous cricket-ers or footballers or something like that?"

"Famous," she said, setting the tea-tray down on the low table in front of the sofa. "Oh no, I don't think they were famous. But they were incredibly handsome, both of them, I can promise you that. They were tall and young and handsome, my dear, just exactly like you."

Once more, Billy glanced down at the book. "Look here," he said, noticing the dates. "This last entry is over two years old."

"It is?"

"Yes, indeed. And Christopher Mulholland's is nearly a year before that—more than *three years* ago."

"Dear me," she said, shaking her head and heaving a dainty little sigh. "I would never have thought it. How time does fly away from us all, doesn't it, Mr. Wilkins?"

"It's Weaver," Billy said. "W-e-a-v-e-r."

"Oh, of course it is!" she cried, sitting down on the sofa. "How silly of me. I do apologize. In one ear and out the other, that's me, Mr. Weaver."

"You know something?" Billy said. "Something that's really quite extraordinary about all this?"

"No, dear, I don't."

"Well, you see, both of these names—Mulholland and Tem-ple—I not only seem to remember each one of them separately, so to speak, but somehow or other, in some peculiar way, they both appear to be sort of connected together as well. As though they were both famous for the same sort of thing, if you see what I mean—like . . . well . . . like Dempsey and Tunney, for example, or Churchill and Roosevelt."

"How amusing," she said. "But come over here now, dear, and sit down beside me on the sofa and I'll give you a nice cup of tea and a ginger biscuit before you go to bed."

"You really shouldn't bother," Billy said. "I didn't mean you to do anything like that." He stood by the piano, watching her as she fussed about with the cups and saucers. He noticed that she had small, white, quickly moving hands, and red finger-nails.

"I'm almost positive it was in the newspapers I saw them," Billy said. "I'll think of it in a second. I'm sure I will."

There is nothing more tantalizing than a thing like this that lingers just outside the borders of one's memory. He hated to give up.

"Now wait a minute," he said. "Wait just a minute. Mulholland . . . Christopher Mulholland . . . wasn't *that* the name of the Eton schoolboy who was on a walking-tour through the West Country, and then all of a sudden . . ."

"Milk?" she said. "And sugar?"

"Yes, please. And then all of a sudden . . ."

"Eton schoolboy?" she said. "Oh no, my dear, that can't possibly be right because *my* Mr. Mulholland was certainly not an Eton schoolboy when he came to me. He was a Cambridge undergraduate. Come over here now and sit next to me and warm yourself in front of this lovely fire. Come on. Your tea's all ready for you." She patted the empty place beside her on the sofa, and she sat there smiling at Billy and waiting for him to come over.

He crossed the room slowly, and sat down on the edge of the sofa. She placed his teacup on the table in front of him.

"*There* we are," she said. "How nice and cosy this is, isn't it?"

Billy started sipping his tea. She did the same. For half a minute or so, neither of them spoke. But Billy knew that she was looking at him. Her body was half turned toward him, and he could feel her eyes resting on his face, watching him over the rim of her teacup. Now and again, he caught a whiff of a peculiar smell that seemed to emanate directly from her person. It was not in the least unpleasant, and it reminded him—well, he wasn't quite sure what it reminded him of. Pickled walnuts? New leather? Or was it the corridors of a hospital?

At length, she said, "Mr. Mulholland was a great one for his tea. Never in my life have I seen anyone drink as much tea as dear, sweet Mr. Mulholland."

"I suppose he left fairly recently," Billy said. He was still puzzling his head about the two names. He was positive now that he had seen them in the newspapers—in the headlines.

"Left?" she said, arching her brows. "But my dear boy, he

never left. He's still here. Mr. Temple is also here. They're on the fourth floor, both of them together."

Billy set his cup down slowly on the table and stared at his landlady. She smiled back at him, and then she put out one of her white hands and patted him comfortingly on the knee. "How old are you, my dear?" she asked.

"Seventeen."

"Seventeen!" she cried. "Oh, it's the perfect age! Mr. Mulholland was also seventeen. But I think he was a trifle shorter than you are; in fact I'm sure he was, and his teeth weren't *quite* so white. You have the most beautiful teeth, Mr. Weaver, did you know that?"

"They're not as good as they look," Billy said. "They've got simply masses of fillings in them at the back."

"Mr. Temple, of course, was a little older," she said, ignoring his remark. "He was actually twenty-eight. And yet I never would have guessed it if he hadn't told me, never in my whole life. There wasn't a *blemish* on his body."

"A what?" Billy said.

"His skin was *just* like a baby's."

There was a pause. Billy picked up his teacup and took another sip of his tea, then he set it down again gently in its saucer. He waited for her to say something else, but she seemed to have lapsed into another of her silences. He sat there staring straight ahead of him into the far corner of the room, biting his lower lip.

"That parrot," he said at last. "You know something? It had me completely fooled when I first saw it through the window. I could have sworn it was alive."

"Alas, no longer."

"It's most terribly clever the way it's been done," he said. "It doesn't look in the least bit dead. Who did it?"

"I did."

"*You* did?"

"Of course," she said. "And have you met my little Basil as well?" She nodded toward the dachshund curled up so comfortably in front of the fire. Billy looked at it. And suddenly, he realized that this animal had all the time been just as silent and motionless as the parrot. He put out a hand and touched it gently on the top of its back. The back was hard and cold, and when he pushed the hair to one side with his fingers, he could see the skin underneath, greyish-black and dry and perfectly preserved.

"Good gracious me," he said. "How absolutely fascinating." He turned away from the dog and stared with deep admiration at the little woman beside him on the sofa. "It must be most awfully difficult to do a thing like that."

"Not in the least," she said. "I stuff *all* my little pets myself when they pass away. Will you have another cup of tea?"

"No, thank you," Billy said. The tea tasted faintly of bitter almonds, and he didn't much care for it.

"You did sign the book, didn't you?"

"Oh, yes."

"That's good. Because later on, if I happen to forget what you were called, then I could always come down here and look it up. I still do that almost every day with Mr. Mulholland and Mr. . . . Mr. . . . ."

"Temple," Billy said. "Gregory Temple. Excuse my asking, but haven't there been *any* other guests here except them in the last two or three years?"

Holding her teacup high in one hand, inclining her head slightly to the left, she looked up at him out of the corners of her eyes and gave him another gentle little smile.

"No, my dear," she said. "Only you."

1962:

The Sailing Club

David Ely

Of all the important social clubs in the city, the most exclusive was also the most casual and the least known to outsiders. This was a small group of venerable origin but without formal organization. Indeed, it was without a name, although it was generally referred to as the Sailing Club, for its sole apparent activity was a short sailing cruise each summer. There were no meetings, no banquets, no other functions—in fact, no club building existed, so that it was difficult even to classify it as a club.

Nevertheless, the Sailing Club represented the zenith of a successful businessman's social ambitions, for its handful of members included the most influential men in the city, and many a top executive would have traded all his other hard-won attainments for an opportunity to join. Even those who had no interest in sailing would willingly have sweated through long practice hours to learn, if the Club had beckoned. Few were invited, however. The Club held its membership to the minimum necessary for the operation of its schooner, and not until death or debility created a vacancy was a new man admitted.

Who were the members of this select group? It was almost impossible to be absolutely certain. For one thing, since the Club had no legal existence, the members did not list it in their

171

Who's Who paragraphs or in any other catalogue of their honors. Furthermore, they appeared reluctant to discuss it in public. At luncheons or parties, for example, the Club might be mentioned, but those who brought up the name did not seem to be members, and as for those distinguished gentlemen who carefully refrained at such times from commenting on the subject—who could tell? They might be members, or they might deliberately be assuming an air of significant detachment in hopes of being mistaken for members.

Naturally, the hint of secrecy which was thus attached to the Sailing Club made it all the more desirable in the eyes of the rising business leaders who yearned for the day when they might be tapped for membership. They realized that the goal was remote and their chances not too likely, but each still treasured in his heart the hope that in time this greatest of all distinctions would reward a lifetime of struggle and success.

One of these executives, a man named John Goforth, could without immodesty consider himself unusually eligible for the Club. He was, first of all, a brilliant success in the business world. Although he was not yet fifty, he was president of a dynamic corporation which had become preeminent in several fields through a series of mergers he himself had expertly negotiated. Each year, under his ambitious direction, the corporation expanded into new areas, snapping up less nimble competitors and spurring the others into furious battles for survival.

Early in his career Goforth had been cautious, even anxious, but year by year his confidence had increased, so that now he welcomed new responsibilities, just as he welcomed the recurrent business crises where one serious mistake in judgment might cause a large enterprise to founder and to sink. His quick rise had not dulled this sense of excitement, but rather had sharpened it. More and more, he put routine matters into the hands of subordinates, while he zestfully attacked those problems that forced from him the fullest measure of daring and skill. He found himself not merely successful, but powerful, a man whose passage through the halls of a club left a wake of murmurs, admiring and envious.

This was the life he loved, and his mastery of it was his chief claim to recognition by the most influential social group of all, the Sailing Club. There was another factor which he thought might count in his favor: his lifelong attachment to the sea and to sailing.

As a boy, he had stood in fascination at the ocean's edge, staring out beyond the breakers to the distant sails, sometimes imagining himself to be the captain of a great ship; at those times, the toy bucket in his hand had become a long spyglass, or a pirate's cutlass, and the strip of reed that fluttered from his fingers had been transformed into a gallant pennant, or a black and wicked skull-and-bones.

At the age of ten, he had been taught to sail at his family's summer place on the shore; later, he was allowed to take his father's boat out alone—and later still, when he was almost of college age, he was chosen for the crew of one of the yacht club entries in the big regatta. By that time, he had come to regard the sea as a resourceful antagonist in a struggle all the more absorbing because of the danger, and a danger that was far from theoretical, for every summer at least one venturesome sailor would be lost forever, far from land, and even a sizable boat might fail to return from some holiday excursion.

Now, in his middle years, John Goforth knew the sea as something more than an invigorating physical challenge. It was that still, but he recognized that it was also an inexhaustible source of renewal for him. The harsh sting of blown spray was a climate in which he thrived, and the erratic thrusts of strength that swayed his little boat evoked a passionate response of answering strength within himself. In those moments—like the supreme moments of business crisis—he felt almost godlike, limitless, as he shared the ocean's solitude, its fierce and fitful communion with the wind, the sun, and the sky.

As time passed, membership in the Sailing Club became the single remaining honor which Goforth coveted but did not have. He told himself: not a member—no, not yet! But of course he realized that this prize would not necessarily fall to him at all, despite his most strenuous efforts to seize it. He sought to put the matter out of his mind; then, failing that, he decided to learn more about the Club, to satisfy his curiosity, at least.

It was no easy task. But he was a resourceful and determined man, and before long he had obtained a fairly accurate idea of the real membership of the Sailing Club. All these men were prominent in business or financial circles, but Goforth found it strange that they seemed to lack any other common character-istic of background or attainments. Most were university men, but a few were not. There was, similarly, a variety of ethnic strains represented among them. Some were foreign-born, even, and one or two were still foreign citizens. Moreover, while some members had a long association with sailing, others seemed to have no interest whatever in the sea.

Yet just as Goforth was prepared to shrug away the matter and conclude that there was no unifying element among the members of the Sailing Club, he became aware of some subtle element that resisted analysis. Did it actually exist, or did he merely imagine it? He studied the features of the supposed Club members more closely. They were casual, yes, and some-what aloof—even bored, it seemed. And yet there was some-thing else, something buried: a kind of suppressed exhilaration that winked out briefly, at odd moments, as though they shared some monumental private joke.

As his perplexing survey of the Club members continued, Goforth became conscious of a quite different sensation. He could not be sure, but he began to suspect that while he was quietly inspecting them, they in turn were examining him.

The most suggestive indication was his recent friendship with an older man named Marshall, who was almost certainly a Club member. Marshall, the chairman of a giant corporation, had taken the lead in their acquaintanceship, which had developed to the point where they lunched together at least once a week. Their conversation was ordinary enough—of business matters, usually, and sometimes of sailing, for both were ardent seamen —but each time, Goforth had a stronger impression that he was undergoing some delicate kind of interrogation which was con-nected with the Sailing Club.

He sought to subdue his excitement. But he often found that his palms were moist, and as he wiped them he disciplined his nervousness, telling himself angrily that he was reacting like a college freshman being examined by the president of some desirable fraternity.

At first he tried to moderate his personality, as well. He sensed that his aggressive attitude toward his work, for exam-ple, was not in harmony with the blasé manner of the Club members. He attempted a show of nonchalance, of indifference

—and all at once he became annoyed. He had nothing to be ashamed of. Why should he try to imitate what was false to his nature? He was *not* bored or indifferent, he was *not* disengaged from the competitive battle of life, and he would not pretend otherwise. The Club could elect him or not, as it chose.

At his next session with Marshall he went out of his way to make clear how fully he enjoyed the daily combat of business. He spoke, in fact, more emphatically than he had intended to, for he was irritated by what seemed to be the other man's ironic amusement.

Once Marshall broke in, wryly, "So you really find the press of business life to be thoroughly satisfying and exciting?"

"Yes, I do," said Goforth. He repressed the desire to add, "And don't you, too?" He decided that if the Sailing Club was nothing but a refuge for burned-out men, bored by life and by themselves, then he wanted no part of it.

At the same time he was disturbed by the thought that he had failed. The Sailing Club might be a worthless objective for a man of his temperament—still he did not like to feel that it might be beyond his grasp.

After he had parted none too cordially from Marshall, he paced along the narrow streets toward the harbor, hoping that the ocean winds would blow away his discontent. As he reached the water's edge, he saw a customs launch bounce by across the widening wake of a huge liner. A veil of spray blew softly toward him. Greedily he awaited the familiar reassurance of its bitter scent. But when it came, it was not quite what he had expected.

He frowned out at the water. No, it was not at all the same.

That winter Goforth became ill for the first time in years. It was influenza, and not a serious case, but the convalescent period stretched on and on, and before he was well enough to do any work, it was spring.

His troubles dated from that illness, he decided; not business troubles, for he had a fine executive staff, and the company did not suffer. The troubles were within himself.

First, he went through a mild depression (the doctors had of course cautioned him of this as an aftereffect), and then an uncharacteristic lassitude, broken by intermittent self-doubts.

He noted, for example, that his executive vice-president was doing a good job of filling in the presidency—and then subsequently realized that this fact had no particular meaning for him. He became uneasy. He should have felt impatient to get back in harness, to show them that old Goforth still was on top. But he had felt no emotion. It was this that disturbed him. Was it simply a delayed result of illness, or was it some inevitable process of aging which the illness had accelerated?

He tested himself grimly. He made an analysis of a stock program proposal worked out by one of the economists. He did a masterly job; he knew it himself, with a rush of familiar pride. In its way, his study was as good as anything he had ever done. No, he was not growing feeble—not yet. The malaise that possessed him was something else, undoubtedly not permanent.

That summer he spent with his family at their place on the shore. He did not feel up to sailing; he watched others sail as he lay on the beach, and was again mildly surprised by his reaction. He did not envy them at all.

In the fall he was back at his desk, in full charge once more. But he was careful to follow the advice of the doctors and the urgings of his wife, and kept his schedule light. He avoided the rush-hour trains by going to work late and leaving early, and two or three times a month he remained at home, resting.

He knew that he once would have chafed impatiently at such a regimen, but now he thought it sensible and had no sensation of loss. As always, he passed the routine problems down to his staff; but now, it seemed, so many things appeared routine that there was not much left on his desk.

The shock came late in winter, when he realized that he had actually turned over to his staff a question of vital importance. It had been well handled, true enough, and he had kept in touch with its progress, but he should have attended to it personally. Why hadn't he? Was he going through some kind of metamorphosis that would end by his becoming a semiactive Chairman of the Board? Perhaps he should consider early retirement . . .

It was in his new condition of uncertainty that he had another encounter with Marshall, this time at a private university club to which they both belonged. Marshall offered to stand him a drink, and commented that he seemed to have recovered splendidly from his illness.

Goforth glanced at him, suspecting irony. He felt fully Marshall's age now, and looked, he thought, even older. But he accepted the drink, and they began to talk.

As they chatted, it occurred to him that he had nothing to lose by speaking frankly of his present perplexities. Marshall *was* older, in point of fact; possibly the man could offer some advice.

And so Goforth spoke of his illness, his slow convalescence, his disinclination to resume his old working pace, even his unthinkable transfer of responsibility to his staff—and strangest of all, his own feeling that it did not really matter, none of it.

Marshall listened attentively, nodding his head in quiet understanding, as if he had heard scores of similar accounts.

At length Goforth's voice trailed off. He glanced at Marshall in mild embarrassment.

"So," said Marshall calmly, "you don't find business life so exciting any more?"

Goforth stirred in irritation at this echo of their previous conversation. "No," he replied, shortly.

Marshall gave him a sharp, amused look. He seemed almost triumphant, and Goforth was sorry he had spoken at all.

Then Marshall leaned forward and said, "What would you say to an invitation to join the Sailing Club?"

Goforth stared at him. "Are you serious?"

"Quite so."

It was Goforth's turn to be amused. "You know, if you'd suggested this two years ago, I'd have jumped at the chance. But now—"

"Yes?" Marshall seemed not at all taken aback.

"But now, it seems of little importance. No offense, mind you."

"I completely understand."

"To put it with absolute frankness, I don't honestly care."

Marshall smiled. "Excellent!" he declared. "That's precisely what makes you eligible!" He winked at Goforth in a conspiratorial way. "We're all of that frame of mind, my friend. We're all suffering from that same disease—"

"But I'm well now."

Marshall chuckled. "So the doctors may say. But you know

otherwise, eh?" He laughed. "The only cure, my friend, is to cast your lot with fellow sufferers—the Sailing Club!"

He continued with the same heartiness to speak of the Club. Most of it Goforth already had heard. There were sixteen members, enough to provide the entire crew for the Club's schooner during its annual summer cruise. One of the sixteen had recently died, and Goforth would be nominated immediately to fill the vacancy; one word of assent from him would be enough to assure his election.

Goforth listened politely; but he had reservations. Marshall did not say exactly what the Club did on its cruises, and Goforth moodily assumed it was not worth mentioning. Probably the members simply drank too much and sang old college songs— hardly an enviable prospect.

Marshall interrupted his musing. "I promise you one thing," he said, more seriously. "You won't be bored."

There was a peculiar intensity in the way he spoke; Goforth wondered at it, then gave up and shrugged. Why not? He sighed and smiled. "All right. Of course. I'm honored, Marshall."

The cruise was scheduled to begin on the last day of July. The evening before, Goforth was driven by Marshall far out along the shore to the estate of another member, who kept the schooner at his private dock. By the time they arrived, all the others were there, and Goforth was duly introduced as the new crewman.

He knew them already, either as acquaintances or by reputation. They included men so eminent that they were better known than the companies or banking houses they headed. There were a few less prominent, but none below Goforth's own rank, and certainly none was in any sense obscure. He was glad to note that all of them had fought their way through the hard competitive years, just as he had done, and then in the course of the evening he slowly came to realize a further fact —that not one of these men had achieved any major triumph in recent years.

He took some comfort from this. If he had fallen into a strange lassitude, then so perhaps had they. Marshall had evidently been right. He was among "fellow sufferers." This thought cheered him, and he moved more easily from group to group, chatting with as much self-possession as if he had been a member of the Club for years.

He had already been told that the ship was in full readiness and that the group was to sail before dawn, and so he was not surprised when the host, a gigantic old man named Teacher, suggested at nine o'clock that they all retire.

"Has the new member signed on?" someone inquired.

"Not yet," said Teacher. He beckoned to Goforth with one huge hairless hand. "This way, my friend," he said.

He led Goforth into an adjoining room, with several of the others following, and after unlocking a wall safe, withdrew a large black volume so worn with age that bits of the binding flaked off in his fingers.

He laid it on a table, thumbed through its pages, and at length called Goforth over and handed him a pen. Goforth noticed the old man had covered the top portion of the page with a blank sheet of paper; all that showed beneath were signatures, those of the other members.

"Sign the articles, seaman," said Teacher gruffly, in imitation of an old-time sea captain.

Goforth grinned and bent over the page, although at the same time he felt a constitutional reluctance to sign something he could not first examine. He glanced at the faces surrounding him. A voice in the background said, "You can read the whole thing, if you like—after the cruise."

There was nothing to do but sign, so he signed boldly, with a flourish, and then turned to shake the hands thrust out to him. "Well done!" someone exclaimed. They all crowded around then to initial his signature as witnesses, and Teacher insisted that they toast the new member with brandy, which they did cheerfully enough, and then went off to bed.

Goforth told himself that the ceremony had been a juvenile bit of foolishness, but somehow it had warmed him with the feeling of fellowship.

His sense of well-being persisted the next morning when in the predawn darkness he was awakened and hurriedly got dressed to join the others for breakfast.

It was still dark when they went down to the ship, each man carrying his sea bag. As he climbed aboard, Goforth was just able to make out the name painted in white letters on the bow: *Freedom IV.*

Since he was experienced, he was assigned a deck hand's job, and as he worked alongside the others to ready sails for hoisting, he sensed a marked change in their attitude.

The Club had its reputation for being casual, and certainly the night before, the members had seemed relaxed to the point of indolence; but there was a difference now. Each man carried out his tasks swiftly, in dead seriousness and without wasted motion, so that in a short time the *Freedom IV* was skimming eastward along the Sound toward the heart of the red rising sun.

Goforth was surprised and pleased. There was seamanship and discipline and sober purpose on this ship, and he gladly discarded his earlier notion that they would wallow about with no program beyond liquor and cards.

With satisfaction, he made a leisurely tour of the ship. Everything was smart and sharp, on deck and below, in the sleeping quarters and galley. Teacher, who seemed to be the captain, had a small cabin forward and it, too, was a model of neatness.

Goforth poked his head inside to admire it further. Teacher was not there, but in a moment the old man stepped through a narrow door on the opposite bulkhead, leading to some compartment below, followed by two other members. They greeted Goforth pleasantly, but closed and locked the door behind them, and did not offer to show him the compartment. He, for his part, refrained from asking, but later in the day he inspected the deck above it and saw that what had seemed earlier to be merely a somewhat unorthodox arrangement of crisscross deck planking was actually a hatchway, cleverly concealed.

He crouched and ran his fingers along the hidden edges of the hatch, then glanced up guiltily to meet Marshall's eyes. Marshall seemed amused, but all he said was, "Ready for chow?"

In the next few days Goforth occasionally wondered what the forward compartment contained. Then he all but forgot about it, for his enjoyment of the voyage was too deep-felt to permit even the smallest question to trouble him. He was more content now than he had been in many months. It was not because he was sailing again, but rather, he believed, because he was actively sharing with others like himself a vigorous and demanding experience. It seemed, indeed, that they formed a little corporation there on the *Freedom IV*—and what a corporation! Even the member who occupied the lowly post of cook's helper was a man accustomed to deal in terms of millions.

Yes, what a crew it was! Now Goforth began to understand the suppressed excitement he had long ago detected as a subtle mark identifying members of the Sailing Club. Theirs was no ordinary cruise, but a grand exercise of seamanship, as if they had decided to pit their collective will against the force and cunning of the ocean, to retrieve through a challenge to that most brutal of antagonists the sense of daring which they once had found in their work . . .

They were searching for something. For a week they sailed a zigzag course, always out of sight of land, but Goforth had not the faintest notion of their whereabouts, nor did he judge that it would be proper for him to inquire. Were they pursuing a storm to provide them with some ultimate test with the sea? He could not be sure. And yet he was quite willing to wait, for there was happiness enough in each waking moment aboard the *Freedom IV.*

On the eighth day he perceived an abrupt change. There was an almost tangible mood of expectancy among the members, a quickening of pace and movement, a tightening of smiles and laughter that reminded him oddly of the atmosphere in a corporation board room, when the final crisis of some serious negotiation approaches. He guessed that some word had been passed among the crew, save for himself, the neophyte.

The men were tense, but it was the invigorating tensity of trained athletes waiting in confidence for a test worthy of their skills. The mood was infectious; without having any idea of what lay ahead, Goforth began to share the exhilaration and to scan the horizon eagerly.

For what? He did not care now. Whatever it might be, he felt an elemental stirring of pride and strength and knew that he would meet whatever ultimate trial impended with all the nerve and daring that his life had stamped into his being.

The *Freedom IV* changed course and plunged due east toward a haze that lay beneath heavier clouds. Goforth thought perhaps the storm lay that way and keenly watched for its signs. There were none, but he took some heart at the sight of another yacht coming toward them, and hopefully imagined that it was retreating from the combat which the *Freedom IV* seemed so ardently to seek.

He studied the sky. The clouds drifted aimlessly, then broke apart for a moment to disclose a regular expanse of blue. He sighed as he saw it, and glanced around at the other crewmen to share his feeling of frustration.

But there was no disappointment on those faces. Instead, the mood of tension seemed heightened to an almost unbearable degree. The men stood strained and stiff, their features set rigidly, their eyes quick and piercing as they stared across the water.

Goforth searched their faces desperately for comprehension, and as it slowly came to him—when at last he *knew*—he felt the revelation grip him physically with a wild penetrating excitement.

He *knew,* and so he watched with fierce absorption but without surprise as the forward hatch swung open to permit what was below to rise to the surface of the deck, and watched still more intently as the crew leaped smartly forward to prepare it with the speed born of long hours of practice.

He stood aside then, for he knew he would need training, too, before he could learn his part; but after the first shot from the sleek little cannon had smashed a great hole in the side of the other yacht, he sprang forward as readily as the others to seize the rifles which were being passed around. And as the *Freedom IV* swooped swiftly in toward the floundering survivors, his cries of delight were mixed with those of his comrades, and their weapons cracked out sharply, gaily, across the wild echoing sea.

1962 Special Award:

This Will Kill You

Patrick Quentin

Harry Lund lay in the bathtub. Above him two pairs of his wife's nylons dangled wetly on the rail which supported the shabby gray-white shower curtain. He could hear Norma preparing Sunday breakfast in the kitchen downstairs.

After twenty-one years of marriage Norma's morning noises were so familiar to him that they brought exact visual pictures. He could see the inevitable cigarette dangling from her mouth while she squeezed oranges on the cluttered enamel table. Norma never dressed on Sunday mornings. He could see her thin body, draped in the old pink quilted robe, bustling about the kitchen.

Every day Harry Lund's aversion to his wife began a fresh attack on his nerves during those moments in the tub. He was a lazy man. He liked his comfort. He liked lolling in warm water, relaxing before the effort of a day at the drugstore, or, better still, relaxing with the knowledge of a long, indolent Sunday ahead. But he could hardly remember a time when he hadn't lain there in the steamy, cramped bathroom taut with hatred.

It was strange, then, to find himself on this particular Sunday morning lying in the same tub, hearing the same kitchen noises, and yet completely free of hate. In fact, the sounds downstairs were almost exhilarating. Even the mental image of his wife's sharp, too-intelligent face with its critical black eyes and short graying hair brought no distaste.

This change of attitude was caused by the fact that he knew now that Norma would not be with him much longer.

He knew this because last night he had decided exactly how and when he was going to kill her.

The thought of murder, flirted with at first and finally embraced as a lover, had lived with him so long that now it had become an old friend. In consequence, he felt no awe at what he had planned to do. No guilt, either. He had let himself forget the shabby motives which had made him lay siege to the plain, enterprising girl who had graduated with him from Pharmacy School and to whom he had never been really attracted. He had forgotten how convenient it had seemed at the time to have for a wife a fully trained pharmacist. He had even forgotten the attractions of her little inheritance which, combined with his, had been sufficient to buy a drugstore and launch his career. He had never admitted that it had been due to her drive and slogging hard work that this career had reached a modest success.

He only knew that he, the handsome Harry Lund, was a figure of tragic suffering chained to a woman who had never appreciated him and whom he could never divorce.

Because he couldn't divorce her. Half the drugstore was her property. Even if he could scrape up enough money to pay her off, she would never sell. He knew that. The store was Norma's whole life and she clung tenaciously to what she wanted.

Having endured so much, then, he viewed murder, this final gesture of rebellion, as almost heroic, certainly as courageous and manly.

And the courage would never have come if it hadn't been for Frances. He realized that. It had been that chance, wonderful meeting with Frances on the bus which had released the true, virile Harry Lund from convention's slavery. Frances was young, dainty, submissive, everything that Norma wasn't. Frances was the type of girl that Harry Lund had deserved from life. And he was almost sure, if he played his cards right, he could get her.

A pleasurable tingle shivered his thickening body when he thought of Frances.

His plans were without flaw. He had gone over and over them in his mind, simplifying, perfecting, like an artist. From the beginning he had rejected drugs as too dangerous for a pharmacist. There were other ways.

"Harry!" Norma's voice, perpetually husky from a smoker's cough, rasped up the stairs.

"Coming, dear." He was surprised at the cordial, almost saccharine tone of his own voice. He must be careful about that. He lumbered to his feet, water streaming off him. More crossly, more convincingly, he added, "Hold your horses, can't you?"

As he dried himself, he studied his reflected body in the steam-stained mirror. Not bad for a man of forty-five. Bit of a paunch, maybe. But a gymnasium would soon fix that up. He concentrated on his face. Harry Lund had always been pleased with his face. Good teeth. Distinguished little mustache. Plenty of hair. Strong eyebrows over eyes that looked straight back at you.

Frances had remarked on his eyes only last week when he had snatched a few hours with her in a restaurant halfway between the city and the outlying suburb where she worked as librarian.

"It was your eyes I liked first. I noticed them right away when you picked up my books in the bus. They're so sincere."

A tiny chill of apprehension came. What would Frances think if she knew he was a married man? How fortunate that, on an adventurous whim, he had introduced himself under an assumed name. Frances was as trusting as she was innocent. She believed his story that he was a widowed salesman from upstate. She would go on believing him. After the thing was over, he could sell the house, the store. He could take Frances away, start a new life.

She need never know.

"For Pete's sake," called Norma. "What are you doing up there? Admiring yourself in the mirror?"

"Coming," called Harry.

He smiled at his reflection so that he could see his firm white teeth.

Neatly dressed, he descended the stairs, thinking: *In a few hours how different everything will be.* The thought was so heady that he wanted to do something youthful, gay, whistle maybe, or slide down the banisters. He moved through the untidy little dining room into the kitchen. Norma, in the old pink robe, was hunched over frying eggs that hissed on the range. She turned, the cigarette drooping from her mouth, giving him that look of keen appraisal which always made him feel transparent.

"My, isn't he beautiful this morning? How about being useful, too, and getting on to those dishes?"

Last night they had not washed the supper dishes. Usually Harry resented the unmanliness of having to work at a sink, but that sunny winter morning it almost pleased him for, as he started to rinse plates, he could look through the window and actually see the place where It Was Going to Happen.

The house was situated in a suburb, half developed before the war and still raw and unfinished, on top of a steep, barren hill. The house was completely his own. He had bought it with money surprisingly bequeathed by an obscure aunt. It was small, inconvenient, and he hated it. But real estate brought large prices these days. He would have no trouble in selling it for a profit.

As the dishes clattered, his study of the view outside was almost covetous. The snowfall of last week still clung to the landscape. It had frozen again during the night. He could just see the elbow of the sharp S-bend where the road swerved down the hillside to the city. Its surface was smooth with ice. An almost sheer drop slid away to the right. Suicide Bend, they called it. Every Sunday afternoon Norma took the car into town to visit with her married sister. A skid on that curve would mean certain death. Especially if the brakes on the ancient sedan were not too good.

Harry Lund was sure that, this particular Sunday afternoon, the brakes would not be too good.

In his mind he saw himself in becoming black, palely acknowledging the sympathy of the neighbors. "It's terrible. . . . like losing my right hand . . . I'm going to sell everything . . . start again somewhere else."

He began to hum under his breath as he piled wet dishes into the rack.

"Listen to him," commented Norma. "Humming. So handsome, so happy this morning. What's happened? Found yourself a beautiful girl friend?"

She laughed her hoarse laugh that was half a cough. There was sarcasm in the laugh, letting him know that she realized how improbable it was that any girl could be interested in a man of his age. An edge of the old hatred pushed up. Norma slammed a plate of fried eggs on the table.

"Come and get it, Don Juan. I guess someone has to feed that body beautiful."

He left the sink and sat down obediently. She sat down opposite him, still smoking, stabbing at her eggs with a fork. She got up again for a house organ issued by some pharmaceutical firm and read while she ate. Norma studied all the new drug literature and, since she had written a couple of articles for *The Pestle and Mortar*, never tired of implying how little he did to keep up with modern medicine.

That was another reason . . .

Harry Lund's hand was trembling slightly as he lifted his coffee cup. It wasn't fear. It was excitement.

After they had cleaned up the kitchen, Norma settled in the living room with her house organ. Under the pretense of chopping wood, Harry slipped out to the garage. He had a knack for tinkering with the car and enjoyed it. He kept an old pair of denim overalls in the garage. He put them on and wormed his way under the car's decrepit chassis. It took very little time to file the brake cable almost through. One violent application of the pedal would snap it. Almost certainly. And he knew Norma's driving as well as his own—and the road. There was no need for brakes until the corner before Suicide Bend and there Norma always jammed them full on.

He took off his overalls, washed his hands in icy water from the faucet, picked up an armful of logs from the woodpile, and went back to the house.

Norma watched him from black, alert eyes over her magazine. "Domestic, too. All the virtues this morning."

He crossed to the fireplace and stooped to lay down the logs. Behind him Norma's voice came: "The roads are terrible, aren't they? Think I should skip Ella?"

One of the logs clattered to the floor. He said with an evenness that made him proud of himself: "She'll be expecting you, won't she? You can't get in touch with her by phone. If you don't show up, she'll be afraid you've had an accident."

"I guess you're right." Norma laughed again, facetiously. "I might as well go, anyway. It'll give you a chance to sneak in a date with your new girl friend . . ."

Harry Lund stood at the kitchen window. Cautiously he had eased the car out of the garage for Norma and left it headed down the road. He had seen her, in her old blue tweed coat, step into the car and drive away. He had run back to the kitchen. Any second now the car would come into view from the window, approaching Suicide Bend. His stomach was fluttering. A curious sensation. Almost as if he was drunk.

The afternoon sunlight beat down on the empty twist of road. Suddenly a car gleamed, Norma's car. He saw it sweep into the bend, topple grotesquely for a second on the brink of the drop, and then plunge over. The sound of wrenched, rattling metal split the silence. A roar, a rumble, fainter as the car hurtled down, down.

He turned away from the window. He wanted to shout, to clap his hands, absurdly to call the boarding house where Frances lived and say: *Marry me, darling. Marry me.*

But he satisfied himself with a smile, the little curled sophisticated smile of an artist who knows that his job was well done.

He went into the living room and turned on the radio loud so that it would seem reasonable he had not heard the crash. He picked up the house organ Norma had been reading. Soon the neighbors would be coming. He would be ready for them.

The front-door buzzer rang shrilly. Harry Lund straightened his handsome red and blue tie and went to answer the door. Mrs. Grant, who lived down the street, stood on the threshold. She was panting.

"Mr. Lund, your wife . . . something happened to the car. It went over Suicide Bend."

Harry Lund put up a hand to cover his fine eyes. "God, no. It's not possible. I thought I heard something, but the radio . . ."

"All the way down," panted Mrs. Grant. "I saw it. Right from the living-room window. Come."

He was running after her through the snowy streets. At Suicide Bend a little group of neighbors was huddled at the roadside. Moaning his wife's name, Harry Lund pushed through them and looked down. Far below in the bed of the valley he saw the car in flames, a twisted wreck of metal. He also saw two men stooped over some blue, half-visible object a little way down the sharp sloping side of the hill. A third man was scrambling away from them up the grade. He came to Harry and pumped his hand.

"She must have opened the door and thrown herself free. She's unconscious, maybe hurt a little. But Doc Peterson's down there and he says she's all right, Mr. Lund. It's a miracle. A miracle . . ."

It was a miracle. Norma had escaped with only a sprained ankle and a shock to her nervous system. The injury was not serious enough for the hospital, but Dr. Peterson confined her to bed for some weeks.

There was no suspicion of a fixed accident. Harry was almost sure of that. At first immense relief kept him from thinking of anything else. But gradually he began to realize that his whole life had become worse. Norma was a difficult patient, demanding constant attention. Her sister Ella, with four children, could offer no assistance. Harry had to hire an expensive day nurse. Without his wife to relieve him, he was obliged to stay all day at the drugstore, snatching a sandwich lunch behind the counter. With his evenings enforcedly dedicated to Norma, there was no chance to see Frances.

He had called her once, feebly ascribing his elusiveness to a succession of business trips. For the first time, Frances' voice had been chilly.

And to make matters worse, he had lost the car and the amount of insurance was much too small to buy a new one, even if a new one had been available. Each morning he had to get up two hours earlier to cook Norma's breakfast before the nurse arrived, and then to trudge down the snow-slushy hill to take the trolley to the store.

But of all the resultant miseries, the new, inescapable intimacy with Norma was the most grueling. The little house had only one bedroom. Constantly smoking, propped up in bed in the pink quilted robe, his wife bossed him, questioning, directing store policy, like a tart-tongued old empress. Something, maybe a half-realized sense of guilt, maybe a tacit admission of her greater strength of character, made him obey meekly. She developed a perverse habit of waking in the early dawn hours and sending him, sleep-stupefied, aching with cold and hatred, to the kitchen for orange juice or a glass of hot milk.

Christmas came, and in a burst of seasonal sentimentality, Norma insisted upon a tree in the bedroom. Harry had to drag it all the way up the icy hill and decorate it with colored balls and pretty little old-fashioned candles under a barrage of sarcastic criticism. The nurse demanded Christmas off. Harry Lund cloood the drugstore, cooked a turkey with the reluctant, neighborly help of Mrs. Grant, and served a meal, with gift-wrapped presents, to Norma in the bedroom. Norma was vivacious and, after domestic champagne, almost flirtatious.

That night Harry Lund knew that, however dangerous it might be, he was going to try to kill her again.

A trivial incident gave him his second idea. Norma was still in bed a few days after Christmas, but she could hobble around with the help of a cane. When she was in the bathroom, Harry came up from the kitchen to find that one of her inevitable cigarettes had rolled, still alight, from the ashtray and was smouldering perilously close to the low, tinder-dry branches of the tree.

Instinctively he stubbed it. But, as he did so, the idea sprang full-born into his mind.

The Retail Druggists' Convention was giving a banquet in two days' time. Norma knew about it and, always conscientious where anything professional was at stake, expected him to go. What if Norma, under the influence of a sedative, should drop asleep and leave a cigarette alight? What if a fire, a sudden, concentrated blaze in the bedroom, should break out while he was at the banquet? The house was insured. He had planned to sell it anyway.

Some sort of time-clock device was all he needed. His tinkerer's mind solved that problem easily. He brought home a couple of cans of lighter fluid from the drug store. All he had to do was to stand one of the Christmas candles under the tree on some of the artificial moss saturated with lighter fluid. The candle would burn down and ignite the moss. The moss would ignite the tree.

Harry Lund felt his manhood returning. That night he smiled at his reflection in the mirror.

It smiled back, reassuringly handsome and decisive.

Half an hour before he was due to leave for the banquet, Harry Lund, spruce in a freshly pressed blue suit, heated milk in the kitchen and dissolved into the glass three strong hypnotic tablets. He carried the glass up to the bedroom.

"Thought you might like your milk before I left."

"Why, how considerate he is." Norma's sharp black eyes studied him with mock admiration. "And doesn't he look dashing tonight!"

She tossed her cigarette down on an ashtray and drank great draughts of the milk. He kept himself from watching her. He moved around the room pretending to tidy up.

"Want the window open, dear?"

"On a night like this? You might help me to the bathroom, though."

When she came out of the bathroom a few minutes later, she was already staggering from sleep. She mumbled confusedly as he half-carried her back to the bed and tucked her in. Soon she turned over on her side and began to breathe deeply.

Carefully Harry Lund arranged his death-trap under the tree, the candle, just the right amount of artificial moss soaked in lighter fluid, at just the right position under a dry limb.

He lit the candle. Half an hour, maybe. Or more. An hour. The tree would flare up. The curtains would catch. In a matter of moments the room would be an inferno.

The little candle flame flickered as he tiptoed out of the room.

While he trudged down the hill to the trolley stop, Harry Lund thought of Frances' young face flushed with love and gratitude as she unwrapped a prettily packed package.

"So you didn't forget my Christmas present after all! Oh, *Spring Lilac*. My favorite perfume. You shouldn't have done it. *So expensive . . .*"

The telephone call came just after the banquet had begun. That morning he had casually mentioned the banquet to Mrs. Grant so that the neighbors would know where to find him. It was Grant himself, announcing excitedly: "Come back at once, Lund! Your house is on fire!"

Feeling important from the drama around him, Harry Lund made breathless excuses and raced for a taxi. As it slithered up the icy hill, he saw fire engines and a milling crowd outside his house. He also saw that, though the flames seemed to be almost extinguished, the upper floor had been completely gutted.

Warm with dangerous excitement, he got out of the taxi. Someone grabbed his arm and started to pull him across the lawn to the next-door neighbor's house. He found himself in a brightly lit living room. Norma was lying on a couch.

Someone was saying: "The smoke woke her up. She managed to crawl out just in time."

Norma's black eyes were fixed on his face, solemn with contrition.

"Harry, I'm so terribly ashamed. My vile habit of smoking in bed. I fell asleep and the cigarette must have set fire to the tree . . ."

The top floor of the house had been demolished, but downstairs there had been little or no damage. The agent from the insurance company did not question the legitimacy of the fire but let Harry know that the condition of the building warranted payment of less than a third of the total policy. With the increased cost of materials and labor, it would take almost all Harry's savings to make his home habitable again.

Owing to the housing shortage, it was impossible to find another place to live. For a short, dismal period, Harry and Norma led a squalorous camping existence on the lower floor of the burnt-out house. Then, by a stroke of luck, their tenants above the drugstore moved to another city and they were able to settle in the tiny two-room apartment there.

Norma could still walk only with difficulty and Dr. Peterson warned that the added shock of the fire should be neutralized by a long rest. But, taking on herself the full blame for the loss of their home, Norma refused to go away or stay in bed. As if in atonement she worked absurd hours in the store, hobbling around with a cane. A few weeks later she collapsed. Dr. Peterson diagnosed a heart condition, prescribed epinephrine, and put her back to bed.

For Harry Lund life had become gray and sour as the ashes of his destroyed bedroom. Twice, when Norma's sister Ella dropped in, he was able to slip away and call Frances, but his excuses were even less convincing and her acceptance of them even more frigid. This was very different from his rosy dreams of *Spring Lilac* and the girl's flushed gratitude.

Vain though he was of his attraction to women, Harry Lund realized that, unless something happened soon, he would lose Frances forever.

As disaster closed in from all sides, Harry Lund's picture of himself as a martyr took on an immense vividness. Life was pummeling him with blows whose strength was out of all proportion to his desserts. And, in consequence, his determination to finish what he had started grew out of all proportion also. No scheme was too reckless for him to consider. Once, at the poison safe in the store, he made up a capsule of potassium cyanide. Only the weak vestiges of a self-preservation instinct kept him from spilling it that night into Norma's bouillon.

But he kept the capsule always in his pocket. He would touch it frequently during the day. It became the one thing that was on his side.

And then the opportunity came. Harry Lund knew that only a man capable of daring and swift decision would have seen it as such. But then he was possessed of both qualities. One evening Norma had asked him to go round to her sister's to borrow a book she wanted. Just before he was about to leave, she had an attack.

Epinephrine! As he looked down at his wife, convulsively gasping for breath in the bed, the name of the drug prescribed by Dr. Peterson seemed to quiver between him and Norma in great red letters. Norma kept ampules of epinephrine and a hypodermic always by her bedside. Proud of her knowledgeability, she had told Dr. Peterson that, if she felt a new attack coming on, she would administer the injection herself. A double dose of epinephrine would certainly kill even Norma.

Who could be suspicious if his wife, alone in the room, had tried to counter an attack and had inadvertently overdosed herself? This was using drugs, but it was using them with a difference—creatively.

His fine eyes bright with self-approval, Harry Lund filled the hypodermic from two ampules. Norma was in a half-coma. She seemed barely conscious of what was happening as he administered the injection.

Scrupulously Harry Lund wiped his fingerprints from the two empty ampules and from the syringe. Holding the ampules in his handkerchief, he brought them in contact with the limp fingertips of Norma's left hand and then let them fall to the floor. With the handkerchief, too, he squeezed the syringe into Norma's right hand and left it where it dropped.

Get out quickly. That was all he had to do, just in case there might be some question about the time of death. Hurry over to Ella's house for a chat about the book Norma wanted.

When he shut the bedroom door, he seemed to be shutting a door forever on his misunderstood past.

Harry had a pleasant talk with Ella, extended through a cup of coffee and a piece of homemade cake. He knew Norma's sister had never liked him, but that day he was so charming that he could see her visibly thaw.

With the book under his arm, he started back to the drugstore. He had given the epinephrine plenty of time. During the next few days, he would need to do some clever acting, but Harry Lund was not worried. His exhibition with Ella had been flawless. He had always known that, if he had wanted to, he could have made a great success on the stage.

Already, as he climbed the drab stairs to the apartment, he had instinctively arranged his face for its necessary expression —the expression of a husband overwhelmed by the discovery of his wife's lifeless body. He was so preoccupied rehearsing the phrases he would use over the phone to Dr. Peterson that he had opened the door and stepped into the bedroom before he was conscious of anything unusual.

Then, as he looked across at the bed, all traces of reality seemed to be sucked out of the world. Because Frances was there. He saw her standing, young, silent, very stiff, at the foot of the bed. She was watching Norma, who lay prostrate under the huddled bedclothes.

As he entered, Frances turned and looked at him. The look was one of unspeakable horror and disgust. He shook himself, staring stupidly. This was in his mind, some vile, cruel trick played by a treacherous imagination.

"Welcome home." Norma's voice sounded from the bed, cracked and weak, but with a ghost of its sarcasm. "Your girl friend just arrived. You poor fool, Harry Lund. Thought I didn't know about her, didn't you? I've known for weeks. A friend of Ella's saw you together in a restaurant. It was easy enough to find out her name, where she lived."

The words fell on him like hammer blows. But it was the horror of Norma's being alive which completed his demoralization. He had pumped enough epinephrine into her to kill anybody. Could nothing kill her? His knees were like water. He tried to grope for some pattern—anything to remove this feeling of helplessness.

Norma's black eyes were watching him sardonically. "I telephoned this poor girl because I thought I should explain. She's not to blame, of course. Used an assumed name, didn't you? Told her you were a widower." A dreadful travesty of the hoarse laugh came. "Guess you thought you were—almost."

She shifted her gaze to the white, rigid Frances. "Three times he tried. First he fixed the brakes of the car. Then he set fire to the house. And now—the epinephrine. He put in a lot of work to get you. You should be flattered."

Harry Lund swung to Frances. Without any control, words spilled out. "Frances, listen to me. Please listen. It isn't true. I didn't . . ."

The icy contempt in her eyes checked him. There was a moment of silence, as awful to Harry Lund as a bomb explosion. Frances turned and walked to the telephone.

Her voice seemed to surge up through the silence. "The police. Get me the police." And then: "Come quickly. There's been an attempted murder at . . ."

Despair brought Harry Lund absolute clarity. He saw, in all

its truth, how pitifully bungled had been his great design. He had lost his car, his house, and now he had lost his girl. The police inevitably would trace the damning connection between the three "accidents." Norma was there as a living testimony against him and, with tormenting irony, Frances would be her witness.

His predicament was without remedy. Somehow, its enormity destroyed in him the worm of fear. His plan had been a magnificent failure. Perhaps that was what his destiny had always been. A magnificent failure. Hadn't all the outstanding figures of tragedy been overwhelmed in the closing scene?

The actor in him rose to its greatest moment. Frances would see him, at least once, as he really was. He felt exalted, high above the pettiness of Harry Lund, druggist. His hand moved to his pocket and closed around the cyanide capsule.

He walked nonchalantly to the bathroom, entered it, and locked the door.

Norma Lund bustled cheerfully around the drugstore, which was now entirely her own. Although she had been bored with her husband for years, some vestige of pity for him still remained. But Norma was a sensible woman with little sympathy for a fool. And that had been Harry's trouble. He had always been a fool.

True, she'd had her own moments of folly. She had only realized that her husband had fixed the brakes a few seconds before the car had toppled over the ravine. Her foolishness had almost cost her her life then. But, once she knew he had tried to kill her and would almost certainly try again, she had made no mistake.

She had rather enjoyed lying in bed, bullying him and keeping him from seeing that girl. It served him right. Later, when she had tasted the sleeping draught in the hot milk, it had been simple to take amphetamine as an antidote in the bathroom. While she pretended sleep she had watched and almost admired Harry's device of the candle and the saturated moss. She had felt a certain pleasure in seeing his house burn, too.

Perhaps she should have gone to the police then. It had been a risk, she supposed, to carry the farce on longer. But, because Harry was a fool, it had not been a dangerous one. The first sham heart attack, artificially induced by digitalis, had fooled even Dr. Peterson. The second attack, which had been sheer acting coupled with the planted props of the hypodermic and the epinephrine ampules filled with sterile water, had seemed to her too obvious a trap even for Harry. But he had lumbered into it like an ox and provided enough evidence to convict him a dozen times over.

Mrs. Grant came into the store for a toothbrush and a bottle of mouthwash. She greeted Norma warmly. Since Harry's suicide, everyone had been particularly kind.

While she reached for the mouthwash, Norma was wondering whether Harry would have killed himself if Frances had not been present during those final moments of his humiliation. Perhaps, by introducing Frances, she had in a way turned from murderee to murderer.

But it was foolish to speculate. Things had gone well for her.

Mrs. Grant was saying: "It's really wonderful the way you manage to run this place all by yourself."

"I do my best." Norma Lund briskly wrapped up the mouthwash. "But sometimes it's hard for a woman all on her own . . ."

1964:

H as in Homicide

Lawrence Treat

She came through the door of the Homicide Squad's outer office as if it were a disgrace to be there, as if she didn't like it, as if she hadn't done anything wrong—and never could or would.

Still, here she was. About twenty-two years old and underweight. Wearing a pink sleeveless dress. She had dark hair pulled back in a bun; her breasts were close together; and her eyes ate you up.

Mitch Taylor had just come back from lunch and was holding down the fort all alone. He nodded at her and said, "Anything I can do?"

"Yes. I—I—" Mitch put her down as a nervous stutterer and waited for her to settle down. "They told me to come here," she said. "I went to the neighborhood police station and they said they couldn't do anything, that I had to come here."

"Yeah," Mitch said. It was the old run-around and he was willing to bet this was Pulasky's doing, up in the Third Precinct. He never took a complaint unless the rule book said, "You, Pulasky—you got to handle this or you'll lose your pension."

So Mitch said, "Sure. What's the trouble?"

"I don't like to bother you and I hope you don't think I'm silly, but—well, my friend left me. And I don't know where or why."

"Boy friend?" Mitch said.

She blushed a deep crimson. "Oh, no! A real *friend*. We were traveling together, and she took the car and went, without even leaving me a note. I can't understand it."

"Let's go inside and get the details," Mitch said.

He brought her into the Squad Room and sat her down at a desk. She looked up shyly, sort of impressed with him. He didn't know why, because he was only an average-looking guy, of medium height, on the cocky side, with stiff, wiry hair and a face nobody remembered, particularly.

He sat down opposite her and took out a pad and pencil. "Your name?" he said.

"Prudence Gilford."

"Address?"

"New York City, but I gave up my apartment there."

"Where I come from too. Quite a ways from home, aren't you?"

"I'm on my way to California—my sister lives out there. I answered an ad in the paper—just a moment, I think I still have it." She fumbled in a big canvas bag, and the strap broke off and the whole business dropped. She picked it up awkwardly, blushing again, but she kept on talking. "Bella Tansey advertised for somebody to share the driving to California. She said she'd pay all expenses. It was a wonderful chance for me. . . . Here, I have it."

She took out the clipping and handed it to Mitch. It was the usual thing: woman companion to share the driving and a phone number.

"So you got in touch?" Mitch prodded.

"Yes. We liked each other immediately, and arranged to go the following week."

She was fiddling with the strap, trying to fix it, and she finally fitted the tab over some kind of button. Mitch, watching, wondered how long *that* was going to last.

Meanwhile she was still telling him about Bella Tansey. "We got along so well," Prudence said, "and last night we stopped at a motel—The Happy Inn, it's called—and we went to bed. When I woke up, she was gone."

"Why did you stop there?" Mitch asked sharply.

"We were tired and it had a vacancy sign." She drew in her

breath and asked anxiously, "Is there something wrong with it?"

"Not too good a reputation," Mitch said. "Did she take all her things with her? Her overnight stuff, I mean."

"Yes, I think so. Or at least, she took her bag."

Mitch got a description of the car: a dark blue Buick; 1959 or 1960, she wasn't sure; New York plates but she didn't know the number.

"OK," Mitch said. "We'll check. We'll send out a flier and have her picked up and find out why she left in such a hurry."

Prudence Gilford's eyes got big. "Yes," she said. "And please, can you help me? I have only five dollars and the motel is expensive. I can't stay there and I don't know where to go."

"Leave it to me," Mitch said. "I'll fix it up at the motel and get you a place in town for a while. You can get some money, can't you?"

"Oh, yes. I'll write my sister for it."

"Better wire," Mitch said. "And will you wait here a couple of minutes? I'll be right back."

"Of course."

Lieutenant Decker had come in and was working on something in his tiny office, which was jammed up with papers and stuff. Mitch reported on the Gilford business and the lieutenant listened.

"Pulasky should have handled it," Mitch said, finishing up. "But what the hell—the kid's left high and dry, so maybe we could give her a little help."

"What do you think's behind this?" Decker asked.

"I don't know," Mitch said. "She's a clinger—scared of everything and leans on people. Maybe the Tansey woman got sick and tired of her, or maybe this is Lesbian stuff. Hard to tell."

"Well, go ahead with an S-4 for the Buick. It ought to be on a main highway and within a five-hundred-mile radius. Somebody'll spot it. We'll see what cooks."

Mitch drove Prudence out to the motel and told her to get her things. While she was busy, he went into the office and spoke to Ed Hiller, who ran the joint. Hiller, a tall stoop-shouldered guy who'd been in and out of jams most of his life, was interested in anything from a nickel up, but chiefly up. He rented cabins by the hour, day, or week, and you could get liquor if you paid the freight; but most of his trouble came from reports of cars that had been left unlocked and rifled. The police had never been able to pin anything on him.

He said, "Hello, Taylor. Anything wrong?"

"Just want to know about a couple of dames that stayed here last night—Bella Tansey and Prudence Gilford. Tansey pulled out during the night."

"Around midnight," Ed said. "She came into the office to make a phone call, and a little later I heard her car pull out."

Time for the missing girl to pack, Mitch decided. So far, everything checked. "Who'd she call?" he asked. "What did she say?"

Hiller shrugged. "I don't listen in," he said. "I saw her open the door and then I heard her go into the phone booth. I mind my own business. You know that."

"Yeah," Mitch said flatly. "You heard the coins drop, didn't you? Local call or long distance?"

Hiller leaned over the counter. "Local," he said softly. "I think."

"Got their registration?" Mitch asked. Hiller nodded and handed Mitch the sheet, which had a record of the New York license plates.

That was about all there was to it. Nobody picked up Bella Tansey and her Buick, Prudence Gilford was socked away in a rooming house in town, and Mitch never expected to see her again.

When he got home that night, Amy kissed him and asked him about things, and then after he'd horsed around with the kids a little, she showed him a letter from her sister. Her sister's husband was on strike, and what the union paid them took care of food and rent and that was about all; but they had to keep up their payments on the car and the new dishwasher, and the TV had broken down again, and could Mitch and Amy help out for a little while—they'd get it back soon.

So after the kids were in bed, Mitch and Amy sat down on the sofa to figure things out, which took about two seconds and came to fifty bucks out of his next paycheck. It was always like that with the two of them: they saw things the same way and never had any arguments. Not many guys were as lucky as Mitch.

The next morning Decker had his usual conference with the Homicide Squad and went over all the cases they had in the shop. The only thing he said about the Gilford business was, the next time Pulasky tried to sucker them, figure it out so he had to come down here, personally, and then make him sweat.

Mitch drew a couple of minor assault cases to investigate, and he'd finished up with one and was on his way to the other when the call came in on his radio. Go out to French Woods, on East Road. They had a homicide, and it looked like the missing Tansey woman.

He found a couple of police cars and an oil truck and the usual bunch of snoopers who had stopped out of curiosity. There was a kind of rough trail going into the woods. A couple of hundred yards in, the lieutenant and a few of the boys and Jub Freeman, the lab technician, were grouped around a dark blue car. It didn't take any heavy brainwork to decide it was the Tansey Buick.

When Mitch got to the car, he saw Bella Tansey slumped in the front seat with her head resting against the window. The right hand door was open and so was the glove compartment, and Decker was looking at the stuff he'd found there.

He gave Mitch the main facts. "Truck driver spotted the car, went in to look, and then got in touch with us. We've been here about fifteen minutes, and the Medical Examiner ought to show up pretty soon. She was strangled—you can see the marks on her neck—and I'll bet a green hat that it happened the night before last, not long after she left the motel."

Mitch surveyed the position of the body with a practiced eye. "She wasn't driving, either. She was pushed in there, after she was dead."

"Check," Decker said. Very carefully, so that he wouldn't spoil any possible fingerprints, he slid the junk he'd been examining onto the front seat. He turned to Jub Freeman, who was delicately holding a handbag by the two ends and scrutinizing it for prints.

"Find anything?" the lieutenant asked.

"Nothing," Jub said. "But the initials on it are B.T.W."

"Bella Tansey What?" the lieutenant said. He didn't laugh and neither did anybody else. He stooped to put his hands on the doorsill, leaned forward, and stared at the body. Mitch, standing behind him, peered over his head.

Bella had been around thirty and she'd been made for men. She was wearing a blue dress with a thing that Amy called a bolero top, and, except where the skirt had pulled up maybe from moving the body, her clothes were not disturbed. The door of the glove compartment and parts of the dashboard were splotched with fingerprint powder.

Mitch pulled back and waited. After about a minute the lieutenant stood up.

"Doesn't look as if there was a sex angle," Decker said. "And this stuff"—he kicked at the dry leaves that covered the earth—"doesn't take footprints. If we're lucky, we'll find somebody who saw the killer somewhere around here." He made a smacking sound with his thin, elastic lips and watched Jub.

Jub had taken off his coat and dumped the contents of the pocketbook onto it. Mitch spotted nothing unusual—just the junk women usually carried; but he didn't see any money. Jub was holding the purse and rummaging inside it.

"Empty?" the lieutenant asked sharply.

Jub nodded. "Except for one nickel. She must have had money, so whoever went through this missed up on five cents."

"Couldn't be Ed Hiller, then," Mitch said, and the gang laughed.

"Let's say the motive was robbery," Decker said. "We got something of a headstart on this, but brother, it's a bad one. Why does a woman on her way to California make a phone call and then sneak off in the middle of the night? Leaving her girl friend in the lurch, too. Doesn't sound like robbery now, does it?"

"Sounds like a guy," Mitch said. "She had a late date, and the guy robbed her, instead of—"

"We'll talk to Ed Hiller about that later," the lieutenant said. "Taylor, you better get going on this. Call New York and get a line on her. Her friends, her background. If she was married. How much money she might have had with her. Her bank might help on that."

"Right," Mitch said.

"And then get hold of the Gilford dame and pump her," Decker said.

Mitch nodded. He glanced into the back of the car and saw the small overnight bag. "That," he said, pointing. "She packed, so she didn't expect to go back to the motel. But she didn't put her bag in the trunk compartment, so she must have expected to check in somewhere else, and pretty soon."

"She'd want to sleep somewhere, wouldn't she?" Decker asked.

"That packing and unpacking doesn't make sense," Mitch said.

Decker grunted. "Homicides never do," he said grimly.

Mitch drove back to headquarters thinking about that overnight bag, and it kept bothering him. He didn't know exactly why, but it was the sort of thing you kept in the back of your mind until something happened or you found something else, and then everything clicked and you got a pattern.

But what with organizing the questions to ask New York he couldn't do much doping out right now. Besides, there was a lot more information to come in.

He got New York on the phone and they said they'd move on it right away; so he hung up and went to see Prudence. He was lucky to find her in.

She was shocked at the news, but she had nothing much to contribute. "We didn't know each other very long," she said, "and I was asleep when she left. I was so tired. We'd been driving all day, and I'd done most of it."

"Did she mention knowing anybody around—anybody in town?" Mitch asked. Prudence shook her head, but he put her through the wringer anyhow—it was easy for people to hear things and then forget them. You had to jog their memories a little. And besides, how could he be sure she was telling all she knew?

He felt sorry for her, though—she looked kind of thin and played out, as if she hadn't been eating much. So he said, "That five bucks of yours isn't going to last too long, and if you need some dough—"

"Oh, thanks!" she said, sort of glowing and making him feel that Mitch Taylor, he was OK. "Oh, thanks! It's perfectly wonderful of you, but I have enough for a while, and I'm sure my sister will send me the money I wired her for."

By that afternoon most of the basic information was in. Locally, the Medical Examiner said that Bella Tansey had been strangled with a towel or a handkerchief; he placed the time as not long after she'd left the motel. The lieutenant had questioned Ed Hiller without being able to get anything "hot." Hiller insisted he hadn't left the motel, but his statement depended only on his own word.

Jub had used a vacuum cleaner on the car and examined the findings with a microscope, and he'd shot enough pictures to fill a couple of albums.

"They stopped at a United Motel the first night," he recapitulated, "and they had dinner at a Howard Johnson place. They ate sandwiches in the car, probably for lunch, and they bought gas in Pennsylvania and Indiana, and the car ate up oil. There was a gray kitten on the rear seat some time or other. They both drove. Bella Tansey had car trouble, and she bought her clothes at Saks Fifth Avenue. I can tell you a lot more about her, but I'm damned if I've uncovered anything that will help on the homicide. No trace in that car of anybody except the two women."

The New York police, however, came up with a bombshell. Bella Tansey had drawn $1,800 from her bank, in cash, and she'd been married to Clyde Warhouse and they'd been divorced two years ago. She'd used her maiden name—Tansey.

"Warhouse!" the lieutenant said.

Everybody knew that name. He ran a column in the local paper—he called it "Culture Corner"—and he covered art galleries, visiting orchestras and egghead lectures. Whenever he had nothing else to write about, he complained how archaic the civic architecture was.

"That's why she had the W on her bag," Mitch said. "Bella Tansey Warhouse. And Ed Hiller didn't lie about the phone call. She made it, all right—to her ex-husband."

Decker nodded. "Let's say she hotfooted it out to see him. Let's say that she still had a yen for him and they scrapped, that he got mad and lost his head and strangled her. But why would he take her dough? She must've had around seventeen hundred with her. Why would he rob her?"

"Why not?" Mitch said. "It was there, wasn't it?"

"Let's think about this," Decker said. "Prudence says Bella unpacked. Did Bella start to go to bed, or what?"

"Prudence doesn't know," Mitch said. "I went into that for all it was worth, and Prudence *assumes* Bella unpacked—she can't actually remember. Says she was bushed and went right to sleep. Didn't even wash her face."

"Well," Decker said, "I guess Warhouse is wondering when we'll get around to him. I'll check on him while you go up there." The lieutenant's jaw set firmly. "Bring him in."

Mitch rolled his shoulders, tugged on the lapels of his jacket, and went out. The first time you hit your suspect, it could make or break the case.

Clyde Warhouse lived in a red brick house with tall white columns on the front. Mitch found him at home, in his study. He was a little guy with big teeth, and he didn't really smile; he just pulled his lips back, and you could take it any way you pleased.

Warhouse came right to the point. "You're here about my former wife," he said. "I just heard about it on the radio, and I wish I could give you some information, but I can't. It's certainly not the end I wished for her."

"What kind of end were you hoping for?" Mitch asked.

"None." The Warhouse lips curled back, telling you how smart he was. "And certainly not one in this town."

"Let's not kid around," Mitch said. "You're coming back with me. You know that, don't you?"

The guy almost went down with the first punch. "You mean —you mean I'm being arrested?"

"What do *you* think?" Mitch said. "We know she phoned you and you met her. We know you saw her."

"But I didn't see her," Warhouse said. "She never showed up."

Mitch didn't even blink.

"How long did you wait?" he asked.

"Almost an hour. Maybe more."

"Where?"

"On the corner of Whitman and Cooper." Warhouse gasped, then put his head in his hands and said, "Oh, God!" And that was all Mitch could get out of him until they had him in the

Squad Room, with Decker leading off on the interrogation.

The guy didn't back down from that first admission. He knew he'd been tricked, but he stuck to his guns and wouldn't give another inch. He said Bella had called him around midnight and said she must see him. He hadn't known she was in town, didn't want to see her, had no interest in her, but he couldn't turn her down. So he went, and he waited. And waited and waited. And then went home.

They kept hammering away at him. First Mitch and Decker, then Bankhart and Balenky, then Mitch and Decker again.

In between they consulted Jub. He'd been examining Warhouse's car for soil that might match samples from French Woods for evidence of a struggle, of Bella's presence—of anything at all. The examination drew a blank. Warhouse grinned his toothy grin and kept saying no. And late that night they gave up on him, brought him across the courtyard to the city jail, and left him there for the night. He needed sleep—and so did the Homicide Squad.

At the conference the next morning, Decker was grim. "We have an ex-wife calling her ex-husband at midnight and making an appointment; we have his statement that he went and she never showed up; and we have a homicide and that's all."

"The dough," Bankhart said.

Decker nodded. "When we find that seventeen hundred, then we might have a case. We'll get warrants and we'll look for it, but let's assume we draw another blank. Then what?"

"Let's have another session with Ed Hiller," Mitch said.

They had it, and they had a longer one with Warhouse, and they were still nowhere. They'd gone into the Warhouse background thoroughly. He earned good money, paid his bills promptly, and got along well with his second wife. He liked women, they went for him, and he was a humdinger with them, although he was not involved in any scandal. But in Mitch's book, he'd humdinged once too often. Still, you had to prove it.

For a while they concentrated on The Happy Inn. But the motel guests either couldn't be found, because they'd registered under fake names with fake license numbers, or else they said they'd been asleep and had no idea what was going on outside.

The usual tips came in—crank stuff that had to be followed

up. The killer had been seen, somebody had heard Bella scream for help, somebody else had had a vision. Warhouse had been spotted waiting on the corner, which proved nothing except he'd arrived there first. Every tip checked out either as useless or a phony. The missing $1,700 didn't show up. Decker ran out of jokes, and Mitch came home tired and irritable.

The case was at full stop.

Then Decker had this wild idea, and he told it to Jub and Mitch. "My wife says I woke up last night and asked for a drink of water, and I don't even remember it."

"So you were thirsty," Mitch remarked.

"Don't you get it?" Decker exclaimed. "People wake up, then go back to sleep, and in the morning they don't even know they were awake. Well, we know Bella packed her bag, and she was in that motel room with Prudence and must have made some noise and possibly even talked. I'll bet a pair of pink panties that Prudence woke up and then forgot all about it. She has a clue buried deep in her mind."

"Granted," Jub said, "but how are you going to dig it up?"

"I'll hypnotize her," Decker said, with fire in his eyes. "I'll ask a psychiatrist to get her to free-associate. Taylor, ask her to come in tomorrow morning, when my mind is fresh. And hers, too."

Mitch dropped in on Prudence and gave her the message, but the way he saw things, the lieutenant was sure reaching for it —far out. Mitch told Amy about this screwy idea of Decker's, but all she said was that tomorrow was payday and not to forget to send the fifty dollars to her sister.

That was why Mitch wasn't around when Prudence showed up. He took his money over to the post office and there, on account he liked to jaw a little, make friends, set up contacts— you never knew when you might need them—he got to gabbing with the postal clerk.

His name was Cornell and he was tired. Mitch figured the guy was born that way. Besides, there was something about a post office that dragged at you. No fun in it, nothing ever happened. All the stamps were the same (or looked the same) and all the clerks were the same (or looked the same) and if anything unusual came up, you checked it in the regulations and did what the rules said, exactly. And if the rules didn't tell you, then the thing couldn't be done, so you sent the customer away and went back to selling stamps.

Which people either wanted or they didn't. There were no sales, no bargains. A damaged stamp was never marked down —it was worth what it said on its face or nothing. There was nothing in between.

Still, the post office was a hell of a lot better than what Decker was doing over at the Homicide Squad, so Mitch handed in his fifty bucks for the money order and said, "It's not much dough, I guess. What's the most you ever handled?"

The clerk came alive. "Ten thousand dollars. Six years ago."

"The hell with six years ago. Say this week."

"Oh. That dame with seventeen hundred dollars. That was the biggest."

Click.

Mitch said cautiously, "You mean Prudence Gilford?"

"No. Patsy Grant."

"P.G.—same thing," Mitch said with certainty. "Same girl. And I'll bet she sent the dough to herself care of General Delivery, somewhere in California."

Cornell looked as if he thought Mitch were some kind of magician. "That's right," he said. "How did you know?"

"Me?" Mitch said, seeing that it all fitted like a glove. Prudence—or whatever her name was—had strangled Bella for the dough, then packed Bella's bag, dragged her out to the car, driven it to the woods, and left it there. And probably walked all the way back. That's why Prudence had been so tired.

"Me?" Mitch said again, riding on a cloud. "I know those things. That's what makes me a cop. Ideas—I got bushels of 'em." He thought of how the lieutenant would go bug-eyed. Mitch Taylor, Homicide Expert.

He walked over to the phone booth, gave his shield number to the operator so he could make the call free and save himself a dime, and got through to the Homicide Squad.

Decker answered. "Taylor?" he said. "Come on back. The Gilford dame just confessed."

"She—*what?*"

"Yeah, yeah, confessed. While she was in here, the strap on her bag broke and she dropped it. Everything fell out—including seventeen money-order receipts for a hundred bucks apiece. We had her cold and she confessed. She knew all about Warhouse and planned it so we'd nail him."

There was a buzz on the wire and Lieutenant Decker's voice went fuzzy.

"Taylor," he said after a couple of seconds. "Can you hear me? Are you listening?"

"Sure," Mitch said. "But what for?"

And he hung up.

Yeah, Mitch Taylor, Homicide Expert.

1966:

The Chosen One

Rhys Davies

A letter, inscribed "By Hand," lay inside the door when he arrived home just before seven o'clock. The thick, expensive-looking envelope was black-edged and smelled of stale face powder. Hoarding old-fashioned mourning envelopes would be typical of Mrs. Vines, and the premonition of disaster Rufus felt now had nothing to do with death. He stared for some moments at the penny-sized blob of purple wax sealing the flap. Other communications he had received from Mrs. Vines over the last two years had not been sent in such a ceremonious envelope. The sheet of ruled paper inside, torn from a pad of the cheapest kind, was more familiar. He read it with strained concentration, his brows drawn into a pucker. The finely traced handwriting, in green ink, gave him no special difficulty, and his pausings over words such as "oral," "category," and "sentimental," while his full-fleshed lips shaped the syllables, came from uncertainty of their meaning.

Sir,
In reply to your oral request to me yesterday, concerning the property Brychan Cottage, I have decided not to grant you a renewal of the lease, due to expire on June 30th next. This is final.

The cottage is unfit for human habitation, whether you consider yourself as coming under that category or not. It is an eyesore to me, and I intend razing it to the ground later this year. That you wish to get married and continue to live in the cottage with some factory hussy from the town is no affair of mine, and that my father, for sentimental reasons, granted your grandfather a seventy-five year lease for the paltry sum of a hundred pounds is no affair of mine, either. Your wretched family has always been a nuisance to me on my estate, and I will not tolerate one of them to infest it any longer than is legal, or any screeching, jazz-dancing slut in trousers and bare feet to trespass and contaminate my land. Although you got rid of the pestiferous poultry after your mother died, the noise of the motorcycle you then bought has annoyed me even more than the cockerel crowing. Get out.

Yours truly,
Audrey P. Vines

He saw her brown-speckled, jewel-ringed hand moving from word to word with a certainty beyond any means of retaliation from him. The abuse in the letter did not enrage him immediately; it belonged too familiarly to Mrs. Vines' character and reputation, though when he was a boy he had known different behavior from her. But awareness that she had this devilish right to throw him, neck and crop, from the home he had inherited began to register somewhere in his mind at last. He had never believed she would do it.

Shock temporarily suspended full realization of the catastrophe. He went into the kitchen to brew the tea he always made as soon as he arrived home on his motorbike from his factory job in the county town. While he waited for the kettle to boil on the oilstove, his eye kept straying warily to the table. The black-edged envelope was like something in a warning dream. He stared vaguely at the familiar objects around him. A peculiar silence seemed to have come to this kitchen that he had known all his life. There was a feel of withdrawal from him in the room, as though he was already an intruder in it.

He winced when he picked up the letter and put it in a pocket of his leather jacket. Then, as was his habit on fine evenings, he took a mug of tea out to a seat under a pear tree shading the ill-fitting front door of the cottage, a whitewashed, sixteenth-century building in which he had been born. Golden light of May flooded the well-stocked garden. He began to re-

read the letter, stopped to fetch a tattered little dictionary from the living room, and sat consulting one or two words that still perplexed him. Then, his thick jaw thrust out in his effort at sustained concentration, he read the letter through again.

The sentence "This is final" pounded in his head. Three words had smashed his plans for the future. In his bewilderment, it did not occur to him that his inbred procrastination was of importance. Until the day before, he had kept postponing going to see the evil-tempered mistress of Plas Iolyn about the lease business, though his mother, who couldn't bear the sight of her, had reminded him of it several times in her last illness. He had just refused to believe that Mrs. Vines would turn him out when a date in a yellowed old document came round. His mother's forebears had occupied Brychan Cottage for hundreds of years, long before Mrs. Vines' family bought Plas Iolyn.

Slowly turning his head, as though in compulsion, he gazed to the left of where he sat. He could see, beyond the garden and the alders fringing a ditch, an extensive slope of rough turf on which, centrally in his vision, a great cypress spread branches to the ground. Higher, crowning the slope, a rectangular mansion of russet stone caught the full light of sunset. At this hour, he had sometimes seen Mrs. Vines walking down the slope with her bulldog. She always carried a bag, throwing bread from it to birds and to wild duck on the river below. The tapestry bag had been familiar to him since he was a boy, but it was not until last Sunday that he learned she kept binoculars in it.

She could not be seen anywhere this evening. He sat thinking of last Sunday's events, unable to understand that such a small mistake as his girl had made could have caused the nastiness in the letter. Gloria had only trespassed a few yards on Plas Iolyn land. And what was wrong with a girl wearing trousers or walking barefoot on clean grass? What harm was there if a girl he was courting screeched when he chased her onto the riverbank and if they tumbled to the ground? Nobody's clothes had come off.

He had thought Sunday was the champion day of his life. He had fetched Gloria from the town on his motorbike in the afternoon. It was her first visit to the cottage that he had boasted about so often in the factory, especially to her. Brought up in a poky terrace house without a garden, she had been pleased and excited with his pretty home on the Plas Iolyn estate, and in half an hour, while they sat under this pear tree, he had asked her to marry him, and she said she would. She had laughed and squealed a lot in the garden and by the river, kicking her shoes off, dancing on the grassy riverbank; she was only eighteen. Then, when he went indoors to put the kettle on for tea, she had jumped the narrow dividing ditch onto Mrs. Vines' land—and soon after came dashing into the cottage. Shaking with fright, she said that a terrible woman in a torn fur coat had come shouting from under a big tree on the slope, spyglasses in her hand and threatening her with a bulldog. It took quite a while to calm Gloria down. He told her of Mrs. Vines' funny ways and the tales he had heard from his mother. But neither on Sunday nor since did he mention anything about the lease of Brychan Cottage, though remembrance of it had crossed his mind when Gloria said she'd marry him.

On Sunday, too, he had kept telling himself that he ought to ride up to the mansion to explain about the stranger who had ignorantly crossed the ditch. But three days went by before he made the visit. He had bought a high-priced suède windcheater in the town, and got his hair trimmed during his dinner hour. He had even picked a bunch of polyanthus for Mrs. Vines when he arrived home from the factory—and then, bothered by wanting to postpone the visit still longer, forgot them when he forced himself at last to jump on the bike. It was her tongue he was frightened of, he had told himself. He could never cope with women's tantrums.

But she had not seemed to be in one of her famous tempers when he appeared at the kitchen door of Plas Iolyn, just after seven. "Well, young man, what do you require?" she asked, pointing to a carpenter's bench, alongside the dresser, on which he had often sat as a boy. First, he tried to tell her that the girl who strayed on her land was going to marry him. But Mrs. Vines talked to the five cats that, one after the other, bounded into the kitchen from upstairs a minute after he arrived. She said to them, "We won't have these loud-voiced factory girls trespassing on any part of my property, will we, my darlings?" Taking her time, she fed the cats with liver she lifted with her fingers from a pan on one of her three small oilstoves. Presently, he forced himself to say, "I've come about the lease of Brychan

Cottage. My mother told me about it. I've got a paper with a date on it." But Mrs. Vines said to one of the cats, "Queenie, you'll have to swallow a pill tomorrow!" After another wait, he tried again, saying, "My young lady is liking Brychan Cottage very much." Mrs. Vines stared at him, not saying a word for about a minute, then said, "You can go now. I will write you tomorrow about the lease."

He had left the kitchen feeling a tightness beginning to throttle him, and he knew then that it had never been fear he felt toward her. But, as he tore at full speed down the drive, the thought came that it might have been a bad mistake to have stopped going to Plas Iolyn to ask if he could collect whinberries for her up on the slopes of Mynydd Baer, or find mushrooms in the Caer Tegid fields, as he used to do before he took a job in a factory in the town. Was that why, soon after his mother died, she had sent him a rude letter about the smell of poultry and the rooster crowing? He had found that letter comic and shown it to chaps in the factory. But something had told him to get rid of the poultry.

He got up from the seat under the pear tree. The strange quiet he had noticed in the kitchen was in the garden, too. Not a leaf or bird stirred. He could hear his heart thumping. He began to walk up and down the paths. He knew now the full meaning of her remark to those cats that no trespassers would be allowed on "my property." In about six months he himself would be a trespasser. He stopped to tear a branch of pear blossom from the tree, and looked at it abstractly. The pear tree was *his!* His mother had told him it was planted on the day he was born. Some summers it used to fruit so well that they had sold the whole load to Harries in the town, and the money was always for him.

Pacing, he slapped the branch against his leg, scattering the blossom. The tumult in his heart did not diminish. Like the kitchen, the garden seemed already to be withdrawn from his keeping. *She* had walked there that day, tainting it. He hurled the branch in the direction of the Plas Iolyn slope. He did not want to go indoors. He went through a thicket of willows and lay on the riverbank staring into the clear, placidly flowing water. Her face flickered in the greenish depths. He flung a stone at it. Stress coiled tighter in him. He lay flat on his back, sweating, a hand clenched over his genitals.

The arc of serene evening sky and the whisper of gently lapping water calmed him for a while. A shred of common sense told him that the loss of Brychan Cottage was not a matter of life and death. But he could not forget Mrs. Vines. He tried to think how he could appease her with some act or service. He remembered that until he was about seventeen she would ask him to do odd jobs for her, such as clearing fallen branches, setting fire to wasp holes, and—she made him wear a bonnet and veil for this—collecting the combs from her beehives. But what could he do now? She had shut herself away from everybody for years.

He could not shake off thought of her. Half-forgotten memories of the past came back. When he was about twelve, how surprised his mother had been when he told her that he had been taken upstairs in Plas Iolyn and shown six kittens born that day! Soon after that, Mrs. Vines had come down to this bank, where he had sat fishing, and said she wanted him to drown three of the kittens. She had a tub of water ready outside her kitchen door, and she stood watching while he held a wriggling canvas sack under the water with a broom. The three were males, she said. He had to dig a hole close to the greenhouses for the sack.

She never gave him money for any job, only presents from the house—an old magic lantern, colored slides, dominoes, a box of crayons, even a doll's house. Her big brown eyes would look at him without any sign of temper at all. Once, when she asked him, "Are you a dunce in school?" and he said, "Yes, bottom of the class," he heard her laugh aloud for the first time, and she looked very pleased with him. All that, he remembered, was when visitors had stopped going to Plas Iolyn, and there was not a servant left; his mother said they wouldn't put up with Mrs. Vines' bad ways any more. But people in the town who had worked for her said she was a very clever woman, with letters after her name, and it was likely she would always come out on top in disputes concerning her estate.

Other scraps of her history returned to his memory—things heard from old people who had known her before she shut herself away. Even Matthews, who used to be her estate keeper and had been a friend of his father's, said that for a time she had lived among African savages, studying their ways with her first husband. Nobody knew how she had got rid of that husband, or the whole truth about her second one. She used to disappear from Plas Iolyn for months, but when her father died she never went away from her old home again. But it was when her second husband was no longer seen in Plas Iolyn that she shut herself up there, except that once a month she hired a Daimler from the county town and went to buy, so it was said, cases of wine at Drapple's, and stuff for her face at the chemist's. Then even those trips had stopped, and everything was delivered to Plas Iolyn by tradesmen's vans or post.

No clue came of a way to appease her. He rose from the riverbank. The sunset light was beginning to fade, but he could still see clearly the mansion façade, its twelve bare windows, and the crumbling entrance portico, which was never used now. In sudden compulsion, he strode down to the narrow, weed-filled ditch marking the boundary of Brychan Cottage land. But he drew up at its edge. If he went to see her, he thought, he must prepare what he had to say with a cooler head than he had now. Besides, to approach the mansion that way was forbidden. She might be watching him through binoculars from one of those windows.

An ambling sound roused him from this torment of indecision. Fifty yards beyond the river's opposite bank, the 7:40 slow train to the county town was approaching. Its passage over the rough stretches of meadowland brought back a reminder of his mother's bitter grudge against the family at Plas Iolyn. The trickery that had been done before the railroad was laid had never meant much to him, though he had heard about it often enough from his mother. Late in the nineteenth century, her father, who couldn't read or write, had been persuaded by Mrs. Vines' father to sell to him, at a low price, not only decaying Brychan Cottage but, across the river, a great many acres of useless meadowland included in the cottage demesne. As a bait, a seventy-five-year retaining lease of the cottage and a piece of land to the riverbank were granted for a hundred pounds. So there had been some money to stave off further dilapidation of the cottage and to put by for hard times. But in less than two years after the transaction, a railroad loop to a developing port in the west had been laid over that long stretch of useless land across the river. Mrs. Vines' father had known of the project and, according to the never-forgotten grudge, cleared a big profit from rail rights. His explanation (alleged by Rufus's mother to be humbug) was that he had wanted to preserve the view from possible ruination by buildings such as gasworks; a few trains every day, including important expresses and freight traffic, did not matter.

Watching, with a belligerent scowl, the 7:40 vanishing into the sunset fume, Rufus remembered that his father used to say that it wasn't Mrs. Vines herself who had done the dirty trick. But was the daughter proving herself to be of the same robbing nature now? He could not believe that she intended razing Brychan Cottage to the ground. Did she want to trim it up and sell or rent at a price she knew he could never afford? But she had plenty of money already—everybody knew that. Was it only that she wanted him out of sight, the last member of his family, and the last man on the estate?

He strode back to the cottage with the quick step of a man reaching a decision. Yet when he entered the dusky, low-ceilinged living room the paralysis of will threatened him again. He stood gazing round at the age-darkened furniture, the steel and copper accoutrements of the cavernous fireplace, the ornaments, the dim engravings of mountains, castles, and waterfalls as though he viewed them for the first time. He could not light the oil lamp, could not prepare a meal, begin his evening routine. A superstitious dread assailed him. Another presence was in possession here.

He shook the spell off. In the crimson glow remaining at the deep window, he read the letter once more, searching for some hint of a loophole. There seemed none. But awareness of a challenge penetrated his mind. For the first time since the death of his parents an important event was his to deal with alone. He lit the lamp, found a seldom used stationery compendium, and sat down. He did not get beyond "Dear Maddam, Supprised to receive your letter . . ." Instinct told him he must wheedle Mrs. Vines. But in what way? After half an hour of defeat, he dashed upstairs, ran down naked to the kitchen to wash at the sink, and returned upstairs to rub scented oil into his tough black hair and dress in the new cotton trousers and elegant windcheater of green suède that had cost him more than a week's wages.

Audrey Vines put her binoculars into her tapestry bag when Rufus entered Brychan Cottage and, her uninterested old bulldog at her heels, stepped out to the slope from between a brace of low-sweeping cypress branches. After concealing herself under the massive tree minutes before the noise of Rufus's motorcycle had come, as usual, a few minutes before seven, she had studied his face and followed his prowlings about the garden and riverbank for nearly an hour. The clear views of him this evening had been particularly satisfactory. She knew it was a dictionary he had consulted under the pear tree, where he often sat drinking from a large Victorian mug. The furious hurling of a branch in the direction of the cypress had pleased her; his stress when he paced the garden had been as rewarding as his stupefied reading of the deliberately perplexing phraseology of her letter.

"Come along, Mia. *Good* little darling! We are going in now."

Paused on the slope in musing, the corpulent bitch grunted, blinked, and followed with a faint trace of former briskness in her bandily aged waddle. Audrey Vines climbed without any breathlessness herself, her pertinacious gaze examining the distances to right and left. She came out every evening not only to feed birds but to scrutinize her estate before settling down for the night. There was also the passage of the 7:40 train to see; since her two watches and every clock in the house needed repairs, it gave verification of the exact time, though this, like the bird feeding, was not really of account to her.

It was her glimpses of Rufus that provided her long day with most interest. For some years she had regularly watched him through the powerful Zeiss binoculars from various concealed spots. He renewed an interest in studies begun during long-ago travels in countries far from Wales, and she often jotted her findings into a household-accounts book kept locked in an old portable escritoire. To her eye, the prognathous jaw, broad nose, and gypsy-black hair of this heavy-bodied but personable young man bore distinct atavistic elements. He possessed, too, a primitive bloom, which often lingered for years beyond adolescence with persons of tardy mental development. But this throwback descendant of an ancient race was also, up to a point, a triumph over decadence. Arriving miraculously late in his mother's life, after three others born much earlier to the illiterate woman had died in infancy, this last-moment child had flourished physically, if not in other respects.

Except for the occasions when, as a boy and youth, he used to come to Plas Iolyn to do odd jobs and run errands, her deductions had been formed entirely through the limited and intensifying medium of the binoculars. She had come to know all his outdoor habits and activities around the cottage. These were rewarding only occasionally. The days when she failed to see him seemed bleakly deficient of incident. While daylight lasted, he never bathed in the river without her knowledge, though sometimes, among the willows and reeds, he was as elusive as an otter. And winter, of course, kept him indoors a great deal.

"Come, darling. There'll be a visitor for us tonight."

Mia, her little question-mark tail unexpectedly quivering, glanced up with the vaguely deprecating look of her breed. Audrey Vines had reached the balustraded front terrace. She paused by a broken sundial for a final look round at the spread of tranquil uplands and dim woods afar, the silent river and deserted meadows below, and, lingeringly, at the ancient trees shading her estate. Mild and windless though the evening was, she wore a long, draggled coat of brown-dyed ermine and, pinned securely on skeins of vigorous hair unskillfully home-dyed to auburn tints, a winged hat of tobacco-gold velvet. These, with her thick bistre face powder and assertive eye pencilling, gave her the look of an uncompromisingly womanly woman in an old-style sepia photograph, a woman halted forever in the dead past. But there was no evidence of waning powers in either her demeanor or her step as she continued to the side terrace. A woman of leisure ignoring time's urgencies, she suggested only an unruffled unity with the day's slow descent into twilight.

The outward calm was deceptive. A watchful gleam in her eyes was always there, and the binoculars were carried for a reason additional to her study of Rufus. She was ever on the lookout for trespassers and poachers or tramps on the estate, rare though such were. When, perhaps three or four times a year, she discovered a stray culprit, the mature repose would disappear in a flash, her step accelerate, her throaty voice lash out. Tradesmen arriving legitimately at her kitchen door avoided looking her straight in the eye, and C. W. Powell, her solicitor, knew exactly how far he could go in sociabilities during his quarterly conferences with her in the kitchen of Plas Iolyn. Deep within those dissociated eyes lay an adamantine refusal to acknowledge the existence of any friendly approach. Only her animals could soften that repudiation.

"Poor Mia! We won't stay out so long tomorrow, I promise! Come along." They had reached the unbalustraded side terrace. "A flower for us tonight, sweetheart, then we'll go in," she murmured.

She crossed the cobbled yard behind the mansion. Close to disused greenhouses, inside which overturned flowerpots and abandoned garden tools lay under tangles of grossly overgrown plants sprouting to the broken roofing, there was a single border of wallflowers, primulas, and several well-pruned rosebushes in generous bud. It was the only evidence in all the Plas Iolyn domain of her almost defunct passion for flower cultivation. One pure white rose, an early herald of summer plenty, had begun to unfold that mild day; she had noticed it when she came out. Raindrops from a morning shower sprinkled onto her wrist as she plucked this sprightly first bloom, and she smiled as she inhaled the secret odor within. Holding the flower aloft like a trophy, she proceeded to the kitchen entrance with the same composed gait. There was all the time in the world.

Dusk had come into the spacious kitchen. But there was sufficient light for her activities from the curtainless bay window overlooking the yard and the flower border in which, long ago, Mia's much loved predecessor had been buried. Candles were not lit until it was strictly necessary. She fumbled among a jumble of oddments in one of the two gloomy little pantries lying off the kitchen, and came out with a cone-shaped silver vase.

Light pattering sounds came from beyond an open inner door, where an uncarpeted back staircase lay, and five cats came bounding down from the first-floor drawing room. Each a ginger tabby of almost identical aspect, they whisked, mewing, around their mistress, tails up.

"Yes, yes, my darlings," she said. "Your saucers in a moment." She crossed to a sink of blackened stone, humming to herself.

A monster Edwardian cooking range stood derelict in a chimneyed alcove, with three portable oilstoves before it holding a covered frying pan, an iron stewpan, and a tin kettle. Stately dinner crockery and a variety of canisters and tinned foodstuff packed the shelves of a huge dresser built into the back wall. A long table stretching down the center of the kitchen was even more crowded. It held half a dozen bulging paper satchels, biscuit tins, piles of unwashed plates and saucers, two stacks of the *Geographical Magazine,* the skull of a sheep, heaped vegetable peelings, an old wooden coffee grinder, a leatherette hatbox, a Tunisian bird cage used for storing meat, several ribboned chocolate boxes crammed with letters, and a traveler's escritoire of rosewood. On the end near the oilstoves, under a three-branched candelabra of heavy Sheffield plate encrusted with carved vine leaves and grapes, a reasonably fresh cloth of fine lace was laid with silver cutlery, a condiment set of polished silver, a crystal wine goblet, and a neatly folded linen napkin. A boudoir chair of gilded wood stood before this end of the table.

When the cold-water tap was turned at the sink, a rattle sounded afar in the house and ended in a groaning cough—a companionable sound, which Mrs. Vines much liked. She continued to hum as she placed the rose in the vase, set it below the handsome candelabra, and stepped back to admire the effect. Pulling out a pair of long, jet-headed pins, she took off her opulent velvet hat.

"He's a stupid lout, isn't he, Queenie?" The eldest cat, her favorite, had leaped on the table. "Thinking he was going to bed that chit down here and breed like rabbits!"

She gave the cats their separate saucers of liver, chopped from cold slices taken from the frying pan. Queenie was served first. The bulldog waited for her dish of beef chunks from the stewpan, and, given them, stood morosely for a minute, as if counting the pieces. Finally, Audrey Vines took for herself a remaining portion of liver and a slice of bread from a loaf on the dresser, and fetched a half bottle of champagne from a capacious oak chest placed between the two pantries. She removed her fur coat before she settled on the frail boudoir chair and shook out her napkin.

Several of these meager snacks were taken every day, the last just after the 11:15 night express rocked away to the port in the west. Now, her excellent teeth masticating with barely perceptible movements, she ate with fastidious care. The bluish light filtering through the grimy bay window soon thickened, but still she did not light the three candles. Her snack finished, and the last drop of champagne taken with a sweet biscuit, she continued to sit at the table, her oil-stained tea gown of beige chiffon ethereal in the dimness.

She became an unmoving shadow. A disciplined meditation or a religious exercise might have been engaging her. Mia, also an immobile smudge, lay fast asleep on a strip of coconut matting beside the gilt chair. The five cats, tails down, had returned upstairs immediately after their meal, going one after the other as though in strict etiquette, or like a file of replete orphans. Each had a mahogany cradle in the drawing room, constructed to their mistress's specifications by an aged craftsman who had once been employed at Plas Iolyn.

She stirred for a minute from the reverie, but her murmuring scarcely disturbed the silence. Turning her head in mechanical habit to where Mia lay, she asked, "Was it last January the river froze for a fortnight? . . . No, not last winter. But there were gales, weren't there? Floods of rain. . . . Which winter did I burn the chairs to keep us warm? That idiotic oilman didn't come. Then the candles and matches gave out, and I used the electricity. One of Queenie's daughters died that winter. It was the year he went to work in a factory."

Time had long ago ceased to have calendar meaning in her life; a dozen years were as one. But lately she had begun to be obsessed by dread of another severe winter. Winters seemed to have become colder and longer. She dreaded the deeper hibernation they enforced. Springs were intolerably long in coming, postponing the time when her child of nature became constantly visible again, busy under his flowering trees and splashing in the river. His reliable appearances brought back flickers of interest in the world; in comparison, intruders on the estate, the arrival of tradesmen, or the visits of her solicitor were becoming of little consequence.

She lapsed back into silence. The kitchen was almost invisible when, swiftly alert, she turned her head toward the indigo blue of the bay window. A throbbing sound had come from far away. It mounted to a series of kicking spurts, roared, and became a loudly tearing rhythm. She rose from her chair and fumbled for a box of matches on the table. But the rhythmic sound began to dwindle, and her hand remained over the box. The sound floated away.

She sank back on the chair. "Not now, darling!" she told the drowsily shifting dog. "Later, later."

The headlamp beam flashed past the high entrance gates to Plas Iolyn, but Rufus did not even glance at them. They were wide open and, he knew, would remain open all night. He had long ceased to wonder about this. Some people said Mrs. Vines wanted to trap strangers inside, so that she could enjoy frightening them when they were nabbed, but other townsfolk thought that the gates had been kept open for years because she was always expecting her second husband to come back.

At top speed, his Riley could reach the town in less than ten minutes. The fir-darkened road was deserted. No cottage or house bordered it for five miles. A roadside farmstead had become derelict, but in a long vale quietly ascending toward the mountain range some families still continued with reduced sheep farming. Rufus knew them all. His father had worked at one of the farms before the decline in agricultural prosperity set in. From the outskirts of the hilly town he could see an illuminated clock in the Assembly Hall tower. It was half past nine. He did not slow down. Avoiding the town center, he tore past the pens of a disused cattle market, a recently built confectionery factory, a nineteenth-century Nonconformist chapel, which had become a furniture depository, then past a row of cottages remaining from days when the town profited from rich milk and tough flannel woven at riverside mills. Farther round the town's lower folds, he turned into an area of diminutive back-to-back dwellings, their fronts ranging direct along narrow pavements.

Nobody was visible in these gaslit streets. He stopped at one of the terraces, walked to a door, and, without knocking, turned its brass knob. The door opened into a living room, though a sort of entrance lobby was formed by a chenille curtain and an upturned painted drainpipe used for umbrellas. Voices came from beyond the curtain. But only Gloria's twelve-year-old brother sat in the darkened room, watching television from a plump easy chair. His spectacles flashed up at the interrupting visitor.

"Gone to the pictures with Mum." The boy's attention returned impatiently to the dramatic serial. "Won't be back till long after ten."

Rufus sat down behind the boy and gazed unseeingly at the screen. A feeling of relief came to him. He knew now that he didn't want to show the letter to Gloria tonight, or tell her anything about the lease of Brychan Cottage. Besides, she mustn't read those nasty insults about her in the letter. He asked himself why he had come there, so hastily. Why hadn't he gone to Plas Iolyn? Mrs. Vines might give way. Then he needn't mention anything at all to Gloria. If he told her about the letter tonight, it would make him look a shifty cheat. She would ask why he hadn't told her about the lease before.

He began to sweat. The close-packed little room was warm and airless. Gloria's two married sisters lived in poky terrace houses just like this one, and he became certain that it was sight of Brychan Cottage and its garden last Sunday that convinced her to marry him. Before Sunday, she had always been a bit offhand, pouting if he said too much about the future. Although she could giggle and squeal a lot, she could wrinkle up her nose, too, and flounce away if any chap tried any fancy stuff on her in the factory recreation room. He saw her little feet skipping and running fast as a deer's.

The torment was coming back. This room, instead of bringing Gloria closer to him, made her seem farther off. He kept seeing her on the run. She was screeching as she ran. That loud screech of hers! He had never really liked it. It made his blood go cold, though a chap in the factory said that screeches like that were only a sign that a girl was a virgin and that they disappeared afterward. Why was he hearing them now? Then he remembered that one of Mrs. Vines' insults was about the screeching.

His fingers trembled when he lit a cigaret. He sat a little while longer, telling himself he ought to have gone begging to Plas Iolyn and promised to do anything if he could keep the cottage. He would work on the estate evenings and weekends for no money; a lot of jobs needed doing there. He'd offer to pay a good rent for the cottage, too. But what he ought to get before going there, he thought further, was advice from someone who had known Mrs. Vines well. He peered at his watch and got up.

"Tell Gloria I thought she'd like to go for a ride on the bike. I won't come back tonight."

"You'll be seeing her in the factory tomorrow," the boy pointed out.

It was only a minute up to the town center. After parking the bike behind the Assembly Hall, Rufus crossed the quiet market square to a timbered old inn at the corner of Einon's Dip. He had remembered that Evan Matthews often went in there on his way to his night job at the reservoir. Sometimes they'd had a quick drink together.

Thursdays were quiet nights in pubs; so far, there were only five customers in the cozily rambling main bar. Instead of his usual beer, he ordered a double whisky, and asked Gwyneth, the elderly barmaid, if Evan Matthews had been in. She said that if he came in at all it would be about that time. Rufus took his glass over to a table beside the fireless inglenook. He didn't know the two fellows playing darts. An English-looking commercial traveler in a bowler sat at a table scribbling in a notebook. Councillor Llew Pryce stood talking in Welsh to Gwyneth at the counter, and, sitting at a table across the bar from himself, the woman called Joanie was reading the local newspaper.

Staring at his unwatered whisky, he tried to decide whether to go to Evan's home in Mostyn Street. No, he'd wait a while here. He wanted more time to think. How could Evan help, after all? A couple of drinks—that's what he needed now. Empty glass in hand, he looked up. Joanie was laying her newspaper down. A blue flower decorated her white felt hat, and there was a bright cherry in her small wineglass.

He watched, in a fascination like relief, as she bit the cherry from its stick and chewed with easy enjoyment. She'd be about thirty-five, he judged. She was a Saturday-night regular, but he had seen her in the Drovers on other nights, and she didn't lack company as a rule. He knew of her only from tales and jokes by chaps in the factory. Someone had said she'd come from Bristol, with a man supposed to be her husband, who had disappeared when they'd both worked in the slab-cake factory for a few months.

Joanie looked at him, and picked up her paper. He wondered if she was waiting for someone. If Evan didn't come in, could he talk to her about his trouble, ask her the best way to handle a bad-tempered old moneybags? She looked experienced and good-hearted, a woman with no lumps in her nature. He could show her the letter; being a newcomer to the town, she wouldn't know who Mrs. Vines was.

He rose to get another double whisky but couldn't make up his mind to stop at Joanie's table or venture a passing nod. He stayed at the counter finishing his second double, and he was still there when Evan came in. He bought Evan a pint of bitter, a single whisky for himself, and, Joanie forgotten, led Evan to the inglenook table.

"Had a knockout when I got home this evening." He took the black-edged envelope from a pocket of his windcheater.

Evan Matthews read the letter. A sinewy and well-preserved man, he looked about fifty and was approaching sixty; when Mrs. Vines had hired him as estate keeper and herdsman, he had been under forty. He grinned as he handed the letter back, saying. "She's got you properly skewered, boyo! I warned your dad she'd do it when the lease was up."

"What's the reason for it? Brychan Cottage isn't unfit for living in, like she says—there's only a bit of dry rot in the floor boards. I've never done her any harm.

"No harm, except that you're a man now."

Uncomprehending, Rufus scowled. "She used to like me. Gave me presents. Is it more money she's after?"

"She isn't after money. Audrey P. Vines was open-fisted with cash—I'll say that for her. No, she just hates the lot of us."

"Men, you mean?"

"The whole bunch of us get her dander up." Recollection lit Evan's eyes. "She gave me cracks across the head with a riding crop that she always carried in those days. I'd been working hard at Plas Iolyn for five years when I got my lot from her."

"Cracks across the head?" Rufus said, sidetracked.

"She drew blood. I told your dad about it. He said I ought to prosecute her for assault. But when she did it I felt sorry for her, and she knew it. It made her boil the more."

"What'd you done?"

"We were in the cowshed. She used to keep a fine herd of Jerseys, and she blamed the death of a calving one on me— began raging that I was clumsy pulling the calf out, which I'd been obliged to do." Evan shook his head. "It wasn't *that* got her flaring. But she took advantage of it and gave me three or four lashes with the crop. I just stood looking at her. I could see she wanted me to hit back and have a proper set-to. Of course, I was much younger then, and so was she! But I only said, 'You and I must part, Mrs. Vines.' She lifted that top lip of hers, like a vixen done out of a fowl—I can see her now—and went from the shed without a word. I packed up that day. Same as her second husband had walked out on her a couple of years before —the one that played a violin."

"You mean . . ." Rufus blurted, after a pause of astonishment. "You mean, you'd *been* with her?"

Evan chuckled. "Now, I didn't say that!"

"What's the *matter* with the woman?" Rufus exclaimed. The mystery of Mrs. Vines' attack on himself was no clearer.

"There's women that turn themselves into royalty," Evan said. "They get it into their heads they rule the world. People who knew little Audrey's father used to say he spoiled her up to the hilt because her mother died young. He only had one child. They traveled a lot together when she was a girl, going into savage parts, and afterward she always had a taste for places where there's no baptized Christians. I heard that her first husband committed suicide in Nigeria, but nobody knows for certain what happened." He took up Rufus's empty whisky glass, and pushed back his chair. "If he did something without her permission, he'd be for the crocodiles."

"I've had two doubles and a single, and I haven't had supper yet," Rufus protested. But Evan fetched him a single whisky. When it was placed before him, Rufus stubbornly asked, "What's the best thing for me to do?"

"Go and see her." Evan's face had the tenderly amused relish of one who knows that the young male must get a portion of trouble at the hands of women. "That's what she wants. I know our Audrey." He glanced again at this slow-thinking son of an old friend. "Go tonight," he urged.

"It's late to go tonight," Rufus mumbled. Sunk in rumination, he added, "She stays up late. I've seen a light in her kitchen window when I drive back over the rise after I've been out with Gloria." He swallowed the whisky at a gulp.

"If you want to keep Brychan Cottage, boyo, *act.* Night's better than daytime for seeing her. She'll have had a glass or two. Bottles still go there regularly from Jack Drapple's."

"You mean, soft-soap her?" Rufus asked with a grimace.

"No, not soft-soap. But give her what she wants." Evan thought for a moment, and added, a little more clearly, "When she starts laying into you—and she will, judging by that letter —you have a go at *her.* I wouldn't be surprised she'll respect you for it. Her and me in the cowshed was a different matter —I wasn't after anything from her. Get some clouts in on her, if you can."

Rufus shook his head slowly. "She said in the letter it was final," he said.

"Nothing is final with women, boyo. Especially what they put down in writing. They send letters like that to get a man springing up off his tail. They can't bear us to sit down quietly for long." Evan finished his beer. It was time to leave for his watchman's job at the new reservoir up at Mynydd Baer, the towering mountain from which showers thrashed down.

"Brychan Cottage belongs to me! Not to that damned old witch!" Rufus had banged the table with his fist. The dart players turned to look; Joanie lowered her paper; the commercial traveler glanced up from his notebook, took off his bowler, and laid it on the table. Gwyneth coughed and thumped a large Toby jug down warningly on the bar counter.

Evan said, "Try shouting at *her* like that—she won't mind language—but pipe down here. And don't take any more whisky."

"I'll tell her I won't budge from Brychan Cottage!" Rufus announced. "Her father cheated my grandfather over the railway—made a lot of money. She won't try to force me out. She'd be disgraced in the town."

"Audrey Vines won't care a farthing about disgrace or gossip." Evan buttoned up his black mackintosh. "I heard she used to give her second husband shocking dressings-down in front of servants and the visitors that used to go to Plas Iolyn in those days. Mr. Oswald, he was called. A touch of African tarbrush in him, and had tried playing the violin for a living." A tone of sly pleasure was in his voice. "Younger than Audrey Vines. One afternoon in Plas Iolyn, she caught him with a skivvy in the girl's bedroom top of the house, and she locked them in there for twenty-four hours. She turned the electricity off at the main, and there the two stayed without food or water all that time."

Evan took from his pocket a tasseled monkey cap of white wool, kept for his journey by motorbike into the mountains. "If you go to see her tonight, give her my love. Come to Mostyn Street tomorrow to tell me how you got on."

"What happened when the two were let out of the bedroom?"

"The skivvy had to go on her neck, of course. Mari, the housekeeper, told me that in a day or two Mrs. Vines was playing her piano to Mr. Oswald's fiddle as usual. Long duets they used to play most evenings, and visitors had to sit and listen. But it wasn't many weeks before Mr. Oswald bunked off, in the dead of night. The tale some tell that he is still shut away somewhere in the Plas Iolyn is bull." He winked at Rufus.

"I've heard she keeps the gates open all the time to welcome him back," Rufus persisted, delaying Evan still longer. It was as though he dreaded to be left alone.

"After all these years? Some people like to believe women get love on the brain. But it's true they can go sour when a man they're set on does a skedaddle from them. And when they get like that, they can go round the bend without much pushing." He rose from the table. "But I'll say this for our Audrey. After Mr. Oswald skedaddled, she shut herself up in Plas Iolyn and wasn't too much of a nuisance to people outside. Far as I know, I was the only man who had his claret tapped with that riding crop!" He drained a last swallow from his glass. "Mind, I wouldn't deny she'd like Mr. Oswald to come back, even after all these years! She'd have ways and means of finishing him off." He patted Rufus's shoulder. "In the long run it might be best if you lost Brychan Cottage."

Rufus's jaw set in sudden obstinate sullenness. "I've told

Gloria we're going to live there forever. I'm going to Plas Iolyn tonight."

When Rufus got up, a minute after Evan had left, it was with a clumsy spring; the table and glasses lurched. But his progress to the bar counter was undeviating. He drank another single whisky, bought a half bottle, which he put inside his elastic-waisted windcheater, and strode from the bar with a newly found hauteur.

She came out of her bedroom above the kitchen rather later than her usual time for going down to prepare her last meal of the day. Carrying a candleholder of Venetian glass shaped like a water lily, she did not descend by the adjacent back staircase tonight but went along a corridor and turned into another, off which lay the front drawing room. Each of the doors she passed, like every other inside the house, was wide open; a bronze statuette of a mounted hussar kept her bedroom door secure against slamming on windy nights.

She had dressed and renewed her make-up by the light of the candle, which was now a dripping stub congealed in the pretty holder. Her wide-skirted evening gown of mauve poplin had not entirely lost a crisp rustle, and on the mottled flesh of her bosom a ruby pendant shone vivaciously. Rouge, lip salve, and mascara had been applied with a prodigal hand, like the expensive scent that left whiffs in her wake. She arrayed herself in this way now and again—sometimes if she planned to sit far into the night composing letters, and always for her solicitor's arrival on the evening of quarter day, when she would give him soup and tinned crab in the kitchen.

She never failed to look into the first-floor drawing room at about eleven o'clock, to bid a goodnight to the cats. The bull-dog, aware of the custom, had preceded her mistress on this occasion and stood looking in turn at the occupants of five short-legged cradles ranged in a half circle before a gaunt and empty fireplace of gray stone. Pampered Queenie lay fast asleep on her eiderdown cushion; the other tabbies had heard the mistress approaching and sat up, stretching and giving themselves a contented lick. Blue starlight came from four tall windows, whose satin curtains were drawn back tightly into dirt-stiff folds, rigid as marble. In that quiet illumination of candle and starlight, the richly dressed woman moving from cradle to cradle, stroking and cooing a word or two, had a look of feudally assured serenity. Mia watched in pedigreed detachment; even her squashed face achieved a debonair comeliness.

"Queenie, Queenie, won't you say goodnight to me? Bowen's are sending fish tomorrow! Friday fish! Soles, darling! *Fish, fish!*"

Queenie refused to stir from her fat sleep. Presently, her ceremony performed, Audrey Vines descended by the front staircase, candle in hand, Mia stepping with equal care behind her. At the rear of the paneled hall, she passed through an archway, above which hung a Bantu initiatory mask, its orange and purple stripes dimmed under grime. A baize door in the passage beyond was kept open with an earthenware jar full of potatoes and onions. In the kitchen, she lit the three-branched candelabra from her pink-and-white holder, and blew out the stub.

This was always the hour she liked best. The last snack would be prepared with even more leisure than the earlier four or five. Tonight, she opened a tin of sardines, sliced a tomato and a hard-boiled egg, and brought from one of the dank little pantries a jar of olives, a bottle of mayonnaise, and a foil-wrapped triangle of processed cheese. While she buttered slices of bread, the distant rocking of the last train could be heard, its fading rhythm leaving behind all the unruffled calm of a windless night. She arranged half a dozen sponge fingers clockwise on a Chelsea plate, then took a half bottle of champagne from the chest, hesitated, and exchanged it for a full-sized one.

Mia had occupied herself with a prolonged examination and sniffing and scratching of her varicolored strip of matting; she might have been viewing it for the first time. Noticing that her mistress was seated, she reclined her obdurate bulk on the strip. Presently, she would be given her usual two sponge fingers dipped in champagne. She took no notice when a throbbing sound came from outside, or when it grew louder.

"Our visitor, sweetheart. I told you he'd come."

Audrey Vines, postponing the treat of her favorite brand of sardines until later, dabbed mayonnaise on a slice of egg, ate, and wiped her lips. "Don't bark!" she commanded. "There's noise enough as it is." Becoming languidly alert to the accumulating roar, Mia had got onto her bandy legs. A light flashed across the bay window. The roar ceased abruptly. Audrey Vines took a slice of bread as footsteps approached outside, and Mia, her shred of a tail faintly active, trundled to the door. A bell hanging inside had tinkled.

"Open, open!" Mrs. Vines' shout from the table was throaty, but strong and even. "Open and come in!"

Rufus paused stiffly on the threshold, his face in profile, his eyes glancing obliquely at the candlelit woman sitting at the table's far end. "I saw your lighted window," he said. The dog returned to the matting after a sniff of his shoes and a brief upward look of approval.

"Thank God I shall not be hearing the noise of that cursed motorcycle on my land much longer. Shut the door, young man, and sit over there."

He shut the door and crossed to the seat Mrs. Vines had indicated. Placed against a wall between the dresser and the inner door, it was the same rough bench on which he used to sit during happier visits long ago. He sat down and forced himself to gaze slowly down the big kitchen, his eyes ranging over the long, crowded table to the woman in her evening gown, to the single, red jewel on her bare chest, and, at last, to her painted face.

Audrey Vines went on with her meal. The silence continued. A visitor might not have been present. Rufus watched her leisurely selection of a slice of tomato and an olive, the careful unwrapping of foil from cheese. Her two diamond rings sparkled in the candlelight. He had never seen her eating, and this evidence of a normal habit both mesmerized and eased him.

"I've come about the letter."

The words out, he sat up, taut in justification of complaint. But Mrs. Vines seemed not to have heard. She sprinkled pepper and salt on the cheese, cut it into small pieces, and looked consideringly at the untouched sardines in their tin, while the disregarded visitor relapsed into silent watching. Three or four minutes passed before she spoke.

"Are you aware that I could institute a police charge against you for bathing completely naked in the river on my estate?"

It stirred him anew to a bolt-upright posture. "There's nobody to see."

She turned a speculative, heavy-lidded eye in his direction. "Then how do I know about it? Do you consider me nobody?" Yet there was no trace of malevolence as she continued. "You are almost as hairy as an ape. Perhaps you consider that is sufficient covering?" Sedate as a judge in court, she added, "But your organs are exceptionally pronounced."

"Other people don't go about with spying glasses." Anger gave his words a stinging ring.

Turning to the dog, she remarked, "An impudent defense from the hairy bather!" Mia, waiting patiently for the sponge fingers, blinked, and Audrey Vines, reaching for the tin of sardines, said, "People in the trains can see."

"I know the times of the trains."

"You have bathed like that all the summer. You walk to the river from Brychan Cottage unclothed. You did not do this when your parents were alive."

"You never sent me a letter about it."

"I delivered a letter at Brychan Cottage today. *That* covers everything."

There was another silence. Needing time to reassemble his thoughts, he watched as she carefully manipulated a sardine out of the tin with her pointed fingernails. The fish did not break. She held it aloft by its tail end to let oil drip into the tin, and regally tilted her head back and slowly lowered it whole into her mouth. The coral-red lips softly clamped about the disappearing body, drawing it in with appreciation. She chewed with fastidiously dawdling movements. Lifting another fish, she repeated the performance, her face wholly absorbed in her pleasure.

She was selecting a third sardine before Rufus spoke. "I want to go on living in Brychan Cottage," he said, slurring the words. The sardine had disappeared when he continued. "My family always lived in Brychan Cottage. It belonged to us hundreds of years before your family came to Plas Iolyn."

"You've been drinking," Audrey Vines said, looking ruminatively over the half-empty plates before her. She did not sound disapproving, but almost amiable. Rufus made no reply. After she had eaten a whole slice of bread, ridding her mouth of sardine taste, she reached for the bottle of champagne. A long time was spent untwisting wire from the cork. Her manipulating hands were gentle in the soft yellow candlelight, and in the quiet of deep country night filling the room she seemed just then an ordinary woman sitting in peace over an ordinary meal, a flower from her garden on the table, a faithful dog lying near her chair.

Making a further effort, he repeated, "My family always lived in Brychan Cottage."

"Your disagreeable mother," Audrey Vines responded, "allowed a man to take a photograph of Brychan Cottage. I had sent the creature packing when he called here. The photograph appeared in a ridiculous guidebook. Your mother knew I would *not* approve of attracting such flashy attention to my estate. My solicitor showed me the book."

Unable to deal with this accusation, he fell into headlong pleading. "I've taken care of the cottage. It's not dirty. I could put new floor boards in downstairs and change the front door. I can cook and do cleaning. The garden is tidy. I'm planning to border the paths with more fruit trees, and—"

"Why did your parents name you Rufus?" she interrupted. "You are dark as night, though your complexion is pale . . . and pitted like the moon's surface." The wire was off the cork. "I wonder were you born hairy-bodied?"

He subsided, baffled. As she eased the cork out, there was the same disregard of him. He jerked when the cork shot in his direction. She seemed to smile as the foam spurted and settled delicately in her crystal glass. She took a sip, and another, and spoke to the saliva-dropping dog.

"Your bikkies in a second. Aren't you a nice quiet little Mia! A pity *he* isn't as quiet, darling."

"Got a bottle of whisky with me. Can I take a swig?" The request came in a sudden desperate burst.

"You may."

She watched in turn while he brought the flat, half-sized bottle from inside his windcheater, unscrewed its stopper, and tilted the neck into his mouth. She took further sips of her wine. Absorbed in his own need, Rufus paused for only a moment before returning the neck to his mouth. About half the whisky had been taken when, holding the bottle at the ready between his knees, his eyes met hers across the room's length. She looked away, her lids stiffening. But confidence increased in Rufus.

He repeated, "I want to live in Brychan Cottage all my life."
"You wish to live in Brychan Cottage. I wish to raze it to the
ground." A second glass of wine was poured. "So there we are,
young man!" She wetted a sponge finger in her wine and
handed it to Mia.

"My mother said the cottage and land belonged to us forever
at one time. Your father cheated us out of . . ." He stopped,
realizing his foolishness, and scowled.

"Mia, darling, how you love your drop of champagne!" She
dipped another sponge finger; in her obliviousness, she might
have been courteously overlooking his slip. "Not good for your
rheumatism, though! Oh, you dribbler!"

He took another swig of whisky—a smaller one. He was sitting in Plas Iolyn and must not forget himself so far as to get
drunk. Settling back against the wall, he stared in wonder at
objects on the long table and ventured to ask, "What . . . what
have you got that skull for? It's a sheep's, isn't it?"

"That? I keep it because it shows pure breeding in its lines
and therefore is beautiful. Such sheep are not degenerate, as are
so many of their so-called masters. No compulsory education,
state welfare services, and social coddling for a sheep!" Rufus's
face displayed the blank respect of a modest person hearing
academic information beyond his comprehension, and she ap-
pended, "The ewe that lived inside the skull was eaten alive by
blowfly maggots. I found her under a hedge below Mynydd
Baer." She finished her second glass, and poured a third.

As though in sociable alliance, he allowed himself another
mouthful of whisky. Awareness of his gaffe about her cheating
father kept him from returning to the subject of the cottage at
once. He was prepared to remain on the bench for hours; she
seemed not to mind his visit. His eyes did not stray from her any
more; every trivial move she made held his attention now. She
reached for a fancy biscuit tin and closely studied the white
roses painted on its shiny blue sides. He waited. The silence
became acceptable. It belonged to the late hour and this house
and the mystery of Mrs. Vines' ways.

Audrey Vines laid the biscuit tin down unopened, and slowly
ran a finger along the lace tablecloth, like a woman preoccupied
with arriving at a resolve. "If you are dissatisfied with the lease-
hold deeds of Brychan Cottage," she began, "I advise you to

consult a solicitor. Daniel Lewis welcomes such small business, I believe. You will find his office behind the Assembly Hall. You have been remarkably lackadaisical in this matter. . . . No, *not* remarkably, since he is as he is! He should live in a tree." She had turned to Mia.

"I don't want to go to a solicitor." After a pause, he mumbled, half sulkily, "Can't . . . can't we settle it between us?"

She looked up. Their eyes met again. The bright ruby on her chest flashed as she purposelessly moved a dish on the table. But the roused expectancy in Rufus's glistening eyes did not fade. After a moment, he tilted the bottle high into his mouth, and withdrew it with a look of extreme surprise. It was empty.

Audrey Vines drank more wine. Then, rapping the words out, she demanded, "How much rent are you prepared to pay me for the cottage?"

Rufus gaped in wonder. Had Evan Matthews been right, then, in saying that nothing was final with women? He put the whisky bottle down on the bench and offered the first sum in his mind. "A pound a week?"

Audrey Vines laughed. It was a hoarse sound, cramped and discordant in her throat. She straightened a leaning candle and spoke with the incisiveness of a nimble businesswoman addressing a foolish client. "Evidently you know nothing of property values, young man. My estate is one of the most attractive in this part of Wales. A Londoner needing weekend seclusion would pay ten pounds a week for my cottage, with fishing rights."

It had become "my cottage." Rufus pushed a hand into his sweat-damp black hair, and mumbled, "Best to have a man you know nearby you on the estate."

"For a pound? I fail to see the advantage I reap."

"Thirty shillings, then? I'm only drawing a clear nine pounds a week in Nelson's factory." Without guile, he sped on, "Haven't got enough training yet to be put on the machines, you see! They've kept me in the packing room with the learners."

"That I can well believe. Nevertheless, you can afford to buy a motorcycle and flasks of whisky." She clattered a plate onto another. "My cottage would be rent-free to the right man. Would you like a couple of sardines with your whisky?"

The abrupt invitation quenched him once more. He lowered

his head, scowling, his thighs wide apart. His hands gripped his knees. There was a silence. When he looked up, she was straining her penciled eyes toward him, as though their sight had become blurred. But now he could not look at her in return. His gaze focused on the three candle flames to the left of her head.

"Well, sardines or not?"

"No," he answered, almost inaudibly.

"Grind me some coffee, then," she rapped, pointing to the handle-topped wooden box on the table. "There are beans in it. Put a little water in the kettle on one of those oilstoves. Matches are here. Coffeepot on the dresser." She dabbed her lips with her napkin, looked at the stain they left, and refilled her glass.

He could no longer respond in any way to these changes of mood. He neither moved nor spoke. Reality had faded, the kitchen itself became less factual, objects on the table insubstantially remote. Only the woman's face drew and held his eyes. But Audrey Vines seemed not to notice this semi-paralysis; she was allowing a slow-thinking man time to obey her command. She spoke a few words to Mia. She leaned forward to reach for a lacquered box, and took from it a pink cigaret. As she rose to light the gold-tipped cigaret at a candle, he said, "Brychan Cottage always belonged to my family."

"He keeps saying that!" she said to Mia, sighing and sitting back. Reflective while she smoked, she had an air of waiting for coffee to be served, a woman retreated into the securities of her distant past, when everybody ran to her bidding.

"What do you want, then?" His voice came from deep in his chest, the words flat and earnest in his need to know.

The mistress of Plas Iolyn did not reply for a minute. Her gaze was fixed on the closely woven flower in its silver vase. And a strange transformation came to her lulled face. The lineaments of a girl eased its contours, bringing a smooth texture to the skin, clothing the stark bones with a pastel-like delicacy of fine young flesh. An apparition, perhaps an inhabitant of her reverie, was fugitively in possession.

"I want peace and quiet," she whispered.

His head had come forward. He saw the extraordinary transformation. Like the dissolving reality of the room, it had the nature of a hallucination. His brows puckering in his effort to concentrate, to find exactness, he slowly sat back, and asked,

"You want me to stay single? Then I can keep Brychan Cottage?"

In a sudden, total extinction of control, her face became contorted into an angry shape of wrinkled flesh. Her eyes blazed almost sightlessly. She threw the cigaret on the floor and screamed, "Did you think I was going to allow that slut to live there? Braying and squealing on my estate like a prostitute!" Her loud breathing was that of someone about to vomit.

With the same flat simplicity, he said, "Gloria is not a prostitute."

"Gloria! Good God, *Gloria!* How far in idiocy can they go? Why not Cleopatra? I don't care a hair of your stupid head what happens to you and that wretched creature. You are *not* going to get the cottage. I'll burn it to the ground rather than have you and that born prostitute in it!" Her hands began to grasp at plates and cutlery on the table, in a blind semblance of the act of clearing them. "Stupid lout, coming here! By the autumn there won't be a stone of that cottage left. Not a stone, you hear!"

Her demented goading held such pure hatred that it seemed devoid of connection with him. She had arrived at the fringe of sane consciousness; her gaze fixed on nothing, she was aware only of a dim figure hovering down the room, beyond the throw of candlelight. "The thirtieth of June, you hear? Or the police will be called to turn you out!"

He had paused for a second at the far end of the table, near the door. His head was averted. Four or five paces away from him lay release into the night. But he proceeded in her direction, advancing as though in deferential shyness, his head still half turned away, a hand sliding along the table. He paused again, took up the coffee grinder, looked at it vaguely, and lowered it to the table. It crashed on the stone floor.

She became aware of the accosting figure. The screaming did not diminish. "Pick that thing up! You've broken it, clumsy fool. Pick it up!"

He looked round uncertainly, not at her but at the uncurtained bay window giving onto the spaces of night. He did not stoop for the grinder.

"Pick it up!" The mounting howl swept away the last hesitation in him. He went toward her unwaveringly.

She sat without a movement until he was close to her. He stopped, and looked down at her. Something like a compelled obedience was in the crouch of his shoulders. Her right hand moved, grasping the tablecloth fringe into a tight fistful. She made no attempt to speak, but an articulation came into the exposed face that was lifted to him. From the glaze of her eyes, from deep in unfathomable misery, came entreaty. He was the chosen one. He alone held the power of deliverance. He saw it, and in that instant of mutual recognition his hand grasped the heavy candelabra and lifted it high. Its three flames blew out in the swiftness of the plunge. There was a din of objects crashing to the floor from the tugged tablecloth. When he rose from beside the fallen chair and put the candelabra down, the whimpering dog followed him in the darkness to the door, as though pleading with this welcome visitor not to go.

He left the motorbike outside the back garden gate of Brychan Cottage, walked along a wicker fence, and, near the river, jumped across the ditch onto Plas Iolyn land. Presently he reached a spot where, long before he was born, the river had been widened and deepened to form an ornamental pool. A rotting summerhouse, impenetrable under wild creeper, overlooked it, and a pair of stone urns marked a short flight of weed-hidden steps. The soft water, which in daytime was as blue as the distant mountain range where lay its source, flowed through in lingering eddies. He had sometimes bathed in this prohibited pool late at night; below Brychan Cottage the river was much less comfortable for swimming.

He undressed without haste, and jumped into the pool with a quick and acrobatically high leap. He swam underwater, rose, and went under again, in complete ablution. When he stood up beside the opposite bank, where the glimmering water reached to his chest, he relaxed his arms along the grassy verge and remained for moments looking at the enormous expanse of starry sky, away from the mansion dimly outlined above the pool.

He was part of the anonymous liberty of the night. This bathe was the completion of an act of mastery. The river was his; returning to its depths, he was assimilated into it. He flowed downstream a little way and, where the water became shallow, sat up. His left hand spread on pebbles below, he leaned negligently there, like a deity of pools and streams risen in search of possibilities in the night. He sat unmoving for several minutes. The supple water running over his loins began to feel much colder. It seemed to clear his mind of tumult. Slowly, he turned his head toward the mansion.

He saw her face in the last flare of the candles, and now he knew why she had tormented him. She had been waiting long for his arrival. The knowledge lodged, certain and tenacious, in his mind. Beyond his wonder at her choice, it brought, too, some easing of the terror threatening him. Further his mind would not go; he retreated from thinking of the woman lying alone in the darkness of that mansion up there. He knew she was dead. Suddenly, he rose, waded to the bank, and strode to where his clothes lay.

His movements took on the neatness and dispatch of a man acting entirely on a residue of memory. He went into Brychan Cottage only to dry and dress himself in the kitchen. When he got to the town, all lamps had been extinguished in the deserted streets. The bike tore into the private hush of an ancient orderliness. He did not turn into the route he had taken earlier that night but drove on at top speed through the marketplace. Behind the medieval Assembly Hall, down a street of municipal offices and timbered old houses in which legal business was done, a blue lamp shone alight. It jutted clearly from the porch of a stone building, and the solid door below yielded to his push.

Inside, a bald-headed officer sitting at a desk glanced up in mild surprise at this visitor out of the peaceful night, and, since the young man kept silent, asked, "Well, what can we do for you?"

1967:

The Oblong Room

Edward D. Hoch

It was Fletcher's case from the beginning, but Captain Leopold rode along with him when the original call came in. The thing seemed open and shut, with the only suspect found literally standing over his victim, and on a dull day Leopold thought that a ride out to the University might be pleasant.

Here, along the river, the October color was already in the trees, and through the park a slight haze of burning leaves clouded the road in spots. It was a warm day for autumn, a sunny day. Not really a day for murder.

"The University hasn't changed much," Leopold commented, as they turned into the narrow street that led past the fraternity houses to the library tower. "A few new dorms, and a new stadium. That's about all."

"We haven't had a case here since that bombing four or five years back," Fletcher said. "This one looks to be a lot easier, though. They've got the guy already. Stabbed his roommate and then stayed right there with the body."

Leopold was silent. They'd pulled up before one of the big new dormitories that towered toward the sky like some middle-income housing project, all brick and concrete and right now surrounded by milling students. Leopold pinned on his badge and led the way.

The room was on the fourth floor, facing the river. It seemed to be identical to all the others—a depressing oblong with bunk beds, twin study desks, wardrobes, and a large picture window opposite the door. The medical examiner was already there, and he looked up as Leopold and Fletcher entered. "We're ready to move him. All right with you, Captain?"

"The boys get their pictures? Then it's fine with me. Fletcher, find out what you can." Then, to the medical examiner, "What killed him?"

"A couple of stab wounds. I'll do an autopsy, but there's not much doubt."

"How long dead?"

"A day or so."

"A day!"

Fletcher had been making notes as he questioned the others. "The precinct men have it pretty well wrapped up for us, Captain. The dead boy is Ralph Rollings, a sophomore. His room mate admits to being here with the body for maybe twenty hours before they were discovered. Roommate's name is Tom McBern. They've got him in the next room."

Leopold nodded and went through the connecting door. Tom McBern was tall and slender, and handsome in a dark, collegiate sort of way. "Have you warned him of his rights?" Leopold asked a patrolman.

"Yes, sir."

"All right." Leopold sat down on the bed opposite McBern. "What have you got to say, son?"

The deep brown eyes came up to meet Leopold's. "Nothing, sir. I think I want a lawyer."

"That's your privilege, of course. You don't wish to make any statement about how your roommate met his death, or why you remained in the room with him for several hours without reporting it?"

"No, sir." He turned away and stared out the window.

"You understand we'll have to book you on suspicion of homicide."

The boy said nothing more, and after a few moments Leopold left him alone with the officer. He went back to Fletcher and watched while the body was covered and carried away. "He's not talking. Wants a lawyer. Where are we?"

Sergeant Fletcher shrugged. "All we need is motive. They probably had the same girl or something."

"Find out."

They went to talk with the boy who occupied the adjoining room, the one who'd found the body. He was sandy-haired and handsome, with the look of an athlete, and his name was Bill Smith.

"Tell us how it was, Bill," Leopold said.

"There's not much to tell. I knew Ralph and Tom slightly during my freshman year, but never really well. They stuck pretty much together. This year I got the room next to them, but the connecting door was always locked. Anyway, yesterday neither one of them showed up at class. When I came back yesterday afternoon I knocked at the door and asked if anything was wrong. Tom called out that they were sick. He wouldn't open the door. I went into my own room and didn't think much about it. Then, this morning, I knocked to see how they were. Tom's voice sounded so . . . strange."

"Where was your own roommate all this time?"

"He's away. His father died and he went home for the funeral." Smith's hands were nervous, busy with a shredded piece of paper. Leopold offered him a cigaret and he took it. "Anyway, when he wouldn't open the door I became quite concerned and told him I was going for help. He opened it then— and I saw Ralph stretched out on the bed, all bloody and . . . dead."

Leopold nodded and went to stand by the window. From here he could see the trees down along the river, blazing gold and amber and scarlet as the October sun passed across them. "Had you heard any sounds the previous day? Any argument?"

"No. Nothing. Nothing at all."

"Had they disagreed in the past about anything?"

"Not that I knew of. If they didn't get along, they hardly would have asked to room together again this year."

"How about girls?" Leopold asked.

"They both dated occasionally, I think."

"No special one? One they both liked?"

Bill Smith was silent for a fraction too long. "No."

"You're sure?"

"I told you I didn't know them very well."

"This is murder, Bill. It's not a sophomore dance or Class Day games."

"Tom killed him. What more do you need?"

"What's her name, Bill?"

He stubbed out the cigaret and looked away. Then finally he answered. "Stella Banting. She's a junior."

"Which one did she go with?"

"I don't know. She was friendly with both of them. I think she went out with Ralph a few times around last Christmas, but I've seen her with Tom lately."

"She's older than them?"

"No. They're all twenty. She's just a year ahead."

"All right," Leopold said. "Sergeant Fletcher will want to question you further."

He left Smith's room and went out in the hall with Fletcher. "It's your case, Sergeant. About time I gave it to you."

"Thanks for the help, Captain."

"Let him talk to a lawyer and then see if he has a story. If he still won't make a statement, book him on suspicion. I don't think there's any doubt we can get an indictment."

"You going to talk to that girl?"

Leopold smiled. "I just might. Smith seemed a bit shy about her. Might be a motive there. Let me know as soon as the medical examiner has something more definite about the time of death."

"Right, Captain."

Leopold went downstairs, pushing his way through the students and faculty members still crowding the halls and stairways. Outside he unpinned the badge and put it away. The air was fresh and crisp as he strolled across the campus to the administration building.

Stella Banting lived in the largest sorority house on campus, a great columned building of ivy and red brick. But when Captain Leopold found her she was on her way back from the drugstore, carrying a carton of cigarets and a bottle of shampoo. Stella was a tall girl with firm, angular lines and a face that might have been beautiful if she ever smiled.

"Stella Banting?"

"Yes?"

"I'm Captain Leopold. I wanted to talk to you about the tragedy over at the men's dorm. I trust you've heard about it?"

She blinked her eyes and said, "Yes. I've heard."

"Could we go somewhere and talk?"

"I'll drop these at the house and we can walk if you'd like. I don't want to talk there."

She was wearing faded bermuda shorts and a bulky sweatshirt, and walking with her made Leopold feel young again. If only she smiled occasionally—but perhaps this was not a day for smiling. They headed away from the main campus, out toward the silent oval of the athletic field and sports stadium. "You didn't come over to the dorm," he said to her finally, breaking the silence of their walk.

"Should I have?"

"I understood you were friendly with them—that you dated the dead boy last Christmas and Tom McBern more recently."

"A few times. Ralph wasn't the sort anyone ever got to know very well."

"And what about Tom?"

"He was a nice fellow."

"Was?"

"It's hard to explain. Ralph did things to people, to everyone around him. When I felt it happening to me, I broke away."

"What sort of things?"

"He had a power—a power you wouldn't believe any twenty-year-old capable of."

"You sound as if you've known a lot of them."

"I have. This is my third year at the University. I've grown up a lot in that time. I think I have anyway."

"And what about Tom McBern?"

"I dated him a few times recently just to confirm for myself how bad things were. He was completely under Ralph's thumb. He lived for no one but Ralph."

"Homosexual?" Leopold asked.

"No, I don't think it was anything as blatant as that. It was more the relationship of teacher and pupil, leader and follower."

"Master and slave?"

She turned to smile at him. "You do seem intent on midnight orgies, don't you?"

"The boy is dead, after all."

"Yes. Yes, he is." She stared down at the ground, kicking randomly at the little clusters of fallen leaves. "But you see what I mean? Ralph was always the leader, the teacher—for Tom, almost the messiah."

"Then why would he have killed him?" Leopold asked.

"That's just it—he wouldn't! Whatever happened in that room, I can't imagine Tom McBern ever bringing himself to kill Ralph."

"There is one possibility, Miss Banting. Could Ralph Rollings have made a disparaging remark about you? Something about when he was dating you?"

"I never slept with Ralph, if that's what you're trying to ask me. With either of them, for that matter."

"I didn't mean it that way."

"It happened just the way I've told you. If anything, I was afraid of Ralph. I didn't want him getting that sort of hold over me."

Somehow he knew they'd reached the end of their stroll, even though they were still in the middle of the campus quadrangle, some distance from the sports arena. "Thank you for your help, Miss Banting. I may want to call on you again."

He left her there and headed back toward the men's dorm, knowing that she would watch him until he was out of sight.

Sergeant Fletcher found Leopold in his office early the following morning, reading the daily reports of the night's activities. "Don't you ever sleep, Captain?" he asked, pulling up the faded leather chair that served for infrequent visitors.

"I'll have enough time for sleeping when I'm dead. What have you got on McBern?"

"His lawyer says he refuses to make a statement, but I gather they'd like to plead him not guilty by reason of insanity."

"What's the medical examiner say?"

Fletcher read from a typed sheet. "Two stab wounds, both in the area of the heart. He apparently was stretched out on the bed when he got it."

"How long before they found him?"

"He'd eaten breakfast maybe an hour or so before he died, and from our questioning that places the time of death at about ten o'clock. Bill Smith went to the door and got McBern to open it at about eight the following morning. Since we know McBern was in the room the previous evening when Smith spoke to him through the door, we can assume he was alone with the body for approximately twenty-two hours."

Leopold was staring out the window, mentally comparing the city's autumn gloom with the colors of the countryside that he'd witnessed the previous day. Everything dies, only it dies a little sooner, a bit more drably, in the city. "What else?" he asked Fletcher, because there obviously was something else.

"In one of the desk drawers," Fletcher said, producing a little evidence envelope. "Six sugar cubes, saturated with LSD."

"All right." Leopold stared down at them. "I guess that's not too unusual on campuses these days. Has there ever been a murder committed by anyone under the influence of LSD?"

"A case out West somewhere. And I think another one over in England."

"Can we get a conviction, or is this the basis of the insanity plea?"

"I'll check on it, Captain."

"And one more thing—get that fellow Smith in here. I want to talk with him again."

Later, alone, Leopold felt profoundly depressed. The case bothered him. McBern had stayed with Rollings' body for twenty-two hours. Anybody that could last that long would have to be crazy. He was crazy and he was a killer and that was all there was to it.

When Fletcher ushered Bill Smith into the office an hour later, Leopold was staring out the window. He turned and motioned the young man to a chair. "I have some further questions, Bill."

"Yes?"

"Tell me about the LSD."

"What?"

Leopold walked over and sat on the edge of the desk. "Don't pretend you never heard of it. Rollings and McBern had some in their room."

Bill Smith looked away. "I didn't know. There were rumors."

"Nothing else? No noise through that connecting door?"

"Noise, yes. Sometimes it was . . ."

Leopold waited for him to continue, and when he did not, said, "This is a murder investigation, Bill."

"Rollings . . . he deserved to die, that's all. He was the most completely evil person I ever knew. The things he did to poor Tom . . ."

"Stella Banting says Tom almost worshiped him."

"He did, and that's what made it all the more terrible."

Leopold leaned back and lit a cigaret. "If they were both high on LSD, almost anyone could have entered that room and stabbed Ralph."

But Bill Smith shook his head. "I doubt it. They wouldn't have dared unlock the door while they were turned on. Besides, Tom would have protected him with his own life."

"And yet we're to believe that Tom killed him? That he stabbed him to death and then spent a day and a night alone with the body? Doing what, Bill? Doing what?"

"I don't know."

"Do you think Tom McBern is insane?"

"No, not really. Not legally." He glanced away. "But on the subject of Rollings, he was pretty far gone. Once, when we were still friendly, he told me he'd do anything for Rollings—even trust him with his life. And he did, one time. It was during the spring weekend and everybody had been drinking a lot. Tom hung upside down out of the dorm window with Rollings holding his ankles. That's how much he trusted him."

"I think I'll have to talk with Tom McBern again," Leopold said. "At the scene of the crime."

Fletcher brought Tom McBern out to the campus in handcuffs, and Captain Leopold was waiting for them in the oblong room on the fourth floor. "All right, Fletcher," Leopold said. "You can leave us alone. Wait outside."

McBern had lost a good deal of his previous composure, and now he faced Leopold with red-ringed eyes and a lip that trembled when he spoke. "What . . . what did you want to ask me?"

"A great many things, son. All the questions in the world." Leopold sighed and offered the boy a cigaret. "You and Rollings were taking LSD, weren't you?"

"We took it, yes."

"Why? For kicks?"

"Not for kicks. You don't understand about Ralph."

"I understand that you killed him. What more is there to understand? You stabbed him to death right over there on that bed."

Tom McBern took a deep breath. "We didn't take LSD for kicks," he repeated. "It was more to heighten the sense of religious experience—a sort of mystical involvement that is the whole meaning of life."

Leopold frowned down at the boy. "I'm only a detective, son. You and Rollings were strangers to me until yesterday, and I guess now he'll always be a stranger to me. That's one of the troubles with my job. I don't get to meet people until it's too late, until the damage"—he gestured toward the empty bed— "is already done. But I want to know what happened in this room, between you two. I don't want to hear about mysticism or religious experience. I want to hear what happened—why you killed him and why you sat here with the body for twenty-two hours."

Tom McBern looked up at the walls, seeing them perhaps for the first and thousandth time. "Did you ever think about this room? About the shape of it? Ralph used to say it reminded him of a story by Poe, 'The Oblong Box.' Remember that story? The box was on board a ship, and of course it contained a body. Like Queequeg's coffin which rose from the sea to rescue Ishmael."

"And this room was Ralph's coffin?" Leopold asked quietly.

"Yes." McBern stared down at his handcuffed wrists. "His tomb."

"You killed him, didn't you?"

"Yes."

Leopold looked away. "Do you want you lawyer?"

"No. Nothing."

"My God! Twenty-two hours!"

"I was—"

"I know what you were doing. But I don't think you'll ever tell it to a judge and jury."

"I'll tell you, because maybe you can understand." And he began to talk in a slow, quiet voice, and Leopold listened because that was his job.

. . .

Toward evening, when Tom McBern had been returned to his cell and Fletcher sat alone with Leopold, he said, "I've called the District Attorney, Captain. What are you going to tell him?"

"The facts, I suppose. McBern will sign a confession of just how it happened. The rest is out of our hands."

"Do you want to tell me about it, Captain?"

"I don't think I want to tell anyone about it. But I suppose I have to. I guess it was all that talk of religious experience and coffins rising from the ocean that tipped me off. You know that Rollings pictured their room as a sort of tomb."

"For him it was."

"I wish I'd known him, Fletcher. I only wish I'd known him in time."

"What would you have done?"

"Perhaps only listened and tried to understand him."

"McBern admitted killing him?"

Leopold nodded. "It seems that Rollings asked him to, and Tom McBern trusted him more than life itself."

"Rollings asked to be stabbed through the heart?"

"Yes."

"Then why did McBern stay with the body so long? For a whole day and night?"

"He was waiting," Leopold said quietly, looking at nothing at all. "He was waiting for Rollings to rise from the dead."

1968:

The Man Who Fooled the World

Warner Law

When my great-uncle, Frank M. Law, died in my house a few
months ago, he left a manuscript. It is a shameless account of
his life, and is in many ways a shocking document. I have
thought long and hard before deciding to let it see print, because a few museums and collectors are going to find themselves with worthless works of art on their hands.

Before you read it, I must explain a few things. I am a television writer and live with my wife, Maria, and our two children
in a fairly large old house high in the Hollywood hills. Melissa
is eleven, and bright and pretty. Peter, at six, is at the age when
one can shout through a closed door, "Peter, whatever you are
doing, stop it!" and nine times out of ten avert a major disaster.

Ever since I could remember, all of us in the American
branch of the Law family had been receiving birthday cards
from our English uncle, Frank, from all over the world. But he
was a man of mystery, and every time I, as a youngster, asked
about him I was shushed. All I knew was that he was my grandfather's half brother—the son of my great-grandfather by his
second wife.

When I was twenty-five I told my grandfather that I was old
enough to know the truth about the man. My grandfather hesi-

tated, sighed, and finally said, "Very well. Frank is a dissolute, drunken scoundrel. He came into a sizable inheritance from his mother, but soon dissipated it on liquor—which has always been his downfall—and loose women and riotous living. He has led a worthless, misspent life."

"Do you ever hear from him?"

"Yes. Once a year he writes me lies about what he is doing. Frank has ever suffered from self-delusion and self-deception."

"Does he ever ask for money?"

"No. All he wants is detailed information about this branch of the family. Why, I do not know."

On the thirteenth of November, 1966, I was watching television in our living room, when the doorbell rang. Maria opened the door. I looked over and saw a man standing there. He was terribly old and shabbily dressed, and was laden with luggage and parcels. His nose was long, and there was a white mustache under it. He was of medium height, gaunt and, now, was panting. We are three miles away from the nearest bus stop, and he must have walked up the hill all the way.

"Yes?" Maria said. "Can I help you?"

"Might this be the abode of one Warner Law?"

"Yes, it is."

"Might he be at home, and receiving?"

"May I ask who is calling?"

"I am his great-uncle, Frank. I have come here to die."

If I were to write for the next fifty years, I could never improve on this as an entrance line. Naturally, I went to the door and asked him to come in.

"You are my great-nephew, Warner?"

"I am. And welcome to my house." I introduced Maria. Melissa came in from the kitchen, and I introduced her.

"My, what a pretty young lady!" *Sotto voce,* to me: "I don't suppose you've got a bit of a nip for a thirsty old man?"

We have an extra bedroom upstairs which we were able to make comfortable for Uncle Frank. Later that afternoon, after he had unpacked and settled in and had knocked off three whiskeys, I said, "You announced that you had come here to die. Are you ill?"

"No, but I am dying, all the same. If I may stay here for a few weeks—I have no other place to go, I must honestly tell you—

I will soon be leaving you for the Great Beyond." He handed me his empty glass. "That was pretty good, such as it was and what there was of it."

Returning with another drink, I asked him how he had happened to come to me.

"Well," he said, "when I was told by a doctor in the Virgin Islands that my life would soon be over, I decided to come to the States and die in the home of your Aunt Clara, in Chicago. Do you know her?"

Indeed I did. She was a severe widow in her sixties, principally known for her fabulous collection of china. Every bit of wall space in her house was covered with plates, and in addition there was a large storeroom in her cellar. In it, plates, cups, saucers, and platters were stacked on shelves from floor to ceiling, on both sides of the room. Aunt Clara told me once that she had ten complete and perfect services, of museum quality.

"She put me up for a week," Uncle Frank continued, and then paused. "But unfortunately there was a bit of an accident."

"Don't tell me you broke one of her plates."

"Well, in a manner of speaking, yes. But it was not my fault at all. The damn ladder wobbles, you see."

"What ladder?"

"The one in the storeroom. One day when Clara was out, you see, I found half a dozen plates on her sink. I thought I would do her a favor and put them away for her. But I could not find where they belonged. Ah! I thought. They must go in the storeroom!"

"Don't tell me you dropped them."

"Well, in a manner of speaking, yes. I took them down there, you see, but could not find their fellow plates on the lower shelves. So I mounted the ladder, the six plates in hand. When I was opposite the top shelf the goddamn ladder suddenly began to wobble and then to fall sideways. It was in order to save myself from a nasty fall that I had to drop the six plates and grab onto the top shelf for support. Unfortunately, however, this damn top shelf had not been adequately secured to the wall, and it came away with me. I might have been killed by all those falling plates. Luckily, I escaped without injury."

"What did Aunt Clara say?"

"I thought it best to pack up and leave before she returned.

I left her a note of explanation, however, and advised her to buy a new ladder."

I could picture Aunt Clara in the hospital, under sedation.

"I then went to her son, Hugh, in Tucson. He said he had heard from his mother, and abused me in the most vicious and vitriolic terms. Soon he slammed the door in my face. So I went to your second cousin, John, in Sacramento. He said he had no room for me, and he suggested you, and gave me the bus fare to come here." He handed me his glass. "Excellent whiskey. Such as it was and what there was of it."

One morning about three, Maria and I were awakened by raucous singing from the living room below. I arose and went and looked down the stairs. Uncle Frank was dancing—quite by himself—and singing, "It's a long way to Tipperar-ee!" He had a drink in his hand and he did a kind of English-music-hall step. "It's a long way to go!" I suddenly realized that he was naked. "It's a long, long way to Tipperar oo!" He had no clothes on at all. "But *my* heart's right there!"

I went to bed without revealing my presence to him.

Somerset Maugham once wrote, "If people were not full of contradictions, life would be unbearable."

Uncle Frank's moral attitudes were certainly contradictory, as evidenced by his proclivity for naked dancing on the one hand, and his aversion to nude women in art on the other. There are a few nudes on my walls, and they outraged him. "Naked women!" he would mutter. "Dirty trash! What've you got these on your walls for, for innocent children to see? Ought to be ashamed of yourself. Dirty trash!"

Later, this almost incredible hangover from Victorian morality was to result in a terrible scene. In school, Melissa had done a crayon version of Botticelli's *Birth of Venus*. In it, one of Venus's hands covers her pubic area, while the other attempts to conceal her breasts. Melissa showed her version round, and we all admired it, including Peter, my son, who was, as usual, sitting by the fire playing with his cars.

Uncle Frank stumbled down the stairs, fairly far gone. Melissa proudly showed him her work. He took one look at it and was furious. "A naked woman! Dirty trash!" His eyes blazed at Maria and me. "Who teaches her to do this kind of filthy thing?" He suddenly tossed the drawing into the fire, and it burst into flame. Melissa screamed and ran up the stairs, crying.

"Dirty trash, dirty trash!" Peter began to shout, his poetic sense appealed to by the rhythm. "Naked woman!" He banged his cars on the floor in time with the refrain. "Dirty trash! Naked woman!"

"Oh, shut up!" I snapped at Peter. And then, angrily, at Uncle Frank: "Can't you learn to behave yourself?"

He looked abashed. "I am sorry. Truly sorry. And you will not have to put up with me much longer. I will be off to the Great Beyond sooner than you think."

Uncle Frank had said this so many times before that Maria and I, being angry with him anyway, did not extend much sympathy.

We have always been sorry we didn't. The next morning, when Uncle Frank did not put in an appearance, Maria went up to see if he was all right. He was dead in his bed—but with a happy smile on his face.

We called our doctor, and in an hour Uncle Frank was out of our house. The kids, luckily, were both in school.

Rather sadly—for we had come to like the old man, despite everything—we went through his things. There was nothing of interest until we came upon his manuscript. It had been written in his own crabbed hand over many years and on all kinds of paper, from hotel stationery to backs of envelopes. It was quite a task to fit it together and to decipher it, but at long last we had a typed copy.

It is in many ways a shameless and shocking document. A good deal of it seems incredible at first, but I have gone to a great deal of trouble to check it out, and have found that in every instance in which corroboration from other sources is available, it is accurate.

I will interrupt from time to time, prefaced by *NOTE*. Otherwise, the manuscript is reproduced as we found it.

How well do I remember my first encounter with W. Somerset Maugham! It was in 1908, on a wintry night in London. I was then twenty-eight years of age. My mother had left me a moderate inheritance, which I fear I was going through rather rapidly. But I gave little thought to the morrow, and devoted myself to pleasure, enjoying the finest of food and wines, and delighting in the company of lovely, agreeable ladies.

On this evening I had escorted two jolly damsels whose names were Flossie and Bessie to a performance of Maugham's charming comedy *Mrs. Dot.* After the play, we crossed the road to the Ivy, a luxurious establishment with thick carpets and sparkling crystal and shining silver.

It was not until I had ordered the third bottle of champagne that I saw W. Somerset Maugham seated at a nearby table with a group of elegantly dressed ladies and gentlemen.

NOTE: Maugham was thirty-four at this time. He had already written eight novels, four successful plays, and a good number of short stories.

I at once decided to pay my respects to him and compliment him on the excellence of his play. I rose and made my way to his table. I might have been a bit unsteady on my feet after the champagne, but my mind was as clear as a bell.

As I came to his table, Maugham was in the course of telling a highly humorous anecdote. He must have felt my breath on his neck, for in a moment he turned in his chair and looked up at me. He was a fairly small man with heavy-lidded eyes and large ears, and he stammered somewhat.

"Can I . . . be of service to you?"

"Somerset, I just wanted to tell you that your play tonight was a real smasher!"

NOTE: One thing always drove Maugham up the walls, and that was being called "Somerset."

"It . . . is very good of you to say so. I . . . appreciate your having come over to . . . tell me." He smiled and nodded—an obvious invitation for me to join him. I took a chair from a nearby table and swung it into place beside Maugham's.

From the banquette, Flossie and Bessie were waving and beckoning to me. I paid no attention. "Pray continue with your anecdote, Somerset."

The lady next to Maugham turned to me with a smile. She was none other than the great actress, Mrs. Patrick Campbell. "I fear we are keeping you from your ladies."

"Give it no mind, madam. It's not every day I have a chance

to natter with Somerset here." Patting his shoulder and smiling warmly, I edged my chair closer to his.

When Flossie had a bit too much of the bubbly she was apt to become overly playful. Now, giggling a little, she took the unopened third bottle of champagne from its cooler and rolled it toward me across the floor. I saw it coming, bouncing and tumbling. So did the headwaiter, who hurried over, but too late. By this time, not having been properly chilled, it had built up so much inner pressure that the cork flew out, wire cage and all, and champagne began to spout all over the feet and red satin gown of Mrs. Patrick Campbell, before whom the bottle had come to rest. In order to protect her, I seized the bottle from the floor and rose and turned it away from her, but, inadvertently and unfortunately, I turned it toward Maugham, whose face was engulfed with a fountain of champagne.

Naturally, I was sorry for this accident and I began to swab his face vigorously with a napkin. He resisted this well-meant action and got to his feet with audible protests.

Mrs. Campbell rose from her chair and shoved me, shouting, "Stop it, you drunken idiot!" Her push threw me off balance, and to save myself from falling I seized a corner of the tablecloth for support, but unfortunately it came with me as I fell, tumbling the crystal and silver and the candelabra this way and that, while the ladies at the table screamed. At Maugham's end of the table was a silver pot of steaming coffee, and this tipped and discharged its contents over his trousers. He cried out at the same moment I fell against him. His chair collapsed into splinters, and I ended up on top of him, on the floor.

Luckily unhurt, I was pulled to my feet by the headwaiter, while a waiter helped Maugham to rise. The headwaiter was unreasonably angry with me, not understanding, of course, that none of this had been my fault. "I must ask you to leave, sir. At once!"

"Not until I have apologized to my friend Somerset here."

On his feet now, his eyes full of rage under eyebrows still foaming with champagne bubbles, Somerset Maugham turned on me furiously. "Damn you, sir! Damn you!"

This was too much. I will not be sworn at. Any man with a normal temperament would have realized that I was not at all to blame for the events which had transpired. The only explanation for his being so unjustifiably rude to me was obvious: Maugham was simply not a gentleman.

I drew myself up. In a chilling tone, I said, "I rather doubt, sir, that I shall ever speak to you again." Having put the bounder in his place, I turned on my heel and strode away, followed by Flossie and Bessie.

During the next week I was twice to chance upon Maugham in the streets of London. The first time was in Piccadilly Circus. I inadvertently bumped into a man who was standing on the corner. He had a folder full of papers in his hand, and, as he stumbled off the curb, he dropped it. It being a windy day, the papers began to blow this way and that across the Circus. Maugham growled in disgust, and then recognized me. "I might have known," he muttered, and then scurried off to try to retrieve his scattered papers amidst the traffic.

Our second meeting was a few days later, on Bond Street. We saw each other at the same time; but he pretended not to have seen me, stopped, and stared into a tobacconist's window. Wishing to apologize for having collided with him, I started toward him. Seeing me coming, he turned away. At this moment a gentleman passed me, hurried up to Maugham, and tapped his shoulder, smiling. Maugham did not deign to turn his head. "I do not wish to speak with you, sir," I heard him say, addressing the shop window. "And I would be grateful if you could contrive, henceforward and for all time, to stay out of my life."

The gentleman flushed in anger. "Very well, Willie. Go to hell!" He turned and hurried off the way he had come—past me. Maugham spun around, saw me, and then saw his friend striding off down the street. Maugham started trotting after him, in some alarm.

"I'm extremely sorry, Somerset," I began, stepping in his way, "but—"

"Oh, shut up!" Maugham snapped as he dodged round me and ran off after his friend.

I continued down the street to my bank, where the manager said that my inheritance had all been spent. I could not understand this, since five hundred pounds had just been credited to my account. My bank manager explained that I had sold some debentures, and the five hundred pounds represented interest accrued after the sale, and would soon be claimed by the purchaser. This would leave me without a shilling.

The English climate had never really agreed with me. I had read a good deal about warmer climes, especially the isles of the South Seas, where one could live on bananas and breadfruit to be had for the picking. Withdrawing the five hundred pounds, I booked passage for Australia, and sailed from London.

I did not trouble my bank manager with the news of my departure. He was a busy man with many problems, and I did not wish to burden him further.

As my ship groped through the fog down the Thames Estuary, I said farewell to London. At least, I mused, as the ship broke into the open sea, I will never again have to encounter that odious man, Maugham. Alas, I was to be dreadfully in error.

.

I settled in Tahiti, a lush and lovely place, then unspoiled by tourists. With the remainder of my capital I purchased an automobile and started a taxi service—one of the very few on the island. This, plus tending the steam boiler in the basement of the local brewery, enabled me to make an adequate living. I was happy and content.

Until one terrible day when I heard—this was in 1916—that none but W. Somerset Maugham had arrived on the island, accompanied by his secretary, a Mr. Gerald Haxton. I at once resolved to stay out of Maugham's way. I had grown a full beard, and eight years had passed since last he had seen me, and I knew he would not recognize me. Regardless, I did not wish to be again the victim of his vile temper.

But this was not to be. One sultry day while I was sleeping in my taxi, someone reached in and nudged me. It was Haxton, with Maugham beside him, dressed dapperly in a white linen suit.

Haxton was a youngish fellow with a patronizing manner. "I say, my good man. Is this vehicle for hire?"

"No."

Haxton said, "See here, my good fellow, we need a motorcar

badly. If you know the Anani house in Mataiea and can take us there, there's ten francs in it for you."

I had slept enough and was low on cash. "Make it twenty. It's a long way."

"Twenty it is," Maugham said. They got in the back of my closed cab. While I drove, Maugham told me that he had come to Tahiti to do research on the painter Paul Gauguin. Did I know anything about him?

I had heard quite a bit about this drunken French painter and his pictures. Mostly of naked women. When I first went to work in the boiler room of the Papeete brewery, there were ten of Gauguin's paintings standing near the coal bin, covered with half an inch of dust. On damp days when the furnace would not catch, I would toss one of them in to get the fire going. It seemed that Gauguin had owed the brewery for beer, but instead of money he had sent over some of his filthy pictures. The man who then owned the brewery was furious, and tossed the worthless canvases into the boiler room. There were still five of them left, but I was not about to tell the noble Mr. Maugham this. Perhaps now they were of some value. The brewery having changed owners twice since, no one but me knew that five of the paintings were still there. And since I had burned some and could burn the rest so far as anyone knew or cared, they were in actuality mine, to do with as I might wish.

I told Maugham I knew nothing about Gauguin. Finally, we drove up to the Anani house, deep in the bush. The three of us got out and went in and met the owner of the house, an old, toothless, flat-nosed Tahitian. Maugham and he conversed in French, of which I had learned some in Tahiti. Maugham was saying that he had come to buy a door. I learned that this Gauguin had once been ill in the Anani house and had run out of things to paint upon.

NOTE: Quite true. Recovering from his illness, Gauguin, having nothing left to paint upon, used the glass panels of three doors which opened into the main room of the Anani house, which was a comparatively modern one by Tahitian standards.

So he had painted some of his filthy pictures on three glass doors. On two of them, almost all the paint had been scraped off idly, as by children's fingernails. But the third was in good condition. Maugham bought it for two hundred francs, which was then worth about four pounds, or twenty dollars.

Maugham asked me if I would use my car tools and take the door off its hinges. I went to work. "Careful! Careful!" Maugham kept muttering as I unscrewed the hinges.

"I *am* being careful!" I took out the last screw, but the hinges still adhered to the door. As I wrested the door free, it slipped out of my hands and fell, but Haxton managed to catch it in mid-air.

"You clumsy clot!" Maugham said. He was in one of his rages.

"Nothing lost, Mr. Maugham."

Very, very slowly, walking about an inch a second, we got the door to my automobile. The only place to put it was in the front seat. But the door was too tall to fit. Two thirds of the door consisted of six panes of painted glass, making up a filthy picture of a naked woman holding a breadfruit. The bottom third was wood.

"Can we not find a wood saw?" asked Maugham.

"Then we could cut off the lower section of wood!" Haxton beamed, proudly and toothily, as if he had just invented the internal-combustion engine or had revealed some great truth to us.

I knew a native chiefess who lived a quarter-mile away who had a wood saw, and so the three of us started out through the bush carrying this two-hundred-franc door. You would have thought it was the goddamn *Mona Lisa*. Finally we got there, and I borrowed the saw and sawed off the lower third, with Maugham and Haxton clucking over me to be careful, as if I were amputating a leg and the patient were about to bleed to death.

When I had finished, Maugham and Haxton themselves carried the glass part of the door back to the car. They got into the back and insisted on holding the door across their laps. We started off, the two of them admonishing me to drive carefully, which I did as well as I was able, the dirt road being full of holes and half-sunken logs and boulders. From the two of them, behind me, I heard the following:

MAUGHAM: "Do you realize, Gerald, the immensity of the treasure we have stumbled upon?"

HAXTON: "It's unique in the world! A Gauguin on glass! It must be worth a bloody fortune!"

MAUGHAM: "I will have it set into that window on the north side of my study."

HAXTON: "I feel almost weak with rapture."

By and by, as we drove along, I began to feel the need of some refreshment, and I pulled up at a little village canteen. I told them I desired a small dollop of cognac. They insisted I wait until we had got the door safely back to Papeete. I told them what they could do with their door, took the car keys, and went into the canteen.

NOTE: *Maugham's own account of the finding of the Anani door corroborates all this, except that he does not mention who drove him to and from the Anani house.*

Half an hour later, a bit of cognac under my belt and feeling better for it, I came out of the canteen and started for my taxi, in which the two were still clutching the door. It was dusk, and I did not see a rock in the road, and I tripped over it and fell. It had been raining, and I fell face down into the mud, and this did not help my temper much.

"Good heavens!" I heard Maugham say. "The man is completely sozzled!"

This was untrue. I went to the driver's door and unlatched it. "I heard that!" I said indignantly. "I wish to state that I am as sober as a coot!" I got into the car.

"I beg of you," Maugham said. "Drive slowly."

Well, I had had about enough of these two snobs and their condescension. As I drove along, I began to sing, "Pack up your troubles in your old kit bag!" We were doing a steady thirty-five. It was nearly dark now, and I had no lights, but I knew the road. "And smile, smile, smile!" We hit a boulder which someone had obviously just placed there, and the car nearly turned over.

"Slow down, damn you!" Maugham cried in alarm.

As I have said, I will not be sworn at. I got the car up to forty. The more they cursed me, the faster I went. We clunked into holes and bounced over logs and once sideswiped a tree. "What's the use of worrying!" I did not give a hoot in hell about the damn door. "It never was worthwhile!"

By the time we reached Papeete my temper had cooled, and I deposited them safely in front of their hotel. I came round the car to Maugham's door and opened it. He was a sorry figure, pale and trembling. So was Haxton. Neither was in any condition to carry the glass door, so I took it from Maugham. "No! Don't touch it!" But I had already started up the steps to the hotel porch.

NOTE: Oh, no!

Unknown to me, the hotel people had recently replaced the nearly rotten old steps with new ones. But instead of four steps, as before, there were now five. Consequently—it was hardly my fault—I tripped over the top step and fell forward onto the porch, the door beneath me. Naturally, it was smashed into a thousand pieces, but the serious thing was that I was cut by the flying glass, and my face and hands were bleeding. I looked up to see Maugham and Haxton staring down at me.

Maugham was breathing heavily. "You fool!" he whispered. "You idiot! You drunken sot! Do you know what you have done?" And then, flying into one of his rages, he kicked me in the rump, crying, "Damn you! Damn you to hell!"

No man swears at me and kicks me in the rump when I am lying in a pool of my own blood. Especially when my only intent was to assist him. I resolved to even the score with Maugham, to teach him a lesson he would not forget for the rest of his life.

Having heard that this Gauguin was often so destitute that he had to paint his dirty pictures on pieces of potato-sack burlap, I rounded up quite a few of these, and then made wood frames that resembled those of the real Gauguins which were still in the boiler room. I stretched the burlap tightly over them and tacked it firmly with rusty nails. In all, I ended up with five canvases.

I was in no great hurry, for his highness, Mr. Maugham, would be in Tahiti until the next steamer arrived. I took my canvases and tied them into a bundle, which I weighted, and canoed out into the lagoon one balmy night. I attached a rope to a permanent navigation buoy and lowered the canvases into the water and left them there.

Next, I took the five Gauguins from the boiler room and studied them in the sunlight, on the beach next to the grass hut in which I lived. They had been near the coal bin since at least 1903, when Gauguin died. I carefully brushed off the coal dust, and wiped the canvases clean with cold water and sponges. When I had finished, they looked as though they had been painted yesterday. Tahiti is humid, and mold is common, but these, having been in a dry place and out of the light, were perfectly preserved.

I should mention here that when I was in school in Yorkshire, I showed a remarkable aptitude for drawing. My mother sent me to a local artist who gave lessons in painting, until an unfortunate accident put an end to both my lessons and the painter's house. No one had told me that turpentine was flammable.

Having therefore been conversant with the basic principles of art, I found Gauguin's paintings both ugly and incompetent. He could not draw, for one thing. He painted flatly, with little perspective or fine detail. Also, he had used a great many ridiculous colors. His oranges were often blue, his coconuts orange, his horses green.

Also, all five of these Gauguins contained naked women. But I resolved to copy them, regardless. I went to the only shop in Papeete which stocked art supplies and bought some sizing mixture, some tubes of oils, some brushes, and a palette.

Then I began to copy the paintings, first on paper, then on cardboard, and then on pieces of wood. After ten days of extremely hard work, I was fairly adept at Gauguin's style, and I decided that I was ready. In the dark of night I went out to the buoy and retrieved my five canvases. They had shrunk nicely. The next morning I washed them with fresh water and left them to dry in the sun. After two days I painted them with the sizing mixture, so they would not drink up the paint.

Then I faced the problem of aging the canvases. There was no one I could ask for advice, so I improvised. I rubbed them with sand, then threw cold coffee on them, and then some beer, and rubbed them with ashes, which I washed off. By the time I had finished they looked to me to be perfect for what I had in mind.

And then I began to paint upon these canvases, copying with great care from the five originals. It turned out to be not so easy as I had imagined. But at last, after two weeks, I had five semigenuine Gauguins. They would not have fooled a true art expert, but they were to fool a greedy person, as you will see.

Because the paint was fresh and could be smelled, I took the paintings out into the lagoon again and let them soak under the buoy for three days. I then brought them ashore and laid them in the sun, face up, for a day. Then, face down for a day. I sprinkled them with old coffee grounds, which I rubbed off with a rough rag. I then wiped them with rancid pork fat, which I scrubbed off with scouring powder. Then, and only then, did I take them to the boiler room, where I sprinkled them with coal dust. I left them there for a week.

Finally, one day, I took the best of my five and wrapped it in newspaper and took it to the hotel where Maugham and Haxton were staying. They were out on the veranda, drinking rum punches.

By now the reader will be thinking that my intention was to pass off my copies as originals, and sell them to Maugham. Not at all. My plan for revenge was far more ingenious.

I had not the slightest doubt that Maugham would accept my copies as genuine. This was 1916, only thirteen years after Gauguin's death. During his lifetime he had sold very few paintings. I had learned from a French civil servant whom I used to taxi about that Gauguin's works were now beginning to change hands, in Paris and London, but for fairly low prices. So anyone capable of forging works of art would have been wasting his time with Gauguin.

In addition, Maugham had no reason to suspect that I had either talent or inclination in this direction. So I approached the two of them on the veranda with the greatest of confidence, though I did not expect a warm welcome.

At the sight of me—our paths had not crossed since the terrible day he kicked me and cursed me—Maugham winced, and turned away.

"Begging your pardon, Mr. Maugham—"

"Be a good fellow and scuttle off," Haxton said.

"I would like to tell you, Mr. Maugham, how sorry I am about that door."

"I would . . . prefer not to . . . discuss it," Maugham stammered, looking into the distance with tragic eyes.

Undaunted, I stood my ground and brought my parcel into view. "Do I understand, sir, that you are interested in the works of this Paul Gauguin?"

Maugham turned slowly back to me. "What have you there?"

"All I can tell you, sir, is that it is a painting, signed 'P G O.' I found it in the boiler room of the brewery where I work." This was the truth. I had put it there, to be sure. But after I had put it there I had found it there again. "Would you care to see it?"

Maugham was a consummate actor. He shrugged. "Why not?" All that gave him away was that his fingers had turned white as they gripped his glass.

I tore off the newspaper and revealed the canvas to them in the sunlight at close range. Their eyes widened, but they did not say a word. Looking at it myself after some passage of time, I had to admit that it was convincingly good. "Looks to be a mite dusty," I said, taking a napkin from the table, dipping it in a glass of water, and proceeding to scrub the painting vigorously.

"Stop it!" said Maugham. "What are you doing!"

This gave me some amusement, considering all I had previously done to the canvas.

Haxton touched Maugham's arm, and they exchanged a conspiratorial smile. "Sit down, my dear fellow. Have a drink with us."

I sat, and a drink soon arrived.

"How did this . . . painting come to be in your possession?" Maugham's tone was casual, but his eyes were unable to leave the painting. "To whom does it . . . belong?"

"To me, sir." I told him about the ten paintings I had found in the boiler room eight years before, and how they had gotten there.

"There are *ten* of them?" Haxton asked, wide-eyed.

"Only five, now. The others I burnt up, to get the furnace going."

"You did what?" Maugham said, his fingers whiter than ever. "Oh, dear!"

"These five," Haxton put in. "Would you consider selling them?"

"I might. I understand they are worth a good deal."

"Oh, no. Oh, no," Haxton said deprecatingly. "Not at all. Besides, they could well be forgeries."

Haxton was really not too bright. If they had no value, who would forge them? But I went along with him. "That they may well be, sir. I had considered that possibility. These forgers, I hear, are ingenious fellows. Suppose, now, that an expert art forger had come to Tahiti some ten years ago, with the sole purpose of forging the works of Gauguin. Not that Gauguins had any value whatever at that time, but this forger had the remarkable foresight to realize that in time they would have. And so he forged ten Gauguins. Desiring to visit some of the other islands while here, but not wishing to carry the forged Gauguins with him, he secreted them in a dry place—the boiler room of the brewery—intending to return and 'discover' them there. But, alas, the interisland schooner ran into a typhoon and sank, with the loss of everyone aboard. And so the forgeries remained there, gathering dust, until I chanced upon them two years later." I had great difficulty in keeping a straight face as I recounted this preposterous fable, but I succeeded. "Grant you," I continued, "it is a rather farfetched set of circumstances, but it is the only way I can imagine that the forgeries came to be in the boiler room."

"Well, I suppose it is a possible explanation," said Haxton.

"Stranger things have happened," Maugham said. I could almost hear his crafty mind working. "Just the same, I should be interested in seeing the other paintings. They might, even as forgeries, have some value as . . . curios."

"Follow me, gentlemen." I rose and started off, and they came after me. Little did they know what I had in store for them, the carrion hunters!

The two of them followed me down the narrow steps to the boiler room of the brewery. It was dark, lit by one high window which admitted a beam of light. In the center of the room was a coal-burning furnace. All around were crates of empty beer bottles. There was a bench under the window, and I invited them to sit.

On a ledge I had previously put a brandy bottle. It was filled with water, but the bottle was brown. "Let me see," I muttered, wandering around in the near darkness, "where would those paintings be?" I found the brandy bottle. "Excuse me, gentlemen. I feel the need of a bit of refreshment." I held the bottle to my lips and drank quite a bit of it. "Where would they be?" I looked about some more. "Good heavens! I fear the native boy has burned them up! What a pity!" I could hear gasps from the bench. "Still, if they are forgeries, as you suspect, it does not matter much." I had some more brandy. "No, wait. Perhaps they are over here." They were. I brought them out of the darkness. "Yes! Here they are!" I threw them on the floor. "My gracious, they are dusty!" I took a stiff broom and began to sweep one of them violently.

"Don't do that!" Maugham cried.

I stopped, and took a rag and whisked off most of the dust, and took them the four paintings. "Here you are, gentlemen. Examine them at your leisure." I went back and had another noisy dollop of "brandy," watching them out of the corner of my eye as they studied one, and then another.

Enough time had gone by for the "brandy" to take effect. I came up to them, unsteadily. "Well, gentlemen? Are they forgeries, or no?"

Maugham and Haxton exchanged a glance. "I very much fear, my good man, that they are," said Haxton.

"And your opinion, Mr. Maugham?"

Maugham hesitated. "It is difficult to tell," he said finally. To give him his due, he was not the barefaced liar Haxton was. "But I would be willing to purchase them from you, and take my chances." But a liar he was, still.

There was a lunatic in Papeete who rolled his eyes in a wild way, although he was harmless and was allowed to roam the streets. I staggered about a bit and let my eyes roll. "No, sir. I will not sell them to you."

"Why not?" Haxton asked.

"Because, gentlemen, they *are* forgeries!" I went over and drained the bottle and then smashed it on the floor.

"Sozzled again!" I heard Maugham whisper.

"How can you be sure?" Haxton asked from across the room.

"Because, gentlemen—I painted them myself!"

"He has lost his mind!" Maugham muttered to his friend.

I staggered back to them. "Yes! I painted them myself! I am a very great artist, you see!"

"Even so," said Maugham, humoring this lunatic, "they have merit of their own, and I am prepared to purchase them anyway."

"They have merit of their own?" I cried in joy. "Oh, thank

you, sir! Thank you! You are the first who has ever appreciated my work!"

"I will give you fifty pounds, for the lot."

"Fifty pounds? Oh, you tempt me, sir. You tempt me. But no." I glowered at them with grim determination. "But no! I only wished to learn from you, who know something of art, if any of my creations were worthwhile."

"Oh, they are, they are!" Haxton shouted.

"No, gentlemen. My work is not for sale. After all, these paintings might fall into the hands of unscrupulous persons who might pass them off as genuine Gauguins! And this must not be!" I picked up four of the paintings from the floor, and seized the fifth from Haxton's hands. "They must be destroyed!" I took them to the furnace and opened the door.

Maugham was on his feet. "No! Stop!"

"They must be destroyed!" I tossed in two of them, and they blazed away.

"You don't know what you're doing!" Haxton screamed.

I threw in the third.

"Stop him!" Maugham cried to Haxton, who came at me.

I picked up a coal shovel and whipped the air with it. "These are my paintings! I can do what I like with them!" I threw in the fourth and the fifth, and slammed the furnace door. "There! It is done!"

"Oh, my God," Maugham moaned.

"But I wish to thank you, Mr. Maugham, for your encouragement. Without it, I might have abandoned my artistic career forever."

I went up the stairs then, leaving them alone in the cellar. My revenge upon his highness, Mr. Maugham, was complete. Even now, I often chuckle over that scene.

NOTE: *Chuckle! It is one of the most dreadful scenes I have ever read. What had Maugham ever done to Uncle Frank, really, except swear at him—and kick him once—under the most severe provocation?*

I heard from one of the hotel maids that Maugham had taken to his bed after the incident in the boiler room and had been unable to work or eat for three days. I began to feel a small measure of remorse. So, since the score between us had been evened, I decided to make amends, so to speak. I went out into the bush to a deserted house, in which I found a glass-paned door very much like the one I had broken. I removed it from its hinges, sawed off the lower third, and took it back to my shack on the beach. I began to paint upon it. I knew, from the five genuine Gauguins (which I still had, of course) that he had often painted the same subject more than once, in different manners.

On the first door, the naked woman holding the breadfruit was on the right. I painted her on the left. A white rabbit was on the left; I painted it on the right. In the original the sea behind the woman was green; I painted it blue.

Because the paint was fresh, I weighted the door and moored it under the sea for a few days. Then I brought it in and baked it in the sun. I tossed pebbles at it. I rubbed it with sand. Then coffee grounds. There was a little puppy who used to come and visit me. I held him up over the glass panes just high enough so that his claws could touch them. Of course, he struggled to get down and, as he did so, his claws scraped off some of the paint. I thought this was very clever of me. When I had finished, the work was delicately distressed, though in slightly better condition than the original door.

I wrapped it in newspaper and went round to the hotel, where the two of them were again seated on the veranda, drinking.

At the sight of me Maugham began to breathe heavily, and his eyes filled with apprehension.

"Go away!" said Haxton firmly.

"Whatever you may have to say," said Maugham, "I do not wish to hear."

Regardless, I approached their table with my door. "I am sorry, Mr. Maugham, about my behavior the other day. I fear that I was emotionally distressed."

"I had . . . considered that possibility," Maugham said.

"I thought it only right that my forgeries should be destroyed. But I have something here, Mr. Maugham, which I think might interest you."

"I do not wish to see it."

"It is a glass-paned door, sir. It reminds me of the one which

I unfortunately destroyed." I took off the newspaper, and they stared at it.

"I beg you, sir. Take it away."

"But why, Mr. Maugham?"

"Because if I evince the slightest . . . interest in it, you will undoubtedly drop it and smash it. Or you will fly into a rage and kick it to pieces. I have had more than enough of you, sir. I simply cannot stand these emotional extravaganzas."

NOTE: Good for Maugham!

Haxton asked, "Do you wish to sell it to Mr. Maugham?"

"Oh, heavens no, sir. I wish to make him a present of it. To make up, in some small way, for the door that I broke."

Maugham studied the door. "Did you happen by any chance to paint this yourself?"

"Oh, yes. Oh, yes. All by myself. Do you think it has merit?"

"When did you paint it?" Haxton asked.

"Oh, a few days ago. Do you think it has merit?"

"A few days ago!" Haxton was out to prove me a liar. He really was a stupid young man. "Why, then, is it so weather-beaten?"

Maugham cleared his throat and tried to catch Haxton's eye with a look which clearly meant, Keep your bloody mouth shut, you idiot! But Haxton did not see it.

"Well, sir, I—that is, I—"

"It has considerable merit," Maugham cut in sharply.

"You are most kind, sir."

The doltish Haxton insisted on opening another keg of peas. "I see that you have signed it 'P G O.' Does not this make it a forgery which should be destroyed?"

"Haxton," Maugham said severely, "I should like to discuss with you the possibility of your swimming to New Zealand!"

"Swimming to . . . ?" The penny finally dropped. "Oh. Yes."

I decided to torture Haxton a bit. "You are right, sir. I had not thought of that. Of course it should be destroyed. I shall go and do so immediately. How stupid of me." I picked up the door.

"Hold on," said Maugham. I did. "I think you were perfectly correct in destroying those . . . forgeries the other day. For the reason that they did not exist before. But the door is another matter. A door painted by Gauguin did exist, until you unfortunately broke it and deprived the world of its beauty. But now you have replaced this door with another, lovelier even than Gauguin's door."

"You have a point there, sir." And so he had.

"So, I beg you to allow me to accept your most . . . gracious gift. I shall take it back to my villa in France and install it as a . . . window. The sun will shine through it and suffuse it with beauty. In order to protect your name—for I am sure you do not wish to be known as a forger of art—"

"Oh, no. No, no."

"—I shall pretend that it was painted by Gauguin. The truth will remain a secret among the three of us. What do you say to that?"

"I think it is a capital idea, sir."

"Would you care to hand the door to Haxton, then?"

I started toward Haxton with it, but could not resist one simulated stumble en route, causing them to gasp. But I put it safely into Haxton's hands, and retreated. "I am leaving for the Marquesas tomorrow," I said, and it was true. "So I shall say good-bye to you both. I hope that we will meet again, one day."

"Ah . . . yes. Of course." Maugham barely managed a smile. "And thank you again."

I left them, looking back only once to see them giggling and chortling together over the door.

I went north to look over the Marquesas because I had wearied of the monotony of life in Tahiti and desired a change of scene. But I found the principal island, Hiva Oa, a dreary place, and resolved to leave by the next boat.

In the town of Atuana, where Gauguin had lived the last years before his death, I visited his grave. It was marked only by an ugly slab of concrete, overgrown with weeds. I had brought a bottle of claret with me, and I spent perhaps an hour there, sipping wine and reflecting.

During the next ten years, I went from job to job, from city to city, from Australia to Tasmania to New Zealand. Unfortunately, I lacked ambition. I only wished to enjoy all that life had to offer, and work was merely a necessary evil.

The only member of the American branch of our family with whom I kept in touch was my half brother, Hartland.

NOTE: *My grandfather.*

By 1928, I had reached bottom. I was living as a guest of the Salvation Army in Wellington, New Zealand. I did not know what in the world to do.

And then I remembered my five original Gauguins, which of course were still with me, carefully and securely wrapped. I had kept in touch with the outside world through the London *Times*, and had learned that Gauguin was receiving more and more recognition as an artist, and that his finer works were now fetching as much as a thousand pounds.

In despair, I realized that I would have to sell one of my Gauguins. I brought them out and studied them. It was agony to part with even one of them, but at last I selected one, and took it to the only art dealer I could locate in Wellington.

A bell tinkled as I walked into a shop hung with dreary, sentimental paintings. A fat little man came from the rear and regarded my shabby attire with some disdain. "Yes?"

"Good morning, sir. I have a painting here which I would like to sell. It is a Gauguin."

"A what?"

"Paul Gauguin. Surely you have heard of him."

"Oh . . . yes. That man in Tahiti. Heard of him, but never seen his work." I unrolled the painting for him and he looked at it. "Crickey Dick! What rubbish! Whoever saw a blue horse, or orange water? The poor blighter must have been nearly blind. Also, he can't even draw!"

I was not going to argue. I merely handed him a sheaf of items about Gauguin I had clipped from the *Times*. "You might care to glance at these, sir." The items included some reproductions in black and white. To give the man his due, he read through them carefully.

Then, grudgingly: "Well, just because I think they're utter rot doesn't mean that some idiot might not buy them. I'll give you twenty pounds for this."

"Twenty pounds! It is worth a thousand!"

"Not to me."

"I am sorry. It is not for sale at that price."

"Fifty, then, and that's my top."

"I'm sorry. No." I left his shop. I was damned if I would sell one of my Gauguins for fifty pounds. I would rather scrub the streets on my hands and knees.

That night, as I was trying to sleep on the relief map that the Salvation Army called a mattress, I remembered what Maugham had said about my door: That since I had destroyed Gauguin's door, it was my duty to replace it, so that the world would not be deprived of a work of art. Despite the false assumption upon which his reasoning was based, there was logic in it. I remembered the five Gauguins I had used, over the years, to get the furnace going. Was not their replacement an obligation on my part to the world—especially as nature and circumstance had combined to make me competent for the task? Could it be that the Lord, whose concern for fallen sparrows was well known, also troubled Himself with the replacement of works of art which His creatures had destroyed out of ignorance? Could it be that, in His infinite wisdom, He had contrived events in such a way as to make me His appointed for the task He wished performed? The thought was so profound that it staggered me; I did not sleep all night. Before morning I knew what I had to do.

Early the next day I started going round Wellington, raising cash. I begged and borrowed from friends and acquaintances, and even strangers on the street. I managed to raise close to three pounds. With this I bought the necessary art materials and a supply of food—mostly tinned beef and crackers, and some cheap wine. Potato sacks and wood for frames were to be had for the picking up.

Some distance out of Wellington I found a deserted beach, on which I built a rude shelter. And I began to copy Gauguins, just as I had in Tahiti.

I was not intending to count these among the five it was my duty to re-create. I was interested only in raising enough capital to enable me to begin my task in proper fashion. And so, this time, I "improved" upon Gauguin greatly. The results were so appalling that I could not bring myself to put his name upon them. But then, Gauguin was always haphazard about signing his works. Sometimes he used "P G O" (whatever that meant), sometimes "P. Gauguin," sometimes just "Gauguin." Sometimes he did not sign them at all.

At the end of a week I had two frightful forgeries, which I "aged," then removed from their frames and took to the art dealer. "I have changed my mind, sir. I might consider selling these two." I unrolled them.

"Well! Why didn't you bring these in the first place? They are head and shoulders above the rubbish you showed me!"

"These were painted at a much later date."

"He finally learned how to draw, I see. That horse *looks* like a horse! And what a lovely blue the sky is. I will give you seventy-five pounds each."

I handed him a recent cutting from the *Times*. In London, one of the Rothschilds had paid two thousand pounds for a Gauguin.

"Very well. A hundred each."

I assented, and took the cash and left. I suddenly knew how a prostitute must feel the first time she takes money from a man.

In those days, two hundred pounds was ample to pay for my first-class passage back to England. On the voyage I remained mostly in my cabin, working on the first two of the five Gauguins I meant to replace. It was not my intention merely to copy my five genuine Gauguins, for these still existed, but rather to create new works in place of those I had destroyed. So I allowed myself a free hand, borrowing various elements from my five to create two new paintings.

By the time my ship reached London, I had two very fine Gauguins, well seasoned in my saltwater bathtub, and then dried and distressed by my usual methods.

Gauguin's naked women continued to upset me, but I reproduced them nonetheless, hopeful that the sight of them would be kept from innocent children.

It was in London that I began to perfect my technique in selling my own Gauguins. Had I had independent means, I would have given them to the world; as it was, I needed money on which to live.

Never did I claim that one of my paintings was a Gauguin. I

merely mentioned that it resembled his work. Nor did I intimate that the painting was for sale. I posed as a collector of
moderate means who suspected that this painting, which had
come into my hands, might well be a forgery. I wished advice
from the wealthy collector, who knew as much about Gauguins
as anyone alive—or so I said. In recent years, scientific tests
have been devised to determine the age of a painting, but they
did not exist at the time of which I write. Consequently, the
genuineness of a Gauguin could only be judged "by guess and
by golly," and anyone who claimed otherwise was either a fool
or a liar.

While the collector pondered, I would carefully point out
those things in the painting which made me suspicious, on
the grounds that Gauguin had never done such and such a
thing in others of his paintings, so far as I knew. The collector, if he had studied Gauguin's work at all, would hide a
knowing smile and pity me for my ignorance. Soon he would
conclude that my suspicions were unfounded, and must
therefore be valueless, and the painting genuine. From that
point on I would let the collector talk me into selling it to
him.

I succeeded in selling both paintings in London, for a total of
five thousand pounds. (When one considers that the pound was
then worth nearly five American dollars, and that the cost of
living was less than half of what it is now—in 1960—one realizes
that this was a considerable sum of money.)

It enabled me to live very well indeed for over four years.
When I finally ran low on money, I settled on a beach in the
north of Spain for a few weeks and painted my third Gauguin.
This I sold in Rome to an Italian prince for three thousand, five
hundred pounds. Good Gauguins were gradually becoming
quite valuable.

Three years later I was close to poverty again, and so
painted my fourth Gauguin, on a Greek island. This I sold to
an Egyptian millionaire for seven thousand pounds, which
kept me in style for another four years. But then, because of
my proclivity for joyous living, I was nearly penniless once
more.

I had only one more Gauguin left to paint, for that was all that
my obligation to the world called for. After the fifth, I had sworn

not to paint another. But if I was to be able to live well for the rest of my life, this last would have to be a truly magnificent Gauguin—and fetch a very high price.

I rented a cottage on the Italian coast and went to work. By then, in 1939, many reproductions of Gauguins were available to me as source material. I spent nearly six weeks on this last Gauguin, and when I had finished it to my satisfaction, it was a masterpiece.

The finished work was quite large for a Gauguin—thirty-eight inches high by twenty-seven inches wide. In the immediate foreground was an exotic plant, with blossoms like yellow butterflies. Behind this was a deep blue pool, streaked with orange. Walking majestically from the pool was a large red horse ridden by a naked Tahitian maiden. Beyond this a group of native children played and splashed about in the pool, under an intricate network of tree branches. Above the entire scene were the mountains of Tahiti, rising to the blue, cloud-dotted sky. Gauguin would have been proud of it, I believe, and would have titled it "The Red Horse."

So magnificent was the painting that I was determined not to let it go for less than twenty-five thousand pounds—an outrageous price, to be sure—which I felt certain I could get. The one thing I failed to take into consideration was that my luck might be running out.

I had read of a certain English duke—I shall not identify him further—reputed to be the richest man in England and an avid art collector. I went to London, called and made an appointment to see him, and took "The Red Horse" to his palace in Regent's Park. His Grace received me in his art gallery, its walls covered with masterpieces. He had three Gauguins, and I was delighted to see that one of them I had painted on my boat trip from New Zealand. I unrolled the canvas for him. He studied it for perhaps five minutes. He was a tall man in his sixties, with a red face and a bristling white mustache. "Where did you get this?" he asked sharply.

I told him about finding five Gauguins in the boiler room, and so forth. If he wished to assume that this was one of them, that was his business.

"Is it for sale?"

"Yes, your Grace."

"At what price?"

"Twenty-five thousand pounds."

"For a Gauguin? You are out of your mind! I bought the last one, there on the wall, for ten."

"If you want this one, your Grace, you will have to pay twenty-five."

"Mmm." He took a magnifying glass and studied the painting, inch by inch. Then he thumbtacked it to a board and paced the room, studying it from various distances. "Y'know, this is a very fine painting. Very fine." He smiled a little. "But I have been collecting art for many years now, and I have developed a kind of sixth sense, you might say." He paused, dramatically. "This, sir, is a forgery!"

I indicated my own Gauguin on his wall. "Did your sixth sense tell you that this Gauguin was genuine?"

"Of course! Knew it the instant I saw it! And my experts agreed with me."

"I see." I removed my painting from the board and rolled it up. "I'm sure you won't mind if I go elsewhere, for another opinion?"

"Elsewhere?" His eyes narrowed.

"To Lord Dodson, for one." This was the duke's most despised competitor in art collecting. "He has several Gauguins, I believe."

"Dodson wouldn't know a Van Gogh from a Titian!"

"Even so." I made as if to leave.

"Wait," said the duke, all faith in his sixth sense draining away. "There is a chance in a hundred that I might be wrong. Tell you what. Leave this with me. There are four experts I would like to call in, to study it."

"Of course, your Grace."

"Come back at four o'clock tomorrow."

I left. I was not concerned. If the same experts who had authenticated my previous Gauguin declared "The Red Horse" to be a forgery, I would simply sell it elsewhere.

The following afternoon the duke received me in his study. My rolled painting was on his desk. He looked at me with a gloating, vindictive smile. "Your painting has been examined, independently, by four experts. They agreed unanimously that it is a forgery."

"I'm sorry to hear that."

"My sixth sense is never wrong."

"I am sure not, your Grace."

"Now that you know for certain that it is a forgery, you will surely not attempt to sell it elsewhere."

"Of course not."

"Good. But just in case you should change your mind, I must tell you that I have had the painting photographed. Copies of it, plus a circular letter stating that it is a patent forgery, will be sent to art dealers, museums, and collectors all over the world. We have our own communications system, for our own protection."

"I see." There went my six weeks of work in Italy. But then, I could always paint another fifth Gauguin.

The duke looked at me severely. "Also, I am forced to tell you, sir, that my sixth sense tells me that you *knew* this painting was a forgery. It is possible that you might try to sell other forgeries in future. For this reason, the circular letter will contain a full description of you, with a warning to beware of any painting you might attempt to sell—especially a painting that is reputed to be a Gauguin."

It was the blackest moment of my life. Not only could I not sell a fifth forgery but now I could not even sell any of my five genuine Gauguins! What was I to do to support myself for the rest of my life? I was in utter despair.

"That will be all," said the duke, rising.

I got to my feet and picked up my painting. At that moment the study door opened behind me. "Hullo!" a man said. "Hope I'm not late for tea."

"Come in, Willie. Come in."

I turned. It was Maugham. He blanched. "Oh, my God! Not you! Not you again!"

Fuddled, the duke asked, "You know this man, Willie?"

"Yes. We met in Tahiti."

"How are you, Mr. Maugham? It has been quite some time."

"The rascal tried to sell me a fake Gauguin!" the duke cried.

"Oh? May I see it?" The duke took it from me and unrolled it for Maugham. "Did he perhaps tell you that he had found it in a boiler room in Tahiti?"

"Yes. Some such rubbish."

Maugham looked at me. "So there were actually six, eh?"

"Yes, sir. There were six."

"What are you talking about?" asked the duke.

"You painted this yourself, didn't you?" Maugham asked me gently.

"Oh, no, sir! No! Please, Mr. Maugham! I could go to prison!"

"It has considerable merit," Maugham said. "It shows really remarkable talent."

I grinned and let my eyes roll a bit. "Do you really think so, sir?"

"I am convinced that you painted it! It is the work of a genius!"

"I did paint it, sir! I did! I did! I painted it all by myself! I am a very great artist, you see."

"By God!" the duke shouted. "You'll go to jail for this! You heard him, Willie. You're a witness."

"Please, your Grace. Please have mercy. You see, sir, despite my genius, no one will buy my paintings. So I have to pretend that they are Gauguins. It is evil of me, I know. It is wrong. I will destroy this at once!" I grabbed for the painting, but Maugham snatched it away and held it behind him. "No, no," he said. "It is too fine a painting to be destroyed." He turned to the duke. "Bertie, I would like a word with you."

"Oh? Oh, of course. *You*—wait outside in the hall!" I went out. "Damn me," the duke bellowed as I shut the door behind me, "I will see that man in jail if it's the last thing I do!"

I went down the hall and found a chair and sat. I could hear the duke shouting and banging his desk. As the minutes went by, his voice quieted, except for an occasional expletive.

After a time the study door opened, and his Grace stalked out to me. I rose. His face was crimson, and his manner gruff. "Take this and be gone," he said, handing me a slip of paper, and then turning and walking away.

It was, as I had expected, a check for twenty-five thousand pounds. It always pays to tell the truth, I have found.

As I write this I am in the Virgin Islands. It is December 17, 1965. I have just learned that Maugham is dead, at ninety-one. Thinking back, I realize that I owe Somerset a great deal. It was he who first encouraged my artistic endeavors, and thus enabled me to live a life of ease and luxury for many, many years.

Knowing that the duke's twenty-five thousand was the only money I would ever earn, I resolved to make it last. And for once in my life I succeeded. I lived fairly modestly here and there in various countries, enjoying my declining years in a quiet way.

In my eighties I moved to the Virgin Islands. Here, in 1965, I suffered a slight stroke. The doctor was staggered to find me still alive, and said that, considering the state of my various organs, I should have died at least ten years earlier. He told me that I would soon be off to the Great Beyond.

Since I did not want to die among strangers, and since my capital was nearly exhausted by then, I decided to go to the States, and to die there in the home of some member of my family.

What of my five genuine Gauguins? I have them with me still, carefully wrapped. I could have sold them but I did not, partly because I loved them so, and partly because I have a devotion to family. And surely, I thought, although my brothers are long gone, there must be, among my nephews and nieces and great-nephews and great-nieces, at least one of them who will be kind enough to take me into his or her home.

When I find such, he or she will have my Gauguins.

So ended Uncle Frank's manuscript. But where were the Gauguins? We had looked through his things and not found them. Had he lost them, or sold them, since writing the above? A little frantic now, Maria and I searched his room again. No Gauguins anywhere. All we found of any interest was a little red fire engine, on the closet shelf.

Could he have hidden them under the lining of his suitcase? It was while exploring this possibility that I found a letter, written on my own stationery:

My dear Warner,

You have received me most kindly. You gave me a home and food and refreshment and a warm bed to die in, and I am grateful to you.

Warner, an old man of eighty-six does not want to die in the gutter, forgotten by the world. It is as simple as that. I wished to be remembered by someone. Not loved, nor admired—merely remembered. That is why I wrote my memoirs. Publish them if you like; everyone in them is now dead.

On the shelf of my cupboard you will find a little fire engine. This is for Peter, for his birthday on the fifth of January.

You will find my Gauguins in your attic, in the old umbrella stand. They are yours, with gratitude. Bless you all, and good-bye.

Your Uncle Frank

I ran up the stairs into our attic. There in our old umbrella stand was a rolled parcel. I nearly fell down the stairs with it.

"It can't be true!" Maria shouted.

"It is!" I carefully placed the parcel on Uncle Frank's bed. "Would you get me a razor blade, please, dear?" I said to my wife.

Maria ran off and soon came back with one. Terribly carefully, I slit open the package. Terribly slowly, I unrolled the layers of paper and oilskin.

Before our eyes was one of the most beautiful paintings I had ever seen. It was a picture of Gauguin's Tahitian mistress, Tahura, bathing their infant son in a lucid pool. Behind them, two native girls stood by with towels. Above them, the jungle rose in undulating forms, the leaves and blossoms red and rust and blue and brown and green. Beyond was a purple sea with little white sails upon it.

So perfectly had the painting been wrapped and preserved that the colors were still vibrant, the canvas flexible. There was no sign of deterioration whatever. Scarcely able to believe what we saw, we examined the other four paintings. Each was exquisite; each was in perfect condition.

Like Uncle Frank, I did not know what in the world to do. Then I thought of George Stasher, a curator at the Los Angeles County Museum of Art. Also lectures at U.S.C.—a Ph.D. and all that. Also, an old friend. I called him at the museum. "George, this is Warner. You've got to come up here right now!"

"I can't. Got to give a lecture on Tintoretto."

"When can you get here?"

"Around six. Has something terrible happened?"

"No! Something wonderful! We need you!"

"Calm yourself, Warner. I'll be there."

At five minutes after six the door opened, and George walked in. He is short and plump, with big eyes and a mustache, and is highly emotional by nature. "What in holy hell is all this about?"

"Don't ask questions!" I shoved our typed copy of Uncle Frank's memoirs into his hands. "Just take this into my den and sit down and read!"

"Calm yourself, Warner. Please. Could I have a Scotch?"

I made it for him and took it into the den, where he was reading and chuckling a bit. "This is amusing—the bit in the Ivy with Mrs. Campbell. But I hardly think it's an emergency."

"Will you read on! Will you just read on and stop talking!"

"Pull yourself together, Warner. Please."

I left him alone to read, and thirty minutes later the door burst open and George ran out, kind of foaming at the mouth. "Where are they?" he shouted.

"Upstairs. Calm yourself, George."

Maria and I took him up to Uncle Frank's room, where the Gauguins were spread out on the bed. George came into the room slowly, and in reverence. He approached the bed, sat on the edge of it, and studied one of the Gauguins. He did not say a word. He looked at the other four, one by one. Then he began to cry. "I'm sorry," he said, "but I have never seen so much beauty at one time in my life."

"I'd better get you another drink," said Maria, leaving.

"Do you think they're genuine, George?"

"I don't know. Let's take them downstairs." We did, and spread them out on the floor. Every time George looked at them he began to sniffle again. "You've got to remember," he told me, "that my field is the Italian Renaissance. Of course, I studied Gauguin in school. But I'm not an expert on him."

"But do you think they are *genuine?*"

"I don't know. I think the five he found in the boiler room were. But are these they?"

Maria came in with more drinks, and George asked her, "Dear one, could I have a razor blade and five envelopes?" She went off. "Nowadays," George said, "it's a fairly simple matter to determine the date of a painting." In a moment Maria returned with the required, and George got on his knees and began gently to scrape a little paint from a corner of each of the paintings. "We have an electronic spectroscope down at the museum." He put the resulting paint flecks into separate envelopes, which he marked. "From these samples of paint we can tell a good deal. We can't tell the precise date, of course, but we can certainly determine if they were painted before 1903, when Gauguin died."

"What would they be worth, if they are real?"

"Well, considering their condition, which is nearly perfect, and considering how beautiful they are, I would say, conservatively, oh . . . a hundred and fifty thousand each."

"But—but that's three-quarters of a million dollars!"

"Yep. So it is."

George left about midnight. Maria and I carefully rewrapped the Gauguins and put them in the hall closet. Then we went to bed. But we did not sleep. I was shopping for a seventy-five-foot motor yacht. I don't know what Maria was buying, but my yacht was going to come first.

The museum opens at ten in the morning. I called at five after and got George. "Well? Well?"

"Will you please calm yourself? Someone else is using the spectroscope. I'll call you as soon as I know anything."

I looked around and didn't see Maria. I went to the head of the stairs and called her.

"She went out, Daddy!" Melissa shouted up at me.

"Where?"

"She had some Christmas shopping to do. And she's having her hair done at two."

"What are you up to?"

"I'm wrapping presents, for a Christmas party at Christine's. Mrs. Smith is picking me up at twelve."

"What's Peter doing?"

"I'm playing with my cars!" came his treble voice.

"Okay. Just keep on doing it. I'm going back to bed. And

Melissa—stay off the phone. I'm expecting a call."

I went back to bed and slept until one and then got up, feeling much more human. I decided to be a devil and have a drink, and went down in my pajamas and bathrobe. Peter was still playing with his cars by the fire. It was a cold and rainy day, and I put another log on the fire.

"Have you had any lunch yet?" I asked.

"Yep. Melissa fixed me three hot dogs."

"Good for Melissa." I went into the kitchen and mixed myself a gin and tonic and waited for George to call. I had another. Then I decided to gloat over the Gauguins a bit. I went to the closet. They were gone.

Who? How? Peter? Melissa? Maria? A burglar? Very calmly I approached Peter. "Tell me, son, did you take anything out of that closet today?"

"No, Daddy. I didn't even open the door." Now, Peter can be a monster but he is always truthful.

Maria? I called the beauty parlor. "Sweetie, did you move the Gauguins?"

"No! Don't tell me they're—"

"They're gone!"

"They couldn't be!"

"They are!"

"Peter?"

"He says not, and I believe him."

"Melissa?"

"She's up at Christine's Christmas party."

There was a long silence at the other end of the line. Then, rather sickly: "Oh, no! *No!*"

"What is it?"

"You know how fond Melissa is of wrapping fancy presents. When I left this morning she said we were running out of wrapping paper!"

"Oh, my God! I'll call you back." I hung up and found Christine's parents' number and called it, but the line was busy. I ran to the front door and shouted to Peter that I'd be back, and jumped down our steps and into the rain, still in my dressing gown and slippers. Christine's house was up the hill a few blocks. We play bridge with her parents. I remembered as I ran that at this kind of children's party, as soon as the presents are opened the wrappings are burned in the fireplace. I ran up that hill like a madman. I lost a slipper and then another. I didn't care. They would now be opening the presents.

I burst in the door of the house. There were about a dozen kids there and three or four mothers. The kids had opened their various presents and were sitting around fighting over them. There was a blazing fire full of papers.

Seeing me dressed as I was, unshaven, hair matted by the rain, with bare feet and wild eyes, and bursting in like this, some of the children began to scream with fright. I didn't care. I saw Melissa across the room and ran to her and picked her up by the throat. "Did you take those paintings out of the hall closet?"

"Yes!" she squeaked as well as she was able.

"Did you use them to wrap your packages with?"

"Warner," said Christine's mother. "Melissa is turning blue."

"Oh. Sorry." I put Melissa down.

"No!" she screamed. "I didn't!"

"Where are they, then?"

Melissa was crying. "In my room! I thought they were pretty, and I put them up in my room!"

"Really!" I could hear Mrs. Smith say from behind me. "We all drink a little too much. But *this* much?"

"I'm sorry, Melissa. I'm sorry." I turned to the ladies. "I'm sorry for this intrusion. Excuse me. Pardon me." I backed to the door. "I'm not myself today." I left.

"And that's for sure!" I heard a woman say behind me.

I ran back down the hill in the rain, and up the steps to my house and into the living room, where Peter was still playing with his cars in front of the fire, and up the stairs to Melissa's room.

The five Gauguins were there, on the walls. She had merely used little pushpins to hold them up. I sat on her bed, gasping for breath and in a state of shock. Peter wandered in. "What's the matter, Daddy?"

"Nothing, Peter. I'm just out of breath."

"You're supposed to call a man named George. Right away."

"Oh? Okay. You be a good boy, now. Daddy loves you." I patted him on the head and went into our bedroom and called George.

"Warner, brace yourself. Our tests show that they've got to be genuine! Congratulations!"

I was too stunned to react. "Thanks, George."

"Warner, I'd like to be able to tell our director about your Gauguins. There's quite a sizable amount in our acquisition fund, and I think he would be most appreciative if he could have first crack. But I won't tell him unless you say I can."

"Sure. Tell him. Sure."

"I'll get back to you."

I called Maria at the beauty parlor and told her all, and she fainted. I told the hairdresser not to worry.

The phone rang again. It was George. "I've spoken to our director. He wants to see the Gauguins as soon as possible. Like in twenty minutes."

"Sure. I'll be home. Bring him up."

I shaved and took a shower and put on my newest clothes. I wanted to look kind of rich, for the director. Then I decided to get the Gauguins and take them downstairs and put them up on the walls, the better to display them.

I went into Melissa's room. They were gone. Now what?

I went downstairs. Peter was playing again in front of the fire. "Peter, what happened to the pictures on the walls of Melissa's room?"

"I took 'em down."

"Oh? And what did you do with them?"

"I burned 'em," he said, indicating the fire.

"You *what?*" In the flames, I saw the last of the Gauguins curl and ignite.

"They were naked women!" Peter shouted. "Dirty trash! Naked women!" He banged in rhythm on the floor with one of his cars. "Naked women! Dirty trash!"

1969:

Goodbye, Pops

Joe Gores

I got off the Greyhound and stopped to draw icy Minnesota air into my lungs. A bus had brought me from Springfield, Illinois, to Chicago the day before; a second bus had brought me here. I caught my passing reflection in the window of the old-fashioned depot—a tall hard man with a white and savage face, wearing an ill-fitting overcoat. I caught another reflection, too, one that froze my guts: a cop in uniform. Could they already know it was someone else in that burned-out car?

Then the cop turned away, chafing his arms with gloved hands through his blue stormcoat, and I started breathing again. I went quickly over to the cab line. Only two hackies were waiting there; the front one rolled down his window as I came up.

"You know the Miller place north of town?" I asked. He looked me over. "I know it. Five bucks—now."

I paid him from the money I'd rolled a drunk for in Chicago and eased back against the rear seat. As he nursed the cab out ice-rimed Second Street my fingers gradually relaxed from their rigid chopping position. I deserved to go back inside if I let a clown like this get to me.

"Old man Miller's pretty sick, I hear." He half turned to catch me with a corner of an eye. "You got business with him?"

"Yeah. My own."

That ended that conversation. It bothered me that Pops was sick enough for this clown to know about it; but maybe my brother Rod being vice-president at the bank would explain that. There was a lot of new construction and a freeway west of town with a tricky overpass to the old county road. A mile beyond a new subdivision were the 200 wooded hilly acres I knew so well.

After my break from the Federal pen at Terre Haute, Indiana, two days before, I'd gotten outside their cordon through woods like these. I'd gone out in a prison truck, in a pail of swill meant for the prison farm pigs, had headed straight west, across the Illinois line. I'm good in open country, even when I'm in prison condition, so by dawn I was in a hayloft near Paris, Illinois, some 20 miles from the pen. You can do what you have to do.

The cabby stopped at the foot of the private road, looking dubious. "Listen, buddy, I know that's been plowed, but it looks damned icy. If I try it and go into the ditch—"

"I'll walk from here."

I waited beside the road until he'd driven away, then let the north wind chase me up the hill and into the leafless hardwoods. The cedars that Pops and I had put in as a windbreak were taller and fuller; rabbit paths were pounded hard into the snow under the barbed-wire tangles of wild raspberry bushes. Under the oaks at the top of the hill was the old-fashioned, two-story house, but I detoured to the kennels first. The snow was deep and undisturbed inside them. No more foxhounds. No cracked corn in the bird feeder outside the kitchen window, either. I rang the front doorbell.

My sister-in-law Edwina, Rod's wife, answered it. She was three years younger than my 35, and she'd started wearing a girdle.

"Good Lord! Chris!" Her mouth tightened. "We didn't—"

"Ma wrote that the old man was sick." She'd written, all right. *Your father is very ill. Not that you have ever cared if any of us lives or dies* . . . And then Edwina decided that my tone of voice had given her something to get righteous about.

"I'm amazed you'd have the nerve to come here, even if they did let you out on parole or something." So nobody had been around asking yet. "If you plan to drag the family name through the mud again—"

I pushed by her into the hallway. "What's wrong with the old man?" I called him Pops only inside myself, where no one could hear.

"He's dying, that's what's wrong with him."

She said it with a sort of baleful pleasure. It hit me, but I just grunted and went by into the living room. Then the old girl called down from the head of the stairs.

"Eddy? What—who is it?"

"Just—a salesman, Ma. He can wait until Doctor's gone."

Doctor. As if some damned croaker was generic physician all by himself. When he came downstairs Edwina tried to hustle him out before I could see him, but I caught his arm as he poked it into his overcoat sleeve.

"Like to see you a minute, Doc. About old man Miller."

He was nearly six feet, a couple of inches shorter than me, but outweighing me forty pounds. He pulled his arm free.

"Now see here, fellow—"

I grabbed his lapels and shook him, just enough to pop a button off his coat and put his glasses awry on his nose. His face got red.

"Old family friend, Doc." I jerked a thumb at the stairs. "What's the story?"

It was dumb, dumb as hell, of course, asking him; at any second the cops would figure out that the farmer in the burned-out car wasn't me after all. I'd dumped enough gasoline before I struck the match so they couldn't lift prints off anything except the shoe I'd planted: but they'd make him through dental charts as soon as they found out he was missing. When they did they'd come here asking questions, and then the croaker would realize who I was. But I wanted to know whether Pops was as bad off as Edwina said he was, and I've never been a patient man.

The croaker straightened his suitcoat, striving to regain lost dignity. "He—Judge Miller is very weak, too weak to move. He probably won't last out the week." His eyes searched my face for pain, but there's nothing like a Federal pen to give you control. Disappointed, he said, "His lungs. I got to it much too late, of course. He's resting easily."

I jerked the thumb again. "You know your way out."

Edwina was at the head of the stairs, her face righteous again. It seems to run in the family, even with those who married in. Only Pops and I were short of it.

"Your father is very ill. I forbid you—"

In the room I could see the old man's arm hanging limply over the edge of the bed, with smoke from the cigarette between his fingers running up to the ceiling in a thin unwavering blue line. The upper arm, which once had measured an honest 18 and had swung his small tight fist against the side of my head a score of times, could not even hold a cigarette up in the air. It gave me the same wrench as finding a good foxhound that's gotten mixed up with a bobcat.

The old girl came out of her chair by the foot of the bed, her face blanched. I put my arms around her. "Hi, Ma," I said. She was rigid inside my embrace, but I knew she wouldn't pull away. Not there in Pops's room.

He had turned his head at my voice. The light glinted from his silky white hair. His eyes, translucent with imminent death, were the pure, pale blue of birch shadows on fresh snow.

"Chris," he said in a weak voice. "Son of a biscuit, boy . . . I'm glad to see you."

"You ought to be, you lazy devil," I said heartily. I pulled off my suit jacket and hung it over the back of the chair, and tugged off my tie. "Getting so lazy that you let the foxhounds go!"

"That's enough, Chris." She tried to put steel into it.

"I'll just sit here a little, Ma," I said easily. Pops wouldn't have long, I knew, and any time I got with him would have to do me. She stood in the doorway, a dark indecisive shape; then she turned and went silently out, probably to phone Rod at the bank.

For the next couple of hours I did most of the talking; Pops just lay there with his eyes shut, like he was asleep. But then he started in, going way back, to the trapline he and I had run when I'd been a kid; to the big white-tail buck that followed him through the woods one rutting season until Pops whacked it on the nose with a tree branch. It was only after his law practice had ripened into a judgeship that we began to draw apart; I guess that in my twenties I was too wild, too much what he'd been himself 30 years before. Only I kept going in that direction.

About seven o'clock my brother Rod called from the doorway. I went out, shutting the door behind me. Rod was taller than me, broad and big-boned, with an athlete's frame—but with mush where his guts should have been. He had close-set pale eyes and not quite enough chin, and hadn't gone out for football in high school.

"My wife reported the vicious things you said to her." It was his best give-the-teller-hell voice. "We've talked this over with mother and we want you out of here tonight. We want—"

"You want? Until he kicks off it's still the old man's house, isn't it?"

He swung at me then—being Rod, it was a right-hand lead—and I blocked it with an open palm. Then I back-handed him, hard, twice across the face each way, jerking his head from side to side with the slaps, and crowding him up against the wall. I could have fouled his groin to bend him over, then driven locked hands down on the back of his neck as I jerked a knee into his face; and I wanted to. The need to get away before they came after me was gnawing at my gut like a weasel in a trap gnawing off his own paw to get loose. But I merely stepped away from him.

"You—you murderous animal!" He had both hands up to his cheeks like a woman might have done. Then his eyes widened theatrically, as the realization struck him. I wondered why it had taken so long. "You've *broken out!"* he gasped. *"Escaped!* a fugitive from—from justice!"

"Yeah. And I'm staying that way. I know you, kid, all of you. The last thing any of you want is for the cops to take me here." I tried to put his tones into my voice. *"Oh!* The *scandal!"*

"But they'll be after you—"

"They think I'm dead." I said flatly. "I went off an icy road in a stolen car in down-state Illinois, and it rolled and burned with me inside."

His voice was hushed, almost horror-stricken. "You mean— that there *is* a body in the car?"

"Right."

I knew what he was thinking, but I didn't bother to tell him the truth—that the old farmer who was driving me to Springfield, because he thought my doubled-up fist in the overcoat pocket was a gun, hit a patch of ice and took the car right off the lonely country road. He was impaled on the steering post, so I took his shoes and put one of mine on his foot. The other I left, with my fingerprints on it, lying near enough so they'd find it but not so near that it'd burn along with the car. Rod wouldn't have believed the truth anyway. If they caught me, who would?

I said, "Bring me up a bottle of bourbon and a carton of cigarettes. And make sure Eddy and Ma keep their mouths shut if anyone asks about me." I opened the door so Pops could hear. "Well, thanks, Rod. It *is* nice to be home again."

Solitary in the pen makes you able to stay awake easily or snatch sleep easily, whichever is necessary. I stayed awake for the last 37 hours that Pops had, leaving the chair by his bed only to go to the bathroom and to listen at the head of the stairs whenever I heard the phone or the doorbell ring. Each time I thought: *this is it.* But my luck held. If they'd just take long enough so I could stay until Pops went; the second that happened, I told myself, I'd be on my way.

Rod and Edwina and Ma were there at the end, with Doctor hovering in the background to make sure he got paid. Pops finally moved a pallid arm and Ma sat down quickly on the edge of the bed—a small, erect, rather indomitable woman with a face made for wearing a lorgnette. She wasn't crying yet; instead, she looked purely luminous in a way.

"Hold my hand, Eileen," Pops paused for the terrible strength to speak again. "Hold my hand. Then I won't be frightened."

She took his hand and he almost smiled, and shut his eyes. We waited, listening to his breathing get slower and slower and then just stop, like a grandfather clock running down. Nobody moved, nobody spoke. I looked around at them, so soft, so unused to death, and I felt like a marten in a brooding house. Then Ma began to sob.

It was a blustery day with snow flurries. I parked the jeep in front of the funeral chapel and went up the slippery walk with

wind plucking at my coat, telling myself for the hundredth time
just how nuts I was to stay for the service. By now they *had* to
know that the dead farmer wasn't me; by now some smart
prison censor *had* to remember Ma's letter about Pops being
sick. He was two days dead, and I should have been in Mexico
by this time. But it didn't seem complete yet, somehow. Or
maybe I was kidding myself, maybe it was just the old need to
put down authority that always ruins guys like me.

From a distance it looked like Pops, but up close you could
see the cosmetics and that his collar was three sizes too big. I
felt his hand; it was a statue's hand, unfamiliar except for the
thick, slightly down-curved fingernails.

Rod came up behind me and said, in a voice meant only for
me, "After today I want you to leave us alone. I want you out
of my house."

"Shame on you, brother." I grinned. "Before the will is even
read, too."

We followed the hearse through snowy streets at the
proper funeral pace, lights burning. Pallbearers wheeled the
heavy casket out smoothly on oiled tracks, then set it on
belts over the open grave. Snow whipped and swirled from
a gray sky, melting on the metal and forming rivulets down
the sides.

I left when the preacher started his scam, impelled by the
need to get moving, get away, yet impelled by another urgency,
too. I wanted something out of the house before all the mourn-
ers arrived to eat and guzzle. The guns and ammo already had
been banished to the garage, since Rod never had fired a round
in his life; but it was easy to dig out the beautiful little .22 target
pistol with the long barrel. Pops and I had spent hundreds of
hours with that gun, so the grip was worn smooth and the
blueing was gone from the metal that had been out in every sort
of weather.

Putting the jeep on four-wheel I ran down through the trees
to a cut between the hills, then went along on foot through the
darkening hardwoods. I moved slowly, evoking memories of
Korea to neutralize the icy bite of the snow through my worn
shoes. There was a flash of brown as a cottontail streaked from
under a deadfall toward a rotting woodpile I'd stacked years
before. My slug took him in the spine, paralyzing the back legs.

He jerked and thrashed until I broke his neck with the edge of my hand.

I left him there and moved out again, down into the small marshy triangle between the hills. It was darkening fast as I kicked at the frozen tussocks. Finally a ringneck in full plumage burst out, long tail fluttering and stubby pheasant wings beating to raise his heavy body. He was quartering up and just a bit to my right, and I had all the time in the world. I squeezed off in mid-swing, knowing it was perfect even before he took that heart-stopping pinwheel tumble.

I carried them back to the jeep; there was a tiny ruby of blood on the pheasant's beak, and the rabbit was still hot under the front legs. I was using headlights when I parked on the curving cemetery drive. They hadn't put the casket down yet, so the snow had laid a soft blanket over it. I put the rabbit and pheasant on top and stood without moving for a minute or two. The wind must have been strong, because I found that tears were burning on my cheeks.

Goodbye, Pops. Goodbye to deer-shining out of season in the hardwood belt across the creek. Goodbye to jump-shooting mallards down in the river bottoms. Goodbye to woodsmoke and mellow bourbon by firelight and all the things that made a part of you mine. The part they could never get at.

I turned away, toward the jeep—and stopped dead. I hadn't even heard them come up. Four of them, waiting patiently as if to pay their respects to the dead. In one sense they were: to them that dead farmer in the burned-out car was Murder One. I tensed, my mind going to the .22 pistol that they didn't know about in my overcoat pocket. Yeah. Except that it had all the stopping power of a fox's bark. If only Pops had run to hand guns of a little heavier caliber. But he hadn't.

Very slowly, as if my arms suddenly had grown very heavy, I raised my hands above my head.

1970:

In the Forests of Riga the Beasts Are Very Wild Indeed

Margery Finn Brown

Take it on faith, make it a handclasp between friends: I am an ordinary woman, unmemorable in looks and endeavors. No one ever followed me home. I never won a prize in a raffle. Once, when I was riding by an open window on a bus, an apple core flew in and gave me a black eye. Later I married, had four children, lived in twenty houses around the earth, gave parties, seamed curtains, dreamed, encountered God, respected beauty, and one Thanksgiving, with my left hand in a splint, cooked dinner for thirty people.

My life has been "usual, simple, and therefore most terrible." Tolstoi? Dostoevski? No matter. What does matter is that since a massive cardiac eight months ago, I am obliged to take quarazine. You say it bluntly: the zine rhymes with *"cousine,"* a word that comes to mind because *Rosenkavalier* is spinning on the record player down the hall, and Ochs is importuning *"ma cousine."* Every note, every hemidemisemiquaver is etched on crystal. None of it matters.

Until eight months ago, music was an integral part of my life. So were books, as necessary to me as breathing in and breathing out. Now when I look at the rows and rows lining the hall— great books, mediocre books, poets, spellbinders, historians, windbags, *flâneurs*, friends—I feel a terrible sadness. This morning I tried again to read Yeats. "What shall I do for beauty, now my old bawd is dead?" The words march valiantly across the page. The meaning sputters through my head like a damp firecracker.

So, you may say. So you cannot enjoy music or read Yeats. So you walk with an obscene white cane and your dreams are stained with the echoes of cigarette smoke. So what? Bear with me, please. We have just left the runway, seat belts are still fastened. To get back to quarazine, its basic ingredient is warfarin. (Warfarin, oddly enough, is the basic ingredient in rat killers.) Quarazine is an anticoagulant. The thinner the mixture, the easier it is for blood to pump up and down the arteries, in and out of the main firehouse, thus lessening the possibility of a "recurring incident," to quote Doctor Chiclets.

How much quarazine do I take? It varies. Every Wednesday I go to Chiclets' office on Sutter Street and have a blood test, to determine the coagulating rate. Every Thursday between one and three, Miss—an old miss—Franklin telephones and says, "Mrs. George Manning? Katherine Manning? Your new dosage until next Wednesday is eleven. Repeat after me, Mrs. Manning, eleven milligrams." Eleven, I say. Eleven, incise it on your heart. Eleven, scrawl it on the Cinderella wallpaper in the bathroom.

I keep quarazine in two phials inside the mirrored medicine chest. The lavender pills are two milligrams. The peach are five milligrams. Eleven is two peach and one half lavender. After I take the quarazine, I close the medicine chest, regard the face in the mirror, and speak to it. I say, "You in there, old tomodachi, you with the sags and the bags and the puffy saucers under the eyes, you have taken your quarazine today. Do not repeat. Repeat, do not repeat today."

Why the ritual?

Thin blood can drown you. It drowns rats.

Stretched out on the mauve-taffeta bed in my room, I am waiting now for Miss Franklin to call. The headboard is a tortured rococo from Venice. The Boulle chest I paid too much for at Butterfield's auction. On top of it are a lamp made from a Waterford candlestick, a princess telephone, and a book bandaged in blue, Yeats.

Yesterday, Wednesday, I went to the doctor's. I am not obliged to remember what happened yesterday. I am not a stone, a lizard. I have free will. I will think how beautiful the light was last night at dusk, the light made Hiroshige blue stripes on the water. I said, "Have you ever seen a more beautiful sunset? My head feels strange."

Before I closed my eyes, I saw my husband and my son exchange a look of utter boredom. (They are not mean, mind you, they don't know how to be mean.) I'm bored with me, too. There is not a damn thing I can do about it while I'm taking quarazine. It has dissolved the inside of my head. There's a forest in there now. It's thick and black. Nothing stirs in the forest. The sun never shines. The growth still grows, chokes. You know the painting by Rousseau, the one where the lion is eating the leopard head first? Rousseau's trees and leaves and branches are shiny-green enamel. Ungloss them. Smudge them black, the lion has finished eating the leopard, the stillness is eternal . . . that is my head.

I am ashamed to tell anyone about the forest. It *is*. I am positive of it. The knowledge comes straight from the "zero bone." Emily Dickinson? Whitman? The zero bone tells you when you have had an encounter. A glance can be an encounter, or a word, a body's spontaneous gesture, the shape of a cloud, autumn leaves burning. You never forget encounters, nor do you search for them: they leap at you, unannounced. An encounter can be like a sunburn. Off peels a layer of skin, exposing a tender red hurting surface that toughens gradually. An encounter can mystify, enlighten, or terrorize. What it can never be is superficial.

Is it true for you? Has your life, like mine, bulged with people? Yet I have had few encounters, fewer still related to joy. A blistering night in Santiago, so long ago air conditioning had not been invented. My back burned with prickly heat. The woman in the next labor room screamed with every breath, *"Madre de Dios. Madre de Dios."* My doctor did not believe in anesthesia, so my first child was born *au naturel.* It took two days.

When I first saw Jamey, he was upside down, a tiny fish, shimmering under a waxy overcoat. The doctor said, "Mrs. Manning, you have been an excellent patient. I am going to give you a whiff of something before I sew you up." I told him to keep it. I didn't want to miss one second of this encounter—an upside-down baby with a pirate's grin and with an impudent gleam in his eye.

Another hot night, years later in Rome, an Embassy reception for R., a famous soprano. I had heard her sing, but never met her before. She wore a chrome-yellow Balenciaga, hoops of perspiration under her arms. Unlike her arrogantly assured stage stance, she looked shy, a please-like-me little girl at her first party. Everyone in Rome had turned out to meet her. Directly ahead of us in line was the British commercial attaché. I remember his guardsman's mustache and rabbity teeth. "In the foddist of Rrrrriga," he said, apropos of something, "the beasts are very wild indeed."

When I was introduced to R., I said good-evening. She looked me right in the eye. "Pray for me," she said. Startled, I said lightly, "Any special time?" There was no answering smile. "All the time," she said, "starting now."

Warrenton, Virginia. A shabby farmhouse with splintery floors and tribes of field mice. I lived there with the children for a year until we could join my husband in Djakarta.

A year is twelve months. He did not write for nine weeks. I found I could function without sleep for two days. Third night, my room would swarm with people, and the people would speak, and my own voice answered, shrilling through the empty dark. One night, I encountered God. He said four words. Did I imagine him? Did He imagine me? The words still live.

So fly a pennant for Warrenton, mute the strings in Djakarta. A mammoth blood-red moon, a hunter's moon, my husband said. The bamboo swayed, swivel-hipped under the window. I cannot even remember the girl's name. All that comes back is the smell of DDT. (Do you know about the parrot Paderewski trained to perch on the piano and say, "You're the greatest, you're the greatest, the greatest"?)

After that night in Djakarta with the hunter's moon, George would never again imitate Paderewski's parrot, and I would never again be his hatchet woman, chopping down his adversaries, making his life free of rent or wrinkle. Which makes neither of us superior. It merely removed one of the hundred reasons we took each other in marriage and bedhood. Vigor, in any event, is a marginal virtue in a woman. If I could create a new façade, I would be lazy and lovely and amiable as the trumpet vine lacing the house where I was born.

Durham, New Hampshire, a brown, shingled house rimmed in Gothic-green. Emmett, my stepbrother—his father married my mother—gets violent every ten years or so. He would never hurt me. We were close as twins. I taught him to ride a bicycle. He paid for my first permanent, caddying. When Father died, the house went to Emmett. I came home to Durham to help him dispose of the incunabula of eighty-some years.

The two of us alone, the night after the funeral, walking down the cellar steps.

"You know how Father hated taxes," Emmett said. "One night last winter he hauled me out of bed and made me bury a wad of treasury notes in the wine cellar. Then I had to cement over it. You're coming with me while I dig it up. I need a witness."

The back of my neck was ice. I kept walking down the steps, too frightened to turn back. "We will have to find Father's ax, won't we, Kate? You wouldn't know where he kept it, would you? I stayed in Durham. I took his crap year in, year out while you roamed, here, there, everywhere. . . . We're going to find that ax if it takes all night, aren't we, Kate?"

Encounters remembered. Deeds done. Words said. Tracer bullets lobbing over the forest. I was named Kate for my Irish grandmother. She dyed her hair with tea leaves and thumped the floor with her blackthorn if the service was poor or people didn't do as she liked. Stay fierce, she used to say, stay lean, Kate, take no man's guff.

Lardy, defanged, I exist in a mauve bedroom, waiting for the phone to ring. If only I didn't have to take quarazine. "If only" is a greased pole to nowhere. All there is is what is. Me. This minute. My left hand. How can I describe my left hand? It has gnawed cuticles, a wedding ring grown too large, grave freckles, wormy blue veins, a medic-alert bracelet on the wrist, a scar on the forefinger where I broke a dish of pickled beets twenty years ago. The framework consists of five fan-shaped bones covered with skin the color of cheese. The bones are cut into five uneven strips, each strip ending in an oval cellophane window. Once, looking down from the loft of a stable, I thought, That's not a horse's back, that's a cello.

Listen: this is quarazine. I am frightened.

Listen: my mother-in-law's lobster claw clamped around your wrist so you would not leave before she finished one of her interminably long, pointless stories. My mother-in-law, a muscled, all-dark-meat woman. Squeaky dentures, lipstick bleeding into the pleats around her mouth, nicotined fingers worked to the bone. She adored George, "my only child, my son, the diplomat." George was ashamed of her. "God's sake, Ma, if you have to label me, just say I'm with the State Department."

Every summer she visited us. The pipes rumbled as she bathed, five o'clock in the morning. The ironing was all finished when we returned at night from a party. No, she wouldn't come, no, she wouldn't "fit in. Besides, I'm allergic to Mexican food." That, George said, was a lot of bushwa. So she went with us to the Troups' in Mexico City. She ate tortillas and drank sangría until she was sick, o, o, *con fuoco* all over the Troups' bathroom.

In the middle of the night, I awoke. The guest-room door had blown open, and I heard her trying quietly to light a match. (Lord, I thought, someday I'll be old and visiting one of my married children, and they'll be whispering in bed, "When is she going home? Lord, I can't stand this much longer.") It wasn't love or pity that impelled me to walk into the guest room. I needed a talisman to ward off my own future. "Mrs. Manning," I said, "can I get you something?" A phlegmy, raspy laugh. Out came the lobster claw. "Listen," she said, "I know I'm a damn nuisance, but I can't seem to help it." The next morning at breakfast, she was the same, lipstick seeping, calliope laugh, trying to woo her son, her only child, the diplomat. The same and never the same again. Martin Buber would say the I-It relationship had changed to an I-Thou. Alan Watts would say the she-ness of she encountered the me-ness of me.

What do I say?

I say our journey is almost over, we're coming in over the airport, the landing gear is down and locked. Yesterday I went to the doctor's. I call him Chiclets for short and for spite. Why do I despise him? Fear, what else? He has wind-colored eyes, furry knuckles, and when he touches you, his hands are deft and contemptuous, like a butcher handling meat. Why should a man so lacking in empathy become a doctor? Geld, more than likely, and status. God is his peer group. Pay homage to the doctor, oh yes, but forget the frank, insult, and mirth. His voice starts out in the lower abdomen, big and scornful, but after winding through fatty detours and truck routes, comes out of his rosebud mouth, minuscule, unvaliant, ridiculous somehow, like a tricycle batting it down the freeway.

"Ah, you have not started smoking again," he says, blowing smoke in my face. "Ah, you have courage." (Not enough, I wanted to say, not enough, you two-bit twot. I heard you browbeating that incontinent old wreck in the hospital.) "As I have said before, Mrs. Manning, quarazine is a powerful drug and your coagulating rate is at best erratic, but never in all my experience have I encountered a reaction such as yours." (Come off it, summer camper, sophomore in life, they should send you back to the worm, you're a waste of love and lust.) "My technician is getting married today. I will draw your blood, make a fist please." (How childish I was when my blood spurted on his shirt, so childishly delighted I found the nerve to ask that bitter-bile question.)

"Mrs. Manning, you may have to take quarazine all your life. It is more than likely, I should say, so you must resign yourself to that probability."

Resigned?

I ride down the elevator of the Medical Arts Building. The blind pencil vendor recognizes my footsteps. "Your feet tapping weak today, Mrs. Manning." I say, "No, Mr. Holliday, I'm fine. How's the world treating you?" "Terrible. . . . No sense knocking it, is they?" Resigned.

I can never be. Dead before I am docile. My neck aches from holding up the forest. I am dispersed. I have nightmares. I am frightened. Things frighten and attract me simultaneously.

The traffic island in front of me. I must cross the street to get a cab home. In the middle of the intersection, there's a pedestrian haven, a small raised triangle. When I'm lucky, I make it across the street without having the light change.

. . .

Today I cannot walk fast enough. I stand on the traffic island, watching the cars arrel-bassing by, the trucks puffing smug and smog, wild-eyed buses so close they eat the breath from my mouth. I look down on my black alligator shoe. Put your little foot right there. Silly jingle. Right there, one inch, and it will all be over, Kate.

Stop pushing. Whoever is pushing me in the small of the back, *stop it.* No need to turn around. I know I am alone on the traffic island. I have no assurance that it would be quick, final, or painless. I could live all chewed up, fresh from the gristmill. Wouldn't that be loverly? When the light changes, I limp across to the cab stand. Be patient, patient. Be valid, invalid. Chop down the forest, but do not make me wait.

I've been waiting all afternoon. Look at the time, ten after three. The neighborhood children are coming home from school, sweater arms lashed around their waists. Elijah, a dilapidated coach dog, crawls out from under the hedge and gives a halfhearted hello.

"Hi, Elijah." I recognize the voice. The new little girl. Can't be five, wears mesh panty hose, and has the whole block in thrall. "Lijah, you know what?"

I pick up the phone before the second ring. It *is* Miss Franklin. I listen, repeat the new dosage, say thank you, hang up.

Lijah, you know what? I have to start taking twenty-two milligrams. *Madre de Dios.* In the hospital it was four milligrams. Then six, nine, eleven, fourteen, fifteen, eighteen. Twenty-two. I'll dissolve. I'll be in fragments.

Leaning on the white tree-stump cane, I walk into the bathroom. The wallpaper I've been meaning to change for years. It cloys—Cinderellas in hoopskirts stepping out of pumpkin coaches. I open the mirrored chest. Twenty-two. That's six peach. Six times five is twenty. One lavender is two. Twenty and two make twenty-two. I fill a cup from the dispenser with water. The pills go down smoothly. I close the medicine chest. Look. I say to the mirror, look, old friend, you with the sags and the bags, you've taken your quarazine today, so do not repeat. Repeat, do not repeat.

I say it.

There is no face in the mirror.

I can see the collar of a faded-blue robe. I can see a corded neck. Above the neck? Nothing. Air. Where the face should be, a square of Cinderella wallpaper.

An optical illusion?

I turn on the light switch. I can hear that humming prelude fluorescent lights always make. I can hear the last trio from *Rosenkavalier* wisping down the hall. My tongue is wet. We have nice water, it's tart and tastes of fresh mermaids. The porcelain sink feels like a porcelain sink—cold, and eternal.

Alles in Ordnung.

I look again in the mirror. The robe, the neck, the air, the wallpaper. I lean over, shaking. I grip my arms tight around my stomach. My heart roars like surf in my ears. Quarazine turned my head into a forest, now it has dissolved my face. Persona means mask. It melted my personal mask. The head, then the face, what comes next? The heart? The zero bone that registers encounters, that labels true feelings and looks ahead and wonders. How will I get through the rest of my days?

The house is cold. I should turn up the thermostat. Feeling the pull of the rug under my slippers, I back into my bedroom, my little mauve vegetable bin. When feelings go, I'll be a vegetable. Carrots, broccoli, o garland me with parsley. The worst has happened. I encountered me. There was no one there.

Memory nags, pulls on my sleeve. A ravenously rough trip to the Aran Islands, all of us strangers, so sopped by the rain we clung together in the snuggery while cows groaned and thudded in the hold. The Guinness flowed like buttermilk. A little runty Dubliner with a tweed cap and yardarm jaw apologized the first time the ship lurched and a wave of Guinness slipped from his glass into my lap. More lurches, more Guinness. There was no place to move to, nor did I show any sign of dismay. Each time his apology was curter, less gracious, till in a fit of exasperation, he growled, "Madame, ye've got to adjist to the whims of nature."

So I must. Nature never rejoices, mourns, never applauds, never condemns. Nature continues. I haven't the energy to cry. I sigh instead, a breathy sigh that nudges the walls like an airy puffball. Somehow it helps, when you are alone and no one can hear you, to sigh deeply, to say, "O dear. Dear me."

Dear me?

Dear nobody.

1971:

Moonlight Gardener

Robert L. Fish

"And the fights! Oh, the fights! Ah, the fights!" Mrs. Williams said piously, leaning forward, her ungainly flowered hat almost toppling, her small china-blue eyes intent upon the young sergeant's unrevealing face. "Awful! *Awful!*" She paused significantly. "Especially the terrible one they had the night before last—Wednesday, it was," she said, and paused again, almost breathlessly. "The night she disappeared," she added meaningfully.

"Disappeared." The sergeant started to write the word down on his lined pad and then stopped halfway to end it in a wiggly squiggle, culminated in an almost vicious dot. He wished, not for the first time, that he had chosen a different line of endeavor for his life's work; he had a strong feeling he knew what was coming.

"Disappeared. That's what I said," Mrs. Williams said sharply. "She hasn't been seen since—and that's disappearance, isn't it?" The edge of poorly concealed disdain tinged her voice. "And then *that man* trying to tell me, when I went over to borrow a cup of sugar—"

"You were out of sugar," the sergeant murmured politely, and carefully printed the word SUGAR on his pad. He hated busybodies of all types, but particularly those like the woman facing him, and not merely because they caused the police a great deal of work that almost inevitably was pointless. He wondered how life must have been in those delightful days before neighbors-within-earshot. Beautiful, without a doubt.

Mrs. Williams's little chin hardened. Her eyes defied him to attempt avoiding the responsibilities of his office with such flimsy tactics. Her well-tended hands clasped themselves more tightly about her purse, as if it might not be safe in this world of predators, even here in the local police station.

"*That man* was trying to tell me," she went on inexorably, a juggernaut not to be stopped, "that she was out shopping. Before eight in the morning, when the stores in town don't open until nine!"

The sergeant made a series of little 9's to border the mutilated DISAPPEARED and the intact SUGAR.

"And she wasn't home all day," Mrs. Williams declared flatly, "because I was watching. And then, this morning, I went over again, because I was worried about her, and *he* comes up with an entirely new story this time, about how she suddenly decided late last night to visit her sister. Which is a bit strange, since she doesn't have a sister and I know that for a gospel fact!"

The sergeant carefully printed NO SISTER on the paper before him, boxed the words neatly with his pencil, and began shading the enclosed parallelogram. He kept his eyes from the rather pretty face of the woman across from him. At the moment, she wasn't all that pretty.

"And how could she possibly have gone away in the middle of the night the way he said—without my hearing, I mean?" Mrs. Williams demanded. "My house is the only one nearby and I'm sure, if Mr. Jenkins had come for her in his taxi—or even if he drove her to either the train or the bus station—I would have heard."

"I'm sure," the sergeant said, and added under his breath, "at any hour, day or night," and he made a series of tiny loops to border the shaded box on his pad. They intertwined with the curved 9's very nicely.

Her blue eyes studied the expressionless face across from her and then dropped to the artistic caligraphy on the pad. Her jaw tightened dangerously, but she kept her voice under control as she brought up her heaviest artillery.

"And then last night," she said, her tone almost vicious, "after two in the morning, he digs up one of the small peach trees in the garden, and then, fifteen minutes later—or maybe a half-hour, no more—I can hear him out there replanting it. And her gone—disappeared—more than twenty-four hours! Now," she said, her tone, her angle of incidence, her entire bearing daring him to downgrade her testimony, "what is your smart-aleck answer to that, young man? Does it make sense for a man to dig up a tree in the middle of the night, and then replant it a half-hour later? Does it? Well?"

The sergeant laid aside the pencil with a certain sense of reluctance and for the first time really studied the woman facing him. The spiteful expression spoiled what he knew might have been beauty under different circumstances; the faint sneer disgusted him. But he couldn't deny the substance of her arguments.

"No," he admitted in his drawl. "No, it doesn't."

"Well! I'm glad you finally realize it, young man. And the money was all hers, too," Mrs. Williams added, almost as an afterthought. She was quite aware that the statement was anti-climactic, but she definitely wanted it included in the record of evidence.

"Money?"

"In the safe-deposit box with her jewels. The money that bought the house, even though everything is in both their names. You wait and see," she added, leaning forward again. "He'll be having it up for sale within a week. He never did a day's work since they married—if he ever did one before, which I seriously doubt!"

There were several moments' silence. The sergeant made the first move, bringing his considerable bulk to his feet, indicating the interview was over. He waited as she came to her five-feet-two-inches of height, looking up at him defiantly.

"I'll take the matter up with the sheriff, ma'am," he said.

"I should certainly hope so, young man," she retorted coldly, studying him once again with eyes that were quite unimpressed. Then she marched from the station house, the fur piece about her neck seeming to hurry to catch up with her.

"I suppose we'll have to check it out," the sheriff said wearily. "I don't know too many people in this town—most of my time is spent over in Bellerville at the county seat—but I do happen to know Charley Crompton. The idea of him doing away with that battle-axe he married is simply ridiculous. If he has a temper, I've never seen it. He's a mouse. If it was the other way around, I might believe it. But Charley! Impossible. At any rate, it's just a rumor from that nosy woman at this stage."

He glanced up at the husky young sergeant. "I don't suppose you've had time to do anything about it yet?"

"Well," the sergeant said, considering, "old Sol Jenkins—he's our taxi here—he didn't pick her up, last night or any other time. He laughed and said he didn't believe she ever took a taxi in her life. They cost money. And if Charley drove her, or if she walked across the fields to the station, nobody caught either the eight o'clock or the midnight train, and that's the last one. And the ticket men at both the train and the bus station don't remember her on any train or bus in the last two days, afternoon or night."

"What about this Mrs. Williams's husband?" the sheriff asked. "Mr. Williams? Does he confirm or deny it?"

"There *is* no Mr. Williams," the sergeant said. His tone commended the shade of Mr. Williams for his wisdom in being the nonexistent spouse of the meddling Mrs. Williams. "She's been a widow over four years." He shook his head. "She's only forty, but I think she's been forty all her life. Doesn't have anything to do all day except sit on the telephone or write letters to the editor of the *Bugle*. She's a feminist. I gather she even had Mrs. Crompton all worked up on the stuff."

The sheriff smiled. "But not your wife?" he said.

"Not yet, at any rate," the sergeant said, and grinned back. The sheriff's smile faded. "Any other neighbors?"

"About a half-mile away, the nearest. Those two houses stand all alone at the end of the road. Around a curve from the others, as a matter of fact. They're pretty isolated."

"I see." The sheriff drummed his fingers and then looked up. "What about that statement regarding money?"

"Well," the sergeant said slowly, frowning, "the money was Mrs. Crompton's—*is* hers, I mean. Everybody in town knew that, but if every man who marries a dollar or two killed his wife for it, we'd be in real trouble. And as far as Charley Crompton telling that busybody neighbor of his that his wife was out shopping, or visiting a sister that doesn't exist, I don't see where he had a duty to tell her anything. If it had been me, I'd have told her my wife was off to Timbuktu, and let her make something of it."

"That's just what she's been doing," the sheriff pointed out. "Still, a man replanting a tree in the middle of the night—well, it seems rather—"

"I know," the sergeant said unhappily, and sighed. "We'll have to look into it a lot deeper, I know."

The man who opened the door of the large old-fashioned house was a nondescript person with thin brown hair pasted against his head and large brown eyes swimming behind thick lenses. He was dressed in slacks and a sweater, neither impressive, and carried a hatchet in a hand one finger of which was heavily bandaged. A honing stone had been tucked under his arm to allow him a free hand with the latch. He took the honing stone from the pit of his arm and allowed the two implements to dangle; they seemed to weigh down his thin arms.

"Hello, Sergeant. What can I do for you?"

"Hello, Charley. Actually, it was your wife I'd hoped to see."

"Well, you can't," Crompton said apologetically. "She isn't here. She's gone away."

"Oh? To visit her sister?"

The smaller man turned his head to stare reproachfully at the house across the road, and down a bit from his. His eyes came back to the patient face of the sergeant.

"Her brother. She has no sister."

"And his name and address?" The sergeant produced a pad and pencil.

"Brown. John Brown." No muscle moved in Crompton's thin face, nor did his hesitant voice reveal anything. He sounded as if he were repeating something by rote. "I don't have his street address or telephone. Chicago is all I know."

"John Brown, Chicago," the sergeant repeated genially, and

wrote it down, not at all perturbed. He looked up from his pad. "I say, Charley, would you mind a lot if we went inside to talk. I mean, standing here in the doorway . . ."

"Do you have a warrant to enter these premises?"

The young sergeant was surprised. He managed to turn his expression into one of slight hurt. "A warrant? To visit an old friend for a few moments? Although," he added, considering it, "I suppose one could be arranged, but it seems a bit foolish."

Crompton's thin lips compressed. He hesitated a moment and then, with a shrug, led the way inside, laying the hatchet and hone on a shelf in the entranceway and continuing into the living room. The sergeant picked the hatchet from its resting place and followed. He lowered his bulk into a chair and studied the instrument in his hand, touching the edge gingerly.

"Quite sharp," he observed.

"I like my tools in order," Crompton said evenly, and continued to watch the other man through his thick glasses.

"Oh? It's a shame it's so stained, then. Other than the honed edge, of course." The sergeant peered more closely. "These brown blotches, for example . . ."

"They're blood, if you want to know," Crompton said abruptly. "I cut my finger yesterday while I was honing it."

"Fingers do bleed like the devil," the sergeant admitted, and placed the hatchet on the floor beside his chair. He looked about the sunlit room and nodded. "A nice place you have here, Charley. I envy you. My wife was saying just the other day how small our house was getting, with two kids here and another on the way. But it's so hard to find a house near enough to the station house not to spend a week's pay on gas, or one that's a decent size any more. A house for sale, that is." A sudden thought struck him. "I don't suppose—well, I don't suppose you have any idea of selling, do you?"

There were several moments of silence as Charley Crompton appeared to gauge the man seated across from him. A mantel clock above the fireplace filled the quiet with a loud and steady ticking.

"I might," Charley Crompton said at last.

"You're sure your wife wouldn't object?"

"No." It was a flat statement, expressionless. Crompton

seemed to feel that the discussion had taken enough of his time. He came to his feet. "Well, sergeant, I'm rather occupied, and if that's all the business you had in mind . . ."

The sergeant rose dutifully and smiled.

"If there's any possibility of the house being up for sale in the near future," he said, "I don't imagine you'd mind greatly if I looked it over? We're really interested, you know." He turned and walked into the kitchen with Crompton on his heels. "Say! This is a nice-sized kitchen. My wife puts a good deal of store by the kitchen. Me, I'm more fussy about the cellar and the yard, the places I spend most of my free time." He opened a door, saw brooms, and closed it. He opened another door. "Stairs to the basement, eh? Do you mind?" He flicked a light switch without awaiting permission, and descended with the smaller man right behind him. He stood and shook his head forlornly. "What a damned shame! What happened to your nice concrete floor?"

"Line under it burst," Crompton said in a rather constricted voice. He cleared his throat. "Line from the sinks over to the septic tank. Had to dig it all up and replace an elbow."

"Tough luck," the sergeant said sympathetically. "Guess contractors weren't much better in those days than they are today. But, other than that, it's a nice dry cellar. Gas heat, too, I see. Well, let's take a look at the back yard, while I'm here. I'm sure you won't mind."

They climbed the steps and walked through the kitchen to the back porch and the enclosed yard. One of the peach trees did, indeed, list slightly, and the fresh earth packed about its base was cleared of grass, reddish-brown in color, like a bad bruise. But the sergeant had been expecting that. What he had not been expecting was to see a second peach tree lying on its side beside a deep excavation, its root ball wrapped in canvas, or a third with a hole begun at its edge and a shovel thrust into the soil there. He glanced at his host.

"Trouble with your peach trees?"

"Tree roots need air," Crompton said. His voice was unnatural, as if he, too, needed air. "My own idea, but it's a valid one. I dig up trees and replant them quite frequently. I—" He paused a moment, eyeing the sergeant as if pleading for belief, and then continued, "It's the truth! They really do, you know. Need fresh air, I mean. They're living creatures; they can't stand not having air. The branches and the leaves get their share, but that's not enough." He shook his head, and behind his thick glasses, his eyes were impossible to interpret. "It's the roots, you see. That's the important part! They need air. It's the truth."

He leaned back, balancing himself on his heels, a trifle breathless, staring at the excavated peach tree and the dark hole it had left behind in the earth.

"A few more hours," he said as if to himself, "and the roots will be fine. Ready to bury again."

The large young sergeant sighed and turned toward the gate leading to the street and his parked patrol car.

"I'll probably be back again," he said conversationally. "I'm sure you won't mind. I'm really quite interested in this house."

"Are you trying to tell me Charley Crompton is a nut?" the sheriff asked. "The last thing from a nut! He's pulling our leg. A policeman shows up at his house and asks where his wife is, and he doesn't even ask why! And that mound in the basement, and that hatchet bit! Cut himself honing the thing the day before, and he's still walking around with the hone the day after!"

"It really was blood, I suppose? Not ketchup, or paint?"

"It was blood, all right. The same type as his. We don't know his wife's type; she never gave anything away, not even blood."

The sergeant turned and paced the room, his large hands locked behind his back, his face grim. He paused and faced the sheriff. "And he *did* have a bad gash under that bandage. I think I'd have preferred to believe him if he didn't." He shook his head, frowning. "More than ten days, and we're where we were when we started. Even further behind, in fact. He's having fun with us, I tell you!"

The sheriff bit at an outcropping of fingernail. "You got your warrant, though, didn't you? I spoke to Judge—"

"Oh, we got the warrant, right enough," the sergeant said darkly, and dropped into his chair, putting a knee against the edge of the desk. "And we dug up the cellar floor. And all we found was an elbow."

"An *elbow?*" The sheriff sat more erect.

"A plumber's elbow," the sergeant said grimly. "Exactly as he told us. New. We dug another three feet down, too, down to solid rock—just in case. She certainly isn't buried there, I can tell you that."

"Could she have *been* buried there?"

"That I don't know," the sergeant said bitterly. "There was more than enough room, but we didn't find any signs. All I know is that she isn't buried there now."

"Nor under the peach trees, either, I gather."

"Nor under anything in the whole damned back yard, and we gave his tree roots all the air they could handle! Ten days and nothing at all!" He shook his head broodingly and then looked up. "Oh, yes. He put the house up for sale this morning. I spoke to Jimmy Glass at the bank; Crompton and his wife exchanged powers of attorney the day they got married, so that's that."

The sheriff frowned. "So what's *his* explanation as to his wife's disappearance?"

"He finally broke down and confessed," the sergeant said bitterly. "According to Charley, they had this big quarrel he was ashamed to admit, and she just up and walked out on him —and of course his pride would never allow him to tell perfect strangers like us about it. They fought and she just upped and away, like that."

"And disappeared into thin air?"

"His idea, or what he says is his idea—is that she probably got to the highway and some kindly soul in a car or a truck picked her up and gave her a lift. That was his second idea. His first was that she caught a Greyhound bus, until I told him we'd checked all the buses. He says he has no idea where she'd head for, but he doesn't expect her back because she's stubborn. He says maybe she went to her brother's, but he honestly doesn't know the address. Just John Brown, in Chicago." He snorted. "And all we got from the cops there, when we asked, were a couple of wisecracks. For which I don't blame them."

The sheriff drummed his fingers. "So what's your idea?"

"My idea," the sergeant began slowly, and then stopped as the telephone at his elbow rang. He picked it up. "Hello?" He cupped the receiver and shook his head dolefully at the sheriff. "Our man on the scene." He uncupped the receiver. "No, Mrs.

Williams. No, Mrs. Williams. Yes, Mrs. Williams. Yes, we are, Mrs. Williams. As much as we can, ma'am. Yes, Mrs. Williams. Yes, we will, Mrs. Williams." He put the receiver back in its cradle and sighed.

"Mrs. Williams," he said, and raised his eyes to the ceiling. "What a woman! She called the other day, all excited. It seems Charley Crompton thought she wasn't home, because he came over and rang her bell and tried to look in the windows. She kept out of sight and then he went back to his house and came out with something bulky and big and put it in the trunk of his car and drove off, and she called us at once. And when we got there, Charley was back, and he had mud all over his tires, red clay like we have down at Wiley Creek, and we searched his trunk, but we never came up with a thing."

"So what's your idea?"

"My idea," the sergeant said, staring at the girly calendar on the wall without seeing it, "is that Charley Crompton has gotten away with murder. My idea is that his wife is buried somewhere in the woods and that, If we ever find her, it will be sheer luck. And that without her body we're in trouble. We don't have a case and we don't have a chance of holding him. My idea is that he went through that rigamarole of digging up trees and ruining a perfect concrete floor because he wanted to rub our noses in a perfect crime."

"Or because it gave him a chance to misdirect your attention while he had her body stored away somewhere else." The sheriff shook his head. "I still can't believe a mouse like Charley Crompton would have the nerve, though, to do a thing like that."

"Believe it," the sergeant said shortly.

"So what do we do?"

The young sergeant swiveled his chair, staring through the window at the deserted square before the old courthouse.

"We wait," he said heavily. "We wait until some Boy Scouts on a hike, or some gang out on a picnic, or some kids necking, or some curious dog, makes what the newspapers call 'a gruesome discovery.' Because one thing is certain: whether she was buried in that house or in that yard at one time or another, she isn't buried there now. That's about the only thing that *is* certain."

The sheriff sighed and swung around and back in his swivel chair.

The mean, petulant, whining voice carried through the still night, threading its way from the garage through the back yard to the house, out-cricketing the crickets. There was an air of continuity about it, as if it had been going on for some time and would continue to go on indefinitely, or until a stop were put to it.

". . . certainly pure nonsense to pick me up in Joliet three stations down the line when the train stops here just as well, same as it was silly to put me on the train there, as if gasoline grew on trees, but of course that wouldn't bother you none—none of it comes out of your pockets and why you insisted on my visiting your mother in the first place heaven only knows, there isn't a thing wrong with her except she's spoiled the way old women are spoiled and she dotes on her darling Charley—darling Charley this darling Charley that— and how her darling Charley could have had any girl he ever wanted, which simply goes to show she doesn't know her darling Charley as well as I do and three weeks with her in that horrible house was no pleasure, locked in that mausoleum with no newspapers, no radio, no television, I don't know how she stands it but you never care what I go through just as long as you get your way—well, that was the last time and if I find you've been up to your usual tricks with girls while I was gone, you'll regret it and you'll regret it where it hurts the most, in the pocketbook."

The gate from the garage to the back yard was opened and closed again.

". . . and for heaven's sake what on earth has happened to that peach tree excavated out of the ground and that lantern alongside? I hope you realize that Chaber's Hardware doesn't give kerosene free and if you want to transplant a tree, the least you can do is do it during the daylight though why you should want to do it at all I can't imagine, the peach trees have been fine ever since I remember—in any event, I want it replanted immediately tomorrow, do you hear? I don't want it lying around and I don't want all that dirt to be tracked into my clean house—"

The kitchen door was swung back; the voice continued, an acid eating through Charley's eardrums.

". . . and leaving the lamp on in the house while you were coming to pick me up all the way to Joliet electricity costs money but you don't care—why should you, you don't pay the bills, and leaving that ugly hatchet on the kitchen counter, I've told you a thousand times the place for your dirty tools is in the cellar—well, at least I see you had the decency to set out two cups of coffee, I only hope you didn't use the electric percolator and leave it on while you were out, electricity isn't free, but you wouldn't think of that, and—"

A sudden pause, and then—"Charles! These cups are dirty—they've been used. If you've been entertaining people in this house while I've been away, that Mrs. Williams from across the street, don't think I'm blind, I see the way you two look at each other. Charles, wait, wait! Charles, who's that in the shadow there? Charles, do you hear me? Charles . . ."

"Hello, dear," said Mrs. Williams quietly, and reached for the kitchen counter and the hatchet there. "Welcome home."

1972:

The Purple Shroud

Joyce Harrington

Mrs. Moon threw the shuttle back and forth and pumped the treadles of the big four-harness loom as if her life depended on it. When they asked what she was weaving so furiously, she would laugh silently and say it was a shroud.

"No, really, what is it?"

"My house needs new draperies." Mrs. Moon would smile and the shuttle would fly and the beater would thump the newly woven threads tightly into place. The muffled, steady sounds of her craft could be heard from early morning until very late at night, until the sounds became an accepted and expected background noise and were only noticed in their absence.

Then they would say, "I wonder what Mrs. Moon is doing now."

That summer, as soon as they had arrived at the art colony and even before they had unpacked, Mrs. Moon requested that the largest loom in the weaving studio be installed in their cabin. Her request had been granted because she was a serious weaver, and because her husband, George, was one of the best painting instructors they'd ever had. He could coax the amateurs into stretching their imaginations and trying new ideas

323

and techniques, and he would bully the scholarship students until, in a fury, they would sometimes produce works of surprising originality.

George Moon was, himself, only a competent painter. His work had never caught on, although he had a small loyal following in Detroit and occasionally sold a painting. His only concessions to the need for making a living and for buying paints and brushes was to teach some ten hours a week throughout the winter and to take this summer job at the art colony, which was also their vacation. Mrs. Moon taught craft therapy at a home for the aged.

After the loom had been set up in their cabin Mrs. Moon waited. Sometimes she went swimming in the lake, sometimes she drove into town and poked about in the antique shops, and sometimes she just sat in the wicker chair and looked at the loom.

They said, "What are you waiting for, Mrs. Moon? When are you going to begin?"

One day Mrs. Moon drove into town and came back with two boxes full of brightly colored yarns. Classes had been going on for about two weeks, and George was deeply engaged with his students. One of the things the students loved about George was the extra time he gave them. He was always ready to sit for hours on the porch of the big house, just outside the communal dining room, or under a tree, and talk about painting or about life as a painter or tell stories about painters he had known.

George looked like a painter. He was tall and thin, and with approaching middle age he was beginning to stoop a little. He had black snaky hair which he had always worn on the long side, and which was beginning to turn gray. His eyes were very dark, so dark you couldn't see the pupils, and they regarded everything and everyone with a probing intensity that evoked uneasiness in some and caused young girls to fall in love with him.

Every year George Moon selected one young lady disciple to be his summer consort.

Mrs. Moon knew all about these summer alliances. Every year, when they returned to Detroit, George would confess to her with great humility and swear never to repeat his transgression.

"Never again, Arlene," he would say. "I promise you, never again."

Mrs. Moon would smile her forgiveness.

Mrs. Moon hummed as she sorted through the skeins of purple and deep scarlet, goldenrod yellow and rich royal blue. She hummed as she wound the glowing hanks into fat balls, and she thought about George and the look that had passed between him and the girl from Minneapolis at dinner the night before. George had not returned to their cabin until almost two in the morning. The girl from Minneapolis was short and plump, with a round face and a halo of fuzzy red-gold hair. She reminded Mrs. Moon of a Teddy bear; she reminded Mrs. Moon of herself twenty years before.

When Mrs. Moon was ready to begin, she carried the purple yarn to the weaving studio.

"I have to make a very long warp," she said. "I'll need to use the warping reel."

She hummed as she measured out the seven feet and a little over, then sent the reel spinning.

"Is it wool?" asked the weaving instructor.

"No, it's orlon," said Mrs. Moon. "It won't shrink, you know."

Mrs. Moon loved the creak of the reel, and she loved feeling the warp threads grow fatter under her hands until at last each planned thread was in place and she could tie the bundle and braid up the end. When she held the plaited warp in her hands she imagined it to be the shorn tresses of some enormously powerful earth goddess whose potency was now transferred to her own person.

That evening after dinner, Mrs. Moon began to thread the loom. George had taken the rowboat and the girl from Minneapolis to the other end of the lake where there was a deserted cottage. Mrs. Moon knew he kept a sleeping bag there, and a cache of wine and peanuts. Mrs. Moon hummed as she carefully threaded the eye of each heddle with a single purple thread, and thought of black widow spiders and rattlesnakes coiled in the corners of the dark cottage.

She worked contentedly until midnight and then went to bed. She was asleep and smiling when George stumbled in two hours later and fell into bed with his clothes on.

Mrs. Moon wove steadily through the summer days. She did not attend the weekly critique sessions for she had nothing to show and was not interested in the problems others were having with their work. She ignored the Saturday night parties where George and the girl from Minneapolis and the others danced and drank beer and slipped off to the beach or the boathouse. Sometimes, when she tired of the long hours at the loom, she would go for solitary walks in the woods and always brought back curious trophies of her rambling. The small cabin, already crowded with the loom and the iron double bedstead, began to fill up with giant toadstools, interesting bits of wood, arrangements of reeds and wild wheat.

One day she brought back two large black stones on which she painted faces. The eyes of the faces were closed and the mouths were faintly curved in archaic smiles. She placed one stone on each side of the fireplace.

George hated the stones. "Those damn stonefaces are watching me," he said. "Get them out of here."

"How can they be watching you? Their eyes are closed."

Mrs. Moon left the stones beside the fireplace and George soon forgot to hate them. She called them Apollo I and Apollo II.

The weaving grew and Mrs. Moon thought it the best thing she had ever done. Scattered about the purple ground were signs and symbols which she saw against the deep blackness of her closed eyelids when she thought of passion and revenge, of love and wasted years and the child she had never had. She thought the barbaric colors spoke of these matters, and she was pleased.

"I hope you'll finish it before the final critique," the weaving teacher said when she came to the cabin to see it. "It's very good."

Word spread through the camp and many of the students came to the cabin to see the marvelous weaving. Mrs. Moon was proud to show it to them and received their compliments with quiet grace.

"It's too fine to hang at a window," said one practical Sunday-painting matron. "The sun will fade the colors."

"I'd love to wear it," said the life model.

"You!" said a bearded student of lithography. "It's a robe for a pagan king!"

"Perhaps you're right," said Mrs. Moon, and smiled her happiness on all of them.

The season was drawing to a close when in the third week of August, Mrs. Moon threw the shuttle for the last time. She slumped on the backless bench and rested her limp hands on the breast beam of the loom. Tomorrow she would cut the warp.

That night, while George was showing color slides of his paintings in the main gallery, the girl from Minneapolis came alone to the Moons' cabin. Mrs. Moon was lying on the bed watching a spider spin a web in the rafters. A fire was blazing in the fireplace, between Apollo I and Apollo II, for the late summer night was chill.

"You must let him go," said the golden-haired Teddy bear. "He loves me."

"Yes, dear," said Mrs. Moon.

"You don't seem to understand. I'm talking about George." The girl sat on the bed. "I think I'm pregnant."

"That's nice," said Mrs. Moon. "Children are a blessing. Watch the spider."

"We have a real relationship going. I don't care about being married—that's too feudal. But you must free George to come and be a father image to the child."

"You'll get over it," said Mrs. Moon, smiling a trifle sadly at the girl.

"Oh, you don't even want to know what's happening!" cried the girl. "No wonder George is bored with you."

"Some spiders eat their mates after fertilization," Mrs. Moon remarked. "Female spiders."

The girl flounced angrily from the cabin, as far as one could be said to flounce in blue jeans and sweatshirt.

George performed his end-of-summer separation ritual simply and brutally the following afternoon. He disappeared after lunch. No one knew where he had gone. The girl from Minneapolis roamed the camp, trying not to let anyone know she was searching for him. Finally she rowed herself down to the other end of the lake, to find that George had dumped her transistor radio, her books of poetry, and her box of incense on the damp sand, and had put a padlock on the door of the cottage.

She threw her belongings into the boat and rowed back to the camp, tears of rage streaming down her cheeks. She beached the boat, and with head lowered and shoulders hunched she stormed the Moons' cabin. She found Mrs. Moon tying off the severed warp threads.

"Tell George," she shouted, "tell George I'm going back to Minneapolis. He knows where to find me!"

"Here, dear," said Mrs. Moon, "hold the end and walk backwards while I unwind it."

The girl did as she was told, caught by the vibrant colors and Mrs. Moon's concentration. In a few minutes the full length of cloth rested in the girl's arms.

"Put it on the bed and spread it out," said Mrs. Moon. "Let's take a good look at it."

"I'm really leaving," whispered the girl. "Tell him I don't care if I never see him again."

"I'll tell him." The wide strip of purple flowed garishly down the middle of the bed between them. "Do you think he'll like it?" asked Mrs. Moon. "He's going to have it around for a long time."

"The colors are very beautiful, very savage." The girl looked closely at Mrs. Moon. "I wouldn't have thought you would choose such colors."

"I never did before."

"I'm leaving now."

"Good-bye," said Mrs. Moon.

George did not reappear until long after the girl had loaded up her battered bug of a car and driven off. Mrs. Moon knew he had been watching and waiting from the hill behind the camp. He came into the cabin whistling softly and began to take his clothes off.

"God, I'm tired," he said.

"It's almost dinner time."

"Too tired to eat," he yawned. "What's that on the bed?"

"My weaving is finished. Do you like it?"

"It's good. Take it off the bed. I'll look at it tomorrow."

Mrs. Moon carefully folded the cloth and laid it on the weaving bench. She looked at George's thin naked body before he got into bed, and smiled.

"I'm going to dinner now," she said.

"Okay. Don't wake me up when you get back. I could sleep for a week."

"I won't wake you up," said Mrs. Moon.

Mrs. Moon ate dinner at a table by herself. Most of the students had already left. A few people, the Moons among them, usually stayed on after the end of classes to rest and enjoy the isolation. Mrs. Moon spoke to no one.

After dinner she sat on the pier and watched the sunset. She watched the turtles in the shallow water and thought she saw a blue heron on the other side of the lake. When the sky was black and the stars were too many to count, Mrs. Moon went to the toolshed and got a wheelbarrow. She rolled this to the door of her cabin and went inside.

The cabin was dark and she could hear George's steady heavy breathing. She lit two candles and placed them on the mantelshelf. She spread her beautiful weaving on her side of the bed, gently so as not to disturb the sleeper. Then she quietly moved the weaving bench to George's side of the bed, near his head.

She sat on the bench for a time, memorizing the lines of his face by the wavering candlelight. She touched him softly on the forehead with the pads of her fingertips and gently caressed his eyes, his hard cheeks, his raspy chin. His breathing became uneven and she withdrew her hands, sitting motionless until his sleep rhythm was restored.

Then Mrs. Moon took off her shoes. She walked carefully to the fireplace, taking long quiet steps. She placed her shoes neatly side by side on the hearth and picked up the larger stone, Apollo I. The face of the kouros, the ancient god, smiled up at her and she returned that faint implacable smile. She carried the stone back to the bench beside the bed, and set it down.

Then she climbed onto the bench, and when she stood, she found she could almost touch the spider's web in the rafters. The spider crouched in the heart of its web, and Mrs. Moon wondered if spiders ever slept.

Mrs. Moon picked up Apollo I, and with both arms raised,

took careful aim. Her shadow, cast by candlelight, had the appearance of a priestess offering sacrifice. The stone was heavy and her arms grew weak. Her hands let go. The stone dropped.

George's eyes flapped open and he saw Mrs. Moon smiling tenderly down on him. His lips drew back to scream, but his mouth could only form a soundless hole.

"Sleep, George," she whispered, and his eyelids clamped over his unbelieving eyes.

Mrs. Moon jumped off the bench. With gentle fingers she probed beneath his snaky locks until she found a satisfying softness. There was no blood and for this Mrs. Moon was grateful. It would have been a shame to spoil the beauty of her patterns with superfluous colors and untidy stains. Her mothlike fingers on his wrist warned her of a faint uneven fluttering.

She padded back to the fireplace and weighed in her hands the smaller, lighter Apollo II. This time she felt there was no need for added height. With three quick butter-churning motions she enlarged the softened area in George's skull and stilled the annoying flutter in his wrist.

Then she rolled him over, as a hospital nurse will roll an immobile patient during bedmaking routine, until he rested on his back on one-half of the purple fabric. She placed his arms across his naked chest and straightened his spindly legs. She kissed his closed eyelids, gently stroked his shaggy brows, and said, "Rest now, dear George."

She folded the free half of the royal cloth over him, covering him from head to foot with a little left over at each end. From her sewing box she took a wide-eyed needle and threaded it with some difficulty in the flickering light. Then kneeling beside the bed, Mrs. Moon began stitching across the top. She stitched small careful stitches that would hold for eternity.

Soon the top was closed and she began stitching down the long side. The job was wearisome, but Mrs. Moon was patient and she hummed a sweet, monotonous tune as stitch followed stitch past George's ear, his shoulder, his bent elbow. It was not until she reached his ankles that she allowed herself to stand and stretch her aching knees and flex her cramped fingers.

Retrieving the twin Apollos from where they lay abandoned on George's pillow, she tucked them reverently into the bottom of the cloth sarcophagus and knelt once more to her task. Her needle flew faster as the remaining gap between the two edges of cloth grew smaller, until the last stitch was securely knotted and George was sealed into his funerary garment. But the hardest part of her night's work was yet to come.

She knew she could not carry George even the short distance to the door of the cabin and the wheelbarrow outside. And the wheelbarrow was too wide to bring inside. She couldn't bear the thought of dragging him across the floor and soiling or tearing the fabric she had so lovingly woven. Finally she rolled him onto the weaving bench and despite the fact that it only supported him from armpits to groin, she managed to maneuver it to the door. From there it was possible to shift the burden to the waiting wheelbarrow.

Mrs. Moon was now breathing heavily from her exertions, and paused for a moment to survey the night and the prospect before her. There were no lights anywhere in the camp except for the feeble glow of her own guttering candles. As she went to blow them out she glanced at her watch and was mildly surprised to see that it was ten minutes past three. The hours had flown while she had been absorbed in her needlework.

She perceived now the furtive night noises of the forest creatures which had hitherto been blocked from her senses by the total concentration she had bestowed on her work. She thought of weasels and foxes prowling, of owls going about their predatory night activities, and considered herself in congenial company. Then taking up the handles of the wheelbarrow, she trundled down the well-defined path to the boathouse.

The wheelbarrow made more noise than she had anticipated and she hoped she was far enough from any occupied cabin for its rumbling to go unnoticed. The moonless night sheltered her from any wakeful watcher, and a dozen summers of waiting had taught her the nature and substance of every square foot of the camp's area. She could walk it blindfolded.

When she reached the boathouse she found that some hurried careless soul had left a boat on the beach in defiance of the camp's rules. It was a simple matter of leverage to shift her burden from barrow to boat and in minutes Mrs. Moon was heaving inexpertly at the oars. At first the boat seemed inclined to travel only in wide arcs and head back to shore, but with patient determination Mrs. Moon established a rowing rhythm that would take her and her passenger to the deepest part of the lake.

She hummed a sea chanty which aided her rowing and pleased her sense of the appropriate. Then pinpointing her position by the silhouette of the tall solitary pine that grew on the opposite shore, Mrs. Moon carefully raised the oars and rested them in the boat.

As Mrs. Moon crept forward in the boat, feeling her way in the darkness, the boat began to rock gently. It was a pleasant, soothing motion and Mrs. Moon thought of cradles and soft enveloping comforters. She continued creeping slowly forward, swaying with the motion of the boat, until she reached the side of her swaddling passenger. There she sat and stroked the cloth and wished that she could see the fine colors just one last time.

She felt the shape beneath the cloth, solid but thin and now rather pitiful. She took the head in her arms and held it against her breast, rocking and humming a long-forgotten lullaby.

The doubled weight at the forward end of the small boat caused the prow to dip. Water began to slosh into the boat—in small wavelets at first as the boat rocked from side to side, then in a steady trickle as the boat rode lower and lower in the water. Mrs. Moon rocked and hummed; the water rose over her bare feet and lapped against her ankles. The sky began to turn purple and she could just make out the distant shape of the boathouse and the hill behind the camp. She was very tired and very cold.

Gently she placed George's head in the water. The boat tilted crazily and she scrambled backward to equalize the weight. She picked up the other end of the long purple chrysalis, the end containing the stone Apollos, and heaved it overboard. George in his shroud, with head and feet trailing in the lake, now lay along the side of the boat weighting it down.

Water was now pouring in. Mrs. Moon held to the other side of the boat with placid hands and thought of the dense comfort of the muddy lake bottom and George beside her forever. She saw that her feet were frantically pushing against the burden of her life, running away from that companionable grave.

With a regretful sigh she let herself slide down the short incline of the seat and came to rest beside George. The boat lurched deeper into the lake. Water surrounded George and climbed into Mrs. Moon's lap. Mrs. Moon closed her eyes and hummed, "Nearer My God to Thee." She did not see George drift away from the side of the boat, carried off by the moving arms of water. She felt a wild bouncing, a shuddering and splashing, and was sure the boat had overturned. With relief she gave herself up to chaos and did not try to hold her breath.

Expecting a suffocating weight of water in her lungs, Mrs. Moon was disappointed to find she could open her eyes, that air still entered and left her gasping mouth. She lay in a pool of water in the bottom of the boat and saw a bird circle high above the lake, peering down at her. The boat was bobbing gently on the water, and when Mrs. Moon sat up she saw that a few yards away, through the fresh blue morning, George was bobbing gently too. The purple shroud had filled with air and floated on the water like a small submarine come up for air and a look at the new day.

As she watched, shivering and wet, the submarine shape drifted away and dwindled as the lake took slow possession. At last, with a grateful sigh, green water replacing the last air bubble, it sank just as the bright arc of the sun rose over the hill in time to give Mrs. Moon a final glimpse of glorious purple and gold. She shook herself like a tired old gray dog and called out, "Good-bye, George." Her cry echoed back and forth across the morning and startled forth a chorus of bird shrieks. Pandemonium and farewell. She picked up the oars.

Back on the beach, the boat carefully restored to its place, Mrs. Moon dipped her blistered hands into the lake. She scented bacon on the early air and instantly felt the pangs of an enormous hunger. Mitch, the cook, would be having his early breakfast and perhaps would share it with her. She hurried to the cabin to change out of her wet clothes, and was amazed, as she stepped over the doorsill, at the stark emptiness which greeted her.

Shafts of daylight fell on the rumpled bed, but there was nothing for her there. She was not tired now, did not need to sleep. The fireplace contained cold ashes, and the hearth looked bare and unfriendly. The loom gaped at her like a toothless mouth, its usefulness at an end. In a heap on the floor lay George's clothes where he had dropped them the night before. Out of habit she picked them up, and as she hung them on a hook in the small closet she felt a rustle in the shirt pocket. It was a scrap of paper torn off a drawing pad; there was part of a pencil sketch on one side, on the other an address and telephone number.

Mrs. Moon hated to leave anything unfinished, despising untidiness in herself and others. She quickly changed into her town clothes and hung her discarded wet things in the tiny bathroom to dry. She found an apple and munched it as she made up her face and combed her still damp hair. The apple took the edge off her hunger, and she decided not to take the time to beg breakfast from the cook.

She carefully made the bed and tidied the small room, sweeping a few scattered ashes back into the fireplace. She checked her summer straw pocketbook for driver's license, car keys, money, and finding everything satisfactory, she paused for a moment in the center of the room. All was quiet, neat, and orderly. The spider still hung inert in the center of its web and one small fly was buzzing helplessly on its perimeter. Mrs. Moon smiled.

There was no time to weave now—indeed, there was no need. She could not really expect to find a conveniently deserted lake in a big city. No. She would have to think of something else.

Mrs. Moon stood in the doorway of the cabin in the early sunlight, a small frown wrinkling the placid surface of her round pink face. She scuffled slowly around to the back of the cabin and into the shadow of the sycamores beyond, her feet kicking up the spongy layers of years of fallen leaves, her eyes watching carefully for the right idea to show itself. Two grayish-white stones appeared side by side, half covered with leaf mold. Anonymous, faceless, about the size of cantaloupes, they would do unless something better presented itself later.

Unceremoniously she dug them out of their bed, brushed away the loose dirt and leaf fragments, and carried them back to the car.

Mrs. Moon's watch had stopped sometime during the night, but as she got into the car she glanced at the now fully risen sun and guessed the time to be about six-thirty or seven o'clock. She placed the two stones snugly on the passenger seat and covered them with her soft pale-blue cardigan. She started the engine, and then reached over and groped in the glove compartment. She never liked to drive anywhere without knowing beforehand the exact roads to take to get to her destination. The road map was there, neatly folded beneath the flashlight and the box of tissues.

Mrs. Moon unfolded the map and spread it out over the steering wheel. As the engine warmed up, Mrs. Moon hummed along with it. Her pudgy pink hand absently patted the tidy blue bundle beside her as she planned the most direct route to the girl in Minneapolis.

1973:

The Whimper of Whipped Dogs

Harlan Ellison

On the night after the day she had stained the louvered window shutters of her new apartment on East 52nd Street, Beth saw a woman slowly and hideously knifed to death in the courtyard of her building. She was one of twenty-six witnesses to the ghoulish scene, and, like them, she did nothing to stop it.

She saw it all, every moment of it, without break and with no impediment to her view. Quite madly, the thought crossed her mind as she watched in horrified fascination, that she had the sort of marvelous line of observation Napoleon had sought when he caused to have constructed at the *Comédie-Française* theaters, a curtained box at the rear, so he could watch the audience as well as the stage. The night was clear, the moon was full, she had just turned off the 11:30 movie on channel 2 after the second commercial break, realizing she had already seen Robert Taylor in *Westward the Women,* and had disliked it the first time; and the apartment was quite dark.

She went to the window, to raise it six inches for the night's sleep, and she saw the woman stumble into the courtyard. She was sliding along the wall, clutching her left arm with her right hand. Con Ed had installed mercury-vapor lamps on the poles; there had been sixteen assaults in seven months; the courtyard

was illuminated with a chill purple glow that made the blood
streaming down the woman's left arm look black and shiny.
Beth saw every detail with utter clarity, as though magnified a
thousand power under a microscope, solarized as if it had been
a television commercial.

The woman threw back her head, as if she were trying to
scream, but there was no sound. Only the traffic on First Avenue, late cabs foraging for singles paired for the night at Max-
well's Plum and Friday's and Adam's Apple. But that was over
there, beyond. Where *she* was, down there seven floors below,
in the courtyard, everything seemed silently suspended in an
invisible force-field.

Beth stood in the darkness of her apartment, and realized she
had raised the window completely. A tiny balcony lay just over
the low sill; now not even glass separated her from the sight; just
the wrought-iron balcony railing and seven floors to the courtyard below.

The woman staggered away from the wall, her head still
thrown back, and Beth could see she was in her mid-thirties,
with dark hair cut in a shag; it was impossible to tell if she was
pretty: terror had contorted her features and her mouth was a
twisted black slash, opened but emitting no sound. Cords stood
out in her neck. She had lost one shoe, and her steps were
uneven, threatening to dump her to the pavement.

The man came around the corner of the building, into the
courtyard. The knife he held was enormous—or perhaps it only
seemed so: Beth remembered a bonehandled fish knife her
father had used one summer at the lake in Maine: it folded back
on itself and locked, revealing eight inches of serrated blade.
The knife in the hand of the dark man in the courtyard seemed
to be similar.

The woman saw him and tried to run, but he leaped across
the distance between them and grabbed her by the hair and
pulled her head back as though he would slash her throat in the
next reaper-motion.

Then the woman screamed.

The sound skirled up into the courtyard like bats trapped in
an echo chamber, unable to find a way out, driven mad. It went
on and on. . . .

The man struggled with her and she drove her elbows into

his sides and he tried to protect himself, spinning her around by her hair, the terrible scream going up and up and never stopping. She came loose and he was left with a fistful of hair torn out by the roots. As she spun out, he slashed straight across and opened her up just below the breasts. Blood sprayed through her clothing and the man was soaked; it seemed to drive him even more berserk. He went at her again, as she tried to hold herself together, the blood pouring down over her arms.

She tried to run, teetered against the wall, slid sidewise, and the man struck the brick surface. She was away, stumbling over a flower bed, falling, getting to her knees as he threw himself on her again. The knife came up in a flashing arc that illuminated the blade strangely with purple light. And still she screamed.

Lights came on in dozens of apartments and people appeared at windows.

He drove the knife to the hilt into her back, high on the right shoulder. He used both hands.

Beth caught it all in jagged flashes—the man, the woman, the knife, the blood, the expressions on the faces of those watching from the windows. Then lights clicked off in the windows, but they still stood there, watching.

She wanted to yell, to scream, "What are you doing to that woman?" But her throat was frozen, two iron hands that had been immersed in dry ice for ten thousand years clamped around her neck. She could feel the blade sliding into her own body.

Somehow—it seemed impossible but there it was down there, happening somehow—the woman struggled erect and *pulled* herself off the knife. Three steps, she took three steps and fell into the flower bed again. The man was howling now, like a great beast, the sounds inarticulate, bubbling up from his stomach. He fell on her and the knife went up and came down, then again, and again, and finally it was all a blur of motion, and her scream of lunatic bats went on till it faded off and was gone.

Beth stood in the darkness, trembling and crying, the sight filling her eyes with horror. And when she could no longer bear to look at what he was doing down there to the unmoving piece of meat over which he worked, she looked up and around at the windows of darkness where the others still stood—even as she stood—and somehow she could see their faces, bruise-purple with the dim light from the mercury lamps, and there was a universal sameness to their expressions. The women stood with their nails biting into the upper arms of their men, their tongues edging from the corners of their mouths; the men were wild-eyed and smiling. They all looked as though they were at cock fights. Breathing deeply. Drawing some sustenance from the grisly scene below. An exhalation of sound, deep, deep, as though from caverns beneath the earth. Flesh pale and moist.

And it was then that she realized the courtyard had grown foggy, as though mist off the East River had rolled up 52nd Street in a veil that would obscure the details of what the knife and the man were still doing . . . endlessly doing it . . . long after there was any joy in it . . . still doing it . . . again and again . . .

But the fog was unnatural, thick and gray and filled with tiny scintillas of light. She stared at it, rising up in the empty space of the courtyard. Bach in the cathedral, stardust in a vacuum chamber.

Beth saw eyes.

There, up there, at the ninth floor and higher, two great eyes, as surely as night and the moon, there were *eyes*. And—a face? Was that a face, could she be sure, was she imagining it . . . a face? In the roiling vapors of chill fog something lived, something brooding and patient and utterly malevolent had been summoned up to witness what was happening down there in the flower bed. Beth tried to look away, but could not. The eyes, those primal burning eyes, filled with an abysmal antiquity yet frighteningly bright and anxious like the eyes of a child; eyes filled with tomb depths, ancient and new, chasm-filled, burning, gigantic and deep as an abyss, holding her, compelling her. The shadow play was being staged not only for the tenants in their windows, watching and drinking of the scene, but for some *other*. Not on frigid tundra or waste moors, not in subterranean caverns or on some faraway world circling a dying sun, but here, in the city, here the eyes of that *other* watched.

Shaking with the effort, Beth wrenched her eyes from those burning depths up there beyond the ninth floor, only to see again the horror that had brought that *other*. And she was struck for the first time by the awfulness of what she was witnessing, she was released from the immobility that had held her like a coelacanth in shale, she was filled with the blood thunder pounding against the membranes of her mind: she had *stood* there! She had done nothing, nothing! A woman had been butchered and she had said nothing, done nothing. Tears had been useless, tremblings had been pointless, she *had done nothing!*

Then she heard hysterical sounds midway between laughter and giggling, and as she stared up into that great face rising in the fog and chimneysmoke of the night, she heard *herself* making those deranged gibbon noises and from the man below a pathetic, trapped sound, like the whimper of whipped dogs.

She was staring up into that face again. She hadn't wanted to see it again—ever. But she was locked with those smoldering eyes, overcome with the feeling that they were childlike, though she *knew* they were incalculably ancient.

Then the butcher below did an unspeakable thing and Beth reeled with dizziness and caught the edge of the window before she could tumble out onto the balcony; she steadied herself and fought for breath.

She felt herself being looked at, and for a long moment of frozen terror she feared she might have caught the attention of that face up there in the fog. She clung to the window, feeling everything growing faraway and dim, and stared straight across the court. She *was* being watched. Intently. By the young man in the seventh-floor window across from her own apartment. Steadily, he was looking at her. Through the strange fog with its burning eyes feasting on the sight below, he was staring at her.

As she felt herself blacking out, in the moment before unconsciousness, the thought flickered and fled that there was something terribly familiar about his face.

It rained the next day. East 52nd Street was slick and shining with the oil rainbows. The rain washed the dog turds into the gutters and nudged them down and down to the catch-basin openings. People bent against the slanting rain, hidden beneath umbrellas, looking like enormous, scurrying black mushrooms. Beth went out to get the newspapers after the police had come and gone.

The news reports dwelled with loving emphasis on the twenty-six tenants of the building who had watched in cold interest as Leona Ciarelli, 37, of 455 Fort Washington Avenue, Manhattan, had been systematically stabbed to death by Burton H. Wells, 41, an unemployed electrician, who had been subsequently shot to death by two off-duty police officers when he burst into Michael's Pub on 55th Street, covered with blood and brandishing a knife that authorities later identified as the murder weapon.

She had thrown up twice that day. Her stomach seemed incapable of retaining anything solid, and the taste of bile lay along the back of her tongue. She could not blot the scenes of the night before from her mind; she re-ran them again and again, every movement of that reaper arm playing over and over as though on a short loop of memory. The woman's head thrown back for silent screams. The blood. Those eyes in the fog.

She was drawn again and again to the window, to stare down into the courtyard and the street. She tried to superimpose over the bleak Manhattan concrete the view from her window in Swann House at Bennington: the little yard and another white, frame dormitory; the fantastic apple trees; and from the other window the rolling hills and gorgeous Vermont countryside; her memory skittered through the change of seasons. But there was always concrete and the rain-slick streets; the rain on the pavement was black and shiny as blood.

She tried to work, rolling up the tambour closure of the old rolltop desk she had bought on Lexington Avenue and hunching over the graph sheets of choreographer's charts. But Labanotation was merely a Jackson Pollock jumble of arcane hieroglyphics to her today, instead of the careful representation of eurhythmics she had studied four years to perfect. And before that, Farmington.

The phone rang. It was the secretary from the Taylor Dance Company, asking when she would be free. She had to beg off. She looked at her hand, lying on the graph sheets of figures Laban had devised, and she saw her fingers trembling. She had to beg off. Then she called Guzman at the Downtown Ballet Company, to tell him she would be late with the charts.

"My God, lady, I have ten dancers sitting around in a rehearsal hall getting their leotards sweaty! What do you expect me to do?"

She explained what had happened the night before. And as she told him, she realized the newspapers had been justified in holding that tone against the twenty-six witnesses to the death of Leona Ciarelli. Paschal Guzman listened, and when he spoke again, his voice was several octaves lower, and he spoke more slowly. He said he understood and she could take a little longer to prepare the charts. But there was a distance in his voice, and he hung up while she was thanking him.

She dressed in an argyle sweater vest in shades of dark purple, and a pair of fitted khaki gabardine trousers. She had to go out, to walk around. To do what? To think about other things. As she pulled on the Fred Braun chunky heels, she idly wondered if that heavy silver bracelet was still in the window of Georg Jensen's. In the elevator, the young man from the window across the courtyard stared at her. Beth felt her body begin to tremble again. She went deep into the corner of the box when he entered behind her.

Between the fifth and fourth floors, he hit the *off* switch and the elevator jerked to a halt.

Beth stared at him and he smiled innocently.

"Hi. My name's Gleeson, Ray Gleeson, I'm in 714."

She wanted to demand he turn the elevator back on, by what right did he *presume* to do such a thing, what did he mean by this, turn it on at once or suffer the consequences. That was what she *wanted* to do. Instead, from the same place she had heard the gibbering laughter the night before, she heard her voice, much smaller and much less possessed than she had trained it to be, saying, "Beth O'Neill, I live in 701."

The thing about it, was that *the elevator was stopped.* And she was frightened. But he leaned against the paneled wall, very well dressed, shoes polished, hair combed and probably blown dry with a hand drier, and he *talked* to her as if they were across a table at L'Argenteuil. "You just moved in, huh?"

"About two months ago."

"Where did you go to school? Bennington or Sarah Lawrence?"

"Bennington. How did you know?"

He laughed, and it was a nice laugh. "I'm an editor at a

religious book publisher; every year we get half a dozen Bennington, Sarah Lawrence, Smith girls. They come hopping in like grasshoppers, ready to revolutionize the publishing industry."

"What's wrong with that? You sound like you don't care for them."

"Oh, I *love* them, they're marvelous. They think they know how to write better than the authors we publish. Had one darlin' little item who was given galleys of three books to proof, and she rewrote all three. I think she's working as a table-swabber in a Horn & Hardart's now."

She didn't reply to that. She would have pegged him as an anti-feminist, ordinarily, if it had been anyone else speaking. But the eyes. There was something terribly familiar about his face. She was enjoying the conversation; she rather liked him.

"What's the nearest big city to Bennington?"

"Albany, New York. About sixty miles."

"How long does it take to drive there?"

"From Bennington? About an hour and a half."

"Must be a nice drive, that Vermont country, really pretty. They went coed, I understand. How's that working out?"

"I don't know, really."

"You don't know?"

"It happened around the time I was graduating."

"What did you major in?"

"I was a dance major, specializing in Labanotation. That's the way you write choreography."

"It's all electives, I gather. You don't have to take anything required, like sciences, for example." He didn't change tone as he said, "That was a terrible thing last night. I saw you watching. I guess a lot of us were watching. It was a really terrible thing."

She nodded dumbly. Fear came back.

"I understand the cops got him. Some nut, they don't even know why he killed her, or why he went charging into that bar. It was really an awful thing. I'd very much like to have dinner with you one night soon, if you're not attached."

"That would be all right."

"Maybe Wednesday. There's an Argentinian place I know. You might like it."

"That would be all right."

"Why don't you turn on the elevator, and we can go," he said, and smiled again. She did it, wondering why she had stopped the elevator in the first place.

On her third date with him, they had their first fight. It was at a party thrown by a director of television commercials. He lived on the ninth floor of their building. He had just done a series of spots for *Sesame Street* (the letters "U" for Underpass, "T" for Tunnel, lowercase "b" for boats, "C" for cars; the numbers 1 to 6 and the numbers 1 to 20; the words *light* and *dark*) and was celebrating his move from the arena of commercial tawdriness (and its attendant $75,000 a year) to the sweet fields of educational programing (and its accompanying descent into low-pay respectability). There was a logic in his joy Beth could not quite understand, and when she talked with him about it, in a far corner of the kitchen, his arguments didn't seem to parse. But he seemed happy, and his girlfriend, a long-legged ex-model from Philadelphia, continued to drift to him and away from him, like some exquisite undersea plant, touching his hair and kissing his neck, murmuring words of pride and barely submerged sexuality. Beth found it bewildering, though the celebrants were all bright and lively.

In the living room, Ray was sitting on the arm of the sofa, hustling a stewardess named Luanne. Beth could tell he was hustling; he was trying to look casual. When he *wasn't* hustling, he was always intense, about everything. She decided to ignore it, and wandered around the apartment, sipping at a Tanqueray and tonic.

There were framed prints of abstract shapes clipped from a calendar printed in Germany. They were in metal Bonniers frames.

In the dining room a huge door from a demolished building somewhere in the city had been handsomely stripped, teaked and refinished. It was now the dinner table.

A Lightolier fixture attached to the wall over the bed swung out, levered up and down, tipped, and its burnished globe-head revolved a full three hundred and sixty degrees.

She was standing in the bedroom, looking out the window, when she realized *this* had been one of the rooms in which light had gone on, gone off; one of the rooms that had contained a silent watcher at the death of Leona Ciarelli.

When she returned to the living room, she looked around more carefully. With only three or four exceptions—the stewardess, a young married couple from the second floor, a stockbroker from Hemphill, Noyes—*everyone* at the party had been a witness to the slaying.

"I'd like to go," she told him.

"Why, aren't you having a good time?" asked the stewardess, a mocking smile crossing her perfect little face.

"Like all Bennington ladies," Ray said, answering for Beth, "she is enjoying herself most by not enjoying herself at all. It's a trait of the anal retentive. Being here in someone else's apartment, she can't empty ashtrays or rewind the toilet paper roll so it doesn't hang a tongue, and being tightassed, her nature demands we go.

"All right, Beth, let's say our goodbyes and take off. The Phantom Rectum strikes again."

She slapped him and the stewardess's eyes widened. But the smile remained frozen where it had appeared.

He grabbed her wrist before she could do it again. "Garbanzo beans, baby," he said, holding her wrist tighter than necessary.

They went back to her apartment, and after sparring silently with kitchen cabinet doors slammed and the television being tuned too loud, they got to her bed, and he tried to perpetuate the metaphor by fucking her in the ass. He had her on elbows and knees before she realized what he was doing; she struggled to turn over and he rode her bucking and tossing without a sound. And when it was clear to him that she would never permit it, he grabbed her breast from underneath and squeezed so hard she howled in pain. He dumped her on her back, rubbed himself between her legs a dozen times, and came on her stomach.

Beth lay with her eyes closed and an arm thrown across her face. She wanted to cry, but found she could not. Ray lay on her and said nothing. She wanted to rush to the bathroom and shower, but he did not move, till long after his semen had dried on their bodies.

"Who did you date at college?" he asked.

"I didn't date anyone very much." Sullen.

"No heavy makeouts with wealthy lads from Williams and Dartmouth . . . no Amherst intellectuals begging you to save them from creeping faggotry by permitting them to stick their carrots in your sticky little slit?"

"Stop it!"

"Come on, baby, it couldn't all have been knee socks and little round circle-pins. You don't expect me to believe you didn't get a little mouthful of cock from time to time. It's only, what? about fifteen miles to Williamstown? I'm sure the Williams werewolves were down burning the highway to your cunt on weekends; you can level with old Uncle Ray. . . ."

"Why are you like this?!" She started to move, to get away from him, and he grabbed her by the shoulder, forced her to lie down again. Then he rose up over her and said, "I'm like this because I'm a New Yorker, baby. Because I live in this fucking city every day. Because I have to play patty-cake with the ministers and other sanctified holy-joe assholes who want their goodness and lightness tracts published by the Blessed Sacrament Publishing and Storm Window Company of 277 Park Avenue, when what I *really* want to do is toss the stupid psalm-suckers out the thirty-seventh-floor window and listen to them quote chapter-and-worse all the way down. Because I've lived in this great big snapping dog of a city all my life and I'm mad as a mudfly, for chrissakes!"

She lay unable to move, breathing shallowly, filled with a sudden pity and affection for him. His face was white and strained, and she knew he was saying things to her that only a bit too much Almadén and exact timing would have let him say.

"What do you expect from me," he said, his voice softer now, but no less intense, "do you expect kindness and gentility and understanding and a hand on *your* hand when the smog burns your eyes? I can't do it, I haven't got it. No one has it in this cesspool of a city. Look around you; what do you think is happening here? They take rats and they put them in boxes and when there are too many of them, some of the little fuckers go out of their minds and start gnawing the rest to death. *It ain't no different here, baby!* It's rat time for everybody in this madhouse. You can't expect to jam as many people into this stone thing as we do, with buses and taxis and dogs shitting themselves scrawny and noise night and day and no money and not enough places to live and no place to go to have a decent think . . . you can't do it without making the time right for some godforsaken other kind of thing to be born! You can't hate everyone around you, and kick every beggar and nigger and *mestizo* shithead, you can't have cabbies stealing from you and taking tips they don't deserve, and then cursing you, you can't walk in the soot till your collar turns black, and your body stinks with the smell of flaking brick and decaying brains, you can't do it without calling up some kind of awful—"

He stopped.

His face bore the expression of a man who has just received brutal word of the death of a loved one. He suddenly lay down, rolled over, and turned off.

She lay beside him, trembling, trying desperately to remember where she had seen his face before.

He didn't call her again, after the night of the party. And when they met in the hall, he pointedly turned away, as though he had given her some obscure chance and she had refused to take it. Beth thought she understood: though Ray Gleeson had not been her first affair, he had been the first to reject her so completely. The first to put her not only out of his bed and his life, but even out of his world. It was as though she were invisible, not even beneath contempt, simply not there.

She busied herself with other things.

She took on three new charting jobs for Guzman and a new group that had formed on Staten Island, of all places. She worked furiously and they gave her new assignments; they even paid her.

She tried to decorate the apartment with a less precise touch. Huge poster blowups of Merce Cunningham and Martha Graham replaced the Brueghel prints that had reminded her of the view looking down the hill toward Williams. The tiny balcony outside her window, the balcony she had steadfastly refused to stand upon since the night of the slaughter, the night of the fog with eyes, that balcony she swept and set about with little flower boxes in which she planted geraniums, petunias, dwarf zinnias, and other hardy perennials. Then, closing the window, she went to give herself, to involve herself in this city to which she had brought her ordered life.

And the city responded to her overtures:

Seeing off an old friend from Bennington, at Kennedy International, she stopped at the terminal coffee shop to have a sandwich. The counter—like a moat—surrounded a center service island that had huge advertising cubes rising above it on burnished poles. The cubes proclaimed the delights of Fun City. *New York Is a Summer Festival,* they said, and *Joseph Papp Presents Shakespeare in Central Park* and *Visit the Bronx Zoo* and *You'll Adore Our Contentious but Lovable Cabbies.* The food emerged from a window far down the service area and moved slowly on a conveyor belt through the hordes of screaming waitresses who slathered the counter with redolent washcloths. The lunchroom had all the charm and dignity of a steel-rolling mill, and approximately the same noise level. Beth ordered a cheeseburger that cost a dollar and a quarter, and a glass of milk.

When it came, it was cold, the cheese unmelted, and the patty of meat resembling nothing so much as a dirty scouring pad. The bun was cold and untoasted. There was no lettuce under the patty.

Beth managed to catch the waitress's eye. The girl approached with an annoyed look. "Please toast the bun and may I have a piece of lettuce?" Beth said.

"We dun' do that," the waitress said, turned half away as though she would walk in a moment.

"You don't do what?"

"We dun' toass the bun here."

"Yes, but I *want* the bun toasted," Beth said firmly.

"An' you got to pay for extra lettuce."

"If I was asking for *extra* lettuce," Beth said, getting annoyed, "I would pay for it, but since there's *no* lettuce here, I don't think I should be charged extra for the first piece."

"We dun' do that."

The waitress started to walk away. "Hold it," Beth said, raising her voice just enough so the assembly-line eaters on either side stared at her. "You mean to tell me I have to pay a dollar and a quarter and I can't get a piece of lettuce or even get the bun toasted?"

"Ef you dun' like it . . ."

"Take it back."

"You gotta pay for it, you order it."

"I said take it back, I don't want the fucking thing!"

The waitress scratched it off the check. The milk cost 27¢ and tasted going-sour. It was the first time in her life that Beth had said *that* word aloud.

At the cashier's stand, Beth said to the sweating man with the felt-tip pens in his shirt pocket, "Just out of curiosity, are you interested in complaints?"

"No!" he said, snarling, quite literally snarling. He did not look up as he punched out 73¢ and it came rolling down the chute.

The city responded to her overtures:

It was raining again. She was trying to cross Second Avenue, with the light. She stepped off the curb and a car came sliding through the red and splashed her. "Hey!" she yelled.

"Eat shit, sister!" the driver yelled back, turning the corner.

Her boots, her legs and her overcoat were splattered with mud. She stood trembling on the curb.

The city responded to her overtures:

She emerged from the building at One Astor Place with her big briefcase full of Laban charts; she was adjusting her rain scarf about her head. A well-dressed man with an attaché case thrust the handle of his umbrella up between her legs from the rear. She gasped and dropped her case.

The city responded and responded and responded.

Her overtures altered quickly.

The old drunk with the stippled cheeks extended his hand and mumbled words. She cursed him and walked on up Broadway past the beaver film houses.

She crossed against the lights on Park Avenue, making hackies slam their brakes to avoid hitting her; she used *that* word frequently now.

When she found herself having a drink with a man who had elbowed up beside her in the singles' bar, she felt faint and knew she should go home.

But Vermont was so far away.

Nights later. She had come home from the Lincoln Center ballet, and gone straight to bed. Lying half-asleep in her bedroom, she heard an alien sound. One room away, in the living room, in the dark, there was a sound. She slipped out of bed and went to the door between the rooms. She fumbled silently for the switch on the lamp just inside the living room, and found it, and clicked it on. A black man in a leather car coat was trying to get *out* of the apartment. In that first flash of light filling the room she noticed the television set beside him on the floor as he struggled with the door, she noticed the police lock and bar had been broken in a new and clever manner *New York Magazine* had not yet reported in a feature article on apartment ripoffs, she noticed that he had gotten his foot tangled in the telephone cord that she had requested be extra-long so she could carry the instrument into the bathroom, I don't want to miss any business calls when the shower is running; she noticed all things in perspective and one thing with sharpest clarity: the expression on the burglar's face.

There was something familiar in that expression.

He almost had the door open, but now he closed it, and slipped the police lock. He took a step toward her.

Beth went back, into the darkened bedroom.

The city responded to her overtures.

She backed against the wall at the head of the bed. Her hand fumbled in the shadows for the telephone. His shape filled the doorway, light, all light behind him.

In silhouette it should not have been possible to tell, but somehow she knew he was wearing gloves and the only marks he would leave would be deep bruises, very blue, almost black, with the tinge under them of blood that had been stopped in its course.

He came for her, arms hanging casually at his sides. She tried to climb over the bed, and he grabbed her from behind, ripping her nightgown. Then he had a hand around her neck and he pulled her backward. She fell off the bed, landed at his feet and his hold was broken. She scuttled across the floor and for a moment she had the respite to feel terror. She was going to die, and she was frightened.

He trapped her in the corner between the closet and the bureau and kicked her. His foot caught her in the thigh as she folded tighter, smaller, drawing her legs up. She was cold.

Then he reached down with both hands and pulled her erect by her hair. He slammed her head against the wall. Everything slid up in her sight as though running off the edge of the world. He slammed her head against the wall again, and she felt something go soft over her right ear.

When he tried to slam her a third time she reached out blindly for his face and ripped down with her nails. He howled in pain and she hurled herself forward, arms wrapping themselves around his waist. He stumbled backward and in a tangle of thrashing arms and legs they fell out onto the little balcony.

Beth landed on the bottom, feeling the window boxes jammed up against her spine and legs. She fought to get to her feet, and her nails hooked into his shirt under the open jacket, ripping. Then she was on her feet again and they struggled silently.

He whirled her around, bent her backward across the wrought-iron railing. Her face was turned outward.

They were standing in their windows, watching.

Through the fog she could see them watching. Through the fog she recognized their expressions. Through the fog she heard them breathing in unison, bellows breathing of expectation and wonder. Through the fog.

And the black man punched her in the throat. She gagged and started to black out and could not draw air into her lungs. Back, back, he bent her further back and she was looking up, straight up, toward the ninth floor and higher. . . .

Up there: eyes.

The words Ray Gleeson had said in a moment filled with what he had become, with the utter hopelessness and finality of the choice the city had forced on him, the words came back. *You can't live in this city and survive unless you have protection . . . you can't live this way, like rats driven mad, without making the time right for some god-forsaken other kind of thing to be born . . . you can't do it without calling up some kind of awful . . .*

God! A new God, an ancient God come again with the eyes and hunger of a child, a deranged blood God of fog and street violence. A God who needed worshipers and offered the choices of death as a victim or life as an eternal witness to the deaths of *other* chosen victims. A God to fit the times, a God of streets and people.

She tried to shriek, to appeal to Ray, to the director in the bedroom window of his ninth-floor apartment with his long-legged Philadelphia model beside him and his fingers inside her as they worshiped in their holiest of ways, to the others who had been at the party that had been Ray's offer of a chance to join their congregation. She wanted to be saved from having to make that choice.

But the black man had punched her in the throat, and now his hands were on her, one on her chest, the other in her face, the smell of leather filling her where the nausea could not. And she understood Ray had *cared,* had wanted her to take the chance offered; but she had come from a world of little white dormitories and Vermont countryside; it was not a real world. *This* was the real world and up there was the God who ruled this world, and she had rejected him, had said no to one of his priests and servitors. *Save me! Don't make me do it!*

She knew she had to call out, to make appeal, to try and win the approbation of that God. *I can't . . . save me!*

She struggled and made terrible little mewling sounds trying to summon the words to cry out, and suddenly she crossed a line, and screamed up into the echoing courtyard with a voice Leona Ciarelli had never known enough to use.

"Him! Take him! Not me! I'm yours, I love you, I'm yours! Take him, not me, please not me, take him, take him, I'm yours!"

And the black man was suddenly lifted away, wrenched off her, and off the balcony, whirled straight up into the fog-thick air in the courtyard, as Beth sank to her knees on the ruined flower boxes.

She was half-conscious, and could not be sure she saw it just that way, but up he went, end over end, whirling and spinning like a charred leaf.

And the form took firmer shape. Enormous paws with claws and shapes that no animal she had ever seen had ever possessed, and the burglar, black, poor, terrified, whimpering like a whipped dog, was stripped of his flesh. His body was opened with a thin incision, and there was a rush as all the blood poured from him like a sudden cloudburst, and yet he was still alive, twitching with the involuntary horror of a frog's leg shocked with an electric current. Twitched, and twitched again as he was torn piece by piece to shreds. Pieces of flesh and bone and half a face with an eye blinking furiously, cascaded down past Beth, and hit the cement below with sodden thuds. And still he was alive, as his organs were squeezed and musculature and bile and shit and skin were rubbed, sandpapered together and let fall. It went on and on, as the death of Leona Ciarelli had gone on and on, and she understood with the blood-knowledge of survivors *at any cost* that the reason the witnesses to the death of Leona Ciarelli had done nothing was not that they had been frozen with horror, that they didn't want to get involved, or that they were inured to death by years of television slaughter.

They were worshipers at a black mass the city had demanded be staged; not once, but a thousand times a day in this insane asylum of steel and stone.

Now she was on her feet, standing half-naked in her ripped nightgown, her hands tightening on the wrought-iron railing, begging to see more, to drink deeper.

Now she was one of them, as the pieces of the night's sacrifice fell past her, bleeding and screaming.

Tomorrow the police would come again, and they would question her, and she would say how terrible it had been, that burglar, and how she had fought, afraid he would rape her and kill her, and how he had fallen, and she had no idea how he had been so hideously mangled and ripped apart, but a seven-story fall, after all . . .

Tomorrow she would not have to worry about walking in the streets, because no harm could come to her. Tomorrow she could even remove the police lock. Nothing in the city could do her any further evil, because she had made the only choice. She was now a dweller in the city, now wholly and richly a part of it. Now she was taken to the bosom of her God.

She felt Ray beside her, standing beside her, holding her, protecting her, his hand on her naked backside, and she watched the fog swirl up and fill the courtyard, fill the city, fill her eyes and her soul and her heart with its power. As Ray's naked body pressed tightly inside her, she drank deeply of the night, knowing whatever voices she heard from this moment forward would be the voices not of whipped dogs, but those of strong, meat-eating beasts.

At last she was unafraid, and it was so good, so very good *not* to be afraid.

. . .

"When inward life dries up, when feeling decreases and apathy increases, when one cannot affect or even genuinely touch another person, violence flares up as a daimonic necessity for contact, a mad drive forcing touch in the most direct way possible."

—Rollo May, *Love and Will*

1975:

The Jail

Jesse Hill Ford

How I found the car was I went with the truck looking for some plows and a harrow and a mowing machine, horse-drawn stuff we had a chance to sell to a fellow who was farming produce on shares—tomatoes, in particular. You can't cultivate tomatoes with a tractor. The sticks are too high. He had located a pair of mules. He was a Do-Right, but that is another story. A Do-Right is a member of a small religion we have in west Tennessee wherein a man pledges that he will *do right* and if a Do-Right is not lazy, he's a fair credit risk. So he needed the implements and I said I'd go look and see if I could locate them over on my grandmother's place.

I got into the truck and drove over there. It was July and I looked over her cotton and beans and saw that everything looked good. She'd built her cage-laying shed spang at the other end of the two thousand acres instead of putting it on the main road like I advised her, and I crossed the stock gaps and the dust powdered on the hood of my green truck. I put up the windows and put the air conditioning on and turned up the music on the country station and presently I saw the laying house and drove on back to the barn, white-painted and neat. I found the key on my ring and unlocked the doors and swung them open and saw the implements almost at once and the stalls just as they had been left, cleaned out and swept after the last mule died. It was a fine old barn and maybe I still would not have found the car except that I went walking down the hall, looking in the big old box stalls and thinking how it was when I was a boy. It was the fourth stall down and when I saw the car, red and low and foreign, with a good bit of dust on it that had filtered down from the old loft above, I took a look at the outer wallboards and could see where they had been removed in order to put the car in there. My first thought was of Sheriff, my little brother, for I well knew his love of cars. And I thought, Well, Sheriff has bought a car and for some reason stored it in here without saying a word to anybody about it. Then I stepped inside the stall and stooped down and rubbed the barn dust off the license plate. New York State, 1965—I crouched there in the silence of the barn and pondered that. I could feel my heart beating. I stood up and opened the car door on the driver's side. It sure needed greasing, for it kind of groaned—a coffin-lid groan—and I looked inside and saw that it was probably British and next saw that it was a Jaguar. You don't see a whole lot of Jaguars in west Tennessee. Fact of the business, you so rarely see one now that the interstate has been put through that there just isn't any telling *when* the *last* Jaguar came through Pinoak, Tennessee. The interstate, which cut us off the mainstream of travel between Florida and the Midwestern states, was opened in 1966.

I saw something on the steering column held by little coil springs and celluloid. I took it off the column and read the name on the New York driver's license. S. Jerome Luben, male, black hair, brown eyes, age 26, address on Riverside Drive, New York City. Nobody with a name like Luben could be mistaken for a member of the Pinoak Missionary Baptist Church. I tossed the license, celluloid, coil springs and all, onto the driver's seat and closed the door. It shut with a sound that was somehow so final I stood there another full minute at least before I could move. The dust of nine years in a mule barn was on my hands.

The year 1965 was the year Sheriff left home for the Marines. I recalled the day he left. I recalled a lot of things, including the way he kept whispering something and nodding to Henry. Henry is the nigger who has worked for my grandmother since he was a little boy: he kind of waited on Sheriff and buddied around with him since Sheriff was little.

Did I say my little brother is spoiled? Spoiled rotten. The baby in the family. My mother thought she was in the change of life and went around eight months thinking he was a tumor and probably malignant until she finally went to the doctor after she had got our family lawyer, Oman Hedgepath, to make her will, which would have left most of her estate for the support of foreign missions. Mother worried about the souls of the heathens. When Ocie Pentecost told her she was pregnant, I think she felt cheated. A month later, here came Sheriff. That is not his name, of course. His real name is Caleb Batsell Beeman Baxter. Mother had an uncle in Somerton whose name was Caleb and he got into real estate and insurance and put his signs up so they read: C. BATSELL BEEMAN FOR EVERYTHING IN REAL ESTATE AND INSURANCE NEEDS. He put that sign on every road leading in and out of town and had a fine income all his life right up to the moment he fell into the wheat bin and suffocated. Wheat is like water: you fall into it and you go under. Uncle Batsell could not swim.

Mother figured Sheriff would be a lawyer like Oman Hedgepath and have a sign on his door and a shingle hanging in the breeze on Main Street, reading: C. BATSELL B. BAXTER, which she thought would make everybody with any law business want to see her youngest son.

As for me, I was never in her mind otherwise than somebody to run everything. To gin cotton during ginning season and combine beans during bean season, to buy hay and manage for the silage and between times build rent houses and work in the store and manage the tractor-and-implement company and make private loans and buy farms and run the sawmill—or, in other words, just like my daddy always did, to run everything and see to everything and mind everything and when there was nothing else to do, to step in behind the meat counter and weigh hams.

Not Sheriff, though. Once it got through her head that he was not a tumor, she saw him in the practice of the law. Then he started to grow up and almost from the first word he spoke, it was obvious that all in the world he would ever want to do would be to be a sheriff and enforce the law. It was all that he spoke about, and because he was the baby, we gave him toy guns and little uniforms and hats and badges. He went around dressed like that and went to school that way. What else would we call him but Sheriff? Everybody in Sligo County thought he was cute as a bug, and during the strawberry festival every year we'd build him a float in the shape of a sheriff's patrol car with little wheels on it and the aerial and all and Sheriff would ride in it, with Henry and a couple of others pulling him in the children's parade. Time and again he won first or got an honorable mention from the judges who come each year from Memphis to judge the parade and the beauty contest.

Then he got to high school and we gave him an automobile and Grandmother gave him police lights for the top of it and my father bought him a siren from Sears. I got him a real badge from a pawnshop in Memphis. It saved us from having to wonder what to do for him when it came Christmas.

If something happened in Pinoak, we had Sheriff as our private police force to investigate things and make arrests and take people over to Somerton to the jail. Nothing official, understand, but a convenience in a small place like Pinoak, where you don't have a police force.

Sheriff, for the most part, confined himself to stopping out-of-state cars if they were speeding or if they looked suspicious. He'd pull them over, get out, walk up to the driver's side and tip his hat. He was young and blond and blue-eyed and had such an innocent face. Yet behind it there was always something that made folks do exactly what he told them to do. Show their driver's license, open their trunk lid, even open their suitcases. He confiscated ever so much liquor and beer, but never went so far as to actually arrest anybody . . . that I ever knew anything about.

He seemed happy and he seemed contented. When he asked if he could have a jail, my father consulted highway patrol. They advised against it. The law in Tennessee did not, they said, let folks operate private jails. That could cause problems, they said. Otherwise, as long as Sheriff never arrested anybody or gave a ticket or fined anybody, he could pretty well do as he pleased, for he was a deterrent to speeders. Pinoak got known far and wide as a speed trap. Back before they opened the interstate, the out-of-state traffic would drive through Pinoak so slow you could walk alongside it the whole two blocks. They'd come at a crawl sometimes, with Sheriff so close behind in his cruiser he was all but bumper to bumper, and Sheriff just daring them to make a wrong move or do anything sudden or reckless.

More than anything else, he liked to stop a car with a New York tag, for when that happened, like as not he'd get a loud-mouth who would start to complain and bitch and raise his voice and Sheriff would end up practically taking the fellow's car apart in front of his eyes. New York drivers were a challenge to Sheriff. Looking at that red car gave me a chill in spite of the heat.

I went outside and stood just beyond the white-painted doors of the mule barn. I could see the cage-laying house and hear the hens and could smell that special odor of hen shit and cracked eggs and ground feed. I saw that Henry's truck was there, so I went down to the packing room and found him. He had collected the eggs and had them in the tank with the vibrator that washes them and he was grading them and putting them in big square cartons of fifty. The cracked ones he broke all the way and put the yolks and whites into big pickle jars to be hauled to the poor farm and to the Somerton jail, because the old and the poor and the prisoners are just as well fed on cracked eggs as on whole ones and cracked eggs come a whole lot cheaper; besides, otherwise we'd have to feed the cracked ones to the hogs. Henry never looked up and the vibrator hummed and the water danced the hen shit off the eggs and the smell of spoiled eggs was in the room. The floor was a little wet. A black-and-white cat was asleep on the sofa Henry had made for himself by welding legs onto a truck seat taken from a wreck.

"S. Jerome Luben," I said. "That mean anything to you?"

He froze, egg in hand, just that quick.

"S. Jerome Luben," I said again.

He dropped the egg and it broke on the wet concrete between his black, down-at-heel shoes.

"Is he dead?" I asked.

Henry reached into the tank for another egg, got one, and then cut off the vibrator. He wiped the egg carefully on the corner of his apron. Flies were worrying about the floor, lighting at the edges of the egg he had dropped.

"Naw, sah, he ain't dead. Leastways he wasn't dead this morning."

"This morning? You saw S. Jerome Luben this morning?"

"Yes, sah. He looked OK to me." Instead of looking at me, he looked at the egg in his hand and pushed with his thumbnail at what might have been a speck on its white, curving surface. "How come you to know about him, sah?"

"I just saw his car."

"Little red automobile."

"Did you knock the wall loose?"

"I prised some of the boards loose. It wouldn't go in if I didn't prise some boards off. But now I nailed 'em back."

"Nine years ago."

"Something lack that," he said, still examining the egg. "It had to be after Christmas, wadn't it?"

"How would I know?" I said.

"It was after Christmas of sixty-five, I b'lieve it was," he said. He never looked blacker. I began to feel something between my shoulder blades in the middle of my back, a cold sensation. He was so utterly still. "Yes, sah. Sixty-five," he said.

"What happened?"

He was quiet a moment. "I tole 'em it was bound to cause trouble."

"Who—told who?"

"Your grandmother, Miss Mettie Bell. And him—Sheriff. He got on her about wanting her to give him a jail—"

"A what?"

"Jail. Tole her wouldn't nothing else make him happy that Christmas if he didn't git him a jail. Jest a teeny little jail. Two cells, he tole her. That's all he wanted Santy to bring him and what if he went away to—where was it he went?"

"Vietnam."

"Nam, that's it. What if he went there and got kilt and hadn't never had him the pleasure of a jail of his own? He started on her in the summertime in weather about like this and she sent to Birmingham for the contractor and they come and built it and she handed him the keys on Christmas Eve. I was standing in the kitchen next to the sink when she handed them keys to him and made him promise he wouldn't abuse his privilege and wouldn't make no trouble and wouldn't tell nobody local from

around here anything about it. She tole me I'd have to feed
anybody he locked up and keep the jail swept and mopped and
cleaned good. She wadn't going to endure with no dirty jail, she
said. So I promised and Sheriff, he promised, too."
I sat down on the sofa. The cat raised her head and gave me
a green stare. Then, closing her eyes again, she laid her head
back down. I heard the vibrator come on.
"S. Jerome Luben," I said. "Is he in the jail?"
"He was this morning when I carried him his breakfast."
"Where the hell is this jail?"
I no sooner asked than something dawned on me. It was like
looking at the flat surface of a pool. You can look ever so long
at the surface and you will see only the reflection of the sky and
the trees, but then, sometimes very suddenly, you'll see below
it—you'll see a fish or a turtle.
It had to be the poison house. We bought farm poisons in such
quantities, all the new poisons and defoliants, the sprays and
powders for controlling everything from the boll weevil to the
cabbage butterfly, plus all the weed killers. I recalled drawing
the check to the Birmingham contractor and wondering why
Grandmother got somebody from Alabama instead of a Somerton builder, but it was Grandmother's money and if she wanted
the poison house set off in a field on the backside of nowhere,
then it was fine with me, because the poisons always gave me
a headache when I had to be around them. I never went to the
poison house, not I or my father or any white man. It gives you
a headache, a poison room does. They say the stuff can collect
in your system and shorten your life. So, for nine years, I'd been
looking at a goddamned jail and had never known what it was.
I had never before wondered why Grandmother would put up
a two-story poison house and have a Birmingham contractor
build it. Hell, *I* could have built the thing. Only when you are
busy as I am all the time, with one season falling on you before
the last one is over—starting with cabbage and strawberries and
rolling right on through corn and soybeans and cotton and
wheat and winter pasture and back to cabbage and strawberries
again—you are so goddamned relieved when anybody will take
even a little something off your back you never wonder about
it and you get so you never ask questions. Nine years can flit past
you like a moth in the dark. You never give it a second thought.

"Henry?"

"Sah?"

"Cut that goddamned thing off and come with me." I stood up, feeling light-headed.

"Cut it *off?*"

"You heard me."

"But I got to grade these eggs—"

"Who feeds him his dinner?"

"Sah?"

"S. Jerome Luben."

He cut off the vibrator, wiped his hands and reached beneath his apron and hauled out his watch. He looked at it and then shucked off the apron and threw it onto the truck-seat sofa before sticking the watch back into the pocket of his gray work trousers.

"No need you to go," he said. He started out and would have gotten in his truck as though to close the matter between us once and for all. I give him credit, He was letting me have my chance to stay out of it.

"Get in my truck, Henry."

He froze again. "You don't have to go," he said.

"My truck."

He gave a sigh and turned then and went slowly to my truck and climbed into the passenger seat and slammed the door. I climbed in beside him and started the engine and felt the air conditioner take hold and start to cool me. It was the first I knew that I was sweating so heavily; it was cold sweat and dried beneath my shirt and left me clammy.

I pulled the gearshift down into drive and accelerated out through the gate, over the stock gap and into the dusty single lane that spun between the pastures, deep and green on both sides of us. Next came cotton acreage, then a bean field with corn standing far down beyond it toward the bottoms, and beyond the corn the groves of virgin cypress timber far down in the flat distance like the faraway rim of the world, as though beyond that contained edge of green there would be nothing else, just blue space and stars. West Tennessee gives that feeling and if you grow up with it, it never leaves you. It's big and lonely and a million miles from nowhere—that's the feeling. I turned through the gate and the tires slapped on the iron pipes spanning the stock gap and the poison house was straight ahead. I pulled around behind it. Sheriff's car was there, parked ramrod straight on the neat gravel apron. On the side of its white front door was a seal and above the seal the word SHERIFF in dark gold, and below the seal in neat black lettering: OFFICIAL BUSINESS ONLY.

The sawed-off shotgun was racked forward against the dashboard and the two-way radio that he always left on was talking to itself when I opened my door, cut the engine and climbed down.

Henry didn't move.

"Get out," I said and slammed my door. He opened his door and climbed down.

"No need you to git mixed into this mess, Mr. Jim," he said, giving me another chance.

The radio in Sheriff's cruiser muttered something, asked something, answered itself.

"Follow me," I said and headed for the door. It was a glassed aluminum storm door and before I opened it, I saw the desk and Sheriff propped up behind it, reading a *True Detective* or some such magazine. His hat was on the costumer in the corner. When I went in, grateful because the building was air conditioned, he didn't stir. Maybe he thinks it's Henry, or maybe he just doesn't care, I told myself.

Henry was behind me. The door clicked shut. Sheriff licked his thumb and turned a page. His blue gaze passed over me as though I didn't exist. He looked almost the same as he had looked the day he left for the Marines, the same tan, the same blond crewcut, the same innocent baby face. Then he saw me. The swivel desk chair creaked and he came forward until his elbows were on the desk. Then I smelled it. Henry had gone by me now into what I saw was a kitchen adjoining the office. I smelled rancid food and unwashed despair and tired mattresses and stale cigarettes—I smelled the smell of every jail in the South, from Miami to Corinth, from Memphis to Biloxi to Charleston to Birmingham—I smelled them all and every little town between. Finally, it is the smell of human fear, the scent of the caged human animal—nine years of that, one year stacked on top of the last, palpable as dust.

"Nice place," I said.

Sheriff looked at me, not sure yet what I knew. Give him credit, he's cool, I thought: my blood, my kin, my flesh. And I had as much hand in spoiling him rotten as anybody. Maybe that's what they teach you at the University of Mississippi, where I played and raised hell for four years before the Army got me. They teach you how to come home and continue to spoil the little brother in the family by letting him do what he damn well pleases. Every family needs one at least with no responsibility at all to burden him. Here sat ours.

"You never seen it before?" Sheriff said. He hollered at Henry: "What you doing in there?"

"Fixin' his dinner, scramblin' his eggs." Henry turned and stood in the kitchen door, holding a pickle jar. I could see the yolks and the whites. So they fed him cracked eggs, the same as any other prisoner in Sligo County. Henry stood patiently. He was looking down at the jar. In the opposite hand he held the lid.

"Fixin' whose dinner?" Sheriff said.

"His—upstairs," said Henry. He didn't look up and his voice was low, a sunken, below-surface sound.

"What the hell you talking about?" said Sheriff.

"He knows," Henry said in the same sunken voice.

"I found the car," I said.

"Oh," said Sheriff.

"The red car and a driver's license and a name."

"Well, now you know about him," Sheriff said. "Figured you or Dad, one was bound to come to the poison house someday. I'd say it was my office and you'd go away and not worry. How come you to find the car, Jim?"

"Just unlucky. A Do-Right wants some old tools and machinery—"

"I told Henry I'd bust his ass if he ever let it out. Didn't I tell you I'd bust your ass, Henry?"

"Yes, sah. Want me to feed him? It's time."

"Goddamn it," Sheriff said. "Goddamn it."

"Just answer me one question," I said. I heard eggs hit the hot skillet.

"Shoot."

"Why would you lock a man up and keep him locked up nine years?"

"You mean Jerome? Why would I keep him so long? It's a fair question. I never intended to leave him in here longer than just overnight to teach him a lesson. He passed through Pinoak that night doing above ninety. I risked my life and never caught him until the son of a bitch was nearly to McKay—lights and siren and giving my car a fit. Goddamn him. He could have been the death of us both. See?" He looked at me with that blue stare of innocence and passed his fingers over the crown of his close-cropped hair. "And he swore at me."

"So you locked him up for nine years. You buried him alive because he cussed you and he was from New York. Do you know how long they'll keep you in prison for this? Did it ever dawn on you?"

"I know all about it," he said.

"God help us," I said. "God *help* us—Henry's in it. I'm in it!"

"Look—go upstairs and talk to him. Please? Go up and let Jerome explain how it happened. He understands it and—" He stopped talking and stood up and took some keys off his belt and went to the steel security door and unlocked and opened it. I climbed the concrete stairs with Sheriff behind me.

There was a hallway at the top with a cell on either side of it and two windows and a toilet and lavatory in each cell. The cell on the right was open and had bookshelves on every wall to the ceiling. The cell on the left was closed. I saw the prisoner, a slender, black-haired man wearing blue jeans and loafers and a T-shirt. He was clean-shaven and his hair was cropped close to his head like Sheriff's and he was working at a typewriter. A book lay open beside him on the desk.

"What's for lunch?" he said. Then he saw me and pushed his chair back. On the cell floor lay the rug that used to be in my grandmother's parlor, a pattern of roses. "Who's this, Sheriff?"

"It's Jim."

"What a surprise. I'm Jerome Luben." He came to the cell door, swung it open and put out his hand to me. We shook hands. "So what brings you here?"

"He found your car," said Sheriff. "And Henry told him."

"You just now found out? Told anybody?" He was handsome in a Jewish way and looked none the worse for wear. There was premature gray at his temples, just a touch.

"Not yet I haven't told anybody," I said.

Luben looked at Sheriff. "Why don't you leave us alone for a few minutes? Tell Henry to hold my lunch. Need to explain things to Jim, don't I?"

Sheriff nodded and turned and went back down the stairs. I heard the security door clank shut.

"We can sit in here, if you like," said Luben, leading the way into the cell on the right. "My library," he said.

I recognized two of Grandmother's parlor chairs and one of her floor lamps.

"You upset, Jim?"

"A little," I said.

"Don't be upset. Because what happened couldn't happen again in a thousand—a million—years. I'm not angry, you see that, don't you?"

"Yes," I said. "But what the hell happened? This is the ruination of my family—the end."

"It's not the end. Listen to me. It's back in 1965, I'm fresh out of Columbia Law School. I'm driving like a bat out of hell, with no respect for anything—asking for it. I've got long hair and a beard and I'm smoking grass and everybody who thinks the war in Vietnam is right is a pissant in my book, shit beneath my feet. Get the picture? I'm bigger and richer and smarter than the world, the entire fucking—pardon me—world. I know Southerners do not use those words."

"Not often, no," I said.

"So your brother stops me. Polite? A complete gentleman. I tell him to eat shit. I hit him. I spit on him. I'm begging him to lock me up so I can be some kind of goddamned martyr and get my ass in jail and my name in the papers and on television and go home to New York and be a fucking hero. Now, understand, my *father* has washed his hands of me three years earlier and put my money in a trust that keeps my checking account overflowing. I mean, he's rich and my mother was rich and she's dead and I've told him what a capitalist pig he is and he hopes to God he will *never* see me again. I'm scorching the highway in the backward, backwoods, medieval South, and who stops me? Your brother."

"Lord have mercy," I whispered.

"He brings me here. He and Henry have to carry me bodily. I'm not cooperating. Then I blew it all to hell."

"How?"

"I demanded my phone call."

"Phone call?"

"Phone call. My lousy phone call. And Sheriff had to tell me there isn't a phone. I said what kind of fucking jail was it with no phone? I said did he realize what was going to happen to him if I didn't get my phone call? Did he know that he had arrested a lawyer—a member of the New York bar, an officer of the court, a graduate of Columbia and much else? Did he know how fucking rich I was? Because I was going to make a career out of him. I had nothing else to do. I was going to make him and Henry and anybody else responsible for building a jail and leaving a phone out of it suffer until they'd wish they had never been born! *Oy!*"

I began to see. I began to see it all. He went on. He was smiling now, that was the wonder of it:

"And he finally had to tell me that his grandmother had built the jail and he wasn't really a sheriff, not even a deputy. I had rolled a joint and was blowing smoke at him and getting high and I told him as soon as he let me out, I'd see his grandmother in prison, and himself, and poor old black-ass Henry. And that did it. He was due to go to the Marines. He had already enlisted. He went away and left Henry to feed me."

I didn't want to let myself think what I was thinking. In the chambers of my mind's memory, I saw the red Jaguar in the mule barn. I heard the door chunk shut; I felt all the finality of our family's situation. Coming down to it, I saw that it was me or S. Jerome Luben.

Luben was saying, "I'm sure Sheriff will keep his word, in which event I'll be free next October. Not that I will leave." He frowned. "I find this hard to believe. I therefore know how difficult it may be for you to believe."

"Believe what, Mr. Luben?"

"That I'm finally rehabilitated. That I love the United States of America, that I'd go to war for my country if asked to serve. That I'd even volunteer. Inward things—I'm clean, I'm thinking straight. He'll unlock the door in October, you'll see."

I knew I'd have to kill him. I felt my heart stagger. He must have seen a change in my face. He looked at me quietly.

"After you're free, what will you do?" I asked. We'd bury him and the automobile. The easiest way would be to poison him, to let him die quietly in his sleep, and just as he had been carried into Sheriff's prison—unresisting but not cooperating—so would he be carried out of it and put deep in the ground. It was the only way.

Luben smiled. "Are you ready for this? I like your brother." My look must have asked him who he was trying to bullshit, because he drew a breath, smiled again and went on talking. All the pressures of New York and the world outside and his troubles with his father and the other members of his family, the drug scene, the antiwar movement, the hippie underground, he was saying, all that passed away once he was locked up here, apparently for life. "All that shit, all those pressures were suddenly gone. I say *suddenly* like it happened overnight, when, of course, it didn't. I was maybe four years getting anywhere with myself, trying to bribe Henry to let me escape, screaming at night. Then I decided to cut my hair and get rid of the beard. Sheriff had already told me I could have anything I wanted within reason, as long as I bought it with my own money. These books, this library, the typewriter—I've got nearly every worthwhile book there is on penology. What started as a lot of shouting back and forth between Sheriff and me became long, leisurely conversations. He taught me how to play dominoes. I used to enter chess tournaments in my other life. Sheriff taught me dominoes—a simple game but really full of genuine American integrity. When I got tired of dominoes, he went home and got his Monopoly set. It was his kindness and his honesty and, at some point, it came to me that I liked him. I saw at last that there had been no forfeiture of equity on his part. You follow me?"

"I'm not sure," I said.

"All I'm saying is that I did wrong. He arrested me and when I threatened him like I did, in effect I locked the door on myself. Now, after ten years, almost, you see the result. You see what I've become."

"Which is what?" I asked. I got the feeling you have when a salesman goes too fast and gets close to selling you a bill of goods. In a desperate way, I wanted to believe there wouldn't be any need to kill him. The thing about him was that he was so goddamned nice and likable and, what's more, his voice and

his accent reminded me of Sheriff's voice, just a touch, or maybe
an echo, but it got to me where I lived. Yet I knew it couldn't
be possible that he was really one of us. He was a New York Jew
and a lawyer and he had to hate us. He was dangerous as a
rattlesnake. "What are you now?" I asked.

"A model prisoner, a rehabilitated man. This is a copy of an
essay for *The American Journal of Penology*," he said, opening
the top drawer of a little olive-green filing cabinet. "Wrote it in
my spare time," he said, laughing a quiet little laugh at his own
joke.

I looked at the title page. "Some Problems of Local Authorities in Administering Small-Community Jails and Lockups" and,
under it, "By Solomon Jerome Luben, B.A., LL.B." "Well, nice,
real nice," I said. My hand was trembling.

"That's nothing. Take a look at these." And he grabbed a long
tube of rolled-up papers from the top of the nearest bookshelf
and started unrolling it on the library table.

Seeing the back of his neck, I thought maybe it would be
better just to shoot him when he wasn't looking. If I knew
Henry and Sheriff, they'd leave that part up to me.

"Don't you want to see this?" he asked.

"All right." And I moved in beside him and looked.

"Front elevation," he said. "Innovative design, eh? Wait till
you see the modern features!"

All I saw was a long building.

"I'm financing the whole thing. We break ground in October,
when I walk out of here. The end of the medieval monstrosity
that has been the bane of every small community in the South."
He peeled the top sheet aside. "Of course, there'll be a wall.
Now, this is your floor plan, your maximum-security block. Dining hall is here. Exercise yard. Library, of course. Kitchen. Sheriff and I have been two years planning this little jewel. Like it?"

I stood dumbfounded. Again he said his fortune was sufficient
to see the place built and maintained. He, S. Jerome Luben,
would be the administrator. Sheriff would provide the prisoners, of course. Henry might need help in the kitchen, with so
many additional mouths to feed. "We'll have to cross that
bridge when we get to it." A dreamy look came into his eyes.
Small-town mayors and city officials would be brought here, in
greatest secrecy, of course, he said. It was his plan to see what

he called "Sheriff's great idea" applied all over the South, for openers. "Ultimately, of course, it will sweep the globe. Once they see how it cuts all the red tape. No criminal lawyers getting some bastard, some baby raper, some fiend out just because his confession got the case thrown out of court. No trial, no court. Just the jail to end all jails, with an indeterminate sentence for everybody. No mail, no phone calls. Just. . . ." And he snapped his fingers.

"Where would you plan to build it?" I asked.

"Why, here, right here! Can you imagine a better location for the first one?" He peeled the next sheet away. "These are below ground—solitary-confinement cells, soundproof, totally dark. I tell you, Jim, when Sheriff and I get through with this thing, it's really going to be something! *Oy!*"

I couldn't think what to say. I couldn't think, period.

"What a plan, what a beautiful fucking plan," Jerome Luben was whispering.

The steel door opened and clanged below. Footsteps on the stairs; it was Henry—bringing the eggs.

1976:

Like a Terrible Scream

Etta Revesz

Me, I just sit here and wait until the man outside push the little button and the door open with a small click and the Father walk out. The Father, I know him since I be five, which is now eight years. I bet he never think he come to see me in lockup. Kid lockup they call it but look like real grown-up jail to me.

I look out the little window for two days now. All I see is sky and maybe a airplane go by. The bed is clean but the floor is cement stone and hard on my leg. It is the door that I hate with much feeling. It is gray and iron, like the brace I wear on my leg. The little square window is high and I am yet too little to see out it and down the hall. I know a man sits there by a high desk and pushes buttons for many doors like I have to my cell. Yesterday I push up tight against the door because I am afraid. I think maybe I am the only one left here. But all I see is the ceiling of the hall and it is gray and not so clean.

It is hard to sit here and see the Father leave. He try. He try hard to make me tell why I do it.

"Confess, my son," Father Diaz say. "Tell me why did you do that terrible thing? You could not have realized. You were not thinking right!"

The good Father he lean his head way down and I think he

cry, but I shake my head. How can I tell him? If I tell him the reason why I have done this it would be all for nothing. So I let him put his hand on my head and I say nothing.

"Kneel, my son," the Father say. "If you cannot tell me, tell God. It will help."

"No, Father," I say. "I cannot kneel."

He look very unhappy then, almost I think he will slap me when he take his hand away from my head. But he does not.

"A boy that cannot kneel and ask forgiveness from God is lost," he say and then go to my iron door and punch the little black button that tell the man at the desk to open up.

Now I sit here on my cot and wait for the Father to leave. My leg is out straight with my iron brace beginning to hurt me. Always at this time when night sounds start, Rita come home and take it off for me and rub my leg. Her hands, always so soft, rub away the stiffness. She talk to me about things outside. Always she ask to see my picture that I make that day. It was Rita that buy the paper and black crayon for me to draw. And last Christmas she bring me a box of paints! How much I do not guess it cost, but I know it cost much.

I feel in my eyes the water begin, but I want not to cry. I look again at Father Diaz's black suit. Like a crow he looks, standing with his arms folded close to his side like wings. I cannot stop my eyes from making tears. I pretend it is because my leg hurts and I try not to think of Rita.

I decide to tell Father Diaz that I cannot kneel because my iron brace does not bend. Then he would not think that all his teaching about God and the Blessed Virgin was for nothing. But it is too late. I hear the click and the door pop open and I am alone again.

Soon they will bring me food. I do not like noodles and cheese. Cheese should be on enchiladas. Noodles and cheese and maybe wheat bread with edges curled up like a dried leaf. Next to it a spoonful of peanut butter which I hate. It glues my tongue to my teeth. I think back to what Rita always bring to me.

Every night before she go to her job she come by the house with a surprise. First she take off my iron brace and rub my leg and then she put the brown bag in my lap and we stick both our heads close to see what big pleasure is there. Sometimes I look up and see her eyes big on me and smiling when I find a bag of candy or a pomegranate or even a new paint brush. At such time I feel a big pain over my heart and my jaw hurt from not crying. Rita she hate for me to cry. How can she know that it is for love of her that I cry?

Sometimes when only Mama and I are home I stop my painting and look out the window. We are high, two stairs up, but I can see the branches of the tree growing from the brown square of land in our sidewalk. It is not very healthy this poor tree, and has dry brown limbs with no leaves much. But still I watch the sun on what leaves are still there. It is when the sun is low and shines even with my tree that I like it best. Long fingers of white light run sharp from the center and when the wind blows everything shoots gold and shining. It is like a sign from God that the day is gone and Rita will run soon into the room and call out.

"Pepito," she calls, "I am here again. Your ugly old sister is here again!"

I pretend I do not hear her and then she come and put her hands around to cover my eyes from behind.

"Guess who it is?" she ask in make-believe man voice.

"My ugly old sister!" I say and then we both laugh. My sister Rita is not ugly. Sometimes she have a day off and she let me draw her picture. She sit by the window quiet while I look at her and put my markings on my paper. Sometimes I forget to move my hand when I look at her. Rita have long black hair and she tie it back so her neck looks very thin. Her mouth is still but when she think I am not watching, her lips move a little and I think she is telling secrets to herself. It is her eyes that I cannot draw so well.

When I look once they are laughing and show a joke ready to be said, but when I look again, I feel I must weep. Once I really start to cry at least a year ago when I was only twelve. Rita rush over and hug me.

"My little Pepito." She touch my cheek. "Does your leg hurt? I will work hard and save—oh, I will save so and will take you to a big hospital where the finest doctors will make a miracle on your leg."

"No," I tell her. I can never lie to Rita even when I want pity. "It is my love for you that make me cry. You are like Sunday music."

She just laugh then and the next day when she come she say, "Here is your Sunday music for your ears to hear on Wednesday!"

I love my Mama and Papa almost as much as I love Rita. But Mama sigh often as she count her beads and wears black instead of colors bright and gay like Rita. I remember long time before, when we first come to city, Mama sing always. Sometimes she dance with Papa when Papa say about the big job he going to get.

"No more driving the junk truck for me," say Papa. "Lucerno family will be on easy street soon."

When Papa finish driving truck for Mr. George Hemfield he go to night school. When I wake up at night from the couch where I sleep because my leg hurt, I see Papa sitting at the kitchen table with books. All is quiet. Only sleeping sounds and the tick-ting of the wake-up clock and the hush sound of the books when Papa close them. Then I hear him push the chair and walk to his bed.

Carlos and Mikos, my big brothers, sleep in the bedroom. They have the big bed and Rita sleep with little Rosa in the little bed. Rosa is very small, only three years, and Rita call her Little Plum. Mama and Papa have the back porch for them. Papa fix it up and when Mama say, "What about the heat, my husband, when the winter come?" Papa he laugh and grab Mama as she pass him to the stove and say, "I will keep you warm—like always!"

"You crazy fellow, not before the children!" And Mama push his hand away like she is mad but I see her lips smile. Mama think I know nothing about life because I stay at home, because I do not run the streets and only walk outside for special days like Easter and Christmas and Cinque de Mayo when the world is spinning to guitar music.

At first when we come to city I go to school but after a while the stairs and long walk is too much. Rita try to carry me but the iron prison on my leg make her tired and once she drop me and the iron bend and cut into my leg. I learn, but not very much. It is hard for me to read the words and the teacher do not call my name very often.

Rita try to help. She is in the high school and she show me to make my letters. But I cannot do well. At my desk I draw pictures of what I want to say. It is much easier and soon the school hall show them on the walls.

One day the Principal give Rita a note for Mama to come and talk with him. Papa he go instead and after a long time in the Principal's office he come out and we walk home. Papa walk very small steps and not even holds my hand from sidewalk to car street. When we get to house Papa pick me up and carry me up to Mama. He hold me very tight and push my face to look behind him but I know he angry, sad angry. He tell Mama that a special teacher is going to teach me at home because they have no place for me at my school.

The teacher come but not for long. After a while another lady come to talk to Mama about budget and say that if Mama bring me to Down-Town I go to special school. Papa get mad and go Down-Town but come back soon. He say nothing and now I stay home and draw much.

I hear the pop of my iron door and a kid like me come in. He is an old one in experience at this place and they let him bring the food. He push open my door with a foot and carry in the tray. I watch him look where to put it.

"Here's your supper, Crip," he say. "Where d'ya want it?"

I sit up and look at what there is to eat. But all I see is red Jello and two pieces of brown bread poked into a sauce of broken meat. I take off the square paper box of milk and tell him to take the tray. He looks worried at me.

"Look, Mex," he speak low. "Not eating won't help."

I shake my head and lean back on my cot and he leaves. It is almost dark now in my little gray room. I can put on a light. It is held away from me in a wire basket like a muzzle for a dog, but I have nothing to look at anyway. So I stand and press against the stone wall so I see up and out the window into the soon night.

In the sky is fuzzy lines of color, like the cotton when you pull it out of the box and it spread fine in your hand. Somewhere I hear a noise and the red and green light of a airplane pass my eyes. So small it is, like a ladybug. So far away and such a small spot, much bigger looks the bird that flies closer to my window, not knowing that night is close and he should be in his nest. I am all alone now in my darkness.

It is like the darkness that came to our house the day Papa

come home from new job hunting. For long days Papa try for new job, after he come home from school and hold high his beautiful piece of paper with gold words saying he is a educated man.

"This is just the beginning," say Papa. "I am just the number one to bring home the High School Certificate. Look, kids," say Papa, "this little piece of paper will be our passport to a new life."

We have a good dinner that night and Mama make a toast. "My man, with all this education, will be *Presidenti* yet!" Papa kiss Mama then and she let us all watch. Rita dance that day. She was fifteen and the next one who would bring home such a paper. But it was not to be.

Papa's paper was only words and no one pull Papa in by the arm and give him a good job. Each day it was harder and harder to see his face at night and each night he have more and more red wine. At last Papa go back to his old job. It was a big truck and Papa was very tired at night after filling it with broken cars and iron and rusty pipes. Soon Mama cry all the time and then Rita stop her school. She come home one day and say she have a fine job that pay much money but she have to work at night. Papa ask who boss is, but Rita say he is Up-Town man and that Papa would not know him.

Rita sleep late now every morning and sometimes she look sad at me when she say goodbye to go for job. Always she look tired and one day she and Mama have big fight. Rita say she move out nearer her job and Mama say, "No," but Rita go anyway. She tell Mama she come every day to see me and bring money every week. The house seem so still now and Mama sit long times with little Rosa on her lap and I hear her say "Little Plum" over and over.

Now for me the day begins when Rita come, for Rita keep her promise. One day she come and after we eat the caramel corn she bring, Rita tell me of a secret she and I will have. It is a plan to make me walk straight without iron brace.

"Pepito," Rita say and put three dollars in my hand, "I want you to hide this and every week I will give you more until there is enough and then we will visit the doctor who fixes legs."

We find empty box that oatmeal come in and cut a hole in the round top big enough to fold money into. It is our secret hiding place and I push the box under the couch where I sleep. Each week Rita add more money, sometimes even more at one time. Our home is not very happy now. With Rita the smiles have gone. Carlos and Mikos are big now. Carlos is in the high school but want to stop and he and Papa fight now. Carlos say to Papa, "Old man, you live on your daughter's hustling!"

I watch as he pull himself up and like a bear try to squeeze the words back into Carlos's mouth. Papa's big hand slaps out at Carlos but he is quick and runs out and down the steps to the street. For the first time I see Papa cry, and when Mama come in and ask, he will not tell her what hurts him.

I cannot sleep that night. I know what hustling is. It is the walking of the streets that a woman does to offer her body to any man who will pay. I have hear Carlos and Mikos talk when they think I sleep. I hear the names of some girls and then rough words and then small swallowed laughter. I am much older than the pain in my legs. I am as old as the new leaves on my poor tree on the sidewalk.

My pillow is hard that night and I close my eyes against my fear. It is then that Rita's face come before my mind. I see her smooth skin and the quick way her body moves and the softness of her breast. I have watched her grow more beautiful in form as in heart. I have made the curve of her with my crayon on white paper. Do not think I look upon her with more than a brother should. But is it wrong to see beauty when it grows before your eyes? Her name is really Margarita, like the white flower with the golden center.

I cannot bear the evil pictures that pass before my eyes, and I cross myself and insist to my mind that Carlos spoke in anger and said a lie. I prefer it so.

When Rita come that next evening I want to tell her what Carlos say so we could laugh about it together and she could slap his face. But I keep silent. When she ask me why I do not smile I tell her a lie. I say my foot hurt.

"Come," she say, "get our box and let us count the money." We open the top and count it in her lap. "We need more," Rita say. "I will work overtime."

I nod for I am afraid to ask and afraid not to ask. For the first time I want Rita to leave.

It is weeks before I sleep well and I blame it on my leg but

I know it is Rita that worry me. Now I look at her more closely as if I expect to see a sign that all was a lie. Once I start to say something.

"A woman that sells her body." I stutter over the words. "What would one call her?"

Rita look at me quick and pulls her lips tight, then smiles. "Don't tell me that my little Pepito is growing up!"

She put her hand on my head and push my hair off my face.

"You do not answer me," I say.

"A prostitute." She turn away from me and her hand drop.

"That is an evil thing for a woman to do, isn't it?" I say.

"It all depends."

She turns and picks up a big bag. "Look what I brought you tonight."

After we eat the big oranges she lean her head against mine and speaks into the room.

"You must not concern yourself with ugly things. You must see only beauty and put it on paper. I do not know any prostitues and neither do you."

She leave soon after and before I sleep that night I curse my brother Carlos and his vile tongue.

It goes on as before now with Rita and me. Soon it is her birthday. She is to be eighteen in a week and I decide to buy her a present. Mama has said that eighteen is a special age for a girl and I want to make it fine for her birthday. The only money I have is under my couch in the oatmeal box. I decide within myself that it would not be wrong to use some of it for Rita's birthday present.

Mama is surprised when I tell her I will go down the stairs and on the street until I explain to her what I want to do. I tell her I have saved some money and I show her the twenty dollars I have in my pocket. She helps me down the first steps and watches me as I walk down the street to where the stores are.

The stores are filled with fine things and I move slowly from one window to the other. Before one I stop a long time and almost decide to buy a small radio. But I think maybe a pretty dress would be better for Rita. A white dress to make her hair blacker than the midnight and the white like snow against her golden skin.

Now I look for a dress shop. Across the street is a large store with dresses like a flower garden. At the corner I stand waiting for the streetlight to change when I hear voices behind me. It is what they say that makes me turn and follow them instead of crossing the street.

I do not know all of them but one boy is Luis. He is older than Rita but was in school with her and sometimes Carlos bring him to the house. It is when I hear him say the name Rita that I decide to follow them.

"Yeah, that damn Rita," one boy say. "Since she move Up-Town into the big time, you can't even touch her any more."

"I hear she's hooked up with some pimp who is really rolling in clover." They all laugh.

My blood! I feel it leave my body and sink to the sidewalk. Surely the earth will open up and these boys will fall into hell! I cannot walk any more. They turn the corner and disappear. My heart is dead inside of me. No longer can I doubt what I feared. No longer can I doubt.

I feel people shove at me as they pass me and still I cannot move. Long later I take steps, slowly down the sidewalk. All the time in the center of my throat is a sore spot I cannot swallow away. Like a terrible scream that has no sound.

It was when my leg hurt so much that I stop and lean my face against the smooth glass of a store window. Cool it feels on my hot cheeks. My eyes I close tight—so tight it hurt. Colors dance in my head and run to stab my heart. My leg beats out the music of pain.

No longer can I stand the ache so I open my eyes again. There, under my look, I see the guns. Like soldiers ready to march when the general shout out a command. They wait quietly, these black snails that carry death inside a shell.

For a long time I look at these guns. Has not Father Diaz said that death is only another life? And a better one?

I move to the store door. It is glass with a wire across it, like the knitting Mama does, all looped together. I put two hands on the door handle. It is stiff and cold like a gun, I think. Down I push and shove open the door. I stumble on a mat and my iron brace rips at the rubber as I pull my leg free. A small bell shakes and makes a ringing. I walk in.

When the police ask me I shake my head and when Mama and Papa cry in the courtroom for children and the judge ask me why I kill my sister on her birthday I still am quiet. They would not understand how hard a thing it was to do. To lose your star when you are thirteen is to walk blind on the earth. Better this way than to see your star fall from the heavens and end in mud. Always to me Margarita will be like her name, pure white on the outside and golden in the center.

And that is why I lie here on this cot with the black of my little room hiding me from the night of nothingness and I am called a murderer.

1977:

Chance After Chance

Thomas Walsh

Padre, everybody in Harrington's called him. Year after year he
dropped in from his furnished room about seven at night, then
drank steadily until three in the morning, closing time; and one
Christmas Eve, very drunk, he curled both arms around his shot
glass, put his head down, and began chanting some kind of
crazy gibberish. Nobody in Harrington's knew what it was—but
maybe, Harrington himself thought later on, maybe it was
Latin. Because little by little, from remarks he let drop about
his earlier life, it became rumored that he had once been a
Roman Catholic priest in a small New England town somewhere near Boston.

He was perhaps in his fifties and in youth must have been a
lusty and physically powerful man. Now, however, the whiskey
had almost finished him. His hands trembled; his face was
markedly lined, weary, and sunken; his shabby alcoholic's jaun-
tiness had a forced ring to it; and he was almost never without
a stubble of dirty gray beard on his cheeks.

One night Jack Delgardo on the next stool inquired idly as to
why they had kicked him out of the church. Was it the whiskey,
Jack wanted to know, or was it women? Did he mean to say they
never even gave him a second chance?

"Well, a chance," Padre admitted, always a bit genially boastful in man-of-the-world conversation. "They found out about a certain French girl over in Holyoke, Massachusetts, and because of her and the booze they told me I'd have to go down to a penitential monastery in Georgia for two years. But bare feet and long hours of prayerful communion with the Lord God would be the only ticket for me in that place, not to mention the dirtiest sort of physical labor day after day. They had no conception at all, however, about the kind of man they were dealing with. So naturally, when I told the monsignor straight out where to go, since I discovered that I had lost the faith by that time, there was no more point in discussing the matter. A long time past, Jack—twenty-odd years."

But Jack Delgardo was not much interested in the Lord God. Besides which, he had just seen his new girl bob in, very dainty and elegant, through Harrington's front door.

"Yeah," he said, rising briskly. "Can't blame you a bit, Padre, for getting the hell out. See you around, huh?"

"Very probably," Padre said, blessing him with humorously overdone solemnity for the free drink. "Always here, Jack. Could you spare me a dollar or two until the first of the month?"

Because the first of the month was when his four checks arrived. In Harrington's he never mentioned that part of his life, but he came from a large and very prosperous family of Boston Irish—Robert the surgeon, Michael the chemist, Edward the engineer, and Kevin Patrick the businessman; and three married sisters and their families who had all settled down years ago in one or another of the more well-to-do Boston suburbs.

But Padre had eventually found himself unable to endure his family any more than he had been able to endure his monsignor. He never failed to detect a slight but telltale flush of shame and apology when they had to introduce him to some friend who dropped by, and he could all too easily imagine the sly knowledge of him that would be whispered from mouth to mouth later on—the weakling of the family, the black sheep, the spoiled youngest of them, and now the drunken, profligate, defrocked priest.

Although having been the spoiled youngest, Padre occasionally thought, might have been the beginning of all his troubles.

Like Robert he might well have been the surgeon, or like Michael the chemist; but as little Joey, always too much loved, always dearest and closest of anyone to the mother, he seemed never once to have had his own life in his hands. As far back as he could remember anything, he could remember Mama and him in a church pew, with sunlight streaming in over them through a stained-glass window, her face lifted up to the high dim altar before them, her lips moving silently, and the rosary beads slipping one by one through her fingers.

Only three or four years old then, Padre had been young enough to believe anything he was told; young enough, in fact, to have believed everything. Only in seminary days had come his first questioning, his first resentment, his first rebellion. So he had written a long letter to his favorite uncle, Uncle Jack, and announced dramatically that he was unable to take the life anymore. So if Uncle Jack could not get Mama to see some sense, he had made up his mind to run away, or even to kill himself.

But in the end he had done neither. He had gone on, and he could also remember, if he ever wanted to, a winter night soon afterward in the kitchen at home, with Uncle Jack and his mother shouting angrily at each other from opposite sides of the table.

"Don't try to make the boy do what he has no inclination at all for," Uncle Jack had cried out at her. "Damn it to hell, Maggie, can't you understand there's nothing half so contemptible in this world as a bad priest? Where in God's name are your brains? It's his life, don't you see? It's not yours. Then let him do what he wants with it, or you'll have to answer for that yourself. It's just the pride you'd feel at having a son in the church—that's why you're bound and determined on it! Why, you're forcing him to—"

Leaning forward shakily, his mother had rested both hands on the table in front of her.

"He'll do what I say!" she had cried back. "He'll have the only true happiness there is in this world. He'll have the collar, I tell you! And you daring to come here tonight and lead him on like this when you never once had the faith that I do, and you never will! What were you all your days but a shame and disgrace to yourself and to the Holy Roman Catholic Church? I know what he wants and what he needs, and better than you. I've prayed to the Blessed Lady every night of my life for it—and she'll answer me! And you'll change that, will you, with your mad carrying on here tonight, and your cursing and swearing at us! Then I take my vow on the thing here and now. From this day on I swear to Almighty God that you and yours will never again enter this house, as I swear to Almighty God that I and mine will never again enter yours! Is that the answer you want? Then there it is. Never again!"

But after that had come the sudden horrible twist of her whole face to one side and her clumsy lurch forward halfway across the table. And after that, Padre could also remember, there had been the family doctor hurriedly summoned, and old Father O'Mara, and up in her bedroom a few minutes after, all the family down on their knees, with Bonnie and Eileen and Agnes all crying, and Father O'Mara leading them on solemnly and gravely in the Litany for the Dying. But Padre had been closest of all to her, as he knew from the day of his birth he had always been, and holding her hand. So. . . .

So. He had gone on. He had done what he had promised her in that moment, if without words. He had got the collar at last. But now, on the first of every month, what he got were the fifty-dollar checks mailed in, one apiece, from the surgeon and the chemist and the engineer and the businessman. To earn them, tacitly understood, he had only to keep himself well away from the city of Boston for as long as he lived. So Harrington's, as the finale of all; so his regular stool at the end of the bar, nearest the rest rooms; so Padre, now hardly more than a shaky and alcoholic shadow of his former self, at the age of not quite fifty-three years old.

There, year after year, he troubled no one and bothered no one, making no friends and no enemies. So he was rather surprised when he was invited up to Jack Delgardo's apartment on Lexington Avenue one January night to meet two of Jack's friends, with a promise that the whiskey would be free and liberally provided for him. And it was. They all had a lot to drink, one after another—a lot even for Padre; and then in half an hour or so, surprisingly enough, it appeared that the conversation had turned to theology.

"But at least you have to believe in God," Jack argued, refilling the glass for him. "You can't kid me, Padre—because a guy has to believe in something, that's all, no matter what he says. And I can still remember what they taught me in parochial school. Once a priest always a priest, the way I got it."

"Quite true," Padre had to agree, smacking his lips over the fine bourbon. "Although I believe the biblical terminology is a priest forever, according to the order of the high priest Melchizedek."

"Yeah, I guess," Eddie Roberts grinned—Steady Eddie, as Jack often referred to him. "Only how do you mean high, Padre? The way you get every night in the week down at Harrington's?"

At that they all laughed, including Padre, although the third man, Pete, did not permit the laugh to change his expression in any way. He had said little so far. He appeared to be studying Padre silently and intently, though not openly, dropping his eyes down to the cigarette in his hand every time Padre happened to glance at him.

"No, not quite like me," Padre said, very jovial about it. "In seminary we used to paraphrase a poem about him, or at least I did. 'Melchizedek, he praised the Lord and gave some wine to Abraham; but who can tell what else he did is smarter far than what I am.'"

"Oh, sometimes you seem smart enough," Steady Eddie put in. "Almost smart enough to know the right score, Padre. I wonder, are you?"

"Classical education," Padre assured him. "Only the best, Eddie, Latin, Greek, and Advanced Theology."

"Yeah, but I thought the theology never took," Jack said, exchanging a quick glance with Pete. "That's what you're always claiming around at Harrington's, isn't it?"

"Well, yes," Padre had to agree once more. "At least these days. Years ago it just happened to strike me all of a sudden that the Lord God Almighty, granting that He exists at all, isn't what most of us are inclined to believe about Him. Look at His record for yourself. Who else, one by one, has killed off every life that He ever created?"

"Yeah, but Sister Mary Cecilia," Jack objected, "used to tell us that no human being ever died, actually. They were transported."

"No, no," Padre corrected grandly. "Transformed, Jack. Into a higher and more superior being, into the spirit; or else, conversely, down into eternal and everlasting hell. And very useful teaching too, let me tell you. Nothing like it for keeping in line everyone who still believes."

"Only you don't believe it anymore?" Pete asked softly.

Padre finished his drink, again smacking his lips over it with great relish. He was very cunning in defending himself at these moments. He'd had much practice.

"I believe," he said, indicating the glass to them, "in what a man sees, hears, tastes, touches, and feels. That's what I believe, gentlemen, and all I believe. Is your bourbon running out, Jack?"

"Yeah, sure," Steady Eddie grinned. "But of course lots of guys talk real big with a few drinks in them. Sometimes you never know whether to believe them or not, Padre."

"So you don't believe in nothing," Pete said, while Jack hurriedly refilled Padre's glass. "Nothing at all. How about money, though? You believe in that?"

"Oh, most emphatically. And in God too. Or at least," Padre amended, trying his new drink, "at least God in the bottle. Which of course means God in the wallet too."

"Yeah, but old habits," Pete said, even more softly. "Hard to break, Padre. Let's suppose somebody ast you to hear a guy's confession, say—and for maybe five or ten thousand dollars? Your specialty too. Right up your alley. Only it wouldn't bother you even one bit?"

"Shrive the penitent," Padre beamed, knowing that he was somewhat overdoing it, as always in discussions of this kind, but unable to restrain himself. Why? He did not know. He did not, as a matter of fact, want to know. It simply had to be done, that was all. Someone had to know the kind of a man He was dealing with. "Solace the afflicted and comfort the dying. I've heard many a confession in my day, and for nothing at all. Very juicy listening too, some of them. You wouldn't believe the things that—"

Pete and Jack exchanged quick glances. Steady Eddie inched forward a bit.

"And then tell us," he whispered, "tell us what the guy said to you afterwards?"

Padre, hand up with the refilled glass, felt an altogether absurd catch of the heart. He had broken many vows in his time, but there was one he had not. He looked over at Eddie, as if a bit startled, then up at Jack, then around at Pete. But this was not fair, something whispered in him. This was active and deliberate malevolence. All his life he had been tried and tried, and beyond his strength; tested and tested; but now at last to betray the only thing he had never betrayed. . . .

Yet he managed to nod calmly. There had to be considered, after all, the kind of man that he was, and what five or ten thousand dollars would mean to him. Could he admit now that he had lied and lied even to himself all these years, and lied to everyone else too? Never! It was not to be thought of for one instant.

"I see," he murmured. "And tell you afterwards. So that's the condition?"

"That's the condition," Pete said. "You still got a priest's shirt and a roman collar, Padre?"

"Here or there," Padre said, still smiling brightly at them, which was very necessary now; nothing but the bold face for it. "Only it's been a very long time, of course. As the old song has it, there's been a few changes made. So I don't know that I could quite—"

Jack Delgardo rubbed a savage hand over his mouth. Steady Eddie replaced his grin with a cold ominous stare. But Pete proved much more acute than either of them. He understood at once why the protest had been made by Padre—not out of strength, but from sudden shrinking weakness; the hidden and unadmitted desire, probably, to be persuaded now even against himself.

"Easiest thing in the world," Pete remarked quietly. "Guy you know, too—so no question about you being a priest, Padre. All you'd have to say is that you've gone back to the church and he'd believe it. Remember Big Lefty Carmichael?"

And Padre did—four or five years ago from Harrington's— but not clearly. He was trying to get the name straight in his head when Jack Delgardo leaned forward to him.

"Well, they let him out," Jack whispered, resting his right hand on Padre's arm, then shaking it, as if to give the most perfect assurance of what he said. "He got sick up in Dannemora Prison, Padre, and now he's dying in a cheap little furnished room over on Ninth Avenue. They can't do a damned thing for him anymore now. They can't even operate. He's just sick as hell and ready to holler cop, see? A friend of his told us. He said that Lefty asked him to bring a priest tomorrow night. So where's any problem?"

That time Padre decided only to sip from his glass. He had begun to feel all drunkenly confused.

"Because what happened," Pete drawled, apparently observing that Padre could not quite place the name, "is that Lefty and two other guys got away with a potful of money three years ago—only they piled up into a trailer truck on Second Avenue, and no one but Lefty got out alive.

"Then the cops grabbed him that night, soon as they identified the two dead guys he always worked with. Grabbed him, Padre—but not the bank money. Well, he couldn't have spent it, of course. No time. And he wouldn't have given it to anyone to hold for him, because he wasn't that stupid. He must have stashed it away somewhere real cute, and whorever he put it, it's still thore. They only let him out of Dannemora yesterday morning and he ain't left the house on Ninth Avenue since he got there. He couldn't have. We've been watching it. We'd have seen.

"OK. So now he wants somebody like you, old Lefty does. No more of the old zip in him, Padre. So if we have the friend tell him about you rejoining the church and all, he's gonna believe it. You're the kind of a priest he wouldn't mind telling his confession to, you know what I mean? You're just like him, the way he'll look at it. You're both losers. Then when he confesses about the bank holdup, all you have to do is tell him he's got to make restitution for what he stole. That's what you'd do, anyway, isn't it? Only this time, of course, soon as he tells you where the money is hid—"

Padre picked up his drink from the coffee table and this time he emptied it. His mind still worked slowly, which irritated him. He could not understand why. So he took good care to conceal whatever he felt, and to smile back at Pete even more arrogantly than before. He reached over to the bourbon bottle with his right hand, lifted it, and solemnly blessed the assembly.

"Absolvo te," he announced then, and in a tone that success-

fully gave just the right touch of derisive priestly unction to what he said. " 'Blessed is he that comes in the name of the Lord.' If it's as simple as that, gentlemen, then I think we're just about agreed on the matter. Let's say somewhere about nine o'clock tomorrow night, then. What's the address?"

Pete was behind the steering wheel, Eddie beside him. Jack Delgardo was crouched forward in the middle of the back seat. It was 9:30 the next night and they were all watching the entrance to a tenement house directly opposite.

About fifteen minutes later Padre came out of the house. He was now shaved cleanly; he wore the black shirt and the Roman collar; and Steady Eddie at once reached back to open the rear door.

"Hey, Padre," he called guardedly. "Over here. We decided to wait for you."

It was a cold January night, with misty rain in the air, but Padre removed his hat a bit wearily in the vestibule doorway. They could see his gray hair then, and the thinly drawn pale face under it—the alcoholic's face. He glanced about, right and left, but did not move until Pete impatiently tapped on the car horn.

Even then, when Jack Delgardo had made room on the back seat, there was a kind of funny look on his face, Steady Eddie thought—a look, for a couple of long seconds, just like he had never seen them before and did not know who they were.

"So how did it go?" Jack Delgardo whispered. "Come on and tell us, Padre. He make his confession to you?"

But for another moment or so Padre only fingered the black hat on his knees, lightly and carefully.

"Yes," he said then. "Yes, he did. He made his confession."

"Then open up," Steady Eddie urged. "What did he tell you? Where's the money, Padre?"

"What?" Padre said. He appeared to be thinking of other matters; like in some damn fog, Jack thought furiously. He did not answer the question. All he did was to keep smoothing the black hat time after time while looking down at it, as if he had never seen that before either. "But first," he added, "I decided that I'd better talk to him a little—to get him into the right mood for the thing. And I had to think up the words to do that, of course—only pretty soon they seemed to be coming out of me all by themselves. Father, he kept calling me—" and he had to laugh here, with a kind of shakily nervous unsteadiness. "It's almost thirty years since anybody called me that, in that way. With respect, I mean. With a certain kind of dependence on me . . . Father."

Eddie got hold of him by the throat angrily and yanked his head up.

"You listen to me, you old lush! Jack asked you something. Where's that money?"

"What?" Padre repeated. He did not seem to understand the question. He was frowning absently. "I had to tell him I'd be around first thing tomorrow morning with the Host," he said. "I think I may have helped him a little. When I gave him Absolution afterwards, he kissed my hand. He actually—"

Pete, who had been staring fixedly ahead through the windshield, his lips compressed, started the car. Nothing more was said. It must have been all decided between them, just as they had decided to wait for Padre while he was still in the house.

They drove onto a dingy street farther west under the shadows of an overhead roadway that was being constructed, and there they drove up and around on a half-finished approach ramp. There was a kind of platform at the top of it, with lumber and big concrete mixers scattered about; before them a waist-high stone parapet; and beyond that the river.

No other cars could be seen, and no other people; no illumination except the intermittent gleam of a blinker light down on the next corner. Red, dark, red, dark. Padre found himself thinking with a curious and altogether aimless detachment of mind. Bitter cold cheer this night against the January rain and against the cluster of faint lights way over on the Jersey side— or not cheer at all, really . . . Father.

"Padre," Pete said, and unlike Eddie in a calm, perfectly controlled manner. "Where's the money?"

Padre might not have heard him at all.

"I had to—comfort him," he said. "But the only thing that came to me was what I had read once in the words of a French Jesuit priest—that a Christian must never be afraid of death, that he must welcome it, that it was the greatest act of faith he would ever make in this life, and that he must plunge joyfully into death as into the arms of his living and loving God. Then I led him on into the Act of Contrition—after I remembered it myself. And somehow I did remember it. Hoist by my own petard, then—" and once more he had to laugh softly. " 'Oh, my God, I am heartily sorry for having offended Thee—' That's how it starts, you know. And once I'd repeated that for him—would any of you have a drink for me?"

Pete got out of the car. So did Eddie. So did Jack Delgardo. One of them opened the door for Padre and took his arm. He got out obediently and then stood there.

"Padre," Pete said. "Where's the money?"

"What?" Padre said. The third time.

There were no more words wasted, just Eddie and Jack Delgardo closing in on him. They were quick about it and very efficient. They got Padre back against the stone parapet, which was some eighty or ninety feet above the river at this point, and there Eddie used his hands, and Jack Delgardo the tip of his right shoe.

There were almost no sounds, just the quick scrape of their feet on the paving, then a gasp, and then Padre falling. After that they allowed him to sit up groggily, muddy brown gutter water all over his black suit, his hat knocked off so that his gray hair could again be seen, and blood on his mouth.

"Now you just come on," Steady Eddie gritted. "We ain't even started on you. You ain't getting away with this, not now. We didn't make you come in with us. You promised you would. So do what we tell you, you phony old lush, or we'll—*Where's that money?*"

By then Padre had straightened against the parapet, supporting himself by his two hands, and breathing with shallow and labored effort.

"But it was never fair," he cried out. "Never fair! I was tempted not in one way during my life but in every possible way—and time after time! And now tonight, up in that room back there, I had to listen to myself saying something—whatever kept coming into my head. And not for him either—but for myself, don't you see? That it didn't matter how often we failed. That we only had to succeed at the end! That it wasn't trial after trial that was given to us. That it was chance after chance after chance! And that if only once, if only once and at the very finish of everything, we could say to Almighty God that we accepted the chance—"

Pete gestured Eddie and Jack Delgardo off and then moved back himself into somewhat better light so that the knife in his hand became clearly visible.

"You know what this is?" he said. "This is a knife. And you know, if you want to go ahead and make me, what I can do with it?"

He proceeded to say. He spoke in a clinically detached manner of various parts of the human body, of their extreme vulnerability to pain, and of what he could do with the knife—if he was forced. Very soon Padre, still hanging onto the parapet, had to turn shuddering away from that voice, and in blind panic. But on one side there was Steady Eddie waiting for him. On the other was Jack Delgardo.

"We'll even give you a square count," Steady Eddie urged, obviously thinking that part important, and at the same time offering a pint bottle of whiskey out of his overcoat pocket. "Honest to God, Padre. Just take a good long drink for yourself —and then think for a minute. Nothing like it, remember? God in a bottle."

And Padre needed that drink. He was beginning to feel the pain now—in his face, in the pit of his stomach, in his right knee. Which would be nothing at all, he realized, to the pain of the knife. Yes, then, he would tell. In the end, knowing himself, he knew he would have to tell.

But was it test after test that had always been demanded of him, venomously and to no purpose? Or was it, as he had found himself saying earlier tonight, chance after chance after chance that was offered—and the chance even now, it might be, to admit finally and for the first time in his life a greater love which, being the kind of man he was, or had insisted he was, he had always denied?

He still could not say. But how queer, it came to him, that the last denial of all, the only promise he had never violated, was now being demanded of him. But as proof of what? Of a thing he believed in his heart even yet, or of a thing he did not believe?

His hands were shaking. He looked at them, at the pint bottle they held, and then at the jagged cluster of rocks almost a hundred feet straight down that he could see at the very edge of the river. He had not drunk from the bottle yet. Now he attempted to and it rolled out of his hands, as if accidentally, onto the parapet.

He wailed aloud, scrambling up desperately for the bottle, and before Steady Eddie could lose his contemptuous grin, before Jack Delgardo, turning his back to the wind, could light the match for his cigarette, and before Pete, now more distant than either of them, could move, Padre was standing erect on top of the parapet.

Pete shouted a warning. Steady Eddie rushed forward. But plunge joyfully, Padre was thinking—the chance taken, the trust maintained, the greater love at last and beyond any question admitted by him. Plunge joyfully!

That was the final thought in his head. After it, avoiding a frantic outward grab for his legs by Steady Eddie, Father Joseph Leo Shanahan moved quickly but calmly to the edge of the parapet, crossed himself there, put up the other hand in a last moment of weakness to cover his eyes—and stepped straight out.

Then the blinker light shone down on a stone ledge empty save for the still corked whiskey bottle, and there were left only the three men, but not the fourth, to gape stupidly and unbelievingly from back in the shadows.

1978:

The Cloud Beneath the Eaves

Barbara Owens

May 10: I begin. At last. Freshborn, dating only from the first of May. New. A satisfying little word, that "new." A proper word to start a journal. It bears repeating: I am new. What passed before never was. That unspeakable accident and the little problem with my nerves are faded leaves, forgotten. I will record them here only once and then discard them. Now—it's done.

I have never kept a journal before and am not sure why I feel compelled to do so now. Perhaps it's because I need the proof of new life in something I can touch and see. I have come far and I am filled with hope.

May 11: This morning I gazed long at myself in the bathroom mirror. My appearance is different, new. I can never credit myself with beauty, but my face is alive and has lost that indoor pallor. I was not afraid to look at myself. That's a good sign.

I've just tidied up my breakfast things and am sitting at my little kitchen table with a steaming cup of coffee. The morning sun streams through my kitchen curtains, creating lacy, flowing patterns on the cloth. Outside it's still quiet. I'm up too early, of course—difficult to break years of rigid farm habits. I miss the sound of birds, but there are several large trees in the yard, so perhaps there are some. Even a city must have some birds.

I must describe my apartment. Another "new"—my own apartment. I was lucky to find it. I didn't know how to find a place, but a waitress in the YWCA coffee shop told me about it, and when I saw it, I knew I had to have it.

It's in a neighborhood of spacious old homes and small unobtrusive apartment houses; quiet, dignified, and comfortably frayed around the edges. This house is quite old and weathered with funny cupolas and old-fashioned bay windows. The front and side yards are small, but the back is large, pleasantly treed and flowered, and boasts a quaint goldfish pond.

My landlady is a widow who has lived here for over forty years, and she's converted every available space into an apartment. She lives on the first floor with several cats, and another elderly lady lives in the second apartment on that floor. Two young men of foreign extraction live in one apartment on the second floor, and I have yet to see the occupant of the other. I understand there's also a young male student living in part of the basement.

That leaves only the attic—the best for the last. It's perfect; I even have my own outside steps for private entry and exit. Because of the odd construction of the house, my walls and ceilings play tricks on me. My living room and kitchen are one large area and the ceiling, being under the steepest slope of the roof, is high. In the bedroom and bath the roof takes a suicidal plunge; as a result, the bedroom windows on one wall are scant inches off the floor and I must stoop to see out under the eaves, for the ceiling at that point is only four feet high. In the bath it is the same; one must enter and leave the tub in a bent position. Perhaps that's why I like it so much; it's funny and cozy, with a personality all its own.

The furnishings are old but comfortable. Everything in my living-room area is overstuffed, and although the pieces don't match, they get along well together. The entire apartment is clean and freshly painted a soft green throughout. It's going to be a delight to live here.

I spent most of yesterday getting settled. Now I must close this and be off to the neighborhood market to stock my kitchen. I've even been giving some thought to a small television set. I've never had the pleasure of a television set. Maybe I'll use part of my first paycheck for that. Everything is going to be all right.

May 12: Today I had a visitor! The unseen occupant from the apartment below climbed my steps and knocked on my kitchen (and only) door just as I was finishing breakfast. I'm afraid I was awkward and ill-at-ease at first, but I invited her in and the visit ended pleasantly.

Her name is Sarah Cooley. She's a widow, small and stout, with gray hair and kind blue eyes. She'd noticed I don't have a car and offered the use of hers if I ever need it. She also invited me to attend church with her this morning. I handled it well, I think, thanking her politely for both offers, but declining. Of course I can never enter a car again, and she could not begin to understand my feelings toward the church. However, it was a grand experience, entertaining in my own home. I left her coffee cup sitting on the table all day just to remind myself she'd been there and that all had gone well. It's a good omen.

I must say a few words about starting my new job tomorrow. I try to be confident; everything else has worked out well. I'm the first to admit my getting a job at all is a bit of a miracle. I was not well prepared for that when I came here, but one trip to an employment agency convinced me that was pointless.

Something must have guided me to that particular street and that particular store with its little yellow sign in the window. Mr. Mazek was so kind. He was surprised that anyone could reach the age of thirty-two without ever having been employed, but I told him just enough of my life on the farm to satisfy him. He even explained how to get a Social Security card, the necessity of which I was not aware. He was so nice I regretted telling him I had a high-school diploma, but I'm sure he would never have considered someone with a mere eighth-grade education. Now my many years of surreptitious reading come to my rescue. I actually have a normal job.

May 13: It went well. In fact, I'm so elated I'm unable to sleep.

I managed the bus complications and arrived exactly on time. Mr. Mazek seemed pleased to see me and started right off addressing me as Alice instead of Miss Whitehead. The day was over before I realized it.

The store is small and dark, a little neighborhood drugstore with two cramped aisles and comfortable clutter. Mr. Mazek is old-fashioned and won't have lunch counters or magazine displays to encourage loitering; he wants his customers to come in, conduct their business, and leave. He's been on that same corner for many years, so almost everyone who enters has a familiar face. I'm going to like being a part of that.

Most of the day I just watched Mr. Mazek and Gloria, the other clerk, but I'm convinced I can handle it. Toward the end of the day he let me ring up several sales on the cash register, and I didn't make one mistake. I'm sure I'll never know the names and positions of each item in the store, but Mr. Mazek says I'll have them memorized in no time and Gloria says if she can do it, I can.

I will do it! I feel safer as each day passes.

May 16: Three days have elapsed and I've neglected my journal. Time goes so quickly! How do I describe my feelings? I wake each morning in my own quiet apartment; I go to a pleasant job where I am needed and appreciated; and I come home to a peaceful evening of doing exactly as I wish. There are no restrictions and no watchful eyes. It's as I always dreamed it would be.

I'm learning the work quickly and am surprised it comes so easily. Gloria complains of boredom, but I find the days too short to savor.

Let me describe Gloria: she's a divorced woman near my own age, languid, slow-moving, with dyed red hair and thick black eyebrows. She's not fat, but gives the appearance of being so because she looks soft and pliable, like an old rubber doll. She has enormous long red fingernails that she fusses with constantly. She wears an abundance of pale makeup, giving her a somewhat startling appearance, but she's been quite nice to me and has worked for Mr. Mazek for several years, so she must be reliable.

I feel cowlike beside her with my great raw bones and awkward hands and feet. We're certainly not alike, but I'm hoping she becomes my first real friend. Yesterday we took our coffee break together, and during our conversation she stopped fiddling with her nails and said, "Gee, Alice, you know you talk just like a book?" At first I was taken aback, but she was smiling so I smiled too. I must listen more to other people and learn.

Casual conversation does not come easily to me.

Mr. Mazek continues to be kind and patient, assuring me I am learning well. In many ways he reminds me of Daddy.

I've already made an impression of sorts. Today something was wrong with the pharmaceutical scales, so I asked to look at them and had them right again in no time. Mr. Mazek was amazed. I hadn't realized it was a unique achievement. Being Daddy's right hand on the farm for so many years, there's nothing about machinery I don't know. But I promised I wouldn't think about Daddy.

May 17: Today I received my first paycheck. Not a very exciting piece of paper, but it means everything to me. I hadn't done my figures before, but it's apparent now I won't be rich. And there'll be no television set for me. I can manage rent, food, and few extras. Fortunately I wear uniforms to work, so I won't need clothes soon.

Immediately after work I went to the bank and opened an account with my check and what remains of the other. I did that too without a mistake. And now it's safe. It looks as though I've really won; they would have come for me by now if she had found me. I'm too far away and too well hidden. Bless her for mistrusting banks; better I should have taken it than some itinerant thief. She's probably praying for my soul. Now, no more looking back.

May 18: I don't work on weekends; Mr. Mazek employs a part-time student. I would rather work since it disturbs me to have much leisure. It's then I think too much.

This morning I allowed myself the luxury of a few extra minutes in bed, and as I watched the sun rise I noticed an odd phenomenon beneath the eaves outside my window. Because of their extension and perhaps some quirk of temperature, the eaves must trap moisture. A definite mist was swirling softly against the top of the window all the while the sun shone brightly through the bottom. It was so interesting I went to the kitchen window to see if it was there, but it wasn't. It continued for several minutes before melting away, and nestled up here in my attic I felt almost as though I were inside a cloud.

This morning I cleaned and shopped. As I was carrying groceries up the steps, Sarah Cooley called me to come sit with her in the backyard. She introduced me to the other widow from the first floor, Mrs. Harmon. Once again Sarah offered her car for marketing, but I said I like the exercise.

It was unusually soft and warm for May, and quite pleasant sitting idly in the sun. A light breeze was sending tiny ripples across the fishpond, and although the fish are not yet back in it I became aware that some trick of light made it appear as though something were down there, a shadowy shape just below the surface. Neither of the ladies seemed to notice it, but I could not make myself look away. It became so obvious to me something was down there under the water that I became ill, having no choice but to excuse myself from pleasant company.

All day I was restless and apprehensive and finally went to bed early, but in the dark it came, my mind playing forbidden scenes. Over and over I heard the creaking pulleys and saw the placid surface of Jordan's pond splintered by the rising roof of Daddy's rusty old car. I heard tortured screams and saw her wild crazy eyes. I must not sit by the fishpond again.

May 19: I was strong again this morning. I lay and watched the little cloud. There is something strangely soothing about its silent drifting; I was almost sorry to see it go.

I ate well and tried to read the paper, but I kept being drawn to the kitchen window and its clear view of the fishpond. At last I gave up and went out for some fresh air. Sarah and Mrs. Harmon were preparing for a drive in the country as I went down my steps and Sarah invited me, but I declined.

Mr. Mazek was surprised to see me in the store on Sunday. They were quite busy and I offered to stay, but he said I should go and enjoy myself while I'm young. Gloria waggled her fingernails at me. I lingered awhile, but finally just bought some shampoo and left.

A bus was sitting at the corner, and not even noticing where it was going I got on. Eventually it deposited me downtown and I spent the day wandering and watching people. I find the city has a vigorous pulse. Everyone seems to know exactly where he's going.

I must have left the shampoo somewhere. It doesn't matter. I already have plenty.

May 20: Today I arrived at the store early. Last week I noticed that the insides of the glass display cases were dirty, so I cleaned them. Mr. Mazek was delighted; he said Gloria never sees when things need cleaning.

Gloria suggested I should have my hair cut and styled, instead of letting it just hang straight; she told me where she has hers done. I'm sure she was trying to be friendly and I thanked her, but I have to laugh when I think of me wearing something like her dyed red frizz.

Mr. Mazek talked to me today about joining some sort of group to meet new people. He suggested a church group as a promising place to start. A church group, of all things! Perhaps he thought I came into the store yesterday because I was lonely and had nothing better to do.

Tonight my landlady, Mrs. Wright, inquired if I had made proper arrangements for mail delivery. Since I've received none, she thought there might have been an error. Again I regretted having to lie. Only the white coats and she would be interested in my whereabouts, and I have worked too hard to evade them.

I am restless and somewhat tense this evening.

May 24: My second week and second paycheck in the bank, and it still goes well.

I've realized with some regret that Gloria and I are not going to be friends. I try, but I'm not fond of her. For one thing, she's lazy; I find myself finishing half of her duties. She makes numerous errors in transactions, and although I've pointed them out to her, she doesn't do any better. I'm undecided whether to bring this to Mr. Mazek's attention. Surely he must be aware of it.

On several occasions this week I've experienced a slight blurring of vision, as though a mist were before my eyes. I'm concerned about the cost involved, but prices and labels have to be read accurately, so it seems essential that I have my eyes tested.

May 26: What an odd thing! The little cloud has moved from under the eaves in my bedroom to the kitchen window. Yesterday when I awoke it wasn't there, and as I was having breakfast, suddenly there it was outside the window, soft and friendly, rolling gently against the pane. Perhaps it's my imagination, but it seems larger. It was there again today, a most welcome sight.

Yesterday was an enjoyable day—the usual cleaning and shopping.

Today was not so enjoyable. Just as I was finishing lunch, I heard voices under my steps where Sarah parks her car. The ladies were getting ready for another Sunday drive and when I looked out, they were concerned over an ominous sound in the engine. Before I stopped to think, I heard myself offering to look at it. All the way down the steps I told myself it would be all right, but as soon as I raised the hood, the blackness and nausea came. I couldn't see and somewhere far away I heard a voice calling, "Allie! Allie, where are you?"

Somehow I managed to find the trouble and get back upstairs. Everything was shadows, threatening. I couldn't catch my breath and my hands wouldn't stop shaking. Suddenly I was at the kitchen window, straining to see down into the fishpond. I'm afraid I don't know what happened next.

But the worst is over. I'm all right now. I have drawn the shade over the kitchen window so I will never see the fishpond again. It's going to be all right.

I wish it were tomorrow and time to be with Mr. Mazek again.

May 30: Gloria takes advantage of him. I have watched her carefully this week and she is useless in that store. Mr. Mazek is so warm and gentle he tends to overlook her inadequacy, but it is wrong of her. I see now she's also a shameless flirt, teasing almost every man who comes in. Today she and a pharmaceutical salesman were in the back stockroom for over an hour, laughing and smoking. I could see that Mr. Mazek didn't like it, but he did nothing to stop it. I've been there long enough to see that he and I could manage that store quite nicely. We really don't need Gloria.

I have an appointment for my eyes. The mist occurs frequently now.

June 2: The cloud *is* getting bigger. Yesterday morning the sun shone brightly in my bedroom, but the kitchen was dim and there was a shadow on the shade. When I raised it a fraction, there were silky fringes resting on the sill. I stepped out on the landing and saw it pressed securely over the pane. It is warm, not damp to the touch—warm, soft, and soothing. I have raised the kitchen shade again—the cloud blots out the fishpond completely.

Yesterday I started down the steps to do my marketing, my eyes lowered to avoid sight of the fishpond, and through the steps I saw the top of Sarah's car. Something stirred across it like currents of water, and suddenly I was so weak and dizzy I had to grip the railing to keep from falling as I crept back up the stairs.

I have stayed in all day.

June 7: I have been in since Wednesday with the flu. I began feeling badly Tuesday, but I worked until Wednesday noon when Mr. Mazek insisted I go home. I'm sorry to leave him with no one but Gloria, but I am certainly not well enough to work.

I came home to bed, but the sun shining through my window made disturbing movements in the room. Everything is so green, and the pulsing shadows across the ceiling made it seem that I was underwater. Suddenly I was trapped, suffocating, my lungs bursting for air.

I've moved my bedding and fashioned a bed for myself on the living-room couch. Here I can see and draw comfort from the cloud. I will sleep now.

June 10: I have been very ill. Sarah has come to my door twice, but I was too tired and weak to call out, so she went away. I am feverish; sometimes I am not sure I'm awake or asleep and dreaming. I just realized today is special—the first month's anniversary of my new life. Somehow it seems longer. I'd hoped.

June 11: I've just awakened and am watching the cloud. Little wisps are peeping playfully under my door. I think it wants to come inside.

June 12: I am better today. Mrs. Wright used her passkey to come in and was horrified to find I'd been so sick and no one knew. She and Sarah wanted to take me to a doctor, but I cannot get inside that car, so I convinced them I'm recovering. She brought hot soup and I managed to get some down.

The cloud pressed close behind her when she came in, but didn't enter. Perhaps it's waiting for an invitation. Poor Mrs. Wright was so concerned with me she didn't notice the cloud.

June 13: Today I felt well enough to go downstairs to Mrs. Wright's and call Mr. Mazek. I couldn't go until after noon— Sarah's car was down there. I became quite anxious, sure that he needed me in the store. He sounded glad to hear my voice and pleased that I am better, but insisted I not come in until Monday when I am stronger.

I am so ashamed. Suddenly wanting to be with him today, I

heard myself pleading. Before I could stop, I told him my entire plan for letting Gloria go and having the store just to ourselves. He was silent so lΓng that I came to my senses and realized my mistake, so I laughed and said something about the fever talking. After a moment he laughed too, and I said I would see him on Monday.

I have let the cloud come in. It sifts about me gently and seems to fill the room.

June 21: Didn't go to the bank today. Crowds and lines begin to annoy me. I will manage with the money and food I have on hand.

Mr. Mazek, bless him, is concerned about my health. I see him watching me with a grave expression, so I work harder to show him I am strong and fine.

I've started taking the cloud to work with me. It stays discreetly out of the way, piling gently in the dim corners, but it comforts me to know it's there, and I find myself smiling at it when no one's looking.

Yesterday afternoon I went to the back stockroom for something, and I'd forgotten Gloria and another one of her salesmen were in there. I stopped when I heard their voices, but not before I heard Gloria say my name and something about "stupid hick"; then they laughed together. Tears came to my eyes, but suddenly a mist was all around me and the cloud was there, smoothing, enfolding, shutting everything away.

A note from Mrs. Wright on my door tonight said that the eye doctor had called to remind me of my appointment. No need to keep it now.

June 23: Sarah's car was here all day yesterday, so I did not go out.

I don't even go into the bedroom now. I am still sleeping on the couch. Because it's old and lumpy, perhaps that's what's causing the dreams. Today I awoke suddenly, my heart pounding and my face wet with tears. I thought I was back there again and all the white coats stood leaning over me. "You can go home," they chorused in a nasty singsong. "You can go home at last to live with your mother." I lay there shaking, remembering. They really believed I would stay with *her!*

Marketed, but did not clean. I am so tired.

June 27: You see? I function normally. I reason, so I am all right. It's that lumpy old couch. Last night the dream was about Daddy choking out his life at the bottom of Jordan's pond. I was out of control when I awoke, but the cloud came and took it all away. Today I fixed my blankets on the floor.

June 28: Dear Mr. Mazek continues to be solicitous of my health. Today he suggested I take a week off—get some rest or take a little vacation. He looked so troubled, but of course I couldn't leave him like that.

Sometimes I feel afraid, feel that everything is slipping away. I am trying so hard.

Maybe I should be more tolerant of Gloria.

July 5: After several hours inside my blessed cloud, I believe I am calm enough to think things through. I have been hurt and betrayed. I cannot conceive such betrayal!

Today I discovered that Gloria is—how shall I say it?—"carrying on" with Mr. Mazek and has evidently been doing so for years. Apparently they were supposed to spend the holiday yesterday together, but Gloria went off with someone else. I heard them through the closed door of Mr. Mazek's little office —their voices were very loud—and Gloria was laughing at him! The cloud came to me instantly and I don't remember the rest of the day.

Now I begin to understand. It explains so many things. At first I was terribly angry with Mr. Mazek. Now I realize Gloria tempted him and he was too weak to resist. The evil of that woman. Something must be done. This cannot be allowed to continue.

July 8: I found my opportunity today when we were working together in the stockroom. I began by telling her my finding out was an accident, but that now she must stop it at once. She just played with her fingernails, smiled, and said nothing until I reminded her he was a respected married man with grandchildren and she was ruining all their lives. Then she laughed out loud, said Mr. Mazek was a big boy, and why didn't I mind my own business.

July 11: I'm afraid it's hopeless. For three days I've pursued and pleaded with her to stop her heartless action. This afternoon she suddenly turned on me, screaming harsh cruel things I can't bring myself to repeat. I couldn't listen, so I took refuge in the cloud. Later I saw her speaking forcefully to Mr. Mazek;

it looked almost as though she were threatening him. What shall I do now?

I am not sleeping well at all

July 12: I have been let out of my job. There is no less painful way to say it. This afternoon Mr. Mazek called me into his office and let me go as of today, but he will pay me for an extra week. I could say nothing, I was so stunned. He said something about his part-time student needing more money in the summer, but of course I know that's not the reason. He said he was sorry, and he looked so unhappy that I felt sorry for him. I know it isn't his fault. I know he would rather have me with him than Gloria. Even the cloud has not been able to save me today

July 16: I have not left here for four days. I know, because I have marked them on the wall the way I did when I was there. Tomorrow I will draw a crossbar over the four little straight sticks.

I think I have eaten. There are empty cans on the floor and bits of food in my blankets.

The cloud sustains mo—whispering, shutting out the pain.

July 19: It is all arranged. Gloria was alone when I went in this morning for my last paycheck. She seemed nervous and a bit ashamed. We were both polite and she went back to Mr. Mazek's office for my pay.

I felt a great sadness. I love that little store. And I have memorized it so well in the time I was allowed to be a part of it. It is fortunate that I know precisely where everything is kept.

At first she refused my invitation to have lunch with me today. She said she begins her vacation tomorrow. But I was persistent, pleading how vital it is to me that we part with no hard feelings between us. Finally she agreed, and I am calm inside the cloud, and strong and confident again.

She came here to my apartment and it went well. Lunch was pleasant and Mr. Mazek's name was never mentioned. I even told her all about myself, and she seemed no more upset than could be expected . . .

Tonight I put a note on Mrs. Wright's door saying I'd been called away for a few weeks. I've moved my heavy furniture in front of the door. I must be very still and remember not to turn on lights. There is enough light from the street to write by and the cloud is here to protect and keep me. I have come a long way. This time it is right.

July: All goes back, goes back. The white coats were wrong. I can't do it.

I saw Daddy again. We stood under the lantern in the big old barn. He showed me all the parts of his old car and how each one of them worked. It felt so safe and good to be with him, and he told me again that I was his good right hand. I wanted

Bad. Oh bad. Everyone said you were crazy. Mean. Your Bible and your praying and church, over and over, your church every night, shouting and praying, never doing anything to help Daddy and me on the farm. Sitting at the kitchen table with your Bible, singing and praying, everything dirty and undone, then into the old car and off to church to shout and pray some more while Daddy and I did all the work.

Never soothed him, never loved him, just prayed at him and counted his sins. Couldn't go to school, made me stay home and work on the farm, no books, books are the devil's tools, had to hide my books in the barn high up under the eaves. Ugly, you're a big ugly child, girl, and you prayed for my soul, prayed for mine and Daddy's souls. Poor sad Daddy's soul.

Took it too hard they said, oh yes, took it too hard, so they sent me away for the white coats to fix and then they made me go back to you, your Bible, and your praying, and everyone said it was an accident, a tragic accident they said, but you knew, you never said but you knew, and you prayed and sang and quoted the Bible and you broke my Daddy's life. In the clouds, girl's always got her head in the clouds, I loved my Daddy and you prayed for souls and went to church every night and every night It is hot in here. It must be summer outside. All the windows are closed up tight and it is very hot here under the eaves. In the clouds

Today: I do not know what day it is. How many days I have been here. Markings on my walls, words and drawings I do not understand. I lie here on the floor and watch my cloud. It sighs and swirls and keeps me safe. I can't see outside it anymore. It is warm and soft and I will stay inside forever. No one can find me now.

Gloria is beginning to smell. Puffy Gloria and her long red

claws. Silly foolish Gloria who didn't even complain when the coffee tasted strange. I have set my Daddy free.

I am in the barn. Night. I am supposed to be milking the cow. I am peaceful, serene. I have done it well and now life will be rich and good. The old car coughs and soon I hear it rattling toward the steep hill over Jordan's pond. It starts down. I listen. Content. The sound fades, a voice, the wrong voice, calling my name: "Allie! Allie, where are you?" The light goes out of the world.

Odaddydaddydaddy, where were you going in the car that night? Wasn't supposed to be you supposed to be her her her

Edgar and Special Awards 1945-1978

Edgars

GRAND MASTER

1978—Aaron Marc Stein
1977—Daphne du Maurier
      Dorothy B. Hughes
      Ngaio Marsh
1976—Graham Greene
1975—Eric Ambler
1973—Ross Macdonald
1972—Judson Philips
1971—John D. MacDonald
1970—Mignon Eberhardt
1969—James M. Cain
1968—John Creasy
1966—Baynard Kendrick
1965—Georges Simenon
1963—George Harmon Coxe
1962—John Dickson Carr
1961—Erle Stanley Gardner
1960—Ellery Queen
1958—Rex Stout
1957—Vincent Starrett
1954—Agatha Christie

BEST NOVEL

1978—*The Eye of the Needle*, Ken Follett (Arbor House)
1977—*Catch Me: Kill Me*, William Hallahan (Bobbs-Merrill)
1976—*Promised Land*, Robert B. Parker (Houghton-Mifflin)
1975—*Hopscotch*, Brian Garfield (M. Evans)
1974—*Peter's Pence*, Jon Cleary (Morrow)
1973—*Dance Hall of the Dead*, Tony Hillerman (Harper & Row)

411

1972—*The Lingala Code*, Warren Kiefer (Random House)
1971—*The Day of the Jackal*, Frederick Forsyth (Viking)
1970—*The Laughing Policeman*, Maj Sjöwall and Per Wahlöö (Pantheon)
1969—*Forfeit*, Dick Francis (Harper & Row)
1968—*A Case of Need*, Jeffery Hudson (World)
1967—*God Save the Mark*, Donald E. Westlake (Random House)
1966—*King of the Rainy Country*, Nicholas Freeling (Harper & Row)
1965—*The Quiller Memorandum*, Adam Hall (Simon & Schuster)
1964—*The Spy Who Came in from the Cold*, John Le Carré (Coward-McCann)
1963—*The Light of Day*, Eric Ambler (Knopf)
1962—*Death of the Joyful Woman*, Ellis Peters (Crime Club)
1961—*Gideon's Fire*, J.J. Marric (Harper & Row)
1960—*Progress of a Crime*, Julian Symons (Harper & Row)
1959—*The Hours Before Dawn*, Celia Fremlin (Lippincott)
1958—*The Eighth Circle*, Stanley Ellin (Random House)
1957—*Room to Swing*, Ed Lacy (Harper & Row)
1956—*A Dram of Poison*, Charlotte Armstrong (Coward McCann)
1955—*Beast in View*, Margaret Millar (Random House)
1954—*The Long Goodbye*, Raymond Chandler (Houghton-Mifflin)
1953—*Beat Not the Bones*, Charlotte Jay (Harper & Row)

BEST FIRST NOVEL

1978—*Killed in the Ratings*, William L. DeAndrea (Harcourt Brace)
1977—*A French Finish*, Robert Ross (Putnam)
1976—*The Thomas Berryman Number*, James Patterson (Little, Brown)
1975—*The Alvarez Journal*, Rex Burns (Harper & Row)
1974—*Fletch*, Gregory Mcdonald (Bobbs-Merrill)
1973—*The Billion Dollar Sure Thing*, Paul Erdman (Scribners)
1972—*Squaw Point*, R.H. Shimer (Harper & Row)
1971—*Finding Maubee*, A.H.Z. Carr (Putnam)
1970—*The Anderson Tapes*, Lawrence Sanders (Putnam)
1969—*A Time of Predators*, Joe Gores (Random House)
1968—*Silver Street*, E. Richard Johnson (Harper & Row)
1967—*Act of Fear*, Michael Collins (Dodd, Mead)

1966—*The Cold War Swap,* Ross Thomas (Morrow)

1965—*In the Heat of the Night,* John Ball (Harper & Row)

1964—*Friday the Rabbi Slept Late,* Harry Kemelman (Crown)

1963—*The Florentine Finish,* Cornelius Hirschberg (Harper & Row)

1962—*The Fugitive,* Robert L. Fish (Simon & Schuster)

1961—*The Green Stone,* Suzanne Blanc (Harper & Row)

1960—*The Man in the Cage,* John Holbrook Vance (Random House)

1959—*The Gray Flannel Shroud,* Henry Slesar (Random House)

1958—*The Bright Road to Fear,* Richard Martin Stern (Ballantine)

1957—*Knock and Wait a While,* William Rawle Weeks (Houghton-Mifflin)

1956—*Rebecca's Pride,* Donald McNutt Douglas (Harper & Row)

1955—*The Perfectionist,* Lane Kauffman (Lippincott)

1954—*Go, Lovely Rose,* Jean Potts (Scribners)

1953—*A Kiss Before Dying,* Ira Levin (Random House)

1952—*Don't Cry for Me,* William Campbell Gault (Dutton)

1951—*Strangle Hold,* Mary McMullen (Harper & Row)

1950—*Nightmare in Manhattan,* Thomas Walsh (Little, Brown)

1949—*What a Body!,* Alan Green (Simon & Schuster)

1948—*The Room Upstairs,* Mildred Davis (Simon & Schuster)

1947—*The Fabulous Clipjoint,* Fredric Brown (Dutton)

1946—*The Horizontal Man,* Helen Eustis (Harper & Row)

1945—*Watchful at Night,* Julius Fast (Farrar & Rinehart)

BEST SHORT STORY

1978—"The Cloud Beneath the Eaves," Barbara Owens *(EQMM)*

1977—"Chance After Chance," Thomas Walsh *(EQMM)*

1976—"Like a Terrible Scream," Etta Revesz *(EQMM)*

1975—"The Jail," Jesse Hill Ford *(Playboy)*

1974—"The Fallen Curtain," Ruth Rendell *(EQMM)*

1973—"The Whimper of Whipped Dogs," Harlan Ellison *(Gallery)*

1972—"The Purple Shroud," Joyce Harrington *(EQMM)*

1971—"Moonlight Gardener," Robert L. Fish *(Argosy)*

1970—"In the Forests of Riga the Beasts Are Very Wild Indeed," Margery Finn Brown *(McCall's)*

1969—"Goodbye, Pops," Joe Gores *(EQMM)*

1968—"The Man Who Fooled the World," Warner Law *(Saturday Evening Post)*

1967—"The Oblong Room," Edward D. Hoch *(Saint Mystery Magazine)*

1966—"The Chosen One," Rhys Davies *(The New Yorker)*

1965—"The Possibility of Evil," Shirley Jackson *(Saturday Evening Post)*

1964—"H as in Homicide," Lawrence Treat *(EQMM)*

1963—"Man Gehorcht," Leslie Ann Brownrigg *(Story Magazine)*

1962—"The Sailing Club," David Ely *(Cosmopolitan)*

1961—"Affair at Lahore Cantonment," Avram Davidson *(EQMM)*

1960—"Tiger," John Durham *(Cosmopolitan)*

1959—"The Landlady," Roald Dahl *(The New Yorker)*

1958—"Over There—Darkness," William O'Farrell *(Sleuth Mystery Magazine)*

1957—"The Secret of the Bottle," Gerald Kersh *(Saturday Evening Post)*

1956—"The Blessington Method," Stanley Ellin *(EQMM)*

1955—"Dream No More," Philip MacDonald *(EQMM)*

1954—"The House Party," Stanley Ellin *(EQMM)*

1953—*Someone Like You,* Roald Dahl (Knopf)

1952—*Something to Hide,* Philip MacDonald (Doubleday)

1951—*Fancies and Goodnights,* John Collier (Doubleday)

1950—*Diagnosis: Homicide,* Lawrence G. Blochman (Lippincott)

1949—*Ellery Queen's Mystery Magazine*

1948—William Irish (Cornell Woolrich)

1947—Ellery Queen

BEST PAPERBACK ORIGINAL

1978—*Deceit and Deadly Lies,* Frank Bandy (Charter)

1977—*The Quark Maneuver,* Mike Jahn (Ballantine)

1976—*Confess, Fletch,* Gregory Mcdonald (Avon)

1975—*Autopsy,* John R. Feegal (Avon)

1974—*The Corpse that Walked,* Roy Winsor (Fawcett Gold Medal)

1973—*Death of an Informer,* Will Perry (Pyramid)

1972—*The Invader,* Richard Wormser (Fawcett Gold Medal)

1971—*For Murder I Charge More,* Frank McAuliffe (Ballantine)

1970—*Flashpoint,* Dan J. Marlowe (Fawcett Gold Medal)

1969—*The Dragon's Eye,* Scott C.S. Stone (Fawcett Gold Medal)

BEST JUVENILE

1978—*Alone in Wolf Hollow,* Dana Brookins (Seabury Press)
1977—*A Really Weird Summer,* Eloise Jarvis McGraw (Atheneum)
1976—*Are You in the House Alone?,* Richard Peck (Viking)
1975—*Z for Zachariah,* Robert C. O'Brien (Atheneum)
1974—*The Dangling Witness,* Jay Bennett (Delacorte Press)
1973—*The Long Black Coat,* Jay Bennett (Delacorte Press)
1972—*Deathwatch,* Robb White (Doubleday)
1971—*Nightfall,* Joan Aiken (Holt, Rinehart & Winston)
1970—*The Intruder,* John Rowe Townsend (Lippincott)
1969—*Danger in Black Dyke,* Winifred Finlay (S.G. Phillips)
1968—*The House of Dies Drear,* Virginia Hamilton (Macmillan)
1967—*Signpost to Terror,* Gretchen Sprague (Dodd, Mead)
1966—*Sinbad and Me,* Kin Platt (Chilton)
1965—*The Mystery of 22 East,* Leon Ware (Westminster Press)
1964—*Mystery of Crans Landing,* Marcella Thum (Dodd, Mead)
1963—*Mystery of the Hidden Hand,* Phyllis A. Whitney
　　　(Westminster)
1962—*Cutlass Island,* Scott Corbett (Little, Brown)
1961—*The Phantom of Walkaway Hill,* Edward Fenton
　　　(Doubleday)
1960—*The Mystery of the Haunted Pool,* Phyllis A. Whitney
　　　(Westminster)

BEST FACT-CRIME

1978—*Til Death Do Us Part,* Vincent Bugliosi and Ken Hurwitz
　　　(Norton)
1977—*By Persons Unknown,* George Jonas and Barbara Amiel
　　　(Grove Press)
1976—*Blood and Money,* Thomas Thompson (Doubleday)
1975—*A Time to Die,* Tom Wicker (Quadrangle)
1974—*Helter Skelter,* Vincent Bugliosi and Curt Gentry (Norton)
1973—*Legacy of Violence,* Barbara Levy (Prentice-Hall)
1972—*Hoax,* Stephen Fay, Lewis Chester and Magnus Linkletter
　　　(Viking)
1971—*Beyond a Reasonable Doubt,* Sandor Frankel (Stein & Day)

1970—*A Great Fall,* Mildred Savage (Simon & Schuster)
1969—*The Case that Will Not Die,* Herbert B. Erhmann (Little, Brown)
1968—*Poe, the Detective,* John Walsh (Rutgers University Press)
1967—*A Private Disgrace,* Victoria Lincoln (Putnam)
1966—*The Boston Strangler,* Gerold Frank (New American Library)
1965—*In Cold Blood,* Truman Capote (Random House)
1964—*Gideon's Trumpet,* Anthony Lewis (Random House)
1963—*The Deed,* Gerold Frank (Simon & Schuster)
1962—*Tragedy in Dedham,* Francis Russell (McGraw-Hill)
1961—*Death and the Supreme Court,* Barrett Prettyman, Jr. (Harcourt Brace)
1960—*The Overbury Affair,* Miriam Allen deFord (Chilton)
1959—*Fire at Sea,* Thomas Gallager (Rinehart)
1958—*They Died in the Chair,* Wenzell Brown (Popular Library)
1957—*The D.A.'s Man,* Harold R. Danforth and James D. Horan (Crown)
1956—*Night Fell on Georgia,* Charles and Louise Samuels (Dell)
1955—*Dead and Gone,* Manly Wade Wellman (University of North Carolina Press)
1954—*The Girl with the Scarlet Brand,* Charles Boswell and Lewis Thompson (Gold Medal)
1953—*Why Did They Kill?,* John Bartlow Martin
1952—*Court of Last Resort,* Erle Stanley Gardner
1951—*True Tales from the Annals of Crime and Rascality,* St. Clair McKelway
1950—*Twelve Against Crime,* Edward D. Radin
1949—*Bad Company,* Joseph Henry Jackson
1948—Regional Murder Series (*Boston Murders* published in 1948), edited by Marie Rodell (Duell, Sloan & Pearce)
1947—*Twelve Against the Law,* Edward D. Radin

BEST CRITICAL/BIOGRAPHICAL STUDY

1978—*The Mystery of Agatha Christie,* Gwen Robyns (Doubleday)
1977—*Rex Stout,* John J. McAleer (Little, Brown)
1976—*The Encyclopedia of Mystery and Detection,* Chris Steinbrunner, Otto Penzler, Marvin Lachman, and Charles Shibuk (McGraw-Hill)

OUTSTANDING MYSTERY CRITICISM

1966—John T. Winterich *(Saturday Review)*
1963—Hans Stefan Santesson *(Saint Mystery Magazine)*
1960—James Sandoe *(New York Herald-Tribune)*
1956—Curtis Casewit *(Denver Post)*
1954—Drexel Drake *(Chicago Tribune)*
1953—Brett Halliday and Helen McCloy
1952—Anthony Boucher *(New York Times* and *EQMM)*
1951—Lenore Glen Offord *(San Francisco Chronicle)*
1950—Dorothy B. Hughes *(Albuquerque Times)*
1949—Anthony Boucher *(New York Times* and *EQMM)*
1948—James Sandoe *(Chicago Sun-Times)*
1947—Howard Haycraft *(EQMM)*
1946—William Weber *(Saturday Review of Literature)*
1945—Anthony Boucher

BEST MOTION PICTURE

1978—*Magic* (William Goldman)
1977—*The Late Show* (Robert Benton)
1976—*Family Plot* (Ernest Lehman)
1975—*Three Days of the Condor* (Lorenzo Semple, Jr., and David Rayfiel)
1974—*Chinatown* (Robert Towne)
1973—*The Last of Sheila* (Stephen Sondheim and Anthony Perkins)
1972—*Sleuth* (Anthony Shaffer)
1971—*The French Connection* (Ernest Tidyman)
1970—*Investigation of a Citizen Above Suspicion* (Elio Petri and Ugo Pirro)
1969—*Z* (Jorge Semprun and Costa Garvis)
1968—*Bullitt* (Alan R. Trustman and Harry Kleiner)
1967—*In the Heat of the Night* (Stirling Silliphant)
1966—*Harper* (William Goldman)
1965—*The Spy Who Came in from the Cold* (Paul Dehn and Guy Trosper)

1964—*Hush, Hush, Sweet Charlotte* (Henry Farrel and Lukas Heller)
1963—*Charade* (Peter Stone)
1961—*The Innocents* (William Archibald and Truman Capote)
1960—*Psycho* (Joseph Stefano; special scroll to Robert Bloch as author of the novel)
1959—*North by Northwest* (Ernest Lehman)
1958—*The Defiant Ones* (Nathan E. Douglas and Harold Jacob Smith)
1957—*Twelve Angry Men* (Reginald Rose)
1955—*The Desperate Hours* (Joseph Hayes)
1954—*Rear Window* (John Michael Hayes)
1953—*The Big Heat* (Sydney Boehm)
1952—*Five Fingers* (Michael Wilson)
1951—*Detective Story* (Phillip Yordan and Robert Wyler)
1950—*The Asphalt Jungle* (Ben Maddow and W.R. Burnett)
1949—*The Window* (based on a story by Cornell Woolrich)
1948—*Call Northside 777* (Quentin Reynolds, Leonard Hoffman, and Jay Dratler)
1947—*Crossfire* (John Paxton)
1946—*The Killers* (Anthony Veiller)
1945—*Murder, My Sweet* (John Paxton)

Special Awards

1978—Special Raven to Alberto Tedeschi for his contribution to the mystery as editor for Il Giallo Mondadori of Italy; Special Awards to Mignon Eberhart and Ellery Queen on the 50th Anniversary of their first published novels
1977—Special Edgar to Allen J. Hubin for a decade as editor of *The Armchair Detective;* Special Edgar to Dilys Winn for *Murder Ink;* Special Award to Lawrence Treat as editor of *The Mystery Writer's Handbook* (Writer's Digest)
1976—Special Raven to *The Edge of Night* TV series (ABC)
1975—Special Edgar to Jorge Luis Borges for his distinguished contribution to the mystery; Special Edgar to Donald J. Sobol for the Encyclopedia Brown books; Special Raven to Leo Margulies, founder and publisher of *Mike Shayne Mystery Magazine*
1974—Special Raven to The Royal Shakespeare Company for its revival of the play *Sherlock Holmes;* Special Raven to CBS

Radio Mystery Theatre; Special Award to Howard Haycraft;
Special Award to Francis M. Nevins, Jr., for *Royal
Bloodline: Ellery Queen, Author and Detective*

1973—Special Edgar to Joseph Wambaugh

1972—Special Awards to Julian Symons, Jeanne Larmoth, and
Charlotte Turgeon

1971—Special Award to Jacques Barzen and Wendell Hertig Taylor
for *A Catalogue of Crime* (Harper & Row)

1969—Special Award to John Dickson Carr in honor of his 40 years
as a mystery writer

1968—Special Award to Ellery Queen on the 40th Anniversary of
The Roman Hat Mystery

1966—Special Rven to *EQMM;* Special Raven to Clayton Rawson

1965—Special Raven to Rev. O.C. Edwards for "The Gospel
According to 007" in *The Living Church*

1963—Special Edgar to Hans Stefan Santesson, editor of *The Saint
Magazine*

1962—Special Edgar to E. Spencer Shew for *Companion to
Murder;* Special Edgar to Philip Reisman for *Cops and
Robbers;* Special Edgar to Frances and Richard Lockridge
on the publication of their fiftieth novel, *The Ticking Clock;*
Special Edgar to Patrick Quentin for his collection of short
stories, *The Ordeal of Mrs. Snow*

1961—Special Edgar to Frederick Knott for his play, *Write Me a
Murder;* Special Edgar to Thomas McDade for his *Annals of
Murder*

1960—Special Edgar to Elizabeth Daly

1959—Special Raven to Gail Jackson, producer of *Perry Mason*
television series; Special Raven to Lucille Fletcher for her
radio play *Sorry, Wrong Number;* Special Raven to David C.
Cooke for his editorship of *Best Detective Stories of the
Year;* Special Raven to Alfred Hitchcock for his contribution
to the mystery

1958—Special Edgar to Alice Wooley Burt for *American Murder
Ballads*

1956—Special Edgar to Meyer Levin for outstanding novel related
to the mystery field *(Compulsion)*

1955—Special Edgar to Henri-Georges Clouzot for writing and
directing *Diabolique*

1954—Special Edgar to Agatha Christie for *Witness for the
Prosecution;* Special Raven to Berton Roueche for true
stories of medical detection, *Eleven Blue Men*

1953—Special Edgar to Mary Roberts Rinehart; Special Raven to

Tom Lehrer for his parodies in song and poem of mystery and crime

1952—Special Edgar to Frederick Knott for his play *Dial M for Murder*

1951—Special Edgar to Ellery Queen for his critical/historical study of the mystery, *Queen's Quorum*

1949—Special Edgar to Sidney Kingsley for *Detective Story;* Special Edgar to John Dickson Carr for *The Life of Sir Arthur Conan Doyle*

1948—Special Edgar to Clayton Rawson for *Clue,* a pioneering magazine of mystery criticism and review; Special Edgar for best foreign-made film, *Jenny Lamour (Quai des Orfèvres)*